WALTER
and
JUNE

WALTER

AND

JUNE

first published as WINTER DOVES

Two Novels by

DAVID COOK

With a new foreword
by the author

An Alison Press Book
Secker & Warburg — London

Walter first published in England 1978,
June first published in England 1979 as Winter Doves,
by The Alison Press/Martin Secker & Warburg Limited
Michelin House, 81 Fulham Road, London SW3 6RB

Reissued in this edition 1989

British Library Cataloguing in Publication Data

Cook, David, *1940–*
    Walter, and, June
    I. Title
    823'.914[F]

    ISBN 0-436-10686-8

Printed in Great Britain by
Redwood Burn Limited, Trowbridge, Wiltshire

For all the patients, nurses
and social workers who helped
me with these two books and
with the making of the film

Foreword

Between the publication of my second novel, *Happy Endings*, and that of *Walter*, four years elapsed. The beginning of that time was taken up by my writing a great deal for television – a play, *Jenny Can't Work Any Faster*, about an autistic girl and her father, a series of nine short plays about children in a foster-home for BBC Schools, and many episodes of an afternoon series, *Couples*, about marriage guidance. I enjoyed all this, spent a fortnight at a school in Gravesend for autistic children, a week in a foster-home near Manchester, and went on courses for marriage guidance counsellors at Rugby. I was greedy for such interesting work and found it hard to refuse, but I am by nature a slow writer, easily panicked by deadlines, and with a strong emotional attachment to my work. I was foolish to undertake so much, particularly in a medium in which emotional attachment to the work may be seen as a threat to the script editor, and the result was a minor nervous breakdown, during which I suffered from depression and could not work at all.

Gradually, during a summer spent in the compulsive evening watering of the garden, and of caring for pigeons which had originally been bought as decoration but which rapidly turned into a responsibility and had to be protected against the depredations of a stoat, the idea of a new novel began to seem itself a form of therapy. It was typical of my state of mind at the time that I chose a subject which was absurdly thematic and extremely depressing. I intended to write a panorama of the unwanted, unloved, the destitute of London in the midst of which I would set a particular example. My novel would cover four hours of time. They would be the four hours between midnight and four a.m., the lowest hours when the old and the sick most usually die, and they would be occupied by the suicide of my protagonist, a lonely and loveless woman, intercutting the stages of her private act of despair with the general panorama of what was happening to those alone and adrift in London, sleeping rough or in hostels, begging, selling themselves, keeping alive with little hope from moment to moment through each long night.

At the idea of all this, I began already to be a little more cheerful, and by the autumn I was confident enough to undertake the research. I grew a beard to disguise myself from recognition (for I had once appeared with a bear on television, presenting a programme for the under-fives, some of whom, with their mothers, might already have joined the legion of the lost), and spent nights among dossers on the concourses of Waterloo and Paddington stations and underneath the arches of Charing Cross; I visited the 'spike', approached the Squatters' Advisory Service and assisted in 'opening-up' a squat. I talked to many people, made many notes; the material accumulated; my only problem was that I seemed to be unable to start the book. To be exact, I did start, more than once. I began to see my central lady. Her name was June. I began to know more about her, to know why she had determined on suicide, why she had made previous attempts and was determined this time not to fail. But whenever I tried to go wider, and take in my metropolitan panorama of despair, I became stuck, and just a woman committing suicide seemed rather short for a novel, almost scanty. What is more, I discovered that I wanted to write a long novel.

Looking back over what, after all, is only twelve years ago from the time of writing this foreword, I am surprised that I cannot remember how or why or exactly when there began to form in my mind during this blocked period a sort of double-image demanding attention. One part of this image was a memory from my days of working in the stockroom of Woolworth's in Preston when I was sixteen, and one of my fellow-workers had been a mentally handicapped boy, Trevor, a little older than I, who swept up, collected rubbish, and did other such odd jobs as were considered suitable for him. The other part was a much more recent memory of two years earlier, when I had been playing Roderigo in a production of *Othello* at the Ludlow Festival. Always on hand, a little younger than I, was Walter, also mentally handicapped, who loved to be with the actors, ran errands for them and hung about backstage so as to be of service in any way they would allow. Walter lived for the annual Festival, and was allowed as a special treat to travel to London with the company at the end of the season in the coach which then carried him back again to Ludlow to wait out another year.

Trevor and Walter! Twenty years separated them in my memory. What had happened to Trevor meanwhile? What might have happened? The double-image merged, and became my Walter, who was neither the Ludlow Walter nor Trevor. I gave him my own birthday, as the first step to becoming him. I forgot about the panoramic view of destitution and despair in London. I began to write my long book.

In fact, it was published as two books, although I was already well into *Winter Doves* before *Walter* appeared. In fact, I had not said goodbye to the dossers and the underside of London at all; they all came back in the second novel; none of the research was wasted. In fact, there was an important place for June's suicide; there was a most important place for June. Even the pigeons (but not the stoat) found a place in my long novel which now in this edition, and to my great pleasure, becomes at last the one book which I first wanted it to be.

After the book – some time after – came the film, which achieved some notoriety, since it was the first of the *Films on Four*, and was shown as the centrepiece of Channel Four's opening night. Later it received a Special Commendation from the jury at the Monte Carlo Festival, and was short-listed for an International Emmy in New York. Then it receded, as films do, particularly those made for television, first into memory, then into oblivion, but meanwhile it had sold a lot of paperbacks of *Walter* and *Winter Doves*, and it induced publishers in those foreign countries in which it was shown to publish the novels in translation.

Many writers whose novels have been turned into films regard the memory, I'm told, like an old bruise which can still hurt when touched, but on balance I enjoyed the experience, first of writing the screenplay, then of helping in various minor capacities during the actual filming; I held the legs of the child Walter as he sat on the railway bridge so as to prevent his falling onto the line below, and I threw pigeons into shot from various cramped positions in Walter's mother's bedroom. I had hoped, when I began thinking about this foreword, that I might be able to come up with a few insights about the essential differences between these two forms of art, except that I am a little leery about writing about either novels or films as "forms of art", and would rather describe them as ways of telling a story. But in fact insights are the business of those who write about art, not those who practise it. Anyone involved in actually making a film rapidly discovers that the considerations which govern the process are financial not artistic.

I had written much for television, mostly for videotape shot in the studio with inserts of location film for the exteriors. Filmed documentaries were common enough on television then, filmed single dramas much less so, though *Film on Four* itself has changed that. So at first I thought, 'This will be a liberating experience. Short scenes. Lots of varied and interesting locations.' I was mistaken, of course. Long scenes were in vogue, I was told; short scenes were old-fashioned. What this really meant was that long scenes are cheap, short scenes expensive. As for the lots of varied exterior locations, they had quite gone out. Almost any interior is cheaper than almost any exterior, since the lighting can be controlled and is not dependent on the English weather. Exteriors, insofar as they can be used at all, should be concentrated in one area, so as not to waste time (and therefore money) in travelling. Even I had not been so foolish as to believe that we would be able to film the Doncaster Pigeon Show, but I had thought we might get about a bit, and it was a shock to discover to what extent the action of the film would have to be confined. Another shock was to be told that *Walter* was a 'period' novel – which put up the cost at once, of course, since 'period' costumes and 'period' vehicles cost more to hire: it had not occurred to me, just turned forty, that my youth and young-manhood had become 'period'. The only insight I have to offer is that, if interesting locations, a large cast and a broad canvas are what you want, you had better stick to reading novels, in which the imaginations of the readers do the work. Imagination is much cheaper than filming.

What made the film, I think, an extraordinarily moving and compelling experience for those who saw it was the performance of Ian McKellen as Walter, and for this I can claim a little credit. I had understudied Ian at the St Martin's Theatre years before in a play called *A Lily in Little India*, and I became convinced, while I was writing the screenplay of *Walter*, that he was the actor to play the part. At the time, Ian was appearing on Broadway as Salieri in Peter Shaffer's *Amadeus*, and I asked my producer, Nigel Evans, for permission to send the screenplay to him. To my delight and relief Ian agreed to play Walter, and for a fortnight before shooting began, he and I and a cheerful cockney male nurse from a mental handicap hospital sat down together, and Ian asked questions, and improvised, and role-played, and we found his costume from boots to flat cap slowly, item by item, the whole process culminating in an expedition by the three of us to Woolworth's and then to the King's Head in Islington, during which we watched members of the public treating Ian as Walter with that guarded goodwill which is customarily extended to the mentally handicapped.

I suppose that the other member of the cast for whom I may claim much more credit was a short-faced tumbler. When it was clear that there really would be a film, I knew that a tame pigeon would be needed to sit on Walter's shoulder, so I set about rearing one. This was a chick who had to be helped out of the egg, the over-tough shell peeled away because he could not break it. I fed him, first with an eye-dropper, then with grains pushed in by hand until he could eat and drink for himself, and he lived with us, and became extremely proprietorial. I named him 'Albie' after Albert Finney so as to give him a good start in the profession, and he took readily to filming, became very attached (at times literally) to Ian's ears, and endured retakes with equanimity. He has given up acting now, and raised several families; it was always clear that his opportunities in film would be limited.

Ian McKellen as Walter, Barbara Jefford as his mother and many other of the performances, and the lighting and camera-work of Chris Menges, they made the film for me, and make me proud to have been part of it. The processes of response to a novel and to a film *are* different, the novel more demanding, more able to reward re-reading, the film more immediate and more enveloping. The processes of writing are similar; characters must be created and, in action, tell a story, which will in some way enlarge or change the understanding of those to whom the story is told. The difference lies in the interpretation which, in a film, is by a team of people, and in a novel within the mind of the reader. The writer is only a small part of any film, the film only a small part of any novel from which it may have been adapted. The novel and film of this long book made up quite a large part of my life. There have been other novels since, and other films, and I shall hope to write more. Meanwhile I still have the pigeons.

David Cook
September, 1988.

xi

JUNE

First published as WINTER DOVES

PART ONE

His Parentage and Birth

I

If you let a man get his way with you, you'll live to regret it

She wanted a child.

First she had wanted to be married. To be married first, and then to have children. That was what women did, if they were to have respect. If they remained unmarried and childless, they became Old Maids, and lacked respect. If they had children without first becoming married, they became Fallen Women, and had no respect at all. It was proper and it was natural for a woman to marry, and thereafter to have a child.

The fact that her own mother had been married and had given birth to a child – to her, Sarah – and had hated both experiences did not deter her. Her mother had merely added fear as an element to the mixture of mainly pleasurable and exciting emotions with which Sarah looked forward to marriage and motherhood. Hips, it seemed, were the problem. Sarah's mother had the narrowest of narrow hips. Consequently Sarah's arrival into the world had been achieved only after the most painful of all deliveries. Sarah's mother spoke with authority for all women who had ever had babies. The hips of none of them had been as narrow as Sarah's mother's hips, the delivery of no baby more painful than the delivery of Sarah. At fifteen, Sarah did not question her mother's authority on the subject of hips.

'You've got them too. You get them from me. You think twice, Sarah, before you let a man go too far. Least done, soonest mended. One moment of pleasure is certainly not worth the pain I went through, giving birth to you.'

3

Sarah's mother went on to say that there were many ways to satisfy a man's desire without permitting actual penetration. 'They've talked to you about it at school, I suppose?' Sarah shook her head. 'They' never meant the other girls, always the teachers, none of whom had ever spoken to the fifteen-year-old Sarah of the ways by which male lust might be satisfied without permitting actual penetration. This was clearly a shortcoming of the educational system, but part of Sarah feared that to admit it would bring forth all the gory details from her mother. Another part of her – the lower part – wished to be enlightened on what to do, and how far it was polite to go.

'You mean, they haven't told you anything?' Again Sarah shook her head. 'Well, I'll be –' but she was never to find out what her mother would be, since a second thought came quick on the heels of the first. 'What about the other girls? They must have talked about it.'

Sarah wasn't sure how to answer this. Then she said, 'Only in a dirty way.'

Mother looked at daughter in a manner that suggested that she was not sure they were related. She could not remember that she had ever put on such airs, though if airs were to be put on at all, she supposed that this was the age for them.

'What's dirty about your body?'

The question did not even seem simple, and was bound to be less simple than it seemed. It would be one of her mother's trick questions, designed to find out exactly how much she knew, and then, having found it, her mother would condemn it all as filth. 'Nothing I hope.' She would not be tricked.

'So should I.' Sarah's mother waited, watching for a flicker of guilt on her daughter's face. 'Do you really mean to tell me you don't know anything?'

'I'm not sure what you're getting at.'

'When and if you get married, there are certain things you have to know about. There's nothing dirty about the way babies are born. Dirt of that kind is all in the mind. But if, as in your case, you'll want to avoid having children, you should be put straight on ways of being fair to your husband, and yet not finding yourself as I did, Sarah, screaming to the Lord for forgiveness because I couldn't bear the pain you were causing me. And don't you expect help from those Sisters of Mercy at the hospital, because they only slap your backside, and call you a ninny. The one who did that to me had never taken a man into her bed in all her life, and she had hips like barn doors. She could have given birth to a wheelbarrow, provided it arrived wheel first.' Sarah closed her eyes. Her mother's imagination was fertile, but seldom expressed as crudely as this.

The silence which followed this speech seemed to be as important as the words of which the speech consisted. Sarah did not know which was worse, to fill the silence or to let it go on for ever. Meanwhile her mother moved around the room, setting the table for tea, refusing to make eye-contact with her daughter, her every movement indicating a continuation of the fury which her daughter had done nothing to provoke. Clearly the silence must be filled. Sarah said, 'I'm sorry.'

Her mother sniffed, and asked her what she felt sorry about.

'About causing you such pain.'

Her mother laid a knife down slowly at the wrong side of a plate, and remained looking down at it for what seemed like an eternity.

Then she spoke in a slow controlled way, measuring her words out carefully as she stared at the knife. 'If you let a man get his way with you, you'll live to regret it. It's sad, because we're both women, and giving men pleasure is what we're made for, but if God makes you too narrow, you'd be better off becoming a nun. Be God's wife. *He* won't force his way into you, without a by-your-leave. I'd been warned about my narrow hips, but I was weak against your father. But he was a big man, you see. And we were married. He said he had every right; it was his right to . . .' Sarah's mother considered the various forms of circumlocution open to her, and chose one '. . . to do it properly. I begged him to allow me to accept him in other ways, but he wouldn't; I think he was puritanical really. Then, when he had forced his way in, I begged him again to be careful. We were fighting. Like animals, I remember. He was what they call "on heat"; he thought it proper for me to fight him, but I was in earnest; I was too frightened for pleasure. Lord! he was a big man. Then there was blood, me being a virgin. I thought he'd damaged me inside for good. I didn't know then that there would be blood, you see. Like you, I hadn't been told. I kept pleading with him to be careful, and withdraw. We were both sweating so much, the sheets were wet with it. Soaking.'

5

She stopped talking, and remained still; the memory of that pain was still painful. Sarah was crying silently, her throat and chest near bursting with the effort not to make a noise. When she could speak, she said 'What happened?'

'You did. You're what happened.' Her mother looked away towards the window. 'He was up inside me so far, there was no way his seed could escape. My only hope was that the seed might be inferior, and not bear fruit, but that was not to be; the seed was fruitful.' Her mother sank slowly into a chair, and continued speaking. 'He came out almost as painfully as he had entered me, and then he slept. I didn't. The sheets were so cold by then, with the sweat cooling off. I thought a lot of funny things as I lay there, with my eyes open all night. I hated him so much. I even thought of creeping downstairs to get my dressmaking scissors. He was sleeping so heavily, I could easily have cut it off, and stopped him wanting me ever again. One snip! He would have bled like a pig, I shouldn't wonder. That seemed fair, when I had already bled for him. I thought a lot about that. I also thought that I was beginning to go mad, with the shock. Nothing seemed real any longer. Not him, pushing and pumping inside me, not his anger because I didn't want to, not his sweat dripping into my face. All unreal.'

She stopped again, this time to remember. It was important to try to be accurate, since this was the first time she had talked about it to anybody.

'I was so completely his property. Pinned down by his arms and his chest. I . . . I lost myself, the moment he took my virginity. It's important, that. You must feel that.'

Sarah nodded.

'I treasured my virginity. It made me feel as if I was somebody.' She looked out of the window at the lawn and the rockery with the different kinds of heather she had planted. 'And his brute strength bled it to death in just a few seconds.' She looked round at Sarah. 'Also he'd been with lots of women before me. He swore he hadn't, of course, but I could tell by the way he handled me. He knew what to do. I could tell at once by the way he pulled me apart. He'd lied to me; he'd said there were no others, but he couldn't have that knowledge without the knowledge of others; he couldn't have the confidence. After that, as long as he went elsewhere for that sort of thing, I kept house for him, and concentrated on you. When the war came, I was glad. Do you know, he never wrote to me once, or I to him. I got the usual telegram when his ship went down, and that was that.'

There was a long pause. Then Sarah said, 'Have you never wanted another man? More gentle.'

Sarah's mother smiled. 'Of course I have. I'm not unnatural. I've teased quite a few in my time, just teased, you know.' She smiled again, and wiped her eyes with the back of her hand. Then she stood. 'Well, there we are. I wasn't expecting to tell you all that. They should teach you at school about all that sort of thing.'

2

We've been and gone and done it, then?

They were going to Southport. She sat opposite him in the train, and thought, 'What have I done?'

The object which prompted this question to enter Sarah's mind was Eric's neck. As they sat down in the compartment, which they had managed to get all to themselves, Eric had removed his scarf, and Sarah had realized that she had never before seen him without one. His neck was so thin and scrawny that she couldn't take her eyes off it.

Here they were, with the train rattling along, taking them to a honeymoon in Southport, and all she could think about was how thin his neck was. He hadn't worn a scarf during the wedding ceremony; he couldn't have; her reason told her that she must have seen Eric's neck before. Yet here it was, naked in the compartment, and she was looking at it as if she were seeing it for the first time.

Eric's mouth was dry. He couldn't stop swallowing, and his Adam's apple shot up and down. Even a sip of alcohol, even a sniff of the cork, went straight to his head, and, feeling that he was no longer in control of himself, he became frightened. Therefore he had not sipped, he had not sniffed the sweet sherry which had been given to him at the small reception held at Sarah's mother's house. He had held a glass in his hand, and pretended to drink from it. The church service had made his mouth dry, since it was important to get it right and to do nothing, say nothing which was not in order and always said. He had hoped that he would find an appropriate moment to go to the bathroom,

8

and drink from the tap. Unfortunately, from the moment he had placed the cheap wedding-ring on Sarah's finger, he had been watched, talked to, joked with; there had been no moment to himself, no opportunity to slip away without making much of it. If he had asked for a non-alcoholic drink, he would have been an object of hilarity to all the men present. His soul thirsted for ginger beer, for squash or Tizer, and they had given him sweet sherry, which he knew better than to touch. None of these men were friends of his. Even the Best Man had been provided by Sarah's mother. He knew no one except the farmer for whom he worked, and who had been unable to attend the wedding because (Eric being away) he had to do the feeding himself. And resented it. He had disapproved strongly that Eric should take a week off work for something as irrelevant as a honeymoon.

He did not understand why, when both he and Sarah were chapel, Sarah's mother had insisted on a church wedding. Sarah had worn white, and an organ had played. There was no organ at the chapel, but white could have been worn there. He would have been less nervous in a more familiar place.

Sarah watched Eric's Adam's apple shooting up and down, and wondered if he were going to be sick. He had behaved strangely all day. He was nervous, of course, but so was she.

'Are you alright, Eric?'

He nodded.

Fascinated by the thinness of his neck, and the way it made his head seem much too large, she began to count the number of times he swallowed, and having started, had to make a positive effort to stop and to look out of the window.

As she watched the countryside move past, she thought how little they knew about each other. They had been for walks, mostly on Sundays after chapel. They had held hands. She knew that he worked on a farm, that he had told her he had been brought up in an orphanage, that he was quiet. He was a quiet man. They had taught him to be quiet at the orphanage. He had never even tried to kiss her. She had thought this odd, but remembering her mother's experience, had put down this apparent lack of passion as a mark in his favour. He certainly wasn't big and muscular as her own father had been. He would never force his attentions where and when they were not wanted. He would be worried about their first night together, more worried than she. She

9

looked again at the stiff white collar around his sunburned neck. She could see the veins standing out, purple on the red neck, squeezed into that solidly starched band of white. And the Adam's apple. No, he would not be difficult to control; he had pulled no one apart; she would be in charge. They had been sitting in the train for half an hour, and all he had found to say in that time was, 'We've been and gone and done it, then?' and all she had said was, 'Yes.' They both looked out of the window. He would be unlike her father; he would not handle her roughly.

They walked from the railway station to the hotel. Eric insisted on carrying both their suitcases, so that he had to stop and change hands every three minutes. On arrival at the entrance hall, Sarah waited for him to go over to the desk and ring the bell, but he stood there, looking around like a puppy which has lost its mother. Sarah rang the bell, and a young girl asked them to sign the register, and then showed them to a large room with a double bed.

Eric put both suitcases on the bed, and began to unpack his own. Sarah noticed that, right at the top, he had packed seven or eight comics. Children's comics! Sarah laughed out loud at the idea of children's comics on a honeymoon, but when Eric turned to find out why she was laughing, his expression was of a child who has discovered that there is no Father Christmas. Both fell silent. Their silence was total. Eric left the comics inside the case, locked it, and placed it on top of the large Victorian double wardrobe. The comics remained there, and were not mentioned.

It was not yet dark, but there seemed to be nothing to do but to go to bed. They undressed, with their backs to each other. Sarah slid into bed first, and kept her back to Eric, who was taking longer to undress, even though he remained in his underwear.

Two hours later, it was dark, and both were still awake. Neither had spoken or moved. They lay side by side with their eyes open, staring into the blackness, each waiting for the other to make a move.

Finally Sarah reached out a hand to find his hand. Almost immediately, her hand was full of a sticky substance. Eric said, 'I'm sorry.' Sarah placed the sticky substance where she thought it should go, and in doing so, found a way of exciting herself.

She was to need that discovery a great deal, later on. 'Sorry' became the word she would fall asleep hearing quite often.

3

A young couple who have just remembered a previous appointment

When Sarah woke the next morning, she saw Eric, already fully dressed, standing by the window, looking out.

She watched him for a long time before he sensed that he was being watched, and turned round. Then they both said, 'Good morning!' in a rather formal way, as one might say it to the newsagent or the postman, and Eric turned back to look out of the window.

The people in the streets below moved mainly in the same direction, like evacuees from a threatened city, carrying with them their most precious possessions, buckets and spades, striped towels, rubber balls and bathing costumes. Prams containing small ill-tempered babies were pushed by women whose thick overcoats announced their belief that the weather would change before lunch.

Eric said, 'We have to be downstairs by quarter past nine, if you want breakfast. I don't mind. I'm not hungry.' They had paid for breakfast; they would eat breakfast. Sarah began to get out of bed, and Eric turned back to look out of the window again, respecting her modesty.

She dressed in silence. Three times Eric cleared his throat, as if about to speak. Finally he did speak, and what he said was, 'Shall we go home?'

He was standing with his face pressed against the window, which was clouded by the steam of his breath. Only the back of his head was towards her. Sarah said, 'Why?'

'I thought if you wanted to, we could. They might not charge us for the whole week. I could start back at work tomorrow. It would mean a bit more money for...' He stopped to consider what the extra money might be used for. 'Mr Davies wasn't keen on me having the whole week off. We could put the money towards furniture.' His voice trailed away. He was exhausted at the length of his speech, and embarrassed at having made such a demand on someone else's attention.

'What would people think?'

'What people?' He had no friends; there would be no one to scoff. Mr Davies would actually be pleased.

'The people at the hotel. All the people who came to the wedding and gave us presents. How would we face them?'

'I'm sorry. I hadn't thought.'

'No.' Even if there were no one else to consider, her mother would have to be faced, if they were to return home after one night of their honeymoon. She might say Eric had been taken ill, but that would not be believed, if he were to begin work again at once. It was not possible. They must stick it out, for the sake of appearances.

They left the bedroom together, he following her. Over breakfast they sat alone in silence, and the waitress who asked them whether they wanted porridge or cornflakes smirked as if the question had a dirtier significance. When the waitress returned to the kitchen, the sound of giggling could be heard from behind the serving-hatch.

They stayed at the hotel the full week. She made no further attempt to touch him, and he slept beside her with what seemed to be as little interest as if they had been married forty years. Sarah told herself that things might improve once they were home again.

Every morning she asked him what he would like to do that day, and every morning he replied that he didn't mind. One day, they went on a coach-trip. It was a Mystery Tour, which passed through Bootle. During the other days, they sat side by side in deckchairs, looking out to sea, each wrapped in separate thoughts, each longing to know what the other was thinking, and neither daring to ask.

One evening was spent at the Concert Party on the Pier. The audience around them roared with laughter at the comedian's jokes, while Sarah and Eric sat in silence, wanting the show to end.

The comedian made two jokes about honeymoon couples, at which the audience laughed even louder than before. Sarah began to sweat, and then to tremble. 'Darling, you've curdled my wee-wee,' the comedian said, and the middle-aged woman in front of them went into a paroxysm of hilarious coughing and was thumped as hilariously on the back by her companion. Sarah found that she had become very frightened; she did not know why. She grabbed Eric by the arm, and pulled him to his feet and along the row of seats, past laughing faces. The comedian noticed two youngish people leaving in the middle of his act, and capitalized on the insult by bringing them to the attention of the rest of the audience. 'There's a young couple, folks, who've just remembered a previous appointment.' Those in front turned to look. Eric closed his eyes, and allowed himself to be led. As they walked up the centre aisle, every face in the audience was turned towards them, and as they reached the back of the auditorium, the audience began to applaud.

'Well, I've often felt like a bit, myself, you know, but I can't say I've been that desperate.' A roar of laughter. There was a lighted sign, which read, 'EXIT', and Sarah willed herself towards it, dragging Eric behind her.

'As my missus always says – always, and this is the truth – "Just keep it on ice for me, Bernard; the waiting's more than half the pleasure."' Laughter. 'Just like the Eskimo, who was engaged to be married. Kept it on ice, but his fiancée broke it off.' Laughter and applause. 'You can't be too careful.' They were through the swing doors and into the foyer.

As the comedian signalled to the pianist that he was ready to go into his 'Getting off' song, he contemplated the advantages there might be in planting two young members of the stage staff to do every night what Sarah and Eric had just done.

For the rest of the week, Sarah and Eric spent their evenings sitting in the lounge of the hotel. Sarah read the back copies of Punch and Woman's Own which lay about there, and Eric, since his comics remained locked in his suitcase upstairs, looked at the photographs in The Field.

On returning home they were to stay with Sarah's mother, until such time as Eric could find a job as a farm labourer which had a tied cottage that went with it.

Sarah's mother met them at the door, wearing a new pink blouse and more make-up than Sarah remembered ever having seen on her mother's face before. She was also wearing ear-rings, the very ornaments which she had once told Sarah that only women of the very lowest character wore. If the Lord had intended women to wear such things, He would, she had told her daughter, have supplied small cup-hooks on their ears. Those had been her words. Now, as she leaned forward to kiss her new son-in-law, miniature replicas of Blackpool Tower were swinging at each side of her face.

'Hello, love!' was all she said to her daughter, but to her son-in-law she said, 'I expect you'd like a nice cup of tea.' Eric nodded.

'Are you sweet enough, or do you take sugar? I like lemon with mine, when I can get them. Such a refreshing taste!' She guided Eric by the shoulders, and lowered him into the most comfortable chair. 'We've got to make him feel at home, haven't we? Start as we mean to go on.' After a sideways glance at Sarah, who stood dumbfounded at this totally new aspect of her mother's character, she added, 'Well, we'll do our best, we hope,' and disappeared into the kitchen.

Sarah looked across at Eric, who was swallowing almost as quickly and as often as he had in the train on the way to Southport, and thought, 'If only she knew!' All that talk! The warnings to keep her legs crossed, and not allow him to go too far. The vivid and detailed accounts of the manifestations of her father's lust. His size. His experience of other women. If only she knew how her daughter had spent this past week! But she would not know. Nobody would be allowed to know.

Sarah's mother made her entrance carrying a tray of tea and cakes, and wearing an apron with frills on it. She said, 'Well, then, how was the weather? Have you had a nice romantic week? You must tell me everything – everything that won't make me blush, that is,' at which Sarah laughed, loudly and suddenly, and found herself unable to stop.

She laughed and laughed, like Little Audrey, while her mother and Eric sat looking at her. Finally she placed the fingers of one hand between her teeth and bit down on them, so as to force herself to stop. Eric's face wore the same expression as when she had laughed at his comics. Her mother would want an explanation, and continue to want it until the want was satisfied. An explanation came

14

to her. She said, 'Mother, what have you got on? That's not Blackpool Tower hanging down from your ear, is it?'

There was a silence before her mother removed both ear-rings from her ears, with a deliberation intended to demonstrate that she was hurt and offended. Then, handing them to her daughter for inspection, she said, 'They're replicas of the Eiffel Tower in Paris, if you must know. They were a present from a very old and dear friend; they're diamanté. But you're quite right, Sarah, as always; they are too dressy for the daytime. I simply wished to please my friend by wearing them when I wanted to put on a bit of a show for your homecoming.' She glanced at Eric, who was studying the pattern of the hearth-rug, with the air of someone who has lost a battle and won the war.

The next two months were the most difficult Sarah had ever endured. Her only refuge was at her work in the drapery shop in town, where she had liking and had respect, from the owner for her pleasant appearance and punctuality, and from the customers for her cheerfulness and civility. She in turn liked her job. It didn't require all the potential which she was sure she had, but because of that she found it relaxing, and it gave her time to think. Now her thoughts and daydreams were no longer of wedded bliss and a cottage, with lupins in the garden and roses round the door, of meals she would cook for her strong but gentle husband, and the attractive and well-mannered children who, with her encouragement and love, would grow and progress from Grammar School to college and on to secure jobs with the Midland Bank and as learned professors – perhaps higher? who knew? – and would in their turn marry, and give her grandchildren swaddled in silk and in cashmere.

Her daydreams now were nightmares, her thoughts of loneliness, of growing too old to have children, of ways to support a jobless husband, of remaining for ever as a lodger in her mother's house, of the impossibility of divorce, which only the upper classes could afford, and of the shame and scandal which would be caused by the only grounds she had for it, non-consummation, since Eric would not, could not, be adulterous. Also she thought of death, her own, Eric's, her mother's.

At home, her mother took every opportunity to corner her. Whenever and wherever they were alone together, her mother

15

would close the door and whisper questions about Eric. Asking what he was like, meaning, what was he like in bed? Asking if she were being careful. Reminding her of the narrowness of her hips. Complaining that Eric spoke so little. Didn't Eric like her? What could she have done to offend him? Yet she had noticed how little he spoke to Sarah, his own wife. Was everything alright between them? Was he resentful at what Sarah was quite rightly denying him? Did Eric blame *her* for this? She knew she shouldn't mention it, but she had to mention it: when Eric came home, the smell of pigs and of cattle on his clothes was impossible to remove from the house. She was not complaining, but the neighbours had inquired whether she were keeping livestock. She wanted Sarah to know that the reason she had stopped buying belly of pork, or pork of any kind, was that the smell on Eric's wellingtons had so strong a relation to the smell of that same animal, and that the associations of that smell had affected the animal's taste to Sarah's mother, so that pork was a meat she could no longer stomach.

Sarah countered all the questions and complaints as best she could. She said that Eric was gentle in bed, that there was no fear as yet of her getting pregnant, and that, as for the smells, Eric was lucky to have a job at all, with so much unemployment about. As for the fresh eggs Eric smuggled home in his pockets, she would like to suggest, without wishing to appear at all rude, that her mother found nothing distasteful about *them*.

To Eric's face, Sarah's mother flirted with him, like a small girl in her first party frock. His lack of response to her attentions was the cause of many of her questions to her daughter.

The other place, besides the drapery shop, where Sarah had time and solitude to think about the future, and what, if anything, she could do to shape it, was in bed with her husband, when, as happened every night, he had turned away from her, squeezed himself into a foetal position, and said, in a very quiet and sad voice, 'Goodnight.'

Two months and three days after their return home from their honeymoon, Sarah decided to take matters into her own hands, so to speak. She had spent many hours at work thinking about it, and had planned, and then replanned, what she intended to do.

The light had been switched off. Eric had rolled himself up, and said his quiet, 'Goodnight.' Gently but firmly, using as much strength as was necessary for the work but no more so as not to alarm him, she pulled his right arm, so that he turned, still in the foetal position, with his knees stuck up in the air to form a tent of the bedclothes. Sarah held each side of his face with her hands, and kissed him firmly on the lips, forcing her tongue into his mouth. Then, still holding his face between her hands, she lifted her face away from his, and said, 'We have to talk about this.'

Her hair hung down on each side of her face, so close to him that he could smell it. He closed his eyes, then lowered his knees, so that for the first time he lay there beneath her, unguarded and passive. From beneath his left eyelid, a tear trickled to the top of his nose, and ran down the side of it. A moment later, his right eye shed water too. Sarah kissed him gently on the tip of his nose, then pressed her lips gently onto each of his eyelids.

'There must be something we can do about it.' She spoke softly, with optimism and tenderness, encouraging a child to take its first step.

He lay still, with his eyes closed. Then his lips began to tremble, and without sound, he mouthed the words, 'I'm sorry. I'm so very sorry.'

The feelings, like floating weeds, which had grown in the base of his stomach, and had accumulated and tied themselves up into the kind of knot one can't undo, now suddenly broke free, and came rushing up into his throat to find release. The corners of his mouth turned down, as he bit hard on his lower lip to stop the feelings escaping, but the force of emotion was too powerful, and first he began to sob, grabbing Sarah's hands and pulling them down so that he was able to turn his face to one side, and then gradually between the sobs there were words, fragmented, some swallowed as they were uttered, some cried out, some whispered, some incoherent, some half-finished. So his feelings poured from him, as his head jerked from side to side as if he were in a fever. His eyes were still closed as tight as he could close them, but the tears still flowed.

'Can't help . . . Help me . . . Takes me . . . by surprise. I do . . . do want . . . do love. Can't . . . control it . . . No warning . . . Me . . . not you . . . My fault . . .' and suddenly, loudly, 'IT'S SO BLOODY UNFAIR', swearing in Sarah's presence for the first time, uttering for what must surely be the first time the clear statement of an unalterable belief, which was that this not so much premature as instantaneous ejaculation was unfair, a trick played on him by

17

some bloody-minded Creator, determined to ensure that the one thing any man could do, he, Eric, would do wrongly, and to no effect but sorrow and embarrassment. He could not believe that it would happen, and yet it happened every time, and every time the surprise and disbelief and shame was as strong as before. Sarah, aware that her mother might already have her ear to the wall, listening for the sound of bed-springs, touched his lips lightly with her forefinger to indicate that he should keep his voice low. She whispered, 'We have to try together. If you turn away from me, I can't help you. It doesn't matter if it takes a long time for you to get better, as long as we keep trying. If we keep touching each other, perhaps you'll get used to me.' Thus, in the year 1923, many years before Masters and Johnson had begun their work among the premature ejaculators of the United States, Sarah's intuition took her towards what was to become an essential principle of Marriage Guidance. The world is full of humble people who have anticipated the discoveries which have made others rich, and died without even a *Times* obituary.

Eric said, 'Hate . . . not being . . . like other . . . They can . . . able . . . I have duties . . . as a husband.' He cleared his throat, and his Adam's apple, Sarah knew, would be bobbing up and down in agonies of embarrassment. She stroked the side of his sunburnt neck with the backs of her fingers. He was not unattractive to her; he did not repel her, as her father had created in her mother feelings of repulsion. 'Should have . . . have told . . . told when . . . Thought . . . Couldn't . . . Talking dirty to mention . . . Telling you . . . dirty talk . . . Not on a Sunday.' They had met, had conducted their courting, had been at least for country walks together, on Sundays. Even if Eric could have brought himself to introduce the topic at all, Sunday would clearly not have been the day for it.

Sarah said, 'How could you know before? Before we were married. How . . .?' But her voice trailed away. If he had tried with other women, and failed, she was not sure she wanted to know about it. If other women knew his secret, then it would be known in the town; there would have been secret sniggers at the wedding. Anyway, she did not want details of that sort from Eric; they did not help her plan. But Eric covered his face with both his hands, and spoke. Once he had begun, he had to tell it all.

He spoke so quietly that she could only hear by putting her ear very close to his mouth, and this tickled, but she bore it. There

18

had been no experience with local women. It had been at the Orphanage. He had told her he had been brought up at an orphanage. He didn't want to offend her; he didn't want it to sound dirty; he hoped she wouldn't laugh at him; he had to tell her. Sarah shook her head, so that her hair brushed against the backs of his hands. She would not laugh at him. He took her hair in his hand, and held it against his face.

There had been a woman at the Orphanage. She was the one who would go round the dormitory at night, tucking everybody up, saying, 'Goodnight. Sleep well.' But for some of the older boys, she did more than tuck them up. She used to put her hand under the blankets, and touch the secret parts of some of the older boys, and play with them, and she would stand close by the side of the bed, and allow them to put their hands up inside her skirt and into her secret parts. But she had laughed at Eric. Because when she touched Eric's secret parts, or if Eric should first put *his* hand up under her skirt, then at once ... immediately ... just as it still was ... always ... every time. And she laughed. There was no excitement, no enjoyment, just surprise and shame. He had thought it was because he was so young, and he had asked the other boys, and they had told him that they had kept their hands within her secret parts for many minutes, in some cases very many, and what it was like up there, inside her, their fingers inside her, how she had become open and wet inside, and had wriggled, and ... and even at the telling, often, at the mere account of it, Eric had experienced the same strange and shameful orgasm, which he did not know was an orgasm, or even what an orgasm was, but only knew that he could not control it or hide the effect. 'It had to be a secret. Otherwise they would have sent her away from the Orphanage. She never told the others about me. But they guessed.'

He stopped, let go of Sarah's hair, buried his face in the pillow, and was biting it. So much regret, and anger, and deep shame. Sarah leaned over him, thinking of all the girls at school who had 'talked dirty', and of all those who, unlike herself, had cried at their first period. She had not cried; she had suddenly felt much older, a woman, and almost of the world. Eric had small golden hairs on the back of his neck, she knew. She put out a hand in the darkness, and touched them. She was a woman, he only a boy who had outgrown his strength. But she had strength, she must use it.

Slowly, while her husband sobbed soundlessly into his pillow, Sarah got to her knees on the bed, and removed the nightdress she was wearing. Then she took one of Eric's hands in hers, and led it around the contour of her body. Using her own fingers to spread out his, she moved his hand over and under and around each of her breasts in turn, down the front of her stomach, then sideways over the curve of her hip, down the outside of her thigh and up the inside to between her legs. As his finger touched her pubic hair, his hand tightened, and he tried to withdraw it, but she held the hand firmly, and refused to let it go. As she lowered herself onto his fingers, she said, 'Don't worry about what happens now. It really doesn't matter,' and forced his fingers inside her, brushing her vulva with one of them.

'We have to love one another, Eric. Because we promised God that we would.' And she thought to herself, 'One day! I can wait. One day he will give me a baby.'

She kissed the back of his schoolboy neck, and, with her fingers intertwined with his and her right arm over him, they both fell asleep.

4

*Everything cost a penny or less, and the eyebrows
of the salesgirls were of little importance*

On the twenty-first of April, 1926, Princess Elizabeth, later to
become Queen of Great Britain, was born. Sarah and Eric had been
married three years, and still they were childless.

Sarah had remained at her job with Tyson's Drapery and was
now the manageress. To young women of a romantic nature, she
sold brightly coloured garters from a card at sixpence each. Such
young women must have too much money for their own good.
Sixpence would buy a pound of stewing-steak which, cooked with
a cow-heel, allowed to cool in a basin, and turned upside down
when the jelly of brawn had set, would be meat for a family for
four days. Sarah disapproved the extravagance, but sold the
ribbons anyway.

She took great pride in her display booth, in which she set
ribbons and cottons, laces and rolls of netting. Thrifty women
came to the shop with their daughters to purchase trimmings with
which to refurbish a handed-down frock so that it could pass for
new. Some of them would bring the frock in with them so as to get
Sarah's advice on how to go about it. She did not sell such customers more than they could afford or needed; her advice was good.

Most of Sarah's customers came to her for Vedonis Egyptian
cotton underpants and vests, and for socks of various sorts – bed-
socks, hiking-socks, ankle-socks, or grey socks for school with red
and black patterns of diamonds at the tops, which turned over.
The pure silk stockings, at three shillings and threepence, were
seldom sold, but remained, wrapped up like treasure, on the shelves

behind the counter. Those women, whose pride would not allow them to go bare-legged to chapel or to work, bought imitation silk at one shilling or seconds at ninepence. White French knickers with lace edges were stocked, and sold for weddings and the honeymoons which followed, sometimes for christenings, seldom for funerals. Sarah herself wore French knickers and imitation silk stockings, below a sensible blouse and skirt, for she had a discount on all goods she bought for herself, and was expected to look her best when serving.

She and Eric now lived in a tied cottage at the end of a row of one-up-and-one-down similar cottages, though theirs had the advantage of a small extra room at the back, in which there was a stone boiler, which had a heavy round wooden lid and an iron grate below it, in which wood or coal could be burned to heat the water. This boiler took up a quarter of the room. The smoke from it was supposed to go out through a pipe at the side of the cottage, but in practice it usually blew back into the room, stinging the eyes of any occupants, and blackening any laundry which had been hung up there to dry. In wet weather, Sarah's blouses for work, which were always crisp and clean, had to be kept away from the boiler, and ironed dry with a flat-iron heated over the fire.

Life at her mother's house had been far more comfortable, but the cottage gave them privacy. Also it was something which Eric himself had acquired by his own work, and this, Sarah hoped, might increase his confidence, and some of that increased self-confidence might find its way into their cold but private bedroom.

The summer passed. Eric worked longer hours at the farm than in winter, and was correspondingly more tired when he got home, so that their love-making, which had improved, regressed again. Sarah found that she was irritable, and less concentrated at work. Her manner was sometimes offhand, and occasional customers complained. She sacked a young girl who had until then shown promise of becoming an efficient saleslady, simply because the girl arrived for work one day with her eyebrows drawn on with a burnt matchstick. It was not the use of the matchstick to which Sarah had objected. This, like top-of-the-milk as face-cream, and soot or salt as toothpowder, might be thought a praiseworthy economy. But the girl had done it so badly, first by not following the natural line of her eyebrows, then by allowing the matchstick line to get smudged, so that she looked like someone who had (for some private reason) pushed her head up the chimney just before leaving the house.

The girl was sacked. It was a mistake. The girl cried, and said what was most likely true, that she would be unable to find another job. Sarah became angry at what she considered to be blackmail, and stood her ground, feeling that if she were to give way, with the other girls looking on, she would no longer be able to control them. So the girl left, and was difficult to replace, none of the many other applicants for her job being even half as competent. Sarah's exasperation was not lessened by hearing that the sacked girl did find another job, with Cohen's Bazaar in Preston, where everything cost a penny or less, and the eyebrows of the salesgirls, whether drawn on properly or not, were of very little importance.

Harvest Festival came and went at the chapel. Flowers and fruit were arranged in various decorative ways to the greater glory of God, before being transferred to the Cottage Hospital, there to be consumed by the patients, but Sarah's womb had borne neither flower nor fruit. She fitted white ankle-socks onto the feet of infants and grey three-quarter-length stockings onto the legs of schoolboys with bruised and blistered knees, but bore no child of her own on which to fit socks of any length or colour. She undressed and re-dressed only her display window, and with less flair and interest than once she had shown, carrying out the task because, if it were not done, the goods there faded or grew dusty and had to be marked down.

Three years more, three more fertile springs, three ripening summers, three Harvest Festivals, three bleak winters, one thousand and ninety-five nights of trial and error. Sarah was now thirty-two years old, Eric thirty-four. Slowly their love-making had improved. Gradually she had brought him to the state in which he took her almost as powerfully as her father had once taken her mother, and as she had laid there, encouraging him to go higher and deeper into her, she had imagined her own father, whom she had never seen, breaking into her mother with his brute force and callous determination, and always it was that image which prompted her orgasm.

One day, in the late spring of 1930, the doctor confirmed that she was pregnant.

By Harvest Festival, she would be round and ripe as the fruit arranged so tastefully about the altar by Mrs Grant and Mrs Williams: she would be as heavy-laden as the sheaves (more usually the sheaf) placed against the pulpit by Miss Burton. But her fruit would not be taken to the Cottage Hospital or feed the old, the sick, and the poor. It was at the Cottage Hospital that her fruit would be delivered, and would be brought forth from there, to grow and thrive; it would see Harvest Festivals long after the Grim Reaper had gathered Sarah and Eric to Him. It would see Christmas as she herself had seen it, as a child (Eric would tell her little about Christmas at the Orphanage), and it would wonder and tremble with excitement at the carol-singing, and the cribs, the home-made mangers, the crêches with their Holy Family and all the animals cut out of cardboard and the cottonwool snow and the tinsel, all lighted by real candles. Later it would play in the cold white magic sent down by God in tiny individual flakes especially for children.

It would love her, and show its love for her. No matter what pain she suffered to give it life; that would be of no account. It would be hers; it would give meaning to her existence. Its future would be her responsibility.

Eric received the news with amazement. Since their marriage, his world had been centred around Sarah and her body. She had shown him how to attain and sustain a prolonged erection, as other men did; he adored her. She had excited him to orgasm, yet it was an orgasm without guilt; it was a release both desired and expected, not an humiliating and guilty surprise. He had sown his seed in a fertile furrow, and his seed had germinated. He was to become a father.

That night Sarah couldn't sleep. Her mind was racing with plans. Nothing must ever go wrong now. She would work out her notice at the shop, and then rest until the baby was born. She was no longer young; there might not be another chance; she must contain her excitement, and keep calm. The Lord had heard her prayers at last. She had said 'Thank You' to Him a thousand times under her breath when in company, aloud when alone. It was not enough; she must make her life a continuous 'Thank You' at least until after the baby's birth, so that He might have no occasion for changing His mind.

Eric lay awake beside her, thinking his own thoughts. Summer was nearly upon them. The hours of work would be longer. There would be haymaking, backbreaking to endure. He remembered the cutting, the turning, the raking, working full out while the weather lasted. Because he did it well, he would again be given the job of standing on top of the horse-drawn cart, and receiving forkfuls of hay from the temporary workers, to stack and make a load that wouldn't fall halfway back to the barn. He had been stabbed twice last year by casual labour, boys from the local Reformatory, hired cheaply. The stabbings had not been intentional, but out of stupidity and boredom and irritation at blistered hands; the boys had had no experience of heaving hay up into the cart with a fork, and had spiked him. He was not looking forward to the summer.

But the news of the baby had made Sarah so happy. He leaned over, and kissed her on the forehead. He moved his hand, just as she had taught him, over and around her breasts and down the centre of her belly, over the curve of her hip, down the outside of her thigh, and then on the inside upwards. But as his hand slid upwards, stroking the inside of her thighs, and just as he was about to move her legs apart as she had shown him, suddenly she squeezed her thighs together, crossed her legs, and then took his hand away, and placed it on the sheet between them.

'Please don't do that any more, Eric. I have to be careful now. It's going to be difficult enough, because of the narrowness of my hips. Try to be patient.'

Eric lay on his back, his hands by his sides, looking at the blackness above and around him. His erection, which they had both worked so long and patiently to achieve, now wouldn't go away, but remained like Cleopatra's Needle as a memorial to their mutual achievement. She had encouraged him to be dominant, praised him when he had thought he might be hurting her. Now she had turned on her side, away from him; for the first time in their marriage, she had turned her back on him. He tried thinking of what he most disliked, such as dogs and mice, so as to fill his mind with what repelled him, and undermine the need he so powerfully felt. But the dogs and mice he imagined were all in a state of copulation. Before his marriage, even as a boy at the Orphanage, the sight of one cow abortively attempting to mount another had been enough to provoke from him an unwanted emission. Miss Barnard had whispered to him, 'You're going to have to practise.' Now he had practised. He had practised through many, many nights with his wife, and practice had at last made perfect. Yet now, when he was at last capable of giving pleasure to himself and her, he was no longer to be allowed to do so. Even he knew that some of the groans and exclamations Sarah had made in the early years had been only to encourage him, but not lately. So why? Why now? If penetration would in some way harm the baby, that was not reason enough; they had experimented in other ways. She had taught him to be dominant, and he would be.

He turned on his side, facing her back. He reached his arm over her body, and touched her breasts. She sighed, and took his hand away, placing it near his own genitals. 'Do what men do when they're on their own. Don't make it difficult.'

He lay as still as he could in the darkness. There was no question of his doing what men do when they're on their own; she must know that. He wasn't on his own; he couldn't do it, not here, lying next to her; the toilet was downstairs in the yard. He felt humiliated and lonely. He had not felt loneliness for so long. He was lonely now, numb with it, apathetic and numb. He turned away from her, and lay awake.

Was it a punishment? They had told him, when he left the Orphanage, that he must never have children, that he must take 'precautions', and they had tried to explain those precautions to him, but even to speak of such things had inflamed his imagination, and his embarrassment had precluded close attention to what was said. They had not explained it well; he had not listened well; he knew that he must not have children, but not why, and Sarah's will was stronger than his incomprehension. It had been in some way important that his father . . . that his father with his sister had . . . that his sister had been sent away . . . that Eric had been taken into the Orphanage . . . they had told him that his parents were dead, but now . . . that it was important; he must remember; he must take precautions; that it was not his fault; he was not to blame; but he must remember.

Was it a punishment? He had not remembered, or at least he had done nothing of what they said. How could he, when it was Sarah who said what they should do? How could he tell her what he himself did not understand, but only knew that it was in some way dirty, because Mr Higgs had looked down at his desk all the time he was talking?

26

Now he was lonely. Sarah had rejected him. Was it a punishment for not remembering what he had been told before he left the Orphanage?

Two hours later, Eric Williams, the product of an incestuous union, fell asleep. At least he had one secret left.

5

Just about the same time as the R 101 was crashing into a field south of Beauvais

At the beginning of October, 1930, Sarah sat up in a hospital bed, feeling pear-shaped, and reading glossy magazines which had been left at the hospital by ladies who could afford such extravagance, with the intention that they should circulate amongst the General Wards to remind the aspiring working classes how they, the other half, lived.

In London, at the Phoenix Theatre, a play called *Private Lives* was to open. The author, Mr Noel Coward, was to appear in one of the two leading roles, Miss Gertrude Lawrence in the other. They would be supported by Miss Adrienne Allen and Mr Laurence Olivier. The play was to be about 'swapping partners', she read, and was bound to be tremendous fun. Advertisements praised the ivory tips of De Reszke cigarettes; Sarah wondered how many people could pronounce the name well enough to ask for a packet at the corner tobacconist's. Mansion Polish was advertised by a peacock in a top hat and spats and a toucan in a shawl; in the glossy magazines even the birds and animals were well turned out. Down below in the hospital yard, a fight had broken out among those members of the unemployed who were queueing for jobs as casual porters or mortuary assistants.

Late on Saturday night of October 4th, Sarah entered labour. It was to last until the early hours of Sunday, October 5th. It was not an unduly protracted labour; there was no remarkable excess of pain, brought about by narrow hips. At much the same time as the British airship R 101 was crashing in flames into a field

28

not far south of Beauvais, Sarah felt her last pain, and gave birth to a baby boy. They had drunk champagne on the flight-deck and in the passenger lounge of the R 101, and toasted the Airship Age. Sarah's child weighed seven pounds, four ounces, and seemed in every way perfectly healthy. Sarah had already decided that he should be called 'Walter', because she fancied the name.

Two weeks after Sarah brought Walter home, the front page of the local paper carried a large photograph of the newly-christened little princess, Margaret, and her mother, the Queen. On an inside page, in much smaller type, and a much more inconspicuous position, it carried the anouncement of Walter's birth. The Queen had not been asked to pay the local paper for publishing her daughter's christening photo, but Sarah and Eric had been asked to pay for announcing Walter, and had, after a quarrel about the cost which Sarah won, done so. Sarah said that all the women of the neighbourhood, who had stared at her in chapel so often and for so long and with such interest, should in fairness have their prolonged curiosity satisfied, and know that she was not barren.

Sarah's mother sat in Sarah's kitchen, her hands resting on the boiler for the warmth it gave off, and watched her daughter breast-feeding Walter. An adjustment had been made to the boiler's chimney, so that it was now possible to sit in the kitchen without being choked by smoke.

She had brought with her two bags of pot-herbs, and a sheep's head, to be boiled into a broth. The sheep's tongue would be left to cook, and then sliced and eaten with mustard.

It was a day in January. Sarah's mother kept her coat on, and Sarah wore a grey army blanket over her shoulders. The cottage was cold and damp, Sarah's mother said, after the warmth of her own house. If Sarah wished Walter to live through the winter, she had better rub his chest with goose-grease and keep him well wrapped up. 'Sounds a bit wheezy to me.' She looked upwards, and sighed at the damp patches on the walls, after which she tut-tutted at the thinness of the curtains and the general lack of furnishings. Sarah's mother made these noises and exclamations every winter, but this January they were louder for Walter.

'And you never screamed?'

'I don't remember. I expect I did. Nobody slapped me, or called me a ninny. They were very considerate.'

'I expect you were drugged, dear. They have these new drugs, to help you bear the pain.'

'If I'd been offered a drug, mother, I'd have refused it. It could have done harm to Baby. Anyway, they didn't offer. No drugs were needed. There was nothing out of the ordinary in my case.'

'There are young girls in our street, as have taken to wearing berets, and chewing gum. You see them every day. There's no respect.' A pause. 'How are you going to manage on one wage?'

'The way others do.'

'Is he alright to you now?'

'I don't know what you mean.'

'I mean what I say. Eric. Is he alright to you?'

'You've not heard me complain.'

'Not recently, no. But then, you don't both sleep in the next room to mine any more. I heard enough in those days to make my hair curl.'

Sarah wanted to reply, 'Eavesdroppers never hear good of themselves,' but it hardly seemed appropriate, so she contented herself with, 'Curly hair would go well with those Eiffel Tower ear-rings your so-called friend gave you.' It was the first time her mother had admitted having listened to what went on between Eric and Sarah in bed. 'You know what they say about nosey-parkers.'

'There's these women in Hungary been poisoning their husbands with arsenic. Fifty, at least. They got it off the midwife. She started up a poison factory, and they went to her for it. Well, nobody would suspect, would they, a midwife; she deals in drugs. Arsenic. They dug the husbands up, and found it in them. It was on the wireless this morning.'

Sarah lifted Walter up to her shoulder, and rubbed his back. He burped, as if in agreement with her opinion of nosey-parkers. 'Good Boy!' Her mother was still wearing the expression of hurt indignation, which Sarah knew so well. 'Anyway, it's what turns out in the end that matters, isn't it?'

Eric's face appeared at the window, before the question could be answered. He smiled, and held up close to the glass something he was clutching between his two hands.

'What's he got?'

'Looks like a bird. Don't let him come in until I've got this blanket round Walter.' Sarah's mother stood with her shoulder to the back door, while Eric rattled at the latch, and Sarah hastily covered Walter against the cold. Then she gave the signal, and her mother opened the door.

'What you lock the door for?'

'She was wrapping the child up, so's he wouldn't catch his death. Not that he mightn't do that any road, considering that there's moss growing on those walls.' Sarah's mother no longer flirted with her son-in-law as she had while he had lived in her house. On the contrary, she now treated him as a person to whom one makes complaints, particularly about his own shortcomings. 'And what's that supposed to be?'

'A racing pigeon.'

'Isn't it going to get left behind, sitting there?'

'There's something wrong with it. Can't seem to fly.'

Sarah looked at the grey bird her husband was clasping, and said, 'Don't you bring it near this child. It might have a disease.' She pressed Walter against her side, and adjusted his blanket.

'I thought he might like to see it.'

'He's sleeping. Take it outside.' Eric turned slowly, and lifted the doorlatch with his elbow. He wished she wouldn't talk to him that way in front of her mother.

The pigeon had landed at the farm where Eric worked, and had showed no sign of wanting to finish whatever race it was engaged in. It had followed him around the yard, and he had stolen a handful of grain to feed it. Once fed, wherever he went, it went. It looked up at him, its head on one side and its bright eyes watching his every move. When his work was over, he had picked it up and brought it home with him.

Eric placed the pigeon in the coalshed next to the outside toilet, leaving it with more stolen grain which he had brought home in his pocket, and a shallow dish of water from which to drink. The pigeon walked steadily to the top of the small pile of coal, and blinked at Eric as he closed the door.

Sarah's mother stood; she would not outstay her welcome. As she buttoned her coat, she nodded towards Walter, and said, 'Are you going to go in for any more, then? Now that Eric's found out how to do it?'

PART TWO

Scenes from his Childhood

I

A good boy eats with a knife and fork, and not with a spoon

When, in later life, he was asked what was his first memory, that was a question which required thought. They had asked him other questions which did not require thought, and they had asked him questions which he could not answer, but this was a question he could answer, except that it required thought.

His first memory was of a girl's face. The girl was giggling, covering her mouth with one hand, and pointing at Walter's face with the other. He was standing beside his mother, leaning against her legs, his arms wrapped round them, holding her skirt. It was his first day at school. He was crying. His mother was trying to explain to the teacher that special allowances had to be made for him, because he was different; he was a late developer, and unable to form words properly. He could identify some objects, but not others.

The teacher told the little girl to go away, but she didn't; she just stood there, laughing. Nevertheless, though she was unable to control her laughter, she continued to keep her mouth covered, because she knew that to laugh at an ugly person is wrong.

All this Walter remembered when they asked him. But he was unable to find words with which to express this memory, so in the end, he said he did not know.

He had been five-and-a-half years old on that first day at school, and his baggy grey trousers, two sizes too big, had revealed that beneath them he still wore nappies and plastic pants. The teacher

35

had noticed this, but had found herself unable to mention it to Walter's mother. His mother herself had intended to inform the teacher that she had not yet been successful in training Walter to give her proper warning when he felt the need to go to the lavatory. Later Walter was to be given the nickname of 'Shitty Pants', and made to sit on his own at the back of the classroom, as far away from the teacher as possible. This placing was a kindness to Walter, for it was at the nearest desk to the door; he was told that he might run out of the class whenever he felt the urge, without raising his hand first to ask permission. The desks in front of him and to his left were kept vacant, and that was a kindness to the other children, Walter's classmates. Whenever unkindness was felt to be necessary for any of those children, by way of punishment, they would be made to sit at one of those two desks. Often, when a child was bored or could think of nothing better to do, he would turn round towards the solitary Walter, squeezing his nose between a thumb and forefinger.

It became clear to the teacher that Walter was unable to concentrate his mind upon even the simplest of sums and that both reading and writing were arts which would be for many years beyond him. So Walter was given a large sheet of what was called sugar-paper – usually dark blue and of a rough texture – and told to draw whatever he wished. Walter drew. He was never asked to stand beside the teacher, and read aloud. He had no idea how letters could be put together to form sounds, and how those sounds, alone and in concert, represented words, and words would come together to form sentences, to form speech, conversation, what was said and written by human beings to each other. Walter's vocabulary consisted of five words which he had learned from his mother, after laborious effort on both their parts.

After a year, it had become clear to many people at the school that Walter was 'different'. The headmistress called Walter to her room, to try to ascertain how different he was.

The interview began by the headmistress asking Walter what day it was. Walter did not know. What had Walter eaten for lunch? Walter could not remember. She pointed to the picture of a cow. What was that? Walter knew what the picture represented; he had seen cows before, but did not know what they were called. Shyly he offered, 'Moo.'

This was distinctly encouraging to the headmistress, being at

least half the right answer. 'Moo what, Walter?' She waited.
Walter was silent. The woman wanted more from him. After a
while, it came to him what more he could give. 'Moo Moo,' he
said. Now he was making a close approximation to the noise a
cow makes. 'Moo Moo Moo.'

'Yes. It's a moo-cow, isn't it?'

Walter was tired now. His imitation of a cow had exhausted
him. He looked towards the window, at the sky outside, trying to
assess by the amount of light how long it would be before his
mother came to collect him.

'Try to pay attention, Walter, when I'm talking.' Walter
blinked, and yawned without remembering to cover his mouth.
'Are you tired?' 'Tired' was not one of the five words included
in Walter's vocabulary, but he had a fair idea of what it meant,
so he nodded without turning to look at the headmistress.

'What I have to decide, Walter, is –' The headmistress had
second thoughts. 'Do you understand the word "decide"?' Walter
looked at the sky outside. 'I mean, do you know what "decide"
means?' The clouds moved. They came together, and moved apart;
they made big patches of white against the blue and split into
smaller bits; sometimes the white was all thick and piled together,
and sometimes it was so thin, you could see the blue through it.
Walter made no sign of understanding or even hearing the headmistress.

'What people are going to want to know from me, Walter, is
this. Are you a backward boy, who doesn't understand, or are you
a boy who has decided to be naughty?'

The only word out of all that which had any meaning for
Walter was the word 'naughty', which was one of the words in his
vocabulary. On hearing it, he turned on the surprised headmistress,
and screamed at the top of his voice, 'Not naughty! Not naughty!'
Thereafter his face crumpled into a silent sobbing. Screwed up like
this, it was even more disturbing than it was in repose.

'Alright now. That's quite enough. I don't want any of that,
Walter. Do you hear me?' His tiny hands were rubbing his eyes,
and his mouth was wide open in silent anguish. 'I'm sure you're
not naughty really. It's just that I have to know what you can
and can't do.' What he was doing at the moment was making her
feel extremely uncomfortable. 'We have to know what to do with
you, Walter. I mean, where to put you. Nobody's going to harm

you. Perhaps you might be better off in a different school; you might be happier there. We only want your happiness. Please, Walter, don't cry like that. It's very unsettling to watch, you know.'

So far Walter had made no sound; this was his own particular way of crying. But the expression on his face and the liberal flow of tears from his eyes had frightened the headmistress. Was he holding his breath? Might he at any moment faint? Was he about to have an epileptic fit? She hoped desperately that someone would come into the room, which was not likely, since she had left instructions that she should not be disturbed. What did one do in case of fits? Her mind flew back to her Girl Guide training many years before. The patient's tongue must be held, she remembered, to prevent its being swallowed. Had Walter perhaps swallowed his tongue already? That might explain the lack of noise. Clearly she was dealing with a highly disturbed child. First his lack of concentration, and now this frightening silent anguish; it was most disconcerting. She attempted to smile, and found that it set on her face. She must take some action, and she would.

'Alright now, Walter, let's play a guessing game. What have I got in here, do you think?' The headmistress unlocked a drawer in her desk, and opened it. From it she took a circular tin box, and pushing it across her desk towards Walter, she said, 'Now, then. You guess what I've got in here. Can you?' With the flourish of a magician performing the final trick in an act which had so far gone almost entirely wrong, she removed the lid from the tin, to reveal an assortment of rather old boiled sweets.

'Which colour would you like?'

Slowly Walter lifted his arm as if it weighed a ton, and flopped his hand down into the middle of the tin of sweets. The motion of his fingers was like that of an excavating-machine on a building-site. They dug down into the sweets, and, having secured as many as his hand would hold, lifted them from the tin. Walter ceased his silent crying, and studied the colours and twists of cellophane wrapping protruding from between his fingers, while the head-mistress quickly replaced the lid on the tin, and the tin in the drawer, and made a mental note to buy more boiled sweets. There had been nothing about them in the Guides' First-Aid Manual, but they semed to be efficacious in dealing with fits.

'Well, there, then! That's better, isn't it? I'll have a talk with your mother, when she comes to collect you, and we'll see what we can do. Alright, then, Walter. No need to go back to your class-room now. The bell's just about to ring for playtime. Why not run along, and find someone nice to play with? Off you go.'

Walter stood, holding the sweets as carefully as one might carry a piece of cut-glass. Slowly he left the room, and behind him the smell of stale pee.

Walter moved around the playground slowly, his arms held up in front of his face, with elbows bent. They were his only protection from the arms, legs, heads and bodies of the other children, who ran and shouted, waving their arms, who might bump into him from the front or the side, or even back into him as they backed away from some pursuer. He had begun by attempting just to stand with his back to a wall, taking no part in the play, but only watching, squinting and blinking his eyes as one child made accidental contact with another. But he had been noticed by an older boy, who had made it his business to patrol the boundaries of the playground, so as to make sure that all newcomers joined in the fun. Any newcomers who declined to join the fun would be challenged by this older boy to a fight. The older boy's name was Addison. His territorial behaviour was the reason why many would-be watchers, many more than Walter, became participant in the exercises of the playground and familiar with the texture of its asphalt surface.

Walter kept to the centre of the playground. Nobody had ever told him of the calm in the eye of the storm, but the same instinct which had kept him to the extreme edge until he was hounded from it by Addison now drove him to the centre, which was not, in fact, calm. He tried to look as if he were joining in the fun; in fact he looked like a blind man moving in fear among a field of cattle. There were fifteen minutes of morning break, fifteen in the afternoon, and a period of free time after Dinner. These periods exhausted Walter more than lessons did or could. When, at the end of each such period, a teacher came into the yard with a handbell, and rang it to signal the end of play, Walter would freeze to the spot, arms up, protecting his face, while the other children darted about, to stand behind each other in neat lines, ready for class, and Walter himself would first be called to, and then fetched by one of the older children, to be placed at the back of his line.

So it was on this day. The old boiled sweets were soon knocked to the ground from his tightly clenched fist, and the other children pushed, and fought, and trod on each other's hands to secure one for themselves. Walter watched this scrabbling without emotion. Something had told him that the possession of sweets put him into physical danger. The loss of them so soon after they had been given was not a disappointment to him, but the assurance of safety.

'Your child needs special help, Mrs Williams. We can't give it to him here. We have tried, but the case is beyond us. To take a single instance, he still wears nappies under his trousers, and sometimes fouls them while he's here at school. That's not right, for a lad over six years old. It shows no sign of changing. Children can be very cruel; they notice such things. I suggest that you keep Walter at home for his own sake until I've had a chance to consult with the Education Department. Then they'll write to you with the name of a Special School. You'll get a letter from County Hall.'

'He can't undo his buttons yet; that's all.' Walter's mother turned away from the headmistress. Through the window she could see other children being collected by other mothers – girls with ringlets bouncing as they rushed forward in greeting, boys swinging school satchels, boys with ties and long socks, held up by garters, beneath short trousers which showed the shapes of their clean little bottoms. In the satchels, there would be exercise-books, with sums all ticked and words copied in small neat writing. The short trousers would have buttons in the front, and the small boys would be capable of handling those buttons, undoing them and doing them up again whenever Nature called. Her own son's trousers had to be two sizes too big to accommodate the nappy and plastic knickers beneath them.

'He just won't thrive here.'

The faces of the children at the school gate resembled their mothers' faces. They were small round clear-skinned faces, portraits in miniature of their parents. They expressed interest and pleasure. Walter sat slouched in the chair in which he had been interviewed, his eyes staring into the middle distance; he was loudly sucking at sweets she had brought him.

'It's only his buttons he can't handle.'

40

She was pleading. The headmistress was embarrassed, and looked at the floor. 'I know he's not a bright child, but he's not . . .' The headmistress had used a word to describe Walter. The word stuck in Sarah's throat, and would not be said.

'It's not a nice word, I know, Mrs Williams, but it has a meaning, and we have to face facts. I'm not saying that Walter might not just be a late developer. If a child does well enough at a Special School, then of course he's sent back to an ordinary school. There's always that possibility.'

Four boys in the playground were playing a game which involved the twisting of ears.

'Will he ever catch up?'

The headmistress noticed that multi-coloured saliva was dripping from Walter's chin onto a rug beside her desk. 'Well, I really couldn't . . . I mean, it's impossible to predict. I don't think one should raise your hopes too high.' Sarah's hopes were not high at all, and might have benefited from being raised. 'I do think Walter will always have problems – problems of what we call "communication". He has a peculiar way of crying, had you noticed? I do think it might be more than an educational problem; I think your doctor should be consulted. I was quite upset by him this afternoon. I simply mentioned the word –' She realized too late that to mention the word again might be to risk a repetition of Walter's peculiar way of crying, so she put one hand up to her mouth and whispered the word 'naughty' in quite a friendly way to this woman, Mrs Williams, the boy's mother, before continuing, 'Frankly I wasn't sure what to do. It's a word which is bound to crop up in any school from time to time. I'm sure that gives you an indication of the kind of problem we're facing.'

Outside a boy of six and a girl of seven were holding hands and whispering secrets to each other.

'And now, if you'll excuse me, I do have a Guide Meeting this evening.' Sarah moved away from the window of the headmistress's study, and took Walter's hand into her own. He stood up, and choked on the sweet he was sucking, and then, after his mother had patted him hard on the back, coughed it out onto the rug, already wet with saliva. His mother bent down to retrieve the sweet.

'No, please don't bother. I'll scrape it up with some waste paper. Please don't get your hands all sticky.'

The large oak door of the school was closed behind them, and they walked together across the playground. Sarah looked back at the door. She had been to school here, many years ago. The oak door, with its Norman arch and its heavy iron hinges, was the same. She remembered having to use both hands to turn the large iron handle. She remembered the fear, the excitement, the reverence she had felt then towards this school, the childhood crushes, the fascination of growing older and wiser, the security and comfort of having friends and being liked. She had been pretty; she had been popular. Nothing in her adulthood had matched the excitement of those children's games.

They reached the wrought-iron railings, the tops of which looked like arrowheads, and passed through the gate. The head of a small boy appeared round the corner of the school wall, its features contorted into a small boy's idea of a village idiot. 'Hey! Shitty Pants! Give us a sweet!' Walter's hand went automatically to the trouser pocket in which he had hidden the sweets his mother had given him, and brought out a mauve boiled sweet. Sarah snatched the sweet from his hand, and threw it over to the other side of the street.

Walter looked up at his mother's face, his eyes squinting at the light of the sky. He saw that she was crying without a sound. Her lips turned down at the corners, and were trembling as she tried to keep the lower lip still by biting it. For Sarah did not wish to be seen weeping in the street, and was determined to take herself in hand.

Walter's grip on his mother's hand tightened, and warned her of the danger of tears. She could sense the anxiety swelling up inside him. Once in a moment of anger she had threatened to give him away to the gypsies whom they had seen camped at the side of the road. He had looked at the large piebald horses, and screamed in terror. He feared all animals, and had nightmares about horses.

His head drooped. He looked down at the stones of the pavement, and they seemed to move towards him. He looked at his school boots, the laces of which he could not tie. (The gypsies' children had bare feet.) His boots moved forward, one overtaking the other. It seemed to him that they were not his boots, the feet inside them not his feet. The feet inside the boots moved, and he did not feel them. If only he could feel them, they would be his,

42

and the boots would be his. He squeezed his toes together (they were certainly his toes), and was reassured by the sharpness of a nail inside the left boot. He had felt that nail before, after his father had put new leather on the soles of the boots. He placed his middle toe over the reassuring nail, and pressed down. He felt the sharp point cut into his toe, and pressed harder until he could feel sticky blood inside his sock. Yes, these were his boots. This was his mother holding his hand. His. The boots, the hand belonged to Walter. This was he. He was Walter. He was here. He was walking. Walter was him. He was Walter.

Now he hardly noticed the cracks between the paving-stones and the bits of silver paper and toffee wrappers. These were his boots moving with his feet inside them. Feet, legs, knees, all belonged to him; he could do what he liked with them. That he should own his whole body both pleased and worried him. His mother had told him that he should take pride in himself, not soil himself or scratch or pick at his skin. *His* skin. Walter began to feel fear again. His whole body belonged to him. It was frightening to be in charge of such a thing. And was he really in charge? He had felt pain sometimes, and had not wished for it. He had experienced being sick, more than once. When that had happened, he had thought, 'What is happening to me? What is inside me that wants to get out? He had seen the producer of his pain. It had rushed out of him, causing him terrifying spasms and retching. This pain-producer was sudden, liquid, acid-tasting, brown in colour, having some resemblance to the vegetable soup he had eaten earlier. It did not belong to him. It lived in his insides, and caused them to hurt, and then rushed out and fell about the room.

So that had been in his body, and he had not controlled it in any way. And there was something behind his forehead also, something that worried him, made him cry, and frightened him. It must be his, since it was inside him, but he couldn't switch it off. Sometimes it gave him headaches. It was like . . . He did not know what it was like; it was like fishes; it was like a bowl, with fishes, too many, which darted about, swimming and slithering about – thoughts and half-thoughts and disconnected parts of thoughts, never joining up, but always swimming and darting about like fish, catching the light for a moment, then gone, never waiting long enough in any place to be clear and apprehended. He could

43

never follow one to see where it went, because the others confused him, taking its place and then, in their turn, twisting away from him, glittering thoughts too slippery for him to hold.

Sometimes, when he rolled his eyes up towards the ceiling and stared hard at that to stop the goldfish from darting about behind his forehead, Walter would be slapped by his mother, and told that he was dreaming again, and that he mustn't look in that funny way because people would think he was simple. He would burst into tears, but that was no answer, because the goldfish only returned, and the same people who would think him simple would say, his mother told him, he was a cry-baby if they saw him weeping. And Walter would rub at his eyelids with the back of his hand, trying to chase away the goldfish, or at least to catch one and make it keep still.

'Please, Walter, be a good boy,' and Walter would reply, 'Want to. Want to.' A good boy was one without goldfish in his head. A good boy smiled, and sat quietly; he used the potty, and cleaned himself afterwards. A good boy ate with a knife and fork, and not with a spoon, but whenever Walter attempted this, his hands shook, and the food dropped back on his plate, or splashed into his lap or on the tablecloth. With a dish and a spoon held close to his face, he could manage quite well, but this was how a baby feeds itself, and Walter was nearly seven years old.

2

A vet with a pill or an injection, administered while she protested love and kindness, could free her

The fire in the grate meant security. The red embers said, 'Continue. We do. Day after day, we are here. We comfort you. Grey and cold in the morning, yet we shall be red again by tea-time.' The flames flickered and reached up. They said, 'Hope. Tomorrow and tomorrow; there is always something. Tomorrow is another day.'

Walter looked at the fire, felt the warmth from it, wondered at how it worked, and was glad his mother got such pleasure from it. What she felt, he felt; it was as simple as that. He was safe when she was happy, unsafe when she was sad. Between those two extremes, there was an infinite variety of moods his mother might feel. At such times, he was uncertain.

Sarah saw Walter watching her, looking up from his place on the rug at her feet. Her awareness of his dependence weighed heavy. If she were to smile, he would smile back, but he would watch her still. And smiling once wasn't enough; she could not smile all the time. To see her worries, fears and doubts reflected back in his face tired her. She felt guilty, like a small child, who has been tormenting an animal, but with none of the pleasure such a child might feel in exercising its power to inflict pain. Walter was like a puppy, licking her hand for approval, like a stray dog at the Dogs' Home, who, if she did not take him home, would be put down, whose tongue, eyes, damp nose, every line of his body, said, 'Please! Please show me I am loved and the world a good place. Reassure me. I only live through you. I can only operate with your good opinion, your approval. Roll me over; tickle my stomach; stroke my head; it is in these ways God's favour is shown. My head is so full of disquiet; smooth it away. Please!'

If only Walter had been born a dog and not a human child, how easy it would be to end her sense of responsibility. A vet with a pill or an injection, administered while she protested love and kindness, could free her. And what then? She was not prepared to consider, 'What then?' Sap bubbled out of a log on the fire, hissing and spitting as it proclaimed its greenness, its life, its unreadiness to burn, its indignation at having been wrongly classified and placed with dead wood. Planted in the earth, it might have sprouted new branches, and grown into a tree. Now its life-juice was being turned rapidly into vapour, and by morning it would be ash, to be sprinkled on the garden to assist other plants to grow.

What if they were weeds, what if it were to assist only weeds?

Walter listened to the noise the green log made, and watched the sap bubbling out. He frowned as he watched, and wished the log to be quiet. To him, it was truly alive; anything which made a noise like that was living. He had watched spiders and woodlice crawl out of logs placed on the fire. He had watched them panic, running upwards to the highest point of the fire to avoid the flames and heat, and then he had seen them taken by the fire, shrivelling up into bits of black and dropping into the flames, where they cracked and hissed. He looked up at his mother, hoping that she would rescue the log before all the sap had gone. Instead she picked up the poker, and pushed the green log further down into the grate. When that log had burned, she would go to bed. She would lie and think about all the tomorrows stretching ahead of her. If Walter had been a dog, avenues which were now closed to her would open. There would be choices to make about her future. Now there was only one choice, which was either to put up with the situation and be as happy as God would allow, or to bemoan her luck and make a virtue of unhappiness.

Her husband did not enter either into the choice she must make as matters were or into the many choices which might open before her had Walter been born a dog.

The red embers glowed, and the weak blue and yellow flames teased the young sapling, as her own mother had teased all the

46

men she had known, once her virginity had been taken by force. 'Tomorrow is another day,' said the mendacious flames, 'Hope!' Tomorrow would be another day just like today, and so onwards. She screwed up her eyes at the thought of it, and then remembered to smile a reassuring smile at the pathetically mournful face of her son. There was no good to be gained in upsetting him before bedtime. Get him to bed, and then cry, if she must. Not in front of him. Don't give him nightmares. There would be time enough, between putting her son to bed and the return of her husband from work, for Sarah to cry.

'Tomorrow is another day.' She would not cry now; she would cry later. 'Tomorrow is another test by God of your love for Him. Are you going to fail that test, and be punished at the last by fire?' The flames licked the log, and took it. 'Glory in God's favours now. Come to Him, and bend your knees in prayer. No one is without sin, none without the need to be forgiven. Place your life before Him. Offer the gift of your self to Him who gave selfhood itself to you. Feel His power, His strength surge up inside you, as you come forward today, glowing with His goodness.' She would cry later, as she prepared Eric's tea. There would be no meat; he could not expect meat in the middle of the week, but it would be hot. 'I can feel the presence of Jesus inside you.' She could feel the presence of Jesus inside her; He was inside her. 'You have true riches, beyond wealth. You have happiness. Am I right?' Yes, He was right. 'Did you ever doubt Him?' Yes, she had doubted Him. 'Are you sure now?' Yes, she was sure. 'Can you feel Him inside you? Can you feel His glory inside you, making you glow?' Yes. 'I see that glow, my sister. I am proud of that glow, my sister. I am proud you have found today, the true, the only love of your life. Stand up before the people, sister. Let the people see you glowing?'

Yes, she was glowing, radiating true happiness, which is expressed in tears, weeping the tears of true happiness, fulfilled and made whole by Him who was so deep within her. 'It is your choice, my brothers and sisters. Only you can make the first step towards Him. He calls, and we come.' He called. She came. 'We give ourselves to Him as Sister Sarah has today. I feel good today, brothers and sisters. One more soul for Jesus. Those tears she weeps are tears of joy. There is a new Sister Sarah walking amongst you from today. Look! Look! They are tears of holy joy.'

47

Walter was frowning, and holding his breath. He had observed the tears of joy; they would give him nightmares. Sarah looked at what Jesus had placed inside her – with such help, with such patient and enduring help from Sarah herself – at what Jesus had placed inside her for nine months. She looked at what Jesus had then drawn forth from within her narrow hips. She held out her hand, and he came and sat on her knee. She cuddled him to her, rocking and weeping. She said, 'I never felt Jesus inside me; you're not a child from Him. I didn't cry for joy. I cried for loneliness; I cried for myself and my wicked thoughts. I tried to seem a different person afterwards. It was all a pretence. I wanted to be accepted by everyone at the chapel. Chapel people. Respectable people. I wanted marriage, and a house on Shear's Brow, over-looking the town. But nobody rushed forward to make a proposal. I waited, teaching Sunday School, and walking home alone. And then . . . And then . . .'

As she talked in a low soothing voice, trying to undo the damage her tears had caused, she became aware that Walter had fallen asleep, and that he was heavy. Then there was a third thought, unconnected as far as she could tell to the others, but it frightened her, and wouldn't go away. The word 'accident' kept pushing its way into her mind. It danced before her, and with it danced Harlequin, with mask and sword. She found that she could not replace these images with any other, no matter how hard she tried. 'Accident.' 'Painless accident.' Children had them every day; the papers were full of them.

'Oh God, what am I thinking about?'

As she asked herself the question, it was answered, though not by God. She knew the answer. She was thinking of herself, of freedom, of tomorrow and all the tomorrows which would follow it, the tomorrows which must follow it. Unless she were careful, and acted now.

3

The most they could do would be to accuse her of being careless

Every day they walked through the streets, hand in hand. She paraded her misfortune. The people who stopped and talked to her always put their heads to one side when they looked down at Walter. Very few of them mentioned him, or talked to him. They assumed that Sarah would rather they ignored him. She felt their pity and their curiosity. She saw their faces, and watched their expressions of relief when the conversation had come to a natural end, or when they had thought of a way of ending it, and were able to move on without impoliteness. She also knew that their seeing her and Walter made them more contented with their own lives.

Other women of her age might have husbands who drank, or looked at, or even chased other women. They might have husbands who had simply grown tired of them, even disliked them, husbands with whom they shared the same house, and that was all. But none of these women was Walter's mother. Her misfortune was their gain.

She had tried staying in the house all day. It was unhealthy. The boredom made her irritable, with herself as well as with Walter. Outside there were things to distract her. At times she was even able to imagine that she was holding the hand of a normal child, the child she had longed for.

At home her awareness of his watching her made her self-conscious. Since no one from County Hall had written to her about a Special School, she tried reading to him, and helping him

49

play with the bricks they had bought for him five years earlier, but she found herself losing her temper too often. If she left one room to go to another, he cried. He seemed happier walking beside her, hand in hand. Sometimes he even seemed interested in the things they saw.

Because of the women she met and the obligatory conversations she did not enjoy, Sarah began taking Walter out into the countryside, where they would meet fewer people whom she knew. Sometimes they would get on a bus, and ride to a park where they were not known at all. At other times, they would just start walking away from the houses and into the country.

Walter never seemed to mind how far they walked. He never whined, or asked to be carried. Anyway, he was too heavy to be carried.

One of these walks took them a long way from the houses, down narrow country lanes where no one saw them. They would have to rest before starting back. Sarah settled on a resting-place where a railway line ran under the road. It was not a bridge, for bridges have humps. The road remained flat, but instead of a hedge on either side, there was a brick wall, about four feet high, under which trains passed at full speed.

Sarah was tall enough to see the trains, and just strong enough to lift Walter up onto the wall for him to see them as they rushed into the short tunnel beneath their feet.

She found herself returning more and more often to this place. The speed of the trains, and the smoke which, when a train passed beneath them, enveloped both the brick wall and themselves, fascinated her. It wasn't only that the fast trains suggested freedom and travel and a new and different kind of life. With Walter sitting on the wall, holding both her hands but looking down at the passing train, she felt her freedom to be more than wishful thinking. Here on the bridge it became a definite possibility. All she had to do was to let go of Walter's hands.

Each time they visited the bridge, they spent longer there, and soon they were going there every day. By the end of two weeks Sarah knew at what time a train would pass beneath them. She knew which were the faster trains, and which seemed to gush the most smoke up at them, hiding Walter's face from hers. Just a few seconds; she only needed a few seconds. As long as she could not see him, she felt sure, she would be able to release his hands from hers.

The most they could do would be to accuse her of being careless. He was known to be backward, but large for his age. She would say he had heard a train coming, and had run on ahead. She would say she had shouted at him to stop, had run as fast as she could, but that he had climbed the wall, had stood on it, been enveloped in smoke, and had become frightened, and had tried to jump down, choosing in panic the wrong side.

She rehearsed the story over and over again inside her head. The recitation of each small detail excited her. Every one must be plausible. Since nobody had ever seen Walter take the initiative and run off on his own, Sarah bought him a small train to play with, and although he ignored it, she would say that he had become fascinated by trains, and that was why he had run on ahead.

Her life would be changed in a very few seconds. There was nothing to keep her with Eric; she need not stay with Eric. She would write away for a post in drapery, somewhere in Manchester, Birmingham or even London. She would rise; she would be at the least a manageress. As for Walter, it was a kindness. How could he ever be happy? If she sighed, he cried; she could not maintain a brave smile all the days of her life. He would be a figure of fun and scorn for the rest of her life, and when she died, they would have no option but to put him away. He would be put away with people who were really mad. Some of them might be violent. It was a kindness.

Day after day for several weeks, they visited the bridge, and each time Walter sat on the wall, holding his mother's hands tightly in his. Sarah closed her eyes when the smoke enveloped them. She moved her fingers inside those of her son, and held her breath. His grip tightened on her hands, as each day she became a little bit braver, and moved her fingers a little more. She tried putting his hands inside hers, but he cried and wanted to get down from the wall. But even with him holding her, she could at any time break free. All it required was a little more strength, a little more determination.

Sarah's strength and determination grew. With every visit to the bridge, she became more positive that her freedom was only a matter of finding the right circumstance, the right moment.

Time passed. Still she had not found circumstance or moment. Every time she helped Walter to jump down from the wall, and they began walking back home, Sarah would feel sadness of an almost overwhelming nature. Every time she would make herself a promise that tomorrow she would be able to pull her hands free from his. With each day that passed, he was growing a little heavier, a little more difficult to lift onto the wall. And his willingness to sit on the wall at all depended on her cheerfulness. Yet the game of pretending that what they were doing was fun, had become harder for her. She had to do it soon.

On a Thursday afternoon, nine weeks after their first visit to the bridge, Sarah was holding Walter's hands, and waiting for the train which gushed the most smoke. While waiting, she talked to him, and patted his hands together. *Pattacake, pattacake, baker's man. We'll bake a cake as fast as we can.* The rhyme distracted him, and the patting of his hands together allowed her to hold his wrists, from which it would be easier to release herself.

They seemed to have been waiting on the bridge for the whole of their lives, and the train wasn't even within hearing distance. She had decided that, whatever happened today, she would never visit the bridge again, unless of course it was necessary to come to explain to those who were making inquiries how the accident had happened. Otherwise she would never stand here again. If she failed today, she never would succeed.

The train was four minutes late. Sarah had run out of rhymes and stories. When she heard the train approaching, she placed an arm round Walter's neck, and kissed him.

She was crying now, telling him that it would be alright, reassuring herself and him that what she was going to do was best for them all. Walter watched with troubled eyes, but did not cry as well, as he would usually have done. He just sat there, and allowed her to squeeze and kiss his hands, and stroke his hair.

She was crying with such force, wiping the tears away with her sleeve, talking and crying as the train came closer to the bridge.

'I love you. I don't want to harm you. Be a good boy for Mummy. It's all for the best. I can't make you well. Please help me this time. Please be a good boy.' Her words ran together, between sobs and gulps for breath. She had worked herself up to meet the right moment, and now her plan had to work. It couldn't not work now.

The smoke from the train made her eyes sting. She closed them, and took two steps back, away from the wall. Her hands were free. No one was holding them. She moved the fingers to make sure, then clenched both fists up tight, and crossed her arms across her chest.

The smoke hung over the bridge far longer than it had ever done before. She thought it was never going to clear. Or was it her eyes? Was it the tears and the stinging which clouded her vision? She wiped her eyes again on her sleeve, and could just make out the shape of a figure sitting on the wall.

She moved towards the figure, and grabbed it to her before it fell. Walter's hands were bleeding. He had gripped the edge of the bricks so hard that they had cut into his palms.

He was shaking, and she helped him down. Not only had she released herself from his grip; she had tried to jolt him off balance. She had failed. They would never come to the bridge again.

Sarah wrapped her handkerchief round Walter's left hand, which was the hand he held out for her to hold, and they started to walk home.

On the next day a letter arrived from County Hall, informing her that a Special School had been found for her son Walter.

4

Is your journey really necessary?

It took forty-three minutes by bus to reach Walter's Special School. Since, as far as Walter knew, it was just another bus-ride, he did not scream until he saw the school, the other children and the teacher into whose care his mother was about to hand him. While Walter screamed on, Sarah spoke to the teacher about her son and his difficulties. And the teacher spoke to Sarah about the importance of what was called 'house-training'. A backward, slow-learning child should be given as much stimulus to learn at home as it was at school. There was a book, which Sarah might be able to borrow from her local Public Library. She wrote the title of the book on a piece of pink paper, rather as if it were a doctor's prescription, and (rather as if it were a prescription) Sarah folded the piece of pink paper, and tucked it into her handbag.

Sarah walked away across the playground, with the sound of Walter's screams echoing inside her head. She had to be back at three thirty to collect him. Considered in terms of the amount of travelling time and the expense, it hardly seemed worthwhile to go home.

She asked, and was directed to the nearest Public Library. She found the book easily, and read it twice, since it was a short book. The necessity for the second reading was that she became sure that she must somehow have misread the first time. Some of the author's suggestions would be likely to send Walter into outright hysterics. There was a section headed, 'Play Wishful Thinking' in which it was suggested that mother and child should act out feelings and thoughts which the child would not otherwise be able to express by giving them to a character in a game. Thus Sarah might pretend that the house was on fire, or that Walter had some dreadful illness which she, as the play-doctor, would cure. Thereby Walter's fear of fire and dreadful illness would be diminished, and also, the author added, with sound practical common sense, 'if it ever does happen, you will both be prepared'.

The most important words for a child to learn were its own name and the word 'Look'. When a child can say its own name, it gains confidence. When it responds to the word 'Look', the world opens up for it. Drawing was good. Sarah must encourage Walter to scribble circles and make straight lines. All children drew houses at some stage of their development and, when Walter drew a house, Sarah must repeatedly ask him the same questions, 'How big are the windows? How small is the door? How much smoke is coming out of the chimney?' (Sarah did not know how one measured the volume of smoke from a chimney, and the book did not tell her.) The question, 'How high is the fence or hedge around the house?' was particularly important, for by the answer might be measured the amount of security felt by the backward child, or – more importantly – lacked.

Later when she asked Walter to draw a house (for he showed no sign of wishing to draw one unasked), he drew a circle, and coloured it red. There were no doors, no windows, no fence, and no smoke. For a long time, Walter's idea of home remained a red circle, and Sarah was left in doubt as to what amount (or lack) of security the red circle signified.

When Walter started at the Special School, he was eight years old, but his mental age was four. Each morning the crying would begin, as Sarah dressed him, ready for the forty-three-minute journey to school.

In the bus, he sat next to the window and sobbed, his eyes red and sore, and his nose running. Sarah held his hand in hers, and used her free hand to point out things of interest, using the word 'Look' as often as posible. 'Look! Cows! Look! Sheep!' But the world was not opened up for Walter by that magic word. Nothing interrupted his sobbing.

He would continue to cry, so the teacher told her, for half an hour every morning after Sarah had left him at the school. He would stand, holding onto a coat-hook in the cloakroom, refusing to let anyone remove his navy-blue gaberdine raincoat, and sobbing his heart out.

Left alone, he would become tired, and sleep for an hour on the floor of the cloakroom, still wearing his raincoat, and when he awoke, it would be as if he were a different Walter. He would remove his raincoat, leave it on the floor, and join the other children to play. He would play as a four-year-old might play, but since all the children at that school were there because they were backward, the fact that Walter was the size of a well-built eight-year-old was not remarkable.

One day in his third week at the school, Walter just stopped crying. He had cried in the bus, but, instead of clinging to the coat-hook, he went straight into the classroom, and began work with plasticine, allowing a teacher to remove his raincoat as he worked.

After that he no longer cried while being dressed for school, or on the bus.

Plasticine, cutting out pictures with blunt round-ended scissors, counting up to ten and playing in the sandpit at one end of the classroom were Walter's principal activities at the Special School for the next four years. He was then twelve years old, had learned very little, but had been, on balance, considerably more happy than not, and Britain had been at war for almost three years.

As a farm labourer, Eric was in a reserved occupation, helping his employer 'Dig For Britain'; indeed, he did considerably the more digging of the two. He continued to smuggle home fresh eggs, and made and set his own wire snares for rabbits, of which, since they were too bulky to hide in his jacket and must be declared to his employer, he was allowed to keep half; on the many occasions on which only one rabbit was caught, it would be chopped in two by the farmer, and a coin tossed to decide who should have which end. Nevertheless, as far as food went, which was, in those days, never far enough, the Williams family fared better than most.

Sarah continued to work with Walter in the evenings, trying to get him to identify objects in picture-books, but even when it was clear that Walter knew what an object was, he could never be persuaded to pronounce its name. She complained to the Head Teacher at the Special School about Walter's lack of progress, reminding her how much time she, Sarah, had spent in travelling to bring Walter to the school and fetch him home. Forty-three minutes ten times a week, forty school weeks in the year, four years at the school. Had the Head Teacher any idea how much that added up to? The Head Teacher opened her mouth to speak, but Sarah, who had worked out the sum herself on a piece of paper the night before, spared her the pain of mental arithmetic. 'One thousand one hundred and forty-six hours and forty minutes. What do you think of that?'

The Head Teacher did not know what to think of it.

'And just in case it has escaped your notice, three out of the four years I've been bringing him here, there's been a war on. There's been petrol rationing, cuts in the bus service, posters everywhere asking me if my journey is really necessary. Well, frankly, I believe I could have saved myself all that travelling time, to say nothing of bus fares. The space on the buses that Walter and I have taken up could have been used by somebody more directly involved with the War Effort, in my view.'

The Head Teacher was not used to the parents of her pupils talking to her in such a manner. Most of them were only too glad to get their children out of the house, and would cut off their tongues rather than offend the source of their relief. Sarah said, 'I could have achieved far more by keeping him at home. and teaching him myself, than what your so-called "Special School" has.'

She had finished. The Head Teacher, who had remained standing while Sarah spoke, unable to break the contact between them, as if mesmerized, turned and moved to the comparative safety of the chair behind her desk. She sat slowly. She did not indicate that Sarah should sit also, but Sarah sat, and discovered that her chair was lower than the Head Teacher's.

The Head Teacher leaned her elbows on her desk, and placed the palms of her hands together. It was a way she had discovered of composing herself.

She began with a silence which was intended to intimidate Sarah, though it did not entirely succeed in making this effect. She said that she did not believe in 'pushing' children. It had been clear from the outset that Walter was only capable of reaching a certain level, and then going no further. She had a great deal of experience with children very like Walter. What was important was that he should be able to mix socially with other children, and at school he did.

Sarah wished to say, 'Yes. With backward children,' but did not.

After the first fortnight, which was always a difficult time, Walter had begun to enjoy coming to school. Sarah must not misunderstand the function of a Special School. It would teach what could be taught to those who could learn, but the Three Rs were not the beginning and end of life in the world; the lives of otherwise restricted and unhappy children might be enriched by Creative Play. The function of a Special School was also to assist parents through a most difficult time. 'We take the strain,' the Head Teacher said, 'We carry a part of the weight. We relax what might otherwise be an intolerable tension, Mrs Williams, in the Home Environment.'

Sarah said she could manage. She had managed before the Special School had been found for Walter, and could again.

'But Walter has to attend school. It's against the law to keep him at home other than for reasons of health. Unfortunately we are the nearest school to your home which is equipped to deal with children like Walter. Please don't think that I don't know what it must be like to have a backward child. I do. All of us here, we all do. But life won't even begin to be easier for you, Mrs Williams, until you accept that backward is what Walter is, and always will be. In two years, he'll be all yours: there'll be nothing more we can do for either of you. It won't be easy for him to find work. Perhaps then you'll wish he were still at school.'

Walter continued to attend the Special School, and Sarah continued to take him there and to collect him, forty-three minutes each way in an unheated bus. The war continued also. Attempts were made to bomb Preston Docks and the Leyland Works nearby, where rubber parts for gas masks were made. Every night, Sarah, Eric and Walter would hear the planes overhead making for Preston, then following the line of the river on to Liverpool and Manchester. They would hear the distant bombing, and see the glow of flames in the sky.

One Sunday, at tea-time, in the small neighbouring village of Lostock Hall, the whole of Ward Street and the houses adjacent were demolished by bombs meant for Leyland. Next day two women arrived at Sarah's door, pushing prams in which they were collecting for the people of Lostock Hall, who had lost everything they had. Sarah gave the women a shilling, Walter's baby clothes (which she had kept in mothballs) and the toys she no longer wished him to play with. Later that day she took him for a walk to see what was left of Ward Street.

Sarah's mother died of cancer of the womb. Neither was a word ever used by Chapel people. The funeral cost twenty-one pounds and fifteen shillings, but since Sarah's mother had been putting twopence a week into the Prudential Insurance Company for much of her adult life in order to meet just such a need, Sarah was well able to pay for it. One hearse and one car to follow it was considered sufficient in time of war, and Sarah had eight pounds of the Insurance money left over.

Sarah inherited her mother's wedding and engagement rings, a string of cultured pearls, and the Eiffel Tower diamanté ear-rings, with various pieces of Victorian furniture, which were moved into the tied cottage, and overcrowded it. She kept the jewellery, but did not wear it; she locked it in a drawer, as her own Insurance for a rainy day. She knew that its value would increase. Sometimes she opened the drawer, and looked at the two rings, the necklace and the glittering Eiffel Tower ear-rings lying there. She had something, no matter how little, if freedom came. Or any other emergency.

Nine months later, Walter's Special School was taken over and used to house prisoners of war and their keepers. To meet the needs of the backward children thus displaced, small Remedial Groups were set up in already existing County Schools, one being only six miles from the village, and this was the one Walter now attended. An added advantage was that the school enjoyed the services of a speech therapist, who visited Walter's Remedial Group once a week.

Walter's speech improved, though he was still difficult to understand. He had never seemed to wish to talk before. That he should do so now, seemed to Sarah a major improvement, which might lead anywhere. However, after fifteen months at the school, he became fourteen, and was obliged to leave, so it led nowhere.

Sarah asked if he might stay on, if only for one more year. But she was told that there were too many handicapped children (the word 'backward' had already begun to go out of fashion), too few schools and teachers. She asked the speech therapist whether Walter might have private lessons, but the fees were more than could be afforded. 'Digging For Britain' may have been vital to the War Effort, but the wage of a farm labourer in 1944 was no more than four pounds a week, and to strike was illegal, even if Eric had ever thought of such a thing. As for Sarah herself, she could not go out to work while Walter was at home; he tied her as effectively at the age of fourteen as he had at three. She opened the drawer, and looked at her mother's jewellery, but the time for that was not yet.

The therapist told her that Walter's speech would improve with time and practice, but that, since he had started so late, it would never be perfect. She gave Sarah some useful hints, and Sarah set one hour a day aside to try to improve the way Walter spoke. His concentration-span was no more than ten minutes at the most, so the lessons would end in arguments and tantrums. Sarah stopped the lessons, and simply corrected him whenever he pronounced a word wrongly.

He was fifteen, and still soiled himself on occasions. To speak the King's English perfectly was not of paramount importance.

5

If you kissed me now, I might get pregnant

'*A penn'orth of chips to grease your lips, and Out . . . Goes . . . You!*
Ip! Dip! Sky blue! Who's it? Not . . . You.
God's words are true. It . . . Must . . . Be . . . You'
Elaine, the eldest of the four girls, was pointing at Walter.

'Oh, no! Not Walter. He never finds us. Do it again.' These
words were spoken by Norma, the smallest of the four girls.
Her hair was ginger, and her face, since this was a fine summer,
was covered with freckles.

'I'm not doing it again. Walter's It. If you don't want to hide,
you can let him catch you. Then you'll be It next time.'

'No fear! I'm not having *that* touch me.'

That was Walter. As Norma said '*that*', she pointed at Walter.
Immediately he covered his mouth with one hand, pointed back at
her and giggled. This was a habit he had acquired at his first
school, the one before the Special School, and it had been reinforced
during his period within a Remedial Group among those who
attended the County School. Any child, confronted with Walter,
would point and giggle. Clearly it was a form of greeting. Therefore
Walter did it. Or perhaps he knew well enough that it was not a
greeting, and pointed and giggled himself to forestall pointing
and giggling in others. Any road, he did it.

'Look at him. He's halfway round the twist. Why do we
always have to play with that?' Walter continued to point.
Bent double now, he acted out the uncontrollable glee and
mockery which were usually directed at him. He was almost
nineteen now. Elaine, the oldest girl, was thirteen.

61

'How would you like it? He can't help being daft, can he?'

Walter stopped his performance. Elaine was his ally. He looked at each of the other girls in turn, waiting to hear whether he were to be allowed to play or not. He composed his face into a tentative smile, and looked first at Pat, then at Ann, finally at Norma, who looked away. Sensing that she was outnumbered, Norma said, 'Oh, alright! Come on, then; let's get started. I wouldn't mind if he could count.'

'You shut your face, ginger nut. Come on, Walter. Cover your eyes up.'

Walter obeyed, his long bony fingers cupped over his protruding eyes, and started to count. He could count, as it happened, but only as far as twenty. This he did aloud, and very loud. At twenty-one, he lowered his voice to a whisper, and began again.

All the girls, including the reluctant Norma, were running, and finding places to hide. Norma was chanting,

> 'One! Two! Three!
> Mother's caught a flea.
> Put it in the teapot, to make a pot of tea.
> Flea jumped out.
> Bit her on the snout.
> In came Walter, with his willy hanging out.'

To all but Norma, the game was more interesting when they contrived to make Walter It. He generated such excitement as he darted about, trying to catch them, they allowing him to get close up to them, and then, just as he was about to touch, outwitting him by turning the other way. The closer he got to catching them, the more excited he became. The excitement was shown in the noises he made and in the saliva which dripped liberally from his mouth. On one occasion he had become so excited that he had stopped suddenly in his tracks, and they had stopped running to watch him as he looked down at the front of his trousers in amazement, feeling the warm piss run down his legs and out through the front of his trousers. And they had laughed, and he had left the game, turning at once on his heels, and had gone – half walking, half running, feeling the wet pants against his legs – home.

Elaine was his ally. She would always let him play, and she persuaded the others. She ran away from him, into the bushes. When he caught up with her, she dodged away just enough to excite him, and then she lunged suddenly towards him, pushing him over, and grabbing him in the crotch. Walter lay on the ground, with Elaine lying on top of him, as she rubbed her hands over the front of his trousers, making his willy go hard.

'You have got one, then?'

Walter placed both hands over his face, and began counting again. He had reached fifteen when Elaine slid her fingers between his fly-buttons, causing two of them to open. She squeezed and rubbed him, and Walter rolled about with an excitement that he couldn't control, his counting forgotten. Then he gave a frightened yelp. Something was happening to him. The tip of his willy itched, and something was bursting out of it, gushing forth like the contents of a squeezed boil. Unlike a boil, it didn't hurt. Walter couldn't think of a word to describe what he felt. The only word that came into his mind was the word 'nice'. It wasn't the right word, but it was the only one he could think of.

Whatever it was that had burst out of him, was sticky. He felt it on Elaine's hand, and on the inside of his trousers.

Elaine wiped her hand on some dock leaves, and said, 'That's what makes babies, Walter. If you kissed me now, I might get pregnant.'

For weeks afterwards, Walter wouldn't go near the Park. He would walk miles to avoid going even round it. It was not that he didn't want to play with the girls. He wanted to very much, and thought about it constantly. But first Elaine might have told the other girls what had happened, and they might laugh at him, and worse, she might be pregnant. He knew what pregnant was. He had seen women, heavy, with large stomachs, and his mother had told him that those women were pregnant. When he had asked what the word meant, she had said, 'Don't worry. It'll never happen to you. By rights, it only happens after you're married, and that you'll never be.'

He remained confused by what Elaine had done to him, and by what she had said, that if they kissed she might become fat and heavy in front like those women. Elaine was only thirteen. Even Walter knew that was much too young to marry.

6

No one was ever really hurt, no one died, and the failures always came out on top

Walter arrived home breathless from having run all the way from the Park. He arrived at the back gate to find his father standing in the back yard, waving a very long bamboo pole at the top of which was a white flag. Walter was told by his father to close the gate quickly, and stand still. He did so, using the gate to lean against, and catch his breath. The substance which Elaine had caused to gush from his willy felt like cold glue. He wondered if it would set hard.

'The buggers are staying out. They won't come sodding home.'

The buggers to which Walter's father referred were Russian High-Flying Pigeons. 'Trust the bloody Russians to be difficult.' Walter looked up, and scanned the sky for any sign of a bird. His father took a referee's whistle from his top pocket, and blew on it as hard as he could. Whereafter Walter heard the sound of a coin being tapped against glass. His mother was standing on the other side of the kitchen window, watching them.

'She's on the bloody warpath, and the sodding buggers won't come down.' Having tapped, Sarah now stood with her arms folded across her chest. 'That's the third time she's done that. Break the bloody window before she's satisfied.'

Sarah was pointing at the Pigeon Loft, which ran the entire length of the back yard. Her meaning was clear. Something would have to be done about those pigeons, if they were to make Eric and Walter late for tea.

The Pigeon Loft was divided into four sections, to house the

64

four different sorts of pigeons which Eric bred, for his interest in pigeons had expanded considerably since his wife and her mother had scorned the solitary racer which had befriended him so long ago. These were not racing pigeons; they were for Show. Consequently it was of the uttermost importance to keep the different sorts of bird apart, so as to control their breeding. The first type of pigeon fancied by Eric were English Long-Faced Tumblers, so named because of their ability to tumble over backwards during flight, or, more strictly, their inability to avoid doing so, since the tumbling which gave entertainment to the onlooker was due to a fault in the inner ears of these birds, which was cultivated by selective breeding. The second type were White-Lace Fantails, which spread out their tails like white lacey fans and inflated their chests so full and high as to make their heads almost disappear. Next were the Turbits, elegantly shaped birds of various colours with inverted necks and tiny bills. Turbits had been inbred until their bills were so tiny that they were unable to feed their own young, which had to be taken from them and fostered, but they were most decorative birds and fit, beholders said, to stand on any mantel – not that they ever would, during their lives, grace a mantel, for, like all pigeons, they were prodigious shitters. Last were the Russian High-Fliers, the wayward birds which were causing Eric so much concern at this moment. Because of their ability to stay high in the air, out of sight of the human eye, a long pole with a flag on it was needed to control their flight. A World Record had been set up by a Mr Wilf Wilmer of Staffordshire, who in June 1943 flew a 'kit' of birds for twenty hours. It was stated at the time that the long twilights in England gave him an unfair advantage over his American rival, a Mr Fred Engelberg of Mespeth, New York, who could only manage a flight of seventeen hours, eighteen minutes.

Eric was now fifty-two. He had left the farm, and become a railway porter. Sarah had insisted, the week after their marriage, that they should have their name on the Corporation Housing List, in case Eric ever wished to change his type of work, so that they were no longer able to live in a tied cottage. By 1943, the Williams name had achieved its slow climb to the top of the List, and they had received a letter informing them that if, after all these years, they still wished a Corporation house, there was one to be had.

The decision had not been an easy one. All Eric knew about was farming; he could not envisage doing any other kind of work. Sarah had assisted him to envisage it, by making a list of all the jobs an unskilled man could do. On that list were the words 'Railway Porter'. They were the only words on the list which had got anything akin to a positive response from Eric.

The following day, Sarah had gone to Preston Station, and put their predicament to the Personnel Officer there. He had been sympathetic. 'Right,' he had said, 'I see the problem. Get different job before leaving work on land, and losing roof over heads.' Sarah had said that was it in a nutshell. The Personnel Officer had agreed to interview Eric on the following day, as a result of which interview Eric gave notice to his employer of long standing, and they had moved into a Corporation house in Bamber Bridge. It was not a new house, but it was a better one, and Sarah was pleased.

Eric was not at first overjoyed with his new job. He had to cycle six miles each way to and from Preston, and the shift system caused inconvenience to the pigeons, who had to get used to having their meals and exercise at different times, depending on whether Eric was on the early or the late shift. This confused the pigeons, as it did Eric, but both adapted. Eric discovered that he quite liked wearing a uniform. It gave him confidence. When he talked (which was seldom to anyone but the pigeons or Walter) he talked as the other porters talked, swearing a lot and saying very little. This annoyed Sarah, who would often remark that if she had known what foul language her husband would bring home from Preston Railway Station, she would have stayed and died of pneumonia in the damp of the tied cottage, rather than to have to listen to her God being blasphemed and her son corrupted by the filth that dropped unashamedly from Eric's lips.

Now Eric rested his long pole for a moment, and used both his hands to shake vigorously an old cocoa-tin filled with small pebbles. The pebbles were to represent the sound of grain. Since they made a louder noise than grain, they were necessary this evening, as the Russians were refusing to answer the call to supper.

The referee's whistle was blown in unison with the rattling of pebbles. This brought another tapping on the window by Sarah. She had given up trying to keep Walter and Eric's tea warm. What she was objecting to most of all was the whistle, since by now everybody within hearing distance knew why it was used, and the regularity of its use reminded the neighbours of her husband's incompetence.

'Can't that bloody woman see I'm doing my best?' Eric rattled the tin of pebbles as hard as he could, and shouted up into the birdless sky, 'Come down, you stupid buggers. My tea's getting cold.' Almost immediately a bird was sighted, just the outline, but it was definitely a bird, and not an aeroplane. After a moment, the bird disappeared, and Eric remarked, 'Probably a sodding eagle with its stomach full of my sodding Russians.' The other possibility to be feared was that some neighbouring pigeon fancier had lured the flock to his own loft, either by using a longer pole or a dropper – a dropper being a comparatively low-flying pigeon, sent up to bring the others down by leading them home to food.

'Go and get Freda.' Walter moved slowly towards the long shed, trying to walk as naturally as possible in case his watching mother should suspect that there was something in his trousers that shouldn't be and insist on an inspection. He had never been able to understand why the shed he was about to enter was called a 'loft', when lofts were above the ceiling and this was on the ground in the back yard.

Seeing Walter go towards the Loft, Sarah opened the kitchen window, and hissed at her husband, 'About time too!' His reply was rendered inaudible by the loud noise of the window's being closed again.

Walter opened the door of the Loft very slowly, and slid inside, leaving as little space for any birds to escape as possible. His presence caused a stir, as pigeons flew about his face, pecking at each other for space, and wing-flicking each other for the occupancy of a perch. Feathers flew and dust rose. The disturbed birds were already wondering what had happened to their supper. Walter closed his eyes, and held one arm over his face for protection. He knew exactly where Freda perched, and could find his way there blindfolded, which now in a sense he was.

Freda was an old bird, a White-Lace Fantail, whose breeding days were past. She was no longer capable of producing offspring beautiful enough to be exhibited at the Harrogate Show or even the London Dairy Show (not that Eric would ever be allowed to travel south to the City of Sin). A more scrupulously professional breeder of Show birds would have wrung Freda's neck more than a year ago, and used her perch and the grain she ate to help him breed a possible winner. But Eric's scruples were of another sort. Freda's job as dropper was to circle around as high as she could, but always so as to be seen from the ground, and to flutter her wings so as to attract the Russians' attention and to remind them that there was food waiting below.

Walter passed through Turbits and through Tumblers. He squeezed carefully though the door in the partition which divided Tumblers from Fantails, and found Freda sitting peacefully on her perch. Being old, she had seen it all before, and was not given to the panic and excessive movement of the younger birds. Walter did as his father had taught him, and placed his left hand just above her head for long enough to distract her and so allow him to slide his right hand under her, securing her legs between his two longest fingers, and holding her wings with his thumb on the one side and the tip of his index finger on the other. She was used to being handled in this way, and her only movement as Walter lifted her from the perch was to cock her head to one side, as if she were asking, 'What is it this time?'

'Good lad! She'll bring 'em down. Won't you, Freda love? Didn't want to disturb you tonight.' Of all the birds in Eric's flock, Freda was his favourite. This was because she was the only bird of his ever to have won a prize. In her youth, Freda had won a cup, and so the cup, and Freda's presence, reminded Eric of the one day in his life when he had been successful.

Eric had taken the bird gently from Walter, and was holding her up to his face, her beak touching his lips. Walter saw that his mother was still standing at the kitchen window, her arms folded across her chest. As he looked, she made a gesture of impatience.

'You'll get them down for me, won't you, my little lovely?' Eric lowered Freda so that she could peck up four grains of hemp from his open palm. She removed the hemp seeds so quickly that it reminded Eric of a Keystone Kops film, in which the Kops were forever jumping in and out of moving vehicles. He remembered particularly how one of them clung for dear life to the trailing hosepipe of a fire-engine, being dragged for miles around sharp corners. But they always got up, and brushed down their ill-fitting uniforms. No one was ever really hurt. No one died, not in those days. And the failures always came out on top.

'If only life was like that!' Eric spoke his private thoughts to Freda. Birds couldn't answer back. 'I wish I could flap my arms, and go up there with you.'

Sarah opened the window again, and shouted, 'Are you going to send that bird up, or are you going to talk it to death first?' And closed the window again, like punctuation.

To Freda, the four hemp seeds she had been given seemed small payment for what she was being required to do, but hemp is what pigeons like best, and she had been called upon so often to collect the Russian High-Fliers, and had always been rewarded at the end of each successful mission with a much larger amount of hemp, with the addition of canary seeds, which pigeons also regard as a delicacy. She knew the score. The sooner she was allowed to get on with the job, and get those stupid Russians down, the sooner everybody could eat.

Eric gave Freda a little assistance by throwing her up into the air. Up she flew, heavy and laborious, slapping her wings together behind her back to attract the Russians' attention. She made four complete circles, then started to fly down again, resting her wings and gliding down, using the wind to conserve her precious energy. The 'kit' of High-Flying Russians returned within the next three minutes. They were given food and a severe talking-to by Eric. Freda herself was given a good handful of mixed seed and grain, which included rape, linseed, millet, maple peas, groats and tares, as well as her two favourites, hemp and canary seed. She did not eat the linseed, which is good for pigeons (being a source of oil) but not much liked by them.

Walter and his parents sat down to their delayed tea, and ate dried-up sausages, lukewarm mashed potatoes and cold boiled carrots. His mother could have eaten hers while it was still at its best, but preferred to sit with them in silence – or to be more exact, without speaking, for she did make small noises of disgust with each mouthful, and left at least half the meal uneaten on her plate. Eric finished all of what he was given, then left the table to read the evening paper. Walter also ate the contents of his plate, wondered about seconds (but there were none), then helped his mother to clear the table and wash up, after which he sat beside her on the settee, and was asked to identify certain objects from the pictures in Woman's Own.

'What's that?'

'Cardigan.' He wondered if his mother would smell what Elaine had squeezed from his willy with such pleasure. He himself could not smell anything extra, but his mother had a special sensitivity about such matters.

'Good. And that?' Sarah had turned to the Cookery Column.

'Pie.'

'Yes, but what do we say?'

Walter thought for a moment. 'A pie.'

'Good. It's *a* pie. Why? Why do we say "a pie"?'

Walter didn't know. He shook his head.

'Don't shake your head.'

Walter discovered that he was becoming angry. He turned his head away, and began humming to himself, to help to remove the anger and frustration he was feeling.

'Don't you know?'

Walter grunted, and continued to hum.

'Then say, "I don't know, mother."'

Walter made noises which approximated to 'I don't know, mother.'

'I don't want noises either, thank you. You can speak very well when it suits you. We don't only do things that we like in this world, my lad. You'll very quickly find that out, after I'm dead, and he's too old and daft to look after you.' She pointed in the direction of the armchair. Eric had placed the evening paper over his face, and was snoring beneath it, so that the Sports Pages rose and fell in time to his breathing. Walter giggled, and pointed to the paper moving up and down.

'Sleep, that's what he's best at. You and him together make a fine pair.' She thought of the evening ahead of her. The emptiness, the pointlessness. The tiny pinpricks behind her eyes warned her of tears. Her mouth quivered. The whole world outside was enjoying its evening, and she was here, trapped in a routine of cleaning and cooking, of fouled bedclothes and snoring. She screwed her eyes up tight, defying them to make water and upset her son. She clenched her teeth, and took a deep breath. She took such breaths every day now. Each day was marked out by them. She saw the days ahead, filled with them. She saw herself in a permanent state of 'holding on'. 'One of the three people in this room,' she thought, 'one of us has to die, before this forever holding on and getting through drives me as silly as Walter.'

70

'Toffee?' He was tugging at her sleeve, saliva running from his mouth to his chin, and then hanging, suspended, before it dropped onto his Fair Isle pullover.

'No, you can't have one. You didn't concentrate at your lessons. Toffees are for when you're good, and you...try...to... CONCENTRATE.' She was almost shouting, spelling each word out slowly, as if she were talking to a two-year-old. How she hated the sound of her own voice, loathed the caricature of a disappointed wife she had become! She had moved away, both from her husband and her son, putting as much distance as there was in the small room between herself and the two men. She had reached the door to the stairs, trapped there, not knowing why or what she intended to do. It was too soon to go up to bed, much too soon. She was in a cage with no exit. The man she had married was snoring, hidden by local gossip and the racing results. Soon they would be lying together in the same bed, back to back, not touching, not speaking, the space between them never to be filled. And the child to whom she had given birth, whom she had reared for nearly nineteen years, was staring at her, wide-eyed and dribbling for toffees. They were on the dresser in a glass bowl. They were given as rewards for good behaviour, enticements to quietness and calm. Her only weapon was to withhold what had already rotted his protruding and uneven teeth. She looked at Walter. As always, he was watching her; whenever they were together, he never took his eyes from her. At eighteen as at seven, he could scream if he sensed fear or even uncertainty in her. And the uncertainty was there. His face was already showing signs of apprehension. It was her own quivering face which looked back at her, horribly distorted as in a fairground mirror. She must go, must get out, if only for an hour, must walk to the Park, scream into the darkness, then look up at the sky and count the stars until she was tired.

Her coat was hanging behind the door. She reached for it, and tried to control herself enough to say, 'I'm going out.' Walter's mouth trembled, and a very small frightened noise emerged. It was enough. The floodgates opened. Sarah slammed the half-opened door, and burst into uncontrollable tears, smashing the glass bowl and the toffees to the floor at the feet of her husband.

'He's your son as well. You take care of him.' The veins in her neck stood out. Walter looked at the broken glass and the toffees,

71

heard his mother's tears, caught and magnified all her rage and frustration and grief and, being unable to deal with emotion on such a scale, went into a fit, rolling about on the floor among the toffees and the broken glass. Eric came abruptly awake. He placed three fingers in Walter's mouth to prevent him from biting his tongue, and Sarah, knowing that in the matter of controlling frightened animals, her ex-farm labourer husband had more experience than she, went out into the back yard, leaned against the Pigeon Loft, and wept.

An hour later, the broken glass and toffees had been cleared away, and Walter sat where they had fallen, doing his favourite jigsaw puzzle. It was in eight large pieces, which he could now fit together and break apart in a matter of four minutes. The jigsaw was a picture of the Pied Piper of Hamelin, dancing down the road, and playing his pipe to charm the rats out of the city. The Piper wore tights and knee-high boots not unlike those worn by Robin Hood in other jigsaws, and the rats which followed him all had smiles on their faces, disarmed of their characteristic rattishness by the calming music of the pipe.

Walter completed the puzzle for the fifth time, and began to break it up, preparatory to completing it for a sixth, but Sarah leaned forward from the chair in which she was sitting, and touched his arm. 'That's enough for tonight. It's bedtime.' Walter put the pieces of jigsaw back into their box, replaced the lid, and returned the box to the cupboard in which it was kept. He came close to his mother, kissed her on the cheek, and said, 'Good night.'

'Good night, Walter. I'll be up to see you in a minute.'

I'll be up to see you in a minute. I'll be up to tuck you in bed. He was eighteen years old. Soon he would be nineteen. She was fifty.

PART THREE

He becomes a Wage-Earner

I

Are you going to make me proud, Walter?
Are you going to do well, and make
me pleased with you?

They sat in Mr Richards' office, he and his mother sitting side
by side. He was wearing his best suit, with a new shirt and a new
tie, tied by his mother. He had cleaned his black shoes, the ones
he wore only on Sundays, three times. Three times he had shown
them to his mother, and three times she had sent him back into
the kitchen to clean them again. Even after that, she had sighed
her sigh of disappointment, and finished them off herself.

She had told him to keep his mouth closed, and to speak only
when spoken to. This would not be easy; Walter's mouth was
almost permanently open, owing to the size of his teeth. He had
watched her sprinkling lavender water inside her blouse. He had
watched her buttoning up the top of her blouse. It was her best
blouse. She had told him to sit up straight and try to look alert.
As he had held out her best coat for her to slip in her arms, she
had said, 'Now this is important. Do you understand?' He had
nodded, and said, 'Yes,' and when she was satisfied with the angle
of her best hat, she had squeezed his hand, and said, 'Good boy!
You do your best, and try to make me proud of you.'

As they sat side by side in the office, Sarah's hands shook with
the strain of trying to make a good impression for them both.
Walter noticed the shaking hands, and listened docilely while she
asked Mr Richards not to be put off by his appearance. 'He's far
more capable than you might think,' she said. Then she smiled at
Walter, for he had remembered to sit up straight, and was doing

75

so, as much as was humanly possible, his knees touching and his arms neatly folded.

Mr Richards asked Walter how old he was, and Walter remembered how old he was, and replied, 'Twenty-one.'

'Can you sweep the floor, Walter?' Mr Richards was speaking in a quiet and gentle voice as if he were talking to a baby. And Walter replied, 'Yes, sir,' and glanced at his mother for approbation, pleased with himself that he had remembered to call Mr Richards 'sir'.

'Just call me "Mr Richards", Walter. No need to be too formal. I haven't been knighted yet, you know.' Then he smiled, and Walter's mother smiled, and laughed the laugh she laughed when she was nervous.

Mr Richards said, 'I'm going to take you upstairs to the Stock Room, and show you a machine, and I want you to tell me truthfully if you think you can work it.'

As they moved from Mr Richards' office out into the shop, they passed the Toiletry Counter, and Walter remembered how good it smelled. He remembered that he had been in this Woolworth's before, several times with his mother. On those occasions she had held his hand with a tight grasp, but today, as they followed Mr Richards through the shop, and Walter tried to slide his hand into his mother's, she pushed him away, and gave a look which he recognized as meaning, 'Don't do that.'

Mr Richards led them into a large lift, and closed the outer door. The door looked to Walter like one side of a concertina, and the inner door looked like trelliswork, which stretched out when it was opened and slid together when closed.

'You'll have to get used to using this. Press the top button for me, please, Walter.' Mr Richards pointed to a row of three buttons on the side of the lift. Walter placed his index finger on the top button, and pressed. Nothing happened. He looked at his mother, who smiled her nervous smile. There was a silence. Mr Richards was watching him. His mother said, 'Press it hard, Walter.' He pressed the top button again, as hard as he could. Still nothing happened. Walter turned to Mr Richards, and said somewhat accusingly, 'Broke.'

'No, it's not.' Mr Richards still maintained his quiet reassuring voice. Then he asked Walter's mother, 'Has he ever been in a lift before?'

'Oh, yes, but not in one like this, I'm afraid. Only the sort where they have a disabled person to press the button for you.'

'What do you think could be wrong with it, Walter?'

Walter waited a moment, gave the matter thought, and repeated, 'Broke.'

'No, it's not broken. Open the door again, and close it.'

Walter did as he was told, sliding back first the trellis, then the concertina. 'Now shut them.' Walter did so, and looked to Mr Richards for further instructions. 'Try again.' Walter pressed the top button, and the lift began to go upwards.

'I did that on purpose, to show you how it works. The lift won't move unless both doors are closed tight. Do you understand, Walter?' Walter nodded, and they arrived at the Stock Room. Mr Richards signalled to Walter to slide back the gates. Walter did so, and the Stock Room was revealed. A group of people who had been standing by or leaning against a large workbench in the centre of the room suddenly began to move about, picking things up or writing things down. The room had become full of activity.

A man in grey overalls came forward to greet Mr Richards. 'Good morning, sir. How are you today?' Mr Richards replied with a sound which was between a grunt and a cough, but did not contain any reminder that he had not been knighted. He said, 'This is Master Walter Williams, who would like to come and work for us, and this lady is his mother.'

The man shook hands with Walter's mother, but not with Walter. Instead he looked Walter up and down. Walter held out his hand to be shaken, having remembered his mother's telling him, 'Always give a good strong handshake. Then people know where they are with you.' But the man did not see Walter's hand, his eyes being on Mr Richards, who was scrutinizing the Stock Room to make sure that all those who were there had a right to be there, and if they had, that they were working.

'Don't let those girls stay chatting up here. Get them back down, down on the floor, behind their counters.'

'Yes, sir.'

'Want you to show Walter how to work the press. What do you think?'

'Well, at least he looks a strong lad. That's what we need.'

Mr Richards placed an arm over the shoulder of the man in grey overalls, and led him on ahead towards the press. Although he spoke in a whisper, both Walter and Sarah could hear what he said.

'Now, he's not very bright, as you can see, but if you think he can do the job, we should give him a trial. They like this sort of thing at Head Office – giving this sort of job to someone who's handicapped. It's less money gone in wages, and good public relations for the shop.' The man nodded, and Mr Richards went on, 'I'm a member of the Round Table. They're very keen on this sort of thing too. Might help in one or two places, see what I mean? Any road, I don't expect you to carry him. If he can't pull his weight, then that's that. Give him a couple of weeks, eh? Trial. What do you think?'

The man replied that he thought it was an excellent idea. Then he turned to Walter, and said, 'This here is a press. The green button starts it, like this.' He pressed the green button, and nothing happened. Walter knew better than to suggest that the press was broken. This would be a test, like the other.

'Oh, yes, I remember now. It's jammed.' The next ten minutes were spent in watching the man in grey overalls dismantle parts of the machine, and attempt to remove some string which had got tangled in the works. Mr Richards grew tired of watching this demonstration, and excused himself by saying he had letters to write.

When the string had been untangled and the various parts replaced, the green button was pressed again, and this time Walter and his mother had the pleasure of hearing the machine make its noise, and watching the top half of it descend to compress cardboard and waste paper into a tight bale. 'Now, that's quite opportune, that happening. It means you'll know never to put string in with the waste. String we keep in a box over there. It gets used up in time.' He pointed to where a large round cardboard drum stood, overflowing with knotted string.

'The red button stops it, like this.' This time the machine obeyed its button, and stopped the pressing and the noise. 'Cardboard and waste paper have to be collected from all the bins in the shop. There are two bins behind every counter.' Walter thought about the Toiletry Counter, and of the girls who worked there, with their faces drawn on them in bright colours.

'Oh, and this floor gets very dusty. So you never put a broom to it before you've first sprinkled water on it with the watering-can you'll find in the Gents. Over here's the skip.' The man pulled at a large square basket on casters. 'You take this down in the lift you came up in, and you empty all the bins into it. Never leave the girls behind their counters without their bins. That just gives them an excuse to come up here to talk to Mike there.' The man pointed to a young man who was standing by the workbench, unpacking boxes of liquorice all-sorts, whereupon the young man grabbed a handful of all-sorts from one of the boxes, and stuffed them into his mouth, winking at Walter. 'Got that?' said the man in the grey overalls. 'Skip down in lift. Bins emptied into skip. Skip back in lift. Remove string and place in drum. Cardboard and waste paper into machine.' Sarah said she was sure that Walter had indeed got it, and would give satisfaction.

He was to be there at half past eight on the following Monday, and leave at six, after he and the trainee floor-walkers had swept out the entire shop. From the back to the front, they would sweep the aisles between every counter. Every sweet wrapper and cigarette packet, every hairpin and comb, every sticky sweet and fly-button had to be swept up and put away, ready for the women who mopped to do their mopping early the following morning.

Sarah and Walter sat side by side on the top deck of the bus going home. Sarah gave him a boiled sweet from her bag. He closed his eyes to unwrap the sweet, then placed it in his mouth, and tried to guess its colour. This was a game they often played. Walter sucked at the sweet, and said, 'Orange,' and Sarah, who had given him a red one, told him he was right. He was not allowed to remove the sweet once it was in his mouth, so he would never know she was lying.

She touched the back of his hand with her leather glove, and said, 'Two weeks' trial they're giving you. Two weeks to test you out. Are you going to make me proud, Walter? Are you going to do well, and make me pleased with you?' Walter nodded, and sucked hard on the red boiled sweet.

'There's a good boy!'

2

An unkind person had once said that the sound of Walter talking was like a fart in a bath of soapy water

Walter was so keen to succeed at his new job that he seldom stood still even for a moment.

He could make sense. The manager of the Stock Room could understand what Walter said. Sometimes. At other times he would ask Walter to stand still, and repeat what he had said. 'Please . . . Mister . . . Hin-gall-ee . . . can some . . . someone . . . help . . . me . . . with this bale?' Walter salivated richly when he was asked to stand still and repeat a sentence out loud, and often Mr Hingley would pretend that Walter had spat in his eye, and say, 'Here, Walter! Watch where you're aiming.' At this Walter would laugh. He didn't know why he laughed, except that laughing seemed to be the safest thing to do. But laughing made him spit even more, and he would have to cover his mouth with a dirty hand.

When Walter laughed, he rocked back and forwards in an exaggerated way, to show people what he was doing. Look! He was laughing. Look! It made people feel better when they saw Walter laughing. They would smile or they themselves would laugh. To those who worked at Woolworth's it seemed that Walter was permanently in a state of good humour.

'Poor Walter! He's a lot happier the way he is, thank God,' though what God had to do with it was something Walter was never able to work out. Laughing was what Walter did best. He was good at his job, but at laughing he was even better.

80

An unkind person had once said that the sound of Walter talking was like a fart in a bath of soapy water.

Mr Hingley had said that without Walter they would all be out of a job. If Walter didn't bale all the cardboard and waste paper, it would mount up so fast and so high that customers would have to climb over it, and crawl about on their hands and knees to find the counters they wanted, saying, ''Scuse me, could you tell me the way to Haberdashery,' and being answered, 'Just keep crawling for two more counters, and it's on your right.'

'What you laughing for?'

'Don't know.'

'Don't *know*?'

'Yes.'

'Don't know was made to know. Is this rubbish yours?' Mr Hingley would point to some straw at his feet.

'No.'

'Whose is it, then?'

'Belongs to Woolworth's.'

'Shift it!'

Walter would laugh, and do as he was told, but a moment later he would be back at Mr Hingley's side, saliva running down from his chin onto his overalls, giggling and pointing to some paper on the floor.

'Do you want this paper, Mr Hin-gall-ee?' Walter's head would nod on each syllable with the effort to get the name right. Mr Hingley would look at Walter, then back to the string he was trying to untangle. It was a game, a game they often played.

Walter would wait, his finger still pointing at the paper on the floor. Then he would make a noise, signifying that his question had not been answered.

The string in Mr Hingley's hands would seem to be even more tangled than it had been when he began to try to unravel it. He hated cutting good string. You couldn't get strong string nowadays. But to spend half an hour untangling three yards of it was not in the best interests of Woolworth's shareholders. Time was money. The string wasn't worth half his hourly rate.

The look Mr Hingley would give Walter would be one of warning. It was a game; they played it often. Walter, enjoying the danger of going too far, would persist. 'Do you want the paper, Mr Hingley? Do you?' Mr Hingley would give a sudden and violent lurch towards Walter, stamping his foot down hard and close to Walter's feet, and shouting, 'No!' into Walter's ear. Then Walter would step back, and mumble to himself in the third person to prove that his actions belonged to the external order of things, and had very little to do with him personally.

'Sometimes he understands everything you say to him,' Walter would mumble, ducking and grabbing to pick up the waste paper and take it to his press, and Mr Hingley would shout over one shoulder to him, 'It wouldn't be lying on the floor if I wanted it, would it, Walter?' Mr Hingley had never met a Woolworth's shareholder. He unravelled string chiefly to put off writing out the Stock Sheet, since he always ordered too much or too little, and the Stock Sheet would show this up. Also his spelling was bad. Mr Hingley hated the thought that the girls in the office would giggle over the words he had spelt wrongly.

'Sometimes he's almost as intelligent as you or me,' Walter would mumble.

'Talking to yourself again, Walter?'

'No, sir.'

'Take you away for that.'

'Yes, sir.'

'Better stop doing it, then, hadn't you?'

'Stop it, then,' Walter would echo, laughing and dribbling onto the paper in his hands.

'Like a bloody parrot you are sometimes, do you know that?'

'No. Do you?' It was a game; they played it often. Walter would rock backwards and forwards on the balls of his feet, putting paper into the press and taking it out again, laughing and dribbling and talking to himself, as he tore up the paper in his hands. 'Face like a parrot too,' he would mutter, 'Wouldn't be seen dead with a hooter like yours, Walter. What a beak! Coooor!' and realizing that Walter was getting over-excited, and that his rocking was becoming faster and faster, Mr Hingley would adopt his serious voice, and say, 'Alright, Walter. Calm down. Stop being silly. Just calm down. Hey! What's on the telly tonight?' and Walter would reply, 'Fursday!' (if the day was Thursday) triumphantly, swinging round from his press and projecting his saliva the full length of the Stock Room.

Then he would go into a familiar routine, which Mr Hingley wisely encouraged, knowing that it would use up some of Walter's excess energy and distract him from being silly and self-derogatory. This was it: Walter's favourite television programme was *Sportsview*, which used for its opening credits a screen split into nine segments, in every one of which a different sporting activity was going on. The music which accompanied these pictures was a rousing tune, which grew and grew in intensity. Walter's routine was to mime all nine of these sporting activities one after another as quickly as he could, humming the rousing music and ending with a robust crescendo.

It was a game; they played it often.

'Where's my bloody Stock Sheet? And shut that row up.' Walter's crescendo was cut short by the boom of a foghorn voice. He covered his mouth with one hand, and used the other to pretend he was busy. Miss Rushden ran the Office, indeed she pretty well ran the whole store. She was a large stout woman, with a voice louder and deeper than most men's voices. Her favourite pleasure in life was to terrify people, and since she was able to do this very easily, her life was given over almost entirely to pleasure. Her feet, hands and other extremities were even larger, in proportion, than the rest of her. This assisted her to dominate anybody she met. In particular she dominated the young ladies of the General Office, to which her own office was adjacent, and which consequently had a very high turnover of staff, two of whom had left after only a week in it, and complained to their doctor of deafness. He had syringed their ears, and told them to stay away from Miss Rushden.

She stood in the doorway, her thick arms folded, and her large left foot tapping. Apart from this noise, there was silence. 'Has everybody in this bloody place gone deaf?' The women who looked after the rows and rows of shelves full of stock had disappeared to the furthest corner of the room, and were hiding behind a stack of ironing boards. The young men who, as part of their training to be floor-walkers, walked no floors, but unloaded and unpacked the merchandise, were hiding in the Gents. Mr Hingley had dropped his only partially unravelled string, and was scribbling numbers on a scrap of paper, whispering them over to himself in an attempt to convince Miss Rushden that he was in the process of working out a most difficult piece of mathematics. Finally he put the back of his hand to his brow, wiped it, and, without looking up, said, 'I haven't had time to do it yet.'

'Haven't had time to *do* it?' Miss Rushden's scornful disbelief rattled the bottles in the Co-op Dairy, ten shops further down the street. 'I can hear everything that goes on in here, you know. You've been playing silly buggers with that monkey over there.' She pointed at a cowering and silent Walter.

The only way Mr Hingley could summon up the courage to match her in volume was to keep his eyes down. His face reddened, and the veins in his neck swelled, as he shouted, 'If you've got a complaint, you know where to take it.'

'Complaint my bloody armpits! You make bloody time. Most of my girls are getting sores on their bums from sitting waiting for you lot.' With that, she stamped her way back to her office, and slammed the door.

Knowing the door to be safely shut, Mr Hingley stuck out his tongue, lifted two fingers, and blew a raspberry. Then he said, 'You'll get me the bloody sack one of these days, Walter.'

The women who looked after the shelves and the young trainee floor-walkers whose training so largely consisted of unloading and unpacking merchandise had come out of hiding, and were standing about, idling the last half hour away.

'What are you doing tonight, Mr Hin-gall-ee?'

Mr Hingley made a gesture as if to strike Walter, and said, 'Get away with you, you dirty-minded hound!' Walter knew this to be a joke, though he did not know in what the joke consisted, or why it should cause the women and the trainee floor-walkers to laugh so much. But it did. It never failed, and he, Walter, had his part in it, since it was always his question which began the joke.

'Do you want this string, Mr Hin-gall-ee?'

'No, Walter, you can keep it.'

'Oh, thank you. Thank you very much, Mr Hin-gall-ee.' Walter was play-acting, pretending that the string was of tremendous importance.

'Use it to hang yourself with.'

A joke again. Walter would extend the joke. 'Strangle you, this could. Round your neck, and pull it tight.' He had placed the string round his own neck, and was making the noises of being strangled.

The young women did not laugh; the trainee floor-walkers did not laugh; Mr Hingley did not laugh at Walter's joke. They looked at him, his head lolling to one side, his tongue protruding, as he made, for their approval, the horrid noises of one who is being strangled.

'You get on my tits sometimes, Walter,' said Mr Hingley.

3

Will all members of the Pygmy Pouter Club please meet in the left-hand corner of the cafeteria?

The Harrogate Fancy Pigeon Show was held that year in the Main Betting Hall of a Greyhound Stadium not far from Preston, owing to the discovery of faults in the electrical equipment of the Exhibition Hall at Harrogate, so Walter and his father did not have the expense and inconvenience of an overnight stay, but were able to bring Amy, their Long-Faced English Tumbler, in a basket that morning in time for judging.

Eric had taken Walter to the Fancy Pigeon Show on three previous occasions. They had taken the train to Harrogate, and stayed overnight at a bed-and-breakfast lodging house.

Walter had enjoyed the Shows, but his father had found it restricting to have Walter in tow. Eric had experienced the abrupt endings to or the tailings-off of conversations, as the people to whom he had been talking had noticed Walter standing close behind him, and had realized that Walter was his son.

Usually Eric would not strike up conversations with people he had never met before. When he had been a farm labourer, he had worked for most of the time on his own, unsupervised, and on the occasions when he had worked in company, as with the hay-makers or with the stockman at lambing time, he had said very little, and very little had been said to him. Even as a porter, he was not of that sociable sort which converses with the passengers. But on one day of the year, during the eleven hours between the Opening of the Show at ten a.m. and its closing at nine p.m., Eric

86

did more talking and more listening than he did in all the rest of the year put together. For three hundred and sixty-four days of the year (three hundred and sixty-five in leap years), he found little of importance to say, and those who spoke to him soon learned that they might rarely expect a reply. But today, the day of the Show, was different. He needed his one day of conversation a year. He thought about and looked forward to little else.

In previous years, those fanciers who could afford it would stay overnight at one of the big Harrogate hotels, and the others like himself, who were less well off, would drop into the Lounge Bar of one of these hotels so as to be able to talk Pigeon Talk with their richer brethren. The wives of those fanciers who stayed in the hotels would wear cocktail dresses, or even long evening dresses, which glittered, and their hair would have been permed for the occasion. Their husbands would wear suits, with collars and ties, and the less rich fanciers who had merely dropped in would wear suits also, so that it would not be easy to tell the rich and the less rich apart. The less rich fanciers would not have brought their wives. Even Eric only brought Walter.

The first time Eric took Walter to the Harrogate Show, they had followed this ritual. Walter had stood in a corner of the Lounge Bar holding a glass of Coca Cola, while Eric had circulated amongst the fanciers. But while discussing the various merits of the Gazzi Silver or Sulphur Tri-Coloured Dragoons with a fancier who specialized in them, Eric had heard three women close by begin to giggle and choke on their drinks. One of them had said, 'I wonder who he belongs to?' and when her husband asked whom they were talking about, had made the unfortunate error of pointing to Walter.

Walter's reaction had been as it always was when anyone pointed towards him. He laughed his loud pretend-laugh so loudly that all conversation in the Lounge Bar came to a halt. Then he covered his mouth with his free hand, and pointed the hand which held the glass of Coca Cola back at the woman who had laughed at him. The liquid from his glass had run down the back of a woman in a low-necked lurex dress, who screamed. Walter had said 'Sorry.' This was another automatic reaction to any action of his own which appeared to have been construed as a fault. Unfortunately he continued to say it several times, until the silence of the other guests in the Lounge Bar had become so strong as almost to be solid, and froze the word on his lips. He had looked towards Eric for support. Eric had avoided his son's eyes until conversation had resumed, and he had been able to bring his own to a natural conclusion. Then he had edged his way round the crowded room towards the door, knowing that Walter would not have let him out of sight, and when he had reached it, allowed his glance to rest for a moment on Walter before giving a tiny cock of his head to indicate that he was going.

Eric had left the hotel, and Walter had followed him, five yards behind. He knew that he had done something wrong, and that his father would be angry. In his hand, he still carried his now empty glass.

The following year, Eric had suggested to Sarah that Walter should be left at home, since his presence disturbed people. But Sarah had replied that if Eric felt too ashamed of his own son to spend one day out of a whole year in his company, doing one of the few things from which Walter got pleasure, then she would wait until he had gone, borrow the neighbour's cat for an hour, and personally place it in the Pigeon Loft.

Since then, Walter had spent the first evening in bed at the bed-and-breakfast lodging house, and stratagems had been devised to keep him standing harmlessly in one place during the Show while his father circulated. This year he was to be in charge of Amy's safety. Security at a Show of Fancy Pigeons is negligible compared to that of a Racing Pigeon Show, where the birds are worth much more since they can win, or be parents to the winners of, large sums of money. Fancy Pigeons are more beautiful, or at least more strange, but they do not win money, and so are worth less. Anyone is allowed to open a cage, and take out a bird to examine it. It would be easy for a stranger to steal Amy, if she were not watched. Even the hands of a benevolent stranger might be germ-laden. Amy herself would become irritable if mauled and pulled about by any Tom, Dick or Harry. Therefore Walter and Eric must take it in turns to stand by her cage, and make sure she was not molested. Walter first.

Walter stood by the cage, which now bore a green ticket, denoting Third in Class. There were many Classes, some having no more than five entries, but the Class for Best Long-Faced English Tumbler, Adult Hen, Self Yellow, had included seven birds (four from the same breeder, two of them entered in his

88

wife's name), so Third in Class was an award to be proud of. Walter was proud. He stood proudly by Amy's cage, protecting her from anyone who might wish to ruffle her feathers. He had not moved for two hours. So far nobody had attempted to open the cage. His father had brought him a pork pie, and had brought Amy some maple peas. He had sent Walter off with a plastic cup to find water, and had allowed Walter to freshen the water in Amy's drinking-bowl himself.

Eric had asked if Walter wished to visit the toilet, and Walter had shaken his head. Were his legs tired? Did he wish to sit down? Again, Walter had shaken his head. So Eric had patted his son's shoulder, and said, 'Good boy!' and walked away again, leaving Amy still in Walter's charge.

Walter looked at the green card attached to Amy's cage, and called her 'Good girl!' He did this several times, and was overheard to do so by several fanciers who were passing. They must have known that he stood in close relation to an award-winning bird.

Eric wandered about, conversing with old acquaintances without the embarrassment of having to admit that the person with him was his son. It was not that people were unkind; it was simply that they didn't know what to say. They didn't know whether to ignore Walter altogether, or to talk to him as one might talk to a small child.

Today there was no such problem. Eric wandered freely, inspecting the many other varieties of pigeons to see how keen the competition was in other classes.

He sympathized with the owner of a Mealy Muffed Tumbler, whose bird had been overlooked in the giving of awards. This owner averred that the bird chosen as First in Class had a crooked beak, and Eric agreed, though secretly he knew that the bird had no such deformity, or if it had, he could not see it.

'The mother's a better bird than the one that won.' Eric could not be sure whether the disappointed fancier was referring to the mother of his own bird or the winning bird, and whether she were better or not would hardly be at issue, since she would be entered in a Class of Adult Hens, whereas the Mealy Muffed Tumbler with (or without) the crooked beak was a Young Hen, so it seemed safer to nod agreement, and move on swiftly to see the Archangels, the Jacobins, the Scandaroons, the British Nuns, the Saxon Priests, the British German Shield Owls (there being

89

no German German Shield Owls), the Stargard Shakers, the Danzig High Fliers, and at last the Oriental Frills.

These were his favourites. Some fanciers called them 'Owls with ties', others 'Gems of the Orient': under either name they were beautiful. He longed to own a pair, and in the 'Selling Off' section of the Show there was a pair to be bought for only two pounds. But he had made Sarah a promise that not even a feather, not even one egg wrapped in cotton wool would he bring back from Harrogate. So instead he spent a whole hour just watching them, and longing.

The two main categories of colour among the Oriental Frills were Satinette and Blondinette. But these were the two main categories merely; within them were Sulphurette, Brownette, Brunette and Turbiteen. Eric gazed at the colours, and the delicate lace-like markings on the wings, and fought with his conscience, and his conscience won. Discretion won. They would be difficult to breed, just like his Turbits, their beaks being so small, almost inverted. No more than the Turbits would they be able to feed their own young; foster-parents would have to be found at the right time. Two pounds would not be the end of the expense. The Loft would need another extension, so as to separate them from the four categories he was already breeding. And of course they would eat. All pigeons eat, and in quantity. Acres of corn in Kansas, of grain ripening on the flat Silesian plain, the hemp plant and the maple pea, all find their way eventually to the fanciers of the Harrogate Show.

'Feel that bird. You tell me what's wrong with that.' A man in a flat cap handed Eric a Red Ribbon-Tailed Indian Fantail. Eric took the bird into his hands, and felt it, not quite sure what he was actually feeling for. It seemed safest to nod, wisely, and to say, 'Very nice. Yes.' The man in the flat cap took the bird from him, smiling. He was pleased. Eric had pleased him. Eric sighed with relief.

'You like it?'

Eric nodded.

'It's cost me a fortune to get a good head on them.'

Eric nodded.

'How d'jou do?' The question did not mean that the man in the flat cap wanted to know how Eric was, but whether he had won anything.

Eric shuffled his feet. 'Only entered one. She came third, though, in quite a large class. I'm well satisfied.'

The man in the flat cap gave Eric a thumbs-up sign, and turned away to place his much-handled bird back in its cage. Eric went on. On his own initiative he started conversations with various breeders who stood, as Walter was standing, before the cages of their champions, and when he was asked how he had done, he would smile modestly, and give the same reply, 'I'm well satisfied.'

And he was. He was satisfied, proud and pleased. Most important of all, he was enjoying himself. This was his one day of the year.

It was not that he knew all there was to know about fancy pigeons, and wished to enlighten the world. But he had an interest; not everyone could say that. From the moment, twenty-four years ago, that Sarah had discovered that she was pregnant, when Eric ceased to be her interest, and she refused any longer to be his, he had lacked an interest until he was adopted by a racing pigeon which had lost its way. Sarah's interest had been her baby. She had undertaken it and, even though the baby, Walter, had turned out not to be a normal baby, an interest of that sort, once undertaken, cannot be renounced. Eric's interest was a comparatively inexpensive hobby, in which he could lose himself, an activity for the most part carried out alone, but an interest shared (as Sarah's was not) by others, by the fancy among whom he moved once a year at the Harrogate Show.

'Do what men do when they're on their own,' Sarah had told him on the night she knew she was pregnant. He had searched for an activity that men do on their own. He had found pigeons.

He supposed that there were couples who got married and lived happily ever after, couples who had normal healthy children, and continued to enjoy each other's bodies, but he also knew that there were others, like himself and Sarah, who grew apart, and never healed together again. Strictly speaking, Walter belonged to them both. But Eric also had his pigeons, and Sarah had nothing. Except Walter.

'Will all members of the Pygmy Pouter Club please meet in the left-hand corner of the cafeteria?' The Tannoy, which was more accustomed to greyhound racing than the placid showing of pigeons, began its announcements with a screech, and ended them with a whistle. 'The Norwich Cropper Club and the Antwerp Smerles Club —' the whistle took over, and drowned out the location of these clubs' meeting-place, but all meetings took place in the cafeteria eventually; those who fancied Antwerp Smerles and Norwich Croppers had only to hang about there, and they would meet their fellows.

Eric returned to Amy's cage, and found Walter moving from foot to foot. He hoped he had arrived in time. 'It's by the Entrance. Go on. Hurry up! I'll look after her.' Walter dashed away in the direction of the Gents.

The Tannoy screeched. 'The Bohemian Brunner Pouter Club and the Barb, Carrier and Scandaroon Club will meet at five o'clock in the cafeteria. Please be prompt.' The Tannoy whistled.

Eric had attended the Tumbler Club meeting just before lunch. (They had met in the cafeteria.) All clubs had to meet at some time during the Show to decide how many Classes each breed of pigeon should have the following year, and to elect a judge for each Class from amongst themselves — a delicate matter, since a judge was required to be a specialist breeder of that Class, and would be debarred, by virtue of his judgeship, from entering birds in it himself. Eric's name had not been put forward as a candidate, but this was not to be expected. He was comparatively new with Tumblers. He had, however, been congratulated on Amy's success, and been bought half a pint of lager. One fellow fancier had even remembered Freda, and had asked after her. It was a day of pride.

'The Birmingham Rollers Club . . .' The Tannoy screeched. 'The Bald and Beard Club . . .' The Tannoy whistled. Walter came running back to his father and to Amy.

'It's alright. No need to run. We're not in any hurry.' Eric looked around to make sure that nobody he knew was within earshot. 'Did you get there in time?' Walter nodded and smiled. 'That's a good boy.'

Walter's legs were tired from standing on the same spot for so long, and Eric's were tired from much walking about. Eric looked at Walter's expression of pleasure at being at the Show, at Amy's success and consequently his father's, and watched it change under his gaze to the expression of one who knows he is under observation, still eager to please but with anxiety creeping into the eagerness, like a dog which waits for you to throw a ball or a piece of wood, and he thought, 'You are not my fault. Even champion pigeons are capable of bearing runts. You're not my fault. Not mine. Nor your own. If anyone is to be blamed, it's my father and my sister.' And even his sister had been under age, and known no better than to do what she was told. Obedience is not a fault.

It was the first time he had ever thought in these terms. He placed an arm over Walter's shoulder. Walter grinned a grin of pleasure.

Eric said, 'Let's go an' have a sit-down, shall we? Amy'll not come to any harm.' But as they started to move, the Tannoy screeched and whistled in a particularly self-important way, preparatory to making the longest announcement made so far that day.

'Ladies and Gentlemen! Fanciers, and those unlike myself, who have the good fortune to be fancied. Our Celebrity Judge is about to choose the pigeon which will be listed in our Hall of Fame.' There was no real likelihood of any list of pigeons being hung up in the Greyhound Stadium, not even in its cafeteria, but a Tannoy is to be allowed a certain licence when it takes the trouble to be comprehensible for more than ten seconds at a stretch. 'Which fortunate bird will be chosen as this year's Best Bird of the Show? Don't wait! Don't wait! Don't hesitate! It only happens once a year. Come to the right-hand corner near the Exit, where our six hopeful beauties are waiting to be scrutinized.'

Fanciers began to drift to the right-hand corner near the Exit. Eric had one last thought about the pair of Oriental Frills, and wondered if they were still for sale. But there was always next year. Better to keep something to look forward to. His arm over Walter's shoulder, he led him towards the six best birds of the Show.

The six finalists were a Blue Gazzi Modena, a Bald Long-Faced Tumbler, a Magpie, a Red Jacobin, a Pouter, and a Double-Crested Trumpeter. 'It'll be the Blue Gazzi Modena,' said the fancier standing on Walter's left foot. 'What do you bet me?' Walter turned and grinned his special grin at the man, and wondered why the man frowned, looked worried and turned away.

The Celebrity Judge took his chrome telescopic judging-stick from his pocket, extended it, poked it between the bars of the cage housing the Blue Gazzi Modena, and touched it, first just under its beak, then on the underside of its tail. The bird responded

93

almost flirtatiously, standing even more erect than before, with its tail stuck up vertically and its head well back. It reminded Walter of a teapot. Then the Judge touched the Pouter, which inflated its crop to such an extent, and strutted so on its long thin legs, that it appeared to have entered a Mr Universe Contest, resembling something which had been squeezed upwards from the bottom to form the shape of an icecream cornet.

The Celebrity Judge took each bird out of its cage several times, and examined it closely. This was a particularly delicate operation in the case of the Double-Crested Trumpeter, which had such long feathers sticking out from the sides of its feet that it could hardly turn round in the cage. The crowd became impatient, and pressed forward against the arms of the Stewards. But the Celebrity Judge would not be rushed into a hasty decision. Judges were not rushed at Crufts or the National Cat Show; *he* would not be rushed.

Finally he took two steps backwards, and nodded to his female Assistant to indicate that he had made up his mind, and, like a surgeon at some trepanning or appendectomy, held out his hand without looking at her, so that there might be placed within it, the coveted blue rosette with gold lettering which would announce 'Best in Show'.

The crowd became silent, remaining pressed tight against the arms of the Stewards. With all attention so concentrated elsewhere it seemed to a small boy who had taken a fancy to a Black-Lace Fantail an ideal moment to open its cage, grasp the unsuspecting bird with both hands, and begin his run towards the Exit. A Steward saw the boy running, shouted, and gave chase. The blue rosette was already within the hand of the Celebrity Judge. He remained immobile. He would not make the presentation while there were distractions. The Steward chasing the thief bumped into a woman, who was holding a Chinese Owl, which was released as she fell over, and took to the air. The woman screamed. Six other Stewards unclasped the arms which had been restraining spectators, and began to push their way through the crowd to join the chase after the small boy. The Celebrity Judge saw, without being able entirely to believe what he saw, that the crowd had actually begun to turn away from the presentation, and having turned, to move.

One bird had already been stolen. People were moving. Amy would be in danger. Walter knew his duty. He began to struggle through the crowd towards Amy's cage. Eric had been pushed onto his knees twice, and his right hand had been trampled by Stewards. Raising his bruised hand and gripping the hem of some fancier's jacket to pull himself to his feet, Eric attempted to follow Walter. In pulling himself up, he pulled the fancier down, and cries pursued him in his own pursuit.

One of the Stewards had reached the small boy, and was pulling him, almost dragging him backwards by the collar of his shirt. Choking, the boy released his grip on the Black-Lace Fantail, which broke free, and flapped clumsily upwards to join the Chinese Owl, leaving the small boy with six black-lace tail-feathers still in his hand.

The crowd gasped as the tailless Black-Lace Fantail attempted to gain height. Walter dodged agitatedly in and out among the fanciers, but made little progress. Eric had decided on a more roundabout route in an attempt to cut Walter off, and had become momentarily lost, beguiled by a row of Voorburg Shield Croppers which he had not seen on his previous tour.

All eyes, except those of Eric, Walter and the Celebrity Judge, were now scanning the high rafters of the Main Betting Hall, trying to spot the exact whereabouts of the Black-Lace Fantail and the Chinese Owl.

There was a very large man blocking Walter's way. Walter looked up at the man, and said, 'Excuse me.' The man removed his gaze for a while from the rafters, and replied, 'Sorry, mate. I don't dance,' breaking thereafter into deep-throated laughter. Walter thought it polite to join in the laughter, while attempting to squeeze past the man, but the man took exception to Walter's unconvincing laugh, and gripping him by the lapels of his jacket, said, 'Here! Watch it,' and pushed him away.

Pushed by the large man, Walter fell hard against a row of cages containing Birmingham Rollers. As the cages fell, their doors opened, and twenty-six frightened Birmingham Rollers took to the air, scattering loose feathers over the crowd like confetti. Seven people in the adjoining aisle were trapped under the fallen cages and confused by the escaping birds. Others who had seen the falling cages in time to dodge them had, in dodging, bumped into still other fanciers, who in their turn knocked over the next aisle of cages, which contained Antwerp Smerles. Fourteen Antwerp Smerles followed the twenty-six Birmingham Rollers, the Chinese

Owl and the tailless Black-Lace Fantail up into the rafters above the upturned faces of the astonished crowd. Feathers of various colours drifted down.

Walter lay where he had been pushed. His back hurt, and he was not sure if he could move. Moreover there were three Birmingham Rollers trapped in their cages beneath him, and if he did move, they might escape.

Eric had found Amy, and was talking to her, trying to calm her down. The freedom of the birds which had escaped seemed to have an unsettling effect on those still behind bars. The Celebrity Judge, in an access of petulance, presented the blue rosette to the Blue Gazzi Modena, with nobody watching, and went off in a huff.

Two Stewards pulled Walter slowly to his feet, while a third attempted to right the three cages beneath him. This had the effect of untrapping the birds, but the ascent of three more Birmingham Rollers to join the throng of birds already in the roof could only be anti-climactic. Walter made first the discovery that he could stand, then that he could walk, left the Stewards, ignoring their advice to visit the First Aid Room, and joined his father at Amy's cage, where the presence of both of the humans who belonged to her had a pronounced calming effect on that prize-winning bird.

Most of the other birds who were still confined were by no means calm. Some rushed the bars of their cages, their crops inflated, their tails down and scraping the floor, making the angry sounds which mean, 'Keep off my territory' at full volume. Others ran their beaks along the bars of their cages, like jailbirds rattling their tin mugs to gain attention. The Tannoy whistled, the Tannoy squeaked, but the sound of three thousand four hundred and thirty-seven discontented pigeons quite drowned out the announcement that the Blue Gazzi Modena had become eligible to have its name inscribed in the Hall of Fame. Even its owner was looking upwards, with the rest of the fanciers, at the forty-five birds which were now circling above them, wondering how they might be reunited with their cages and whether any of the Antwerp Smerles were his.

4

You fall asleep and Jesus decides if he wants you to live with him in Paradise

Walter walked along the back alley which separated the back yards of Bancroft Street from the back yards of Crossley Street. Three small children were racing each other from one end of the alley to the other. Walter stopped as they approached him, and pressed himself against the wall, not wishing to knock any of them down, or to spoil the chance of any one runner by being in his way. The child running along the gutter in the middle of the alley had the advantage, since the cobblestones on either side were damp and slippery.

Walter was no longer allowed to enter the house by the front door on his return from Woolworth's, because, apart from the dirt he had accumulated about himself, his mother had often found sticky things on the carpet, which he had brought in on the soles of his shoes. Toffees dropped by children, paint from a can which a careless assistant had allowed to fall from the counter, jam, honey, even glue, all these had at one time or another been innocently carried home on Walter's shoes.

Sarah had thought of supplying her son with one pair of shoes to travel in and another to work in, but her knowledge of the time it took him to tie and untie his shoe-laces and that his work-shoes would get dirtier and dirtier because he would never remember to bring them home to be cleaned, made her decide against this plan. Besides, if Walter continued to get substances of various sorts stuck to the soles of his work-shoes, and these substances accumulated, he would eventually have great difficulty in walking, and would give offence to customers by standing several feet

97

taller than they. Or the work-shoes would be lost, or even stolen, and Walter would know no better than to tread the ever-sticky floors of Woolworth's in his stockinged feet.

Walter enjoyed the walk from the bus. He would walk briskly on his toes, with his arms swinging, and his head thrown back to study the sky. He would whistle, in a tuneless, but optimistic tone. When he reached the alley, sometimes he would jump as high as he could, so as to look over into the back yard of a neighbour. He liked entering the house from the back, because it gave him a chance to say 'Hello' to his father's pigeons, peeping at them through the slats Eric had put on to the Loft for light and ventilation.

This evening his step was particularly springy, and his lips were pursed in an extra effort to make a louder and more tuneful whistle. The day had been successful. He had helped – no, he had taken a leading part – in cleaning up four jars of raspberry jam, which had fallen from the arms of a Counter Assistant who was working out her week's notice, given for persistent lateness. The jam had slipped from her grasp right outside Mr Richards' office. Mr Richards, who had given her notice in the first place, now shouted at her, and sent her up to the General Office to collect the money owing to her, with instructions to leave the building at once.

Walter had stepped in at once to start cleaning up the mess. Under the supervision of one of the floor-walkers (Mr Sykes, whose promotion was well overdue), he had cleared away the jam and broken glass, and had washed the floor in what seemed like record time. When all this was done, all that Mr Richards had to say to Mr Sykes was that the display on Haberdashery was a disgrace to his department, but he had placed an arm round Walter's shoulder, and had thanked him warmly, and told him once more what he had often told him, and always in a loud voice so that others could hear, 'I don't know what I'd do without you, Walter. The best thing I ever did was taking you on.' The girls behind the counters within earshot had looked at one another, and smiled, and they had smiled at Walter, and Walter had grinned up into the face of Mr Richards, and had said, 'Thank you, Mr Richards.'

He was still smiling at the memory when he reached the back yard of his parents' house. He remembered to close the gate behind him. Then he peered between the slats of the Loft, and said,

'Hello, pigeons.' The birds stood side by side on their perches, almost all of them in pairs. Some stood on one leg (for whatever reason Walter did not know), some used both legs to support themselves, and some crouched in a sitting-down position. One White-Lace Fantail crouched thus, quivering one of its wings and making a low throaty noise to show approval, while its partner pecked gently and lovingly round the crouching pigeon's head and neck. Eric had explained to Walter that this is how pigeons show affection for each other. The crouching bird opened and closed its eyes, enjoying the love-making. Its eyelids came up from below to cover the eye, instead of coming down like the eyelids of human beings.

Walter watched the pigeon's eyes, fascinated. The standing bird placed its beak inside that of the crouching bird, and both rocked their heads from side to side. Walter knew that this was called 'billing'. The crouching bird quivered and cooed more strongly, and the standing bird placed first one leg and then the other on its partner's back. The bird beneath lifted its tail, and, with a flap of wings to steady itself, the bird above placed its tail sideways and under the loved one's tail. No more. They had mated. It was February, almost spring. Soon there would be eggs to look for, the days before hatching to be counted, then the tiny feather- less bodies and extra food to be given to all those birds whose eggs had hatched and who were feeding them a kind of cheese produced from between their feathers in their breasts, then the featherless bodies become slowly feathered, a persistent squeaking from the nest and the young squabs fed now with digested grain pumped into voracious mouths from the crops of parent birds who would need even more food while doing so. By the time the young squabs began to pick some grain for themselves the parents would already have mated again; more eggs would be expected. It never occurred to Walter that this activity of his father's pigeons had anything to do with what had happened to him in the Park.

The White-Lace Fantails who had just mated were billing again. If they had been free, not confined in a Loft, they would have taken to the sky in a flight of mutual congratulation at having successfully passed sperm from cock to hen in spite of the difficulty caused by the shape of their tails. Forgetting to remove his jam- stained shoes, Walter rushed into the house to tell his father what he had just seen.

'Dad!' There was nobody in the kitchen. Usually at this time, his mother would be there to supervise the cleaning of shoes. Walter sensed that something was wrong. Nobody had answered his call, and there was nothing being cooked on the stove.

He opened the door to the living-room. His mother was sitting at the dining table, opposite a woman who occasionally came to the house with a catalogue from which his mother would choose things to buy. The woman would leave the catalogue with Sarah for a few days, and she would use it for Walter's lessons, pointing to pictures of objects, the names of which he had then to tell her.

Today there was no catalogue on the table. Between his mother and the woman there was a teapot, milk jug, sugar bowl and two cups and saucers. He stood by the door, holding it open, and waiting for his mother to speak. She did not speak. She turned her face to the window, and lifted the handkerchief she was clasping, so that it covered her eyes. Her face was red.

Had the woman done something bad to his mother? This woman had never looked at Walter directly, on any of the occasions when she had come with the catalogue. She had never looked into his eyes. Whenever she had spoken to Walter in the past, she had looked at the ground, or to one side of him. And now, when she turned to face him, she looked at the carpet, and said, 'Hello, Walter.'

Walter nodded. She would not see him nod. She was not looking at his head.

'What are you going to tell him?' the woman said to Walter's mother. Walter's mother kept the handkerchief over her eyes, and shook her head.

Something was wrong. Perhaps his mother had an ache in her head. The woman should not pester her. Walter wished she would go away. The clock on the mantel ticked out the seconds, and Walter listened to it. He had never noticed that it had so loud a tick before.

'Do you want me to go?'

His mother nodded. The woman drank what tea was left in her cup, and stood up. 'You know where I live, if there's . . .?' Walter's mother nodded again. She knew where the woman lived. Who did not?

The woman was going. Whatever was wrong would soon not be wrong any more. Walter's mother said, 'Thank you,' to the woman.

'Not at all. We all need help at times like this.' The woman looked at Walter for the first time in her life. 'It won't be easy,' she said. 'I'll be off, then.'

She had gone. She had moved out of the living-room and into the hall, and Walter had heard the front door close behind her. He remembered his shoes, went quickly back into the kitchen before his mother could speak, bent down, and began to untie the laces. When the shoes were off, he placed them on a page of the previous evening's paper, and placed the paper in a corner. As he turned from doing so, he saw his mother standing by the kitchen door.

'More sticky soles?' Walter nodded. Her face was red and puffed up. She had been crying, but was not now.

'Better clean them now, then. Before you forget.' Walter took the oldest knife from the cutlery drawer, and began to scrape raspberry jam from the soles of his shoes.

'What is it? Chewing-gum again?' Walter shook his head.

'What, then?'

'Jam.'

'What sort?' She leaned against the sink for support. 'Or don't you know?' If she kept talking, she might be able to prevent herself from screaming or going mad. She might just be able to hold on long enough for the rage inside her to pass. The almost overwhelming desire to let go, to break everything in sight, to scream and cry until she was exhausted, must be contained. Words would help. If she could keep him answering questions, he wouldn't catch on yet. Not yet. She wasn't ready for that. Yet. Already he was watching her, with that frightened apprehensive look.

'Did you drop it?'

He didn't understand.

'The jam. Was it you who dropped it?'

He shook his head. 'I cleaned it ... Cleaned it for Mr Richards.'

'Good boy!' She was biting hard on her lower lip, to stop it trembling. 'Will they give you more money, do you think?'

Walter shrugged his shoulders, and shook his head. He discovered that he was no longer looking forward to telling her how Mr Richards had placed an arm around his shoulder, and praised him for all to hear.

'What's that supposed to mean?' Her voice was harder now.

'Is it because you don't know, or you don't think they'll give you more money, or you don't understand the question? Shrugging your shoulders, that's no good to anybody.' Someone had to be strong with him. Someone had to try. She would sell her mother's rings and the cultured pearls. The ear-rings wouldn't be worth much.

'It was raspberry . . . I think.' He had removed the sticky jam from his shoes. The jam was grey now, made grey by the dust from the floor of the Stock Room. In amongst the grey mess, there were tiny splinters of broken glass, sparkling.

'What shall I . . . ?' He was holding out the crumpled newspaper containing jam and splinters of glass.

'What do you usually do with it?' She must hold on. She must be strong.

'Fire!' He emphasized the word, as if she were the one in doubt.

'We don't have a fire. It's nearly spring.'

'Yes . . . Fantails mated.' His face showed pleasure. Exaggerated pleasure, the pleasure of having observed something special.

He would never mate. Not her son. And she would never. Never again. 'Bully for them.' She remembered her husband's excitement when the first eggs of the season were laid. 'Bully for them.' Mother Nature was carrying on in the Pigeon Loft as if nothing had happened. But Eric was dead.

'Tell Dad.' He screwed the newspaper tighter, building up the excitement of his discovery.

'Put that in the bin.' She watched him bend down and place it in the pedal-bin.

'Where is he?' He had completed his task, and was watching her closely, looking for some clue that would explain the difference in her manner.

'Where's he gone?' They had played a game when he was small, in short cotton trousers over nappies, played it still when he was 'just a late developer', continued to play it as he grew, might even sometimes, if she were in a good mood and prepared to allow childishness in her wage-earning son, play it now. 'Where's he gone?' She would hide her thumb or even a sweetie within her fingers to make him giggle. He sang the words to her, as once she had sung to him. 'Where's he gone?'

She turned her head away to hide the trembling lips. 'Where's he gone?' He had caught her look, and moved to face her, with an anxious searching gaze which broke her heart. She had failed, was crying inaudibly, suffering pain in her throat and chest so as not to make a noise. Her whole body shook with the effort of control. Tears dripped onto the floor from her chin. She was leaning against the back door, her face pressed into the corner, shaking, taking in gulps of breath she didn't want. Why should she breathe?

He watched her, silent now and still, feeling the darkness at the base of his stomach grow. This was the feeling he recognized as fear; his vocabulary was not yet so wide as to include the word, but he knew the feeling well; it was what you felt just before a scream burst out of you. His mother was not in control, and he was frightened. The feeling was getting worse, and she wouldn't look at him, wouldn't help him, hold him, even for a moment touch him. He pressed himself against her, clutching at her blouse, his arms around her waist. She was struggling to free herself, shouting at him to let go, protecting her face from his greasy, spotty, anxious, animal's face, fighting off a son who was taller, stronger than she, whose head was a weight on her shoulder, and whose need to be cuddled made her sick.

As she pushed him away, flaying around wildly with her arms and shouting between sobs, he started his scream. It was a long continuous earsplitting scream of terror, punctuated by the stamping of his feet. As he topped up with breath so as to make the scream persist, he bit the back of his own hand. She rounded on him, first striking him across the face, then gripping the hair at the back of his neck, pulling him towards the sink, and pushing his head under the cold-water tap.

He made no resistance after her slap across his face. The fact that she had taken control relieved much of the fear he felt. The cold water struck the back of his head; he felt it slide down the sides of his face and neck, and wet the collar of his shirt. His body relaxed. He watched the water run from the end of his nose into the sink, and circle the plug-hole, and concentrated on the feel of it. Sarah was pressing his neck to keep his head down, but since he did not resist, she loosened her grip, then removed it, and reached for a drying-up cloth.

Walter remained obediently where he was, with his head under the tap, until she turned off the water, placed the drying-up cloth over his head, and guided him into the living-room.

She sat on the settee, and Walter lay on it in the foetal position, with his wet head resting in her lap. She moved the drying-up cloth slowly and gently back and forth to dry his face and hair. After a while she said, 'Your dad's gone to sleep for a very long time. We won't see him again, until we fall asleep forever. Then we'll meet him again, where and when God wants us to. It's hard for you to understand, I know. But even though we shall miss him ...'

She could not go on. She would not miss Eric; her tears were not for that. All through her married life until now, she had still preserved some thoughts, some hope of freedom, or at least of relief. Now Eric had found that freedom; he had relief. Her tears were for herself, not her husband. She was trapped, still trapped, forever trapped with a twenty-seven-year-old-late-developer. It was comic. Here he lay on her lap, this *thing* she had made. From now on, she was totally responsible for Walter. The trap had tightened; the wire round her neck was pulling. She was like a rabbit which hadn't the sense to draw back while the noose was still slack. If only she had left, run away all those years ago, used her mother's jewellery to go somewhere, anywhere at all! If! The head in her lap moved, and she must speak to it.

'Even though I know you'll miss him a lot, you've got to remember that he's happy now, where he is. He has no problems, you see. You must be glad for him. We all have to fall asleep some time, but when we do, it's a sleep of peace. Jesus calls us to him, and we are glad to be called. That's the day of Reckoning. You fall asleep, and Jesus decides if He wants you to live with Him in Paradise. Only those who have been good get to live forever with Jesus. We won't see your dad any more, but Jesus will look after him.'

Gently she began to rock Walter's head, so that his whole body moved backwards and forwards. His wet hair had left a damp patch on her dress. It would dry out. If she rocked him for long enough, she might be able to convince herself as well as her son of the truth of what she had just told him. She had to. There had to be a point to it all. There must be some compensation for life; that was only fair. She began to sing.

'*Jesus loves me. This I know,*
For the Bible tells me so ...'

104

They remained in the same position for well over an hour, Sarah singing hymns, passing from one to another without pausing, and remembering all the words as if she had written them herself. Walter was reassured by the closeness of his mother. Only one thing worried him, and that was the problem of how he was going to be able to stay awake. He did not wish to fall asleep, as it seemed his father had done, for he did not wish to be called by Jesus yet. Not yet.

> 'Shall we gather at the river,
> The beautiful, beautiful river?
> Gather with the saints at the river,
> Which flows by the hand of God?'

5

*Even the girls who had left their counters to have
a quiet smoke behind the stacks of detergents
would remark on his silence*

The day after Walter had been told that his father was with
Jesus, his mother woke him at the usual time, and he caught the
bus he always caught. The conductor joked with him, as was
usual, but Walter didn't respond. He was silent.

The Walter who laughed his braying pointing laugh, the
Walter who giggled, the Walter who made people feel good
because they were not he, the Walter who comforted the unsure
by showing them that not all madness is tragic, was having a day
off.

Today the tonic and comforter of the passengers on the early
morning bus sat in silence, and stared into the middle distance,
and when the bus reached the stop at which Walter got off, the
conductor had to shake him.

'Are you alright, lad?'

Walter didn't answer.

He walked from the bus stop to the Staff Entrance of Woolworth's. He stood, as he always stood, waiting for Mr Hingley
to unlock the lift gates, and press the button for the lift which
would take them up to the Stock Room, but this morning, instead
of giggling and pointing when Mr Hingley dangled the keys in
front of his face prior to pulling them away just as Walter made
a grab for them, Walter did not grab; he did not giggle. He only
stared at the concrete, and at the empty crisp bags and cigarette
packets and at the silver paper which blew about the yard.

Mr Hingley ruffled Walter's Brylcreemed hair, and said, 'What's up with thee?'

Walter was silent.

'You've got a face like a month of Mondays.' Still getting no reply, he followed Walter's gaze down to the ground, and said, 'Yes, I want you to clean up this yard today. I'll get one of the other lads to help you.'

'Are you sick?' They were now in the lift. Walter shook his head.

When he had changed into his overalls, he went to his press, and started to make a bale.

Jean, who looked after the shelves of soap-powders, detergents, pan-scourers and disinfectants, arrived singing. She was always good-humoured, known for it. She said nobody would apply for a job at Woolworth's without a very odd sense of humour. She was unmarried, and looked after her mother. She had steel-grey hair, cropped short, and wore wire-rimmed spectacles, and both her chin and nose were pointed. Her shelves were the closest to Walter's press.

She skipped around the Stock Room twice, taking her overcoat off as she did so in the manner of an extremely clumsy stripper, and singing, 'I've Got a Handful of Songs to Sing You'. After a while she caught the eye of Mr Hingley, who gestured at her to be quiet, and pointed at Walter's back.

Jean frowned, not understanding the meaning of the gesture. But clearly it concerned Walter, so she tiptoed over to him, shouted, 'Got you!' and engaged him in a mock fight, pulling his neck back with one arm and holding him in a half-nelson with the other.

Usually Walter enjoyed these mock wrestling matches. He liked the attention. But today, he went limp, and gave no resistance.

Jean let him go, and moved round to look into his face. His eyes refused to meet hers. Instead he took a step back away from her, and bent down to pick up the tool he used to cut the baling-wire.

'Hey, sweetheart, what's wrong? Come on, tell me. What's the matter?' She crouched down quickly before he could get up, placing an arm around his shoulder, and talking to him as if he were a baby.

Walter said, 'S'nuffing. It's alright.' Then, after he had resumed his work, he added, without directing the statement at anybody in particular, 'Jesus wanted him,' and then, after thought, 'I'll look after the pigeons.'

There had been other times when Walter had been silent, when he had sulked, but they had always occurred after he had started work, and the cause was always known. If he had been wrongly accused of falling down in his duties, and he felt the fault was not his, he would first protest loudly, shouting the name of the real culprit, spitting as he did so, and justifying his innocence with arms flying wildly about his head. If his justification were ignored, and he were told to shut up and get on with it, then he would sulk. Walter sulking became the centre of a circle of general emotional discomfort. His shoulders were always round, and appeared to become rounder. His face and jaw were always long, and appeared to become longer. And he was quiet. This was an unnatural quietness; it was the quietness of a Walter not laughing to himself or talking in the third person or playing both parts in a duologue only imperfectly remembered from a previous evening's television programme. The heavy silence, the silence of Walter, the unnatural hang-dog silence would affect everyone else who worked in the Stock Room. Even the girls who had left their counters down below, to come visiting friends and to have a quiet smoke behind the stacks of detergents, even they would remark on the silence, and would say, 'What's up with Walter, then?'

Then someone would take his side, and talk in an exaggeratedly loud voice about what a good worker he was, and how the store could not operate without him. 'Imagine,' the someone would say, 'the piles of cardboard boxes filling the spaces between the counters.' Wonder would be expressed at the inevitable consequences to Woolworth's should Walter ever slacken, of the enormous fines the Council would impose on Mr Richards, as his rubbish swelled out into the High Street, bringing traffic to a stop and immobilizing the Town Centre.

Then Mr Hingley would place an arm around Walter's shoulder, and ask him for a special favour. The favour was always the same. It was that Walter should move some stock in the Confectionery Department. And Mr Hingley would wink at Walter, and at the very same moment, Miss Evans, who was in charge of the Confectionery, would announce in her clear gentle precise voice, 'I shall be incommunicado, Mr Hingley, for the next quarter of an hour,' and off she would go to visit the Ladies.

Everyone knew that the stock Walter was sent to move did not exist, and that he would spend fifteen minutes pretending to try to find it, while stuffing his mouth with a half-pound bar of milk chocolate or a large slice of coconut slab, and that thereafter the heavy silence would be over, and Walter himself again.

But that was not to be today. Today was different. Today a Walter they had never known before had come to work, a Walter who went about his work silently and methodically, ignoring or seeming not to hear the voices of concern.

Each in turn of those who worked in the Stock Room expressed concern; each in turn tried to find out from Walter what was wrong.

Gwyneth, whose wide domain included plants, seeds, garden tools, gents' socks, shirts, ties and underwear, asked Walter in her warm Cornish accent what had happened to upset him. Walter maintained that he was alright. 'Well, you'm don't look alright, Walter; you'm don't, really.' She pulled the bright red hair-ribbon from her long dark ringlets, shook them, and retied the knot so as to secure the ringlets from the side of her face. But Walter only looked away.

Mike, the young man whom Walter had first seen stuffing liquorice all-sorts into his mouth, when Walter had come with his mother for the interview with Mr Richards, was told to take Walter and two brooms down to the back yard, and clean it. 'What's the matter, kiddo?' he said to Walter in the lift. Walter looked at the bristles on his yard-brush, and remained silent.

In the back yard they found Lynn, one of Mike's many girl-friends. Most of Lynn's time was spent in leaning against the wall of the yard, hoping that Mike would be sent down to unload a lorry. Mike was quick, funny and energetic. Very little of this energy went into the unloading of lorries; it was divided almost equally between sex and the attempt to create a belief in all the people whom Mike ever met that he was slick, clever, ambitious and, above all, charming. To Walter he seemed just like a whirl-wind of activity. Everything Mike did was done with a flourish. Mike unpacking a case – throwing, catching, slamming down – was not a young man performing a routine job, but a paradigm of manager-material pitching in.

Since much of Mike's conversation with Lynn was conducted while catching or throwing boxes from lorry to ground or from ground to lift, and since one of the regular drivers was a Jehovah's Witness, Mike and Lynn had invented a code so as not to offend the godly. In this code, Lynn's privy member was called 'Janey', Mike's 'Big John': Mike was not one to sell himself short. Mike and Lynn believed that the sentence, 'Janey thinks it's time Big John came to visit her,' would be thought by a Jehovah's Witness or any other eavesdropping third party to refer to mutual friends, and the reply, 'Big John says he's got nothing to wear, and he's broke' (meaning that Mike was unfortunately without a condom and had no money to buy any) would only support this misapprehension.

Walter started in the far corner of the yard, sweeping the rubbish towards the lift. Mike left his yard-brush leaning against the wall, and pressed Lynn into a corner, where no one but Walter could see that his hands were inside her clothes.

'Is Janey better?' ('Is your period over?')

'Yes, thank you. She's getting lonely.'

'Oh, yes, she is, i'nt she? I can feel that. She's saying, "Come up and see me sometime." '

'What about tonight?'

'What about right now?'

'Don't be daft.'

'There's only Walter. He wouldn't even know what we were doing.'

Walter's bowed shoulders, Walter's elongated face, were still mute signs of the pain he felt at Jesus's having taken his father, and his sense of the unfairness that a body couldn't so much as go to sleep without being removed by Jesus in this way, but Lynn could not read the signs. She said, 'What's the matter with him, anyway?'

'Dunno. He's sulking. Come on, it's months since we had a stander.'

'Not here, Mike. That Jehovah's Witness might turn up with a lorryload of John Innes Compost, and want to bless us.'

'He's not due for weeks. Here, come on, let us. We've only got to take 'em down a bit.'

'No, not with him brushing away over there. Send him upstairs, then we'll see.'

'I can't do that. They'll want to know where I am. If he tells them I'm with you, they'll all be down here, wanting to watch.'

'Cheeky buggers!'

'Come on! Just let Big John walk in, and have a look around. Just a bit of stock-taking.'

'No, he's watching. Look! He keeps turning round.'

And Walter was turning round. His sense of unfairness had increased to include the fact that Mike was not doing any of the sweeping, though that would not have bothered him on an ordinary day.

'Sod that fucking Walter! Hey, Fuck-Face, keep your eyes down. There are pound notes in that rubbish.'

Usually Walter would have laughed his braying laugh at that, and pointed. But not today. He looked away, his shoulders bowed, and began to sweep again.

Mike turned back to Lynn; the lower half of him had never turned away. 'Christ!' he said, 'I think I've creamed my jeans.' He moved a little away from her, held the broad leather belt he was wearing away from his twenty-eight-inch waist, and wriggled his small tight little bottom about. 'That's better,' he said.

'Tonight.'

'Big John can't screw you tonight, darling. He's got to go to sodding Evening Class.'

By now, Walter had almost finished sweeping the yard. Lynn and Mike kissed, Mike picked up his brush again, and Lynn walked off down the alley towards the High Street.

Mike stood leaning on his brush, with the lift doors open, waiting for Walter to finish. 'You're a pain in the anus, you are, Walter,' he said. 'Do you know that?'

6

You've not been yourself today, Walter. Now, that's not like you

The day passed, and as always at five o'clock a loud bell sounded in the store downstairs to announce the end of trading for the day. At each cash register, the Counter Assistant rang up 'No Sale', and left the cash register open so that one of the girls from the General Office could check the money, which would be transferred to leather bags. Most of the counters were then covered with dark green sheets, except for Cosmetics, Confectionery and Groceries, which were covered with white sheets.

Each Counter Assistant then stood to attention at that corner of the counter which was nearest the door to the Cloak Room.

As the Counter Girls stood to attention, and the girls from the General Office checked and emptied the tills, Mr Richards, the Manager, would make his tour of inspection. He would walk the aisles between the counters, appraising each girl's appearance, and choosing at random a counter from which he would pull the green or the white sheet like a bullfighter making a pass. Then he would inspect the display. If he should spot untidiness or a price-card upside down, he would shout to the floor-walker who had sinned, and the unfortunate man would come running to correct his error and to ask forgiveness.

On hearing the bell sound from downstairs, the four young trainee floor-walkers in the Stock Room would grab brooms from the corner where they were kept, jostling and arguing in order to attain the broom with most bristles. Then they would stand in the lift, shouting and swearing at Walter to hurry. Walter always

112

took his time, and this evening the time he took was even longer. Usually it was part of the ritual that he would complain of being left a broom with insufficient bristles. He would keep the others waiting while he insisted that Mr Hingley should inspect his balding broom and promise to order a new one. But not this evening. This evening, although he was slower than usual, he made no complaint, no request for a new broom. His time was taken in silence.

Finishing early meant no more to Walter than a longer wait for his bus home. To the young trainee floor-walkers, it meant sex, films, alcohol, food, the television, more food, and sleep. Usually as the lift descended to the shop floor, they would crowd Walter into a corner, and tickle him until, laughing hysterically, he slid to the floor, imploring them to stop, but enjoying the attention. By doing so they hoped to disrupt the solemnity and silence of Mr Richards' inspection, but Walter had always stopped laughing by the time the lift had reached the ground floor.

Today there was silence in the lift, and no tickling. Walter leaned his back against the side of the lift, and stared down at the floor. His manner did not encourage tickling. The young trainee floor-walkers looked at each other, but said nothing.

The lift reached the shop floor, and one of the boys opened the gates. Seeing that the inspection was not yet over, they waited where they were. Finally Mr Richards nodded to the Assistant Manager, and a second bell sounded. Then the Counter Girls rushed towards the Cloak Room, elbowing each other to get out, and treading on each other's feet. The moving mass of rust-brown overalls, coming from all directions and squeezing through one narrow doorway, looked like a highly organized army of worker ants, evacuating a nest infected with DDT.

The trainee floor-walkers and Walter moved to the back of the store. Each taking an aisle, they began sweeping towards the glass doors at the front of the shop. All eyes scanned the floor for treasure. Silver, copper, even pound notes had, at one time or another, been found. These, being without identification of owner-ship, might safely be kept. A wallet or purse would usually be handed in, depending on who found it, and whether he thought he had been seen picking it up.

Walter moved forwards slowly, disturbed at the prospect of

going home to his mother. It would be different now. She would probably cry again, and that would frighten him.

Then his thoughts moved to pigeons. He visualized the Russian High-Fliers, soaring ever onwards and upwards, higher and higher. Would he ever be able to get them down? The clouds, within which they might become lost, reminded him of Paradise, where even at this very moment his father would be standing in front of Jesus. Would his father have been asked to take off his jacket and trousers in order to wear white flowing robes like those Jesus wore? Walter found it difficult to imagine his father in flowing robes of any colour. Unlike Jesus and the disciples, Walter's father had no beard, and his hair was far from long. It had been cut regularly once a fortnight in the style he had always asked for, which was short back and sides.

'Leave that, Walter. I want to have a word with you.'

Walter hadn't noticed Mr Richards approach him, partly because of his preoccupation with the sartorial arrangements of Jesus, and partly because Mr Richards habitually crept about, and took his staff by surprise, so that his nickname among them was 'Pussyfoot'.

Now Mr Richards first placed his hand on Walter's shoulder, then walked ahead of him to the Manager's Office. Once inside, he closed the door carefully, and placed this time, not a hand, but a whole arm round Walter's shoulder.

'I'm worried about you, Walter. Mr Hingley's worried about you; he told me so, and that means I worry too. You've not been yourself today. Now, that's not like you, Walter. Mr Hingley says you won't tell anyone why. I want to help. You're a good worker. I'd hate to have to let you go.'

Walter looked up into Mr Richards' face. His hair was short, like that of Walter's father, but he did have a small neat moustache. Walter half-closed his eyes, and tried to picture Mr Richards without his dark brown pin-striped suit, but with long white robes. Just as he had tried to imagine his father's first meeting with Jesus, he now tried to imagine Jesus faced with Mr Richards. It was difficult. He strained to do it. A picture began to form, then fell to pieces again. No matter how hard he tried, he couldn't think what Mr Richards and Jesus could possibly find to say to each other.

'What are you squinting like that for?'

Walter opened his eyes fully.

'Do you hear what I'm saying?' The white robes finally fell away, like a vampire's body turning to dust, and were replaced by the brown pin-striped suit.

'Yes, sir.'

'Well, then?' Mr Richards applied more pressure to Walter's left shoulder. This was not punishment, but encouragement. The boy needed it. Mr Richards was proud of the way he had with people. They responded to him. He could not have reached his present position without the talent for provoking such a response, which was, even at first meeting, the response of follower to leader, and not just to any leader, but to a leader who knew where he was going.

'Well come on, lad. Spit it out.' Mr Richards moved to his desk, and sat at it, commandingly, yet with warmth and friendship. This was strategy – the open hand combined with the subtle reminder of who the leader is. As Mr Richards sat in the leader's chair, Walter laughed, then quickly covered his mouth with his right hand.

'What's so funny?'

Walter moved the hand from his mouth. 'You said "spit".'

Mr Richards looked at Walter with incomprehension.

Walter explained. 'People don't like it. Me. Spitting. Tell me not to.'

Mr Richards grunted, still unconvinced that what he had said had held any humour. Then he looked at his watch, and said, 'Well, I haven't much time. You'd better get back to sweeping the floor. Do try to be more of your old self tomorrow. I can't have all my staff depressed by you. Go on, then.'

Walter said, 'Yes, sir,' and began to leave the office. At the door, he turned. 'I'm sorry, Mr Richards, sir. I've not felt very well today. My dad's went to live with Jesus yesterday. He won't be coming home any more. But I'll try to be more myself tomorrow.' Then Walter closed the office door behind him, and the manager sat for a full five seconds with his mouth open.

At the end of that time, discovering his mouth to be still open, he closed it, and swallowed. He put his hand down to the side waistband of flesh that protruded from beneath the bottom of his waistcoat and the top of his trousers, and felt it. He must get more exercise. He must take up tennis again; he really must; no

115

need to take his turn on the Public Courts; he could afford to join a Tennis Club. Before he turned the light out and left the office, he made a hurried note on his Memo Pad, *Walter's dad dead. Tell Hingley* and then beneath it as an afterthought, *Consider small increase wages. What do we pay him now?*

By now the floor had been swept and the rubbish disposed of, and the four trainee floor-walkers were back in the lift, waiting for Walter. Mike had already entered in his pocket diary the length of time it had taken them to sweep the floor. He did this every working evening. The record stood at fifteen minutes, twelve seconds. Mike's ambition was to complete the whole operation in thirteen minutes flat, and catch an earlier bus home. Tonight, owing to Walter's sloth and his subsequent absence, the time had been twenty-one minutes, five seconds.

The trainee floor-walkers tapped their feet, and sighed with frustration. When they saw Walter come out of Mr Richards' office, they shouted to him to hurry.

Walter took his time. His thoughts were elsewhere. As he drew closer, Mike and Clifford, one of the other boys, came impatiently out of the lift, grasped Walter by the lapels of his jacket, and pulled him violently into the lift. The lift gates were slammed shut, and abuse of every kind was hurled at Walter. Questions as to why he had been taken to the manager's office went unanswered. Walter looked at the floor.

Then Ernie, who was not known for bright ideas, had one. He told Walter that, as Mr Hingley had wanted to get away early, he had entrusted Mike with the key, and that, since Walter had kept them all waiting, they had decided to lock him in for the night. Stanley, the fourth trainee floor-walker, offered that it could all be explained away later as a mistake. They would simply say that they had been unable to find Walter, and had assumed that he had gone home.

Though Ernie's idea had been to tease Walter, the first part of the tease was true. Mike did have the keys. Walter had seen Mr Hingley give them to him. And the boys' manner, as they elaborated the tease, was serious. Walter listened as their enthusiasm built. He looked from one to another, trying desperately to catch one of them smiling, which would tell him it was a joke. But none smiled. All were serious. They were determined, they said, to teach him a lesson.

The lift reached the Stock Room, and Clifford and Mike pushed Walter out of it in front of them, and then stood, one on either side, guarding him while Ernie and Stan went to the Wash Room to wash their hands and collect their coats.

Walter stood, flanked by his two guards, still in his overalls with the balding broom still in his hand. Minutes passed. Hours. Several years passed. Mike shouted to the boys in the Wash Room to hurry, then took Walter's broom out of his hand, and placed it in the corner with the others.

With one guard away, Walter, terrified, made a bid for freedom, by dashing back into the lift, and sliding the trellis gate shut. Unfortunately, Mike's reactions were quicker than Walter's. Before the gate was completely closed, he had rushed to the lift, getting his foot in the way of the gate, and preventing it from closing.

Walter kicked desperately at Mike's foot, trying to dislodge it. Mike pulled at his side of the gate, and Walter pushed as hard as he could at the other. Walter was stronger than Mike, but Mike outwitted him by relaxing his pull for a moment, so that Walter relaxed his push in order to concentrate on dislodging the foot. Then Mike applied his entire strength, taking Walter by surprise, and pulling the gate open far enough to get his whole body into the lift.

Walter backed away into the far corner, and crouched low, his arms lifted to protect his face. As Mike approached, he slid down onto the floor, making himself into as near the shape of a ball as he could, huddling with his knees up to protect his privates, his arms covering his head to protect his face and skull. He began to moan and whine, like a small child who has just been told it is to be punished, begging not to be kicked, not to be hurt, slobbering out a flow of words, almost indistinguishable, running into each other. 'Please. No. Don't. Sorry. Don't hurt me. Got to go home tonight. Please don't. No. Good boy. I'll be a good boy.'

Mike stood still. He did not wish to approach closer, for the closer he got, the more agonized and pitiful were Walter's pleas for clemency. But Mike did not feel pity; he felt sick. Ill. His stomach gurgled, and he felt a stale taste in his mouth. He was disgusted by Walter, disgusted by what he himself was doing, something which had started out as a joke, a game, and was no longer a game. The cringing heap of humanity in the corner

117

upset him because he knew that something in him had wanted to see it, to hold this position of power, to create fear in another. Now it had turned sour, and his stomach rejected it.

He did not know that Walter's pleas for clemency were automatic, almost rehearsed, had been learned and practised in the school playground, and used often in circumstances similar to the one he found himself in now.

The others were standing near the lift, waiting for Mike to do something. The pause had lasted too long. It was impossible to kick the body now. All his spite, anger, and excitement had drained away. He said, 'Get up.'

Walter made a moaning noise, covered his face with his hands, and pretended to sob. The noise convinced no one, and made Mike angry again. The others waited.

Mike tried to decide what to do. He had been forced by the lump in the corner into the role of bully. The fake sobbing continued, and Mike moved forward, lifted Walter to his feet, and brought him out of the lift and over to the bench used for unpacking.

'Don't be bloody stupid, Walter. Nobody's going to hurt you.'

Walter kept his face covered, and continued his moaning. He leaned his elbows on the bench, and Mike tried to prise Walter's hands away from his face, to see whether any real tears accompanied the disturbing noise.

By now the other boys were losing interest. Clifford and Ernie moved to the lift, and stood in it, waiting. Walter continued to moan and to resist Mike's efforts to uncover his face. Stanley tapped Mike on the shoulder, and performed an elaborate mime, indicating that the four of them should go for a drink, leaving Walter behind to cool off.

Mike got the message, and backed away from Walter to the lift. The last few feet were a scramble, and, as the lift gate was slammed and the Down button pressed, Walter took his hands from his face, and listened to the jollity from the four trainee floor-walkers as they descended to ground level, from which they would proceed to Yates' Wine Lodge.

Walter rushed to the lift, and shouted after them, pleading to be let out. There was no reply. He listened. The outer gate of the lift below was being locked. He heard a voice shout, 'Goodnight, Walter. Sweet dreams.' It was Mike's voice.

Walter shouted, 'I'll tell me dad.' No reply. He pressed his right ear against the lift gate, and listened. No sound. He turned, and looked round the empty Stock Room, which was getting darker. The long aisles, shelved at either side, ran away from him through gloom into pitch blackness. He remembered that he no longer had a dad to tell. He was alone.

He gripped the gate of the lift with both hands, and listened. He could hear scratching. It came out of the darkness from the end of the aisle he was facing. Something was scratching in the blackness, a quiet scratching; there was someone there, where no one should be. He gripped the lift tighter. The scratching noise persisted, and then a shadow moved across the floor of the Stock Room. Walter inhaled, and kept the breath inside his chest for as long as he could. Someone was in the Stock Room with him. He was not alone. But why didn't this someone wish to be seen? The scratching drew closer. He was trapped with – he did not know what with. He began to whimper. He knew that the noise would attract attention, but could not help himself. He dared not move. His coat was in the Wash Room, and he badly wanted to use the lavatory, but he dared not move. He waited.

Another shadow moved slowly over what was left of the light on the Stock Room floor. Somewhere inside Walter's head, a fact isolated itself from the frightened fishes. Shadows were made by things. They were made by people and by things. Since he could see shadows, there must be things to make them. He kept his head still, and peered into the darkness. He did not wish to see whatever was in the Stock Room with him, but to close his eyes would be even more frightening. His eye-movements took in the skylight. As he looked at it, it grew darker, then light again. The first fact was joined by another fact, and already the fishes swam less madly, as fear receded. For Walter had seen something like this before, in summer, when the Stock Room would sometimes be flooded with sunlight, then grow darker, then sunny again. Clouds were not things, but they made shadows by passing in front of the sun.

The shadows were made by clouds. It was nothing to be afraid of.

They had pretended; they had teased him; they had not locked the gate; they would not. Walter had become brave. He moved slowly, sideways, towards the Wash Room, reached it without incident, used the lavatory, collected his coat. He would press the button, and bring the lift up to the Stock Room. He would travel in it to the ground level, and find that the outer door was unlocked. They had teased him; that was all. They would be waiting to laugh at him. They would laugh, and he too, Walter, would laugh. They would never lock Walter in the store, for Mr Richards would hear of it, and he would give them all the sack.

He opened the door of the Wash Room with caution. It was darker now, and the small unexpected noise of a creaking floorboard as he crossed the Stock Room brought back his fear. The distance from the Wash Room to the lift was further than he had remembered it.

As he lifted his hand to press the lift button, the scratching began again, this time even louder and closer. *Clouds did not cause scratching.* His hand froze on the button. There was a squeal. Walter turned his head quickly. Two bright eyes were staring back at him. There was nothing else to see, just blackness, and the eyes on a level with his own. Walter lifted the hand he would have used to press the button towards his mouth instead. The eyes moved. They moved towards him. Walter bit hard at his fingers. The squealing noise began again, louder. The eyes were getting closer. Walter's mouth opened. The squealing came from just below the staring eyes. Walter squealed.

The Stock Room cat jumped from the line of shelves it had been patrolling onto the bench which was used for unpacking. It had its own unpacking to do, but not yet, not for a while. First it must tease and frighten the mouse it carried in its mouth.

Walter was shaking, and very close to tears. He watched the cat release the mouse from its mouth, and stalk it. He watched its limping run, backwards and forwards across the bench, each time easily outwitted by the cat, which cuffed it into changing direction and trying to move faster. Walter drew in breath with each blow the mouse received.

The game went on, and Walter watched, until the cat cuffed the mouse so hard that it slid across the bench, and fell off the other side onto the floor. Alive, but injured, it began to limp towards the safety of the shelves, but the cat was there first, jumping from the bench to cut off its escape, and start the game all over again. Walter turned his attention back to the lift button. After all, the cat was only doing what it was supposed to do.

The lift arrived. Walter entered it. It descended. He slid the inner gate open, and tried the outer gate. It was locked.

He was unable to believe it. They couldn't have. He listened. Perhaps they were on the other side of the gate, waiting for him. There was no sound beyond what came from the High Street at the end of the alley. He tried again to pull the outer gate open, banging at it, shouting, kicking at the gate with his foot. Someone must hear him.

He waited, knowing that no one would hear. They had gone; they had left him on his own. He would be late home.

He pressed the button that would take the lift to the level of the shop floor. Perhaps there he could attract somebody's attention.

In the store, he closed the gates of the lift behind him. It was a habit he had been made to acquire, since, if the gates were left open, the lift would go neither up nor down.

The back of the store was in darkness, but at the front there was light from the streetlamps outside. He gazed round the covered counters, and saw the head and shoulders of a woman. He moved quickly towards her. 'Please! I can't get out. They've locked me in.' The woman was made out of plaster. She was a plaster head and shoulders, wearing jewellery and a headscarf.

There was light at the front of the store, light beyond the thick glass windows. He would go towards it. There would be people in the street, and they would help him.

He pressed his face against the plate glass, making signs to the passers by. Most did not notice him. Of those who did, some smiled, or waved back. They could not hear his shouts for help or understand what the wild waving of his arms was intended to signify.

'I'll be late home.' As he shouted, his voice echoed in the empty store. 'I'll be late home.' A young man in a duffel coat stopped, and came closer to the glass, 'They've locked me in. I've got to feed the pigeons.' The young man could not make out what Walter was saying, and, having raised Walter's hopes of rescue, made a dismissive gesture, and walked on.

The heating system of the store had switched itself off and, even with his overcoat on, Walter was still cold. Spring, but still cold. Fewer of the pigeons' eggs would hatch because of it. It would be warmer away from the glass door, but back there, at the back of the shop, it was dark. He held on to the counters, feeling his way.

121

Sweets and Cosmetics were nearest the front, then Soaps, Shampoos, Combs, Hairslides. Right at the back there would be Household Wares, and among them, some cheap rugs. He would lie down, and cover himself. His mother would come looking for him, or she would phone the police. He only need wait.

There was nothing he could do. He passed Men's Socks, Braces and Ties. There was nothing there to warm him. He could not remember what was on the next counter, nor could he see. He lifted the sheet which covered it, and felt. Lampshades. He couldn't be far from Rugs now.

From the next counter came the ticking of at least fifty alarm clocks, each with a different tick, and each (he knew, having seen them by daylight) telling a different time. Whichever was right, he should be home by now, and his mother would be worried.

He reached Household Wares, and located the rugs by feeling for them. They were stacked against the back wall of the store. He would be warmer if he sheltered behind a counter. He dragged a bundle of rugs behind the nearest counter, and lay down on it, reserving one rug to place over himself.

He lay, and listened. He could hear the ticking of the different clocks, but as if in the distance now. There were other odd noises for which he could find no reason. He had expected it to be silent here, apart from the clocks, but the small creaks and taps and scraping sounds, some at regular intervals and some sudden, worried and frightened him. Most of these noises were, in fact, due to the contraction of metal pipes and of wood as the temperature fell, but Walter could not know that. To him they were people, moving about the store. Once, he had been told, one of the women who arrived early to mop the floor had discovered an old tramp behind some cardboard boxes, where he had hidden himself the night before. He had remained in the store all night for warmth and chocolate. He must have sampled every kind of biscuit there was on sale, for all the tins were without lids.

The old tramp entered Walter's mind, and remained there. With every new sound, Walter imagined the old man's face leaning over his, and the shower of biscuit crumbs that would fall from his mouth into Walter's staring eyes.

At four minutes to eleven, Mike and the other trainee floorwalkers were urinating against the outer door of the stock-lift.

They urinated with cheerful abandon, enjoying the release of pressure from bladders which had been filled in the warmth of Yates' Wine Lodge.

Clifford had announced that he was about to hand in his notice, and train to be accepted by the Meteorological Office. This announcement had reminded the other three how dissatisfied they were with the progress of their careers. It was not that, like Clifford, they wished to study the mysteries of cumulus and cirrus, but unloading lorries, unpacking, checking, sweeping out the store was not the kind of life they had dreamed of. Mike had lost four girlfriends, each of whom at different times had looked through the glass of the shop doors, and seen him sweeping the floor with Walter. 'Thought you told me you were a manager,' they had each said. Mike had explained that in order to become a manager, one had first to be a floor-walker, in order to be a floor-walker, first a trainee floor-walker, and that in Woolworth's, trainee floor-walkers swept the floor as an important part of their training. Even Mike had been unable to make this statement carry enough plausibility to convince the girls.

'Where's that bloody key? Hey! come on! The poor bugger must have shit himself by now.' Mike found the key, and, after several attempts, inserted it into the lock.

'There we are! Never been known to miss a hole.' They giggled, and held each other up. The outer gate was slid back, the button pressed, and the lift arrived. They began to argue over which of them was to go in, one or all. Since they all wanted to see Walter's face, they would all go.

The lift rose to the Stock Room, and they staggered out, looking for Walter. They called his name, but there was no answer. The cat hissed at Stanley, resenting this interruption to its work.

'Bloody spooky in here! He's probably down in the shop, stuffing himself with chocolate.' Back into the lift they all went, and the lift descended to the shop floor.

When the lift stopped, Clifford drew the gate back as quietly as he could. The other three put their index fingers vertically against their mouths, and tried not to giggle.

Clifford took a sheet from one of the counters, and draped it over his head, pretending to be a ghost. The others tiptoed out of the lift, and did the same. Their impersonation was made a little less effective by the necessity of lifting the sheets up at the front so as to be able to see where they were going, but they made a virtue of this necessity by flapping the sheet fronts about in what they reckoned to be a ghostly manner. So they began their search.

They found Walter easily. Like the old tramp, he snored. Standing over him, they began to make howling noises, as a dog is said to do when someone has died. Mike began this sound, and the others took it up, building it, harmonizing, flapping their sheets over Walter's face.

He woke to this. He screamed. There were things, a howling noise, movement. The impersonation of ghosts was wasted on him, for he could see nothing clearly, but whatever was there was enough to inspire terror. He scrambled to his feet, tripped on the rug, fell, and rose again. Wherever he turned, some thing was in his way. He fought with one, wrestling with it, knocking it down, and heard the sound of bone crack hard against the corner of a counter. The thing he had been fighting lay there, and didn't get up. The howling stopped. He could hear the sound of his own frightened breathing.

What had hit the corner of the counter had been Stanley's head. It was unheard of that Walter should fight anyone, inconceivable that he could win. Hampered as they were by sheets, Mike, Ernie and Clifford came at Walter, angry now, determined to punish him.

Screaming and howling the three shapes moved against Walter, who screamed also, not in anger, but in fear. One of them caught him by the belt of his overcoat, and swung him round. Another struck him across the face. Walter's nose bled copiously. Then he was on the floor, slipping in his own blood, and the things were on top of him. He struggled, bit, and kicked. He scrambled to his feet, and reached out for some support. The things tried to drag him back down.

Walter's hands gripped something on the counter, something heavy; he had found the weighing-scales on Confectionery. He gripped the scales firmly, but as he felt his feet slipping again, and the force of the things pulling him down, he flung them with as much strength as he had left towards the glass doors. They crashed through one of the doors. Walter let out a kick at the things which were pulling him, struggled free, and escaped through the hole and the splintered glass, falling into the arms of a policeman.

'What do you think *you're* doing?' the policeman said. Walter's nose was spurting blood and he had a long deep cut in his hand and wrist from the splintered glass of the door. He pointed back into the interior of the shop, and the blood from his wound dripped, black in the sodium lighting of the street, onto the pavement.

Walter was taken home in a police car, having had his hand and nose treated at the hospital. Stanley, who had concussion, was kept in overnight for observation. Mike and Ernie were allowed to go home after having made a statement to the police.

On seeing the glass break, Clifford had rushed to the back of the shop, and hidden behind some cardboard boxes. By the time the cleaners arrived, he had hidden himself in the Stock Room, and by the time the Stock Room staff had arrived, he had used the lift to make his escape. His resignation was sent by post. He wrote that he would rather forfeit his holiday pay than work out his two weeks' notice.

Mike and Ernie stuck to the story they had told the police. It was Mike's story, and Ernie had simply nodded, and signed a joint statement. They claimed that both of them had been trying to protect Walter against Stanley and Clifford, who had a grudge against Walter, and intended to get their own back by frightening him.

Walter was not required either to confirm or to deny this story, either by the police or Mr Richards. Stanley was instructed not to return to work, and his cards were sent to him, without the enclosure of a reference which would have helped him to get another job. Stanley at first felt some slight bitterness at the unfairness of this treatment, but being, as Mike well knew, of an equable temperament decided that, since the story was partly true (for he, as much as the others, *had* intended to frighten Walter), and since references were only of use in the getting of posh jobs, he did not greatly mind. Instead he applied for, and got, a job as a builder's labourer, removing fireplaces from posh houses, and was paid twice as much as he had been receiving as a trainee floor-walker.

Mr Richards told Mike and Ernie that he did not entirely believe their story, and stopped two pounds a week from their wages until the replacement glass for the doors had been paid for. Indeed, nobody in the Stock Room believed the account Mike had given of the affair, and all knew that the only reason Mr Richards had accepted it was because Mike was the most likely trainee floor-walker to succeed. Consequently the atmosphere in the Stock Room for the following fortnight was of cool politeness. After that, memories became blurred, and three months later Mike was told to come to work in a smart suit with a collar and tie. No longer a trainee, he was a fully fledged floor-walker.

PART FOUR

His mother is taken by Jesus

1

She had never asked him before what he was thinking

Sleeping. He always slept well. She stood, watching him sleep, had risen earlier from her own bed than was necessary, in order to stand over him while he slept. Sleeping, she could bear him. If he slept for ever, she would be content.

Yet the face on the pillow never ceased to make her angry. She herself had been pretty, and had been told so, more than once. His father had looked – not handsome, not even passably good-looking, since his neck had been long and thin like a bird's neck, but at least *alright*: Eric had looked alright. But Walter, sleeping, Witless Walter, was a mistake made by nature, and God had chosen not to correct it. The heavy hooded eyelids, closed now over bulging eyes. The hooked nose, which resembled a joke nose one might buy at the seaside, with an elastic band to hold it over one's real nose. The large pointed jaw, and protruding teeth, yellow and green where they stuck out sharply from the gums. The oily sallow skin and tiny white-headed pimples.

Leaning over him, close to his sleeping face, she whispered, 'You must be the ugliest person in this town, and you spent nine months inside me.' His breath was foul. 'Constipated. Must be. Never thinks to tell me these things.'

She moved away, and sat against the wall on a straight-backed chair to watch him. There was plenty of time. She spoke to God, as she had spoken many times before. 'Why has my life been so ill arranged, Lord? Why allow me only one child, and that an ill-put-together, foul-smelling, dribbling lump of ugliness?' God might have replied that she had never tried to make another, that although matrimony was a holy state and sanctified for the procreation of children, she had denied her husband access to her womb after it had once been filled, so that He, God, could hardly be held responsible for any subsequent barrenness. But God was old and wise and knew well the futility of argument with a complaining woman. He permitted her to continue.

'I won't mince words with you, Lord. Not now; I'm too old.' She never had minced words. God sighed, and wondered whether a sparrow somewhere might be falling, to distract His attention. 'I've visited Your chapel twice every Sunday, since I was taken there, at five years old, to Sunday School. Almost sixty years, multiplied by fifty-two, then doubled. I can't begin to count the hours I've sat on hard benches or knelt on a prayer-stool to Your greater glory, and tried to cast everything from my mind but Your face.' It would be the face of Christ she meant; the other two persons of the Trinity didn't have a face. The Face composed itself in patience, and continued to listen. 'I never believed those pictures with the halo. Not like that. Not You. You had to be more beautiful in my mind, more masculine than any of those. Man was made in Your likeness.' She looked across at the sleeping figure. 'Is this what You look like? Is Walter made in Your likeness? Is that Your likeness, a physically grotesque man of twenty-seven, with the brain of an infant? Why?'

Why the years of soiled blankets and sheets, the crying, shouting, screaming? Why the hope that he would improve, would learn, that with age he would change, would become at least less of an embarrassment? God had made that hope, had allowed it to persist, kept Sarah at it. Had His intention been to punish? If so, for what? 'Everybody has thoughts. Thoughts they shouldn't have. Unnatural.' Everybody must have those thoughts sometimes, the shameful, unnatural thoughts, which slipped into her mind and clung, like spiders clinging to the side of the bath. You might wish to wash them away down the dark plug-hole, and clean yourself, but there would be no hole in your mind down which to wash them, so they would persist.

But everyone would have such thoughts; it was unfair to punish her. God was unfair and heartless. She had complained to Him so often, and He never took any notice. Walter's mother wiped the tears from her face with a small lace handkerchief which smelt of lavender. She returned the handkerchief to the pocket of her apron, and went over to the bed. It was time to wake her son.

The first thing he saw every morning was her face.

Sleeping was like being dead. She would shake him out of sleep at half past seven every morning. He didn't like it. He was drowned, and she would pull him to the surface with a long rope. He would struggle, but the rope would only become tighter. The water round him would bubble, pulling him down, water up his nostrils and inside his head, hair flattened over his eyes.

He would come up slowly, gulping at the air when he reached the top.

'Come on, Walter. You can't lie there forever.'

That's what she always said, every morning. The water was warm. He liked it above his head. Not having to think. You can't ever go backwards. Even when you remember last week, you can't go there. The clock keeps ticking, moving you on. When you're in a pleasant bit of time, why can't you just stop there?'

She shook him. He nodded. Alive, there was time to pass, things to remember, other people asking questions. Rules.

She watched him all the time. All the time, his mother watching. She said they were tied together by a rope he couldn't see. He always did as he was told now, yet she got no pleasure, not even when he was good. She used to like him to remember things. Now she liked nothing. Smile; he had seen her smile. But he could no longer remember her smile.

The first thing he saw every morning was her face. It was not like his own. Her face was small, round and shiny. She did not wear make-up like the Counter Girls. It was dirty stuff; she did not hold with it. 'Come on! Out you get!' He closed his eyes, remembering the warmth of the water, and she shook him.

Her eyes were not hooded like his. 'Move, will you?' He sat up, blinking. His mother's eyes did not stick out, but fitted with the rest of her face. They were red this morning, because she cried for him.

She took his ankles, and swung them round so that his feet were off the bed and touching the cold linoleum.

Her nose was not like the top half of a parrot's beak. He did not go to school any more; he was too old now to go to school. They had called him names, 'Parrot Face' and 'Witless Walter'.

Her teeth did not stick out. They were false now, because she was old; he had seen them out of her mouth.

She stood back from the bed, and watched him. She would remain to make sure that he stood up, his body entirely leaving the bed. She would not leave the room until he had taken his pyjamas off. He could tell her he was alright now, but she would stand there; she would not go. He would whine, but she would wait.

He took off his pyjama jacket. She should know now that he had grown out of messing himself; it was a subject no longer mentioned. He dropped his pyjama trousers to the floor, and turned round on the spot. No need for words now. Looks were enough.

She left him, and went into the bathroom. He heard the sound of water running, wrapped a towel around his waist, and sat on the bed until she called for him.

He sat on the toilet, while she waited outside the door, listening. He made water, but nothing else.

'I'll give you something this morning to make your bowels move. And if you have to go while you're at work, remember to clean yourself properly. And wash your hands.'

The sound of the toilet being flushed brought her into the bathroom. He sat in the lukewarm water, while she slid the lavender-scented soap all over his body. He didn't shout now, or scream, or make any noises to stop her. He didn't struggle. He just sat there.

She slid her soapy hands all over his chest, back and legs. She never touched his willy. She would point to that, and give him the soap. 'Do it some more. Come on. More soap. Between your legs.'

She was standing now, and she had the towel ready. As he stepped out of the bath, she turned her head away. 'You must be rotten inside, the way your breath smells.'

He stood there while she dried his back, legs and buttocks, rubbing them hard. 'If you can't do Number Twos in the morning, you must tell me. Alright?' He nodded. 'No sense in leaving it until you've got to smelling like a parrot's cage. What will they think at work?'

He didn't know what they would think.

'Don't know was made to know. If people complain about you,

you'll be out of a job. Woolworth's customers don't want you breathing down their necks, not with that breath.'

She finished drying his face, neck, ears and feet. He did the rest. He had clean underwear every other day. She would watch to make sure he wore it.

As I get into my clothes, I tell myself aloud what I have to remember. 'Don't dawdle!' 'You're slouching, Walter. Stand up straight.' 'Pay attention.' 'You are a cross for my back, Walter, you really are.' All my socks are darned. She does them well. I won't wear nylon socks. I'd rather break things up than wear socks that squeak and crackle. She knows now not to buy them. I taught her. 'It's not worth the screaming fits, even though wool is more expensive.' I wear a navy-blue suit to go to work in. At work I wear an overall. Seventy-four bus, that's what I get. 'Not the Forty-seven, Walter. Silly blockhead! Seventy-four, not Forty-seven. Mill Hill, Chorlton, Flixstead. The number Six goes to Flixstead too. You don't want that.' I sit on my bed, rocking, taking time to dress. She watches. 'Number Two is a Special. Only bring it out at holiday times. Always clean, Number Two.' I laugh because she has to wait for me. No, Forty-seven's not my bus, not for going home on. Seventy-four. 'There you are, you see. You're alright, Walter. Walter's alright. Only eleven pence to the shilling, but he knows what it's about.'

'Are you ready?'

I look at her and laugh, rocking backwards and forwards as I sit on the bed. She shakes her head, and looks at the linoleum on my bedroom floor. I stop laughing, and try to see what she is looking at. But there's nothing there, only the pattern.

'Li No Lee Um. Not lino, Walter. Linoleum.'

Breakfast was on the table. She would lay it out the night before, and come down before she woke him, to cook the rest. She couldn't sleep.

She sat beside him, not facing him. She had the view out of the window to look at, and did not have to look at him. He swung his legs backwards and forwards as he ate. Whenever she heard them bang against the chair, she shouted at him to stop.

She wouldn't eat until after he had left the house.

She stared out of the window. She only looked at him to see whether he had finished.

She could feel him looking at her with those bulging eyes. The hooded lids blinked as he grinned and chortled to himself. How could she know what he was thinking?

If anyone looks at me, I point my finger at them, and start to laugh. I throw my head back, and laugh until they turn away. She taught me. At school, they would do that to me, and when I told her, she said, 'Do it to them back, then,' but if I waited for them to do it first, I felt sad inside, and couldn't laugh. So I started to laugh at them before they had time to laugh at me. I put my hand over my mouth, and pointed, and laughed. It made them angry, and they called me names. Then they stopped laughing at me. They would pretend I was not there. Then I would laugh to myself. I started laughing a lot then. I keep myself ready, in case somebody who doesn't know me should point at me and laugh. I'm laughing to myself now. It annoys her.

She woke me up.

Scooping food into his mouth like an animal! Dribbling as he giggled insanely, and let the cornflakes drop from his mouth back into the bowl! The noise he made! She felt like sitting at table with cotton wool stuffed in her ears.

What did he think of her? There had to be something going on inside that head. What was he thinking about that he found so funny?

'What are you thinking about, Walter?'

Walter stopped shovelling cornflakes into his mouth, and looked at her. She had never asked him such a question before. He stared at her for some time, then laughed again half-heartedly, and lowered his head to continue eating. She leaned forward, and grabbed hold of the hand which held the spoon.

'I want an answer.'

Again he looked at her, and tried to smile. Her expression told him that she was in earnest. He would have to speak.

'Thinking, Walter. I want to know what you're thinking about.' Though she said it with force, she knew the danger. He was stronger than she. Frightened, he might up-end the table.

'Thinking?' He was laughing again. It was clear that she was angry. Perhaps she thought he had been thinking of dirty things. She had warned him of what God might do if he were to allow himself to think in a dirty way. One of the boys in the Stock Room had shown him a magazine, and forced him to look at it when he would have turned his head away. Did she know? Did she think he was thinking about that? He did not know what he had been thinking about.

She used her other hand to remove the spoon from him. 'Answer me, will you? What were you thinking about?'

'No. Not them.'

'Them what?'

'I don't like mucky books. "Look at those, Walter. What a pair of knockers, eh? Cor! You could suffocate between those, eh"?'

'What are you talking about?'

'I didn't look. Honest. Cross my heart, and hope to die.' He made the sign of the cross, somewhere in the region where he thought his heart might be. 'Mucky ladies in mucky books.'

She turned away from him, and looked again at the view outside the window. He saw that she was biting her lower lip. Her false teeth were worn down more at one side of her mouth than the other. That was the side she chewed.

'Got your bus fare?' He nodded. 'What's your kerb drill?' He told her, singing it like a television commercial.

She walked with him down the path to the gate. He preferred her not to, but she always did, unless there was snow, or it was raining hard. She stood on tiptoe to kiss him on the side of his cheek. He hated her doing this. He knew the neighbours watched. It was better when she kissed him in the hall, where nobody could see.

'Don't come out with me.'

'Why not? I want to. It's not raining.'

The neighbours felt sorry for her. He had heard them say so.

'*You're a martyr to put up with it.*'

'Nonsense. He's no trouble really.'

'*But you take such care.*'

'I have to. He is mine. Only God knows why, and He's not saying.'

'*Thank Goodness he's got a job.*'

'Yes, that's a blessing. I kiss him every morning you know.'

135

'Yes, we've seen you.'
'I think to myself, "Would I really be sorry if God took him?" '
'You'd miss him, surely?'
'God made him, so He should have to clean up, after he's messed himself all over the house.'
'He doesn't still do that, does he?'
'No. Not any more.'
'What will he do when you're gone?'

All the conductors on the Seventy-Four knew him. They knew where he'd want to get off. They knew his name; they'd say, 'Good Morning, Walter.' He would point and laugh at them. They liked him doing that. One of them would tease him about girlfriends, just like Mr Hin-gall-ee did at work. 'What were you up to last night, eh? How far did she let you go?'
I laugh. He laughs. They laugh. 'Did you get your oats, then?' They laugh. He laughs. So I laugh.
He didn't understand the question, but the passengers laughed, and seemed to like him. Sometimes the conductor (whichever it was) would pull his cap down over his eyes. His large nose would stop it going further. 'Here's our Casanova here! Here's sexy Walter!'
He would get off at Yates' Wine Lodge, and walk past Boots', Ravel's and Owen Owen's. There was an alley by the side of Woolworth's where he worked. The lorries had to back up that alley in order to deliver goods. He would walk up it, and into the back yard, and then he would wait outside the doors of the lift which would take him up to the Stock Room. Every morning, he would be early, and he would stand and wait for Mr Hin-gall-ee to unlock the gates of the lift, before he could get in it.
'Morning, Walter. Eager to get at it?' That's what he always said. And Walter would say, 'Yes, Mr Hin-gall-ee,' and rub his hands together.
He would take his jacket off, and hang it in the Gents' Wash Room. He had to wear a brown overall, so that the customers would know he worked for Woolworth's when he asked them to let him pass with the rubbish. But before he saw any customers, he had first to clear the Stock Room floor of any cardboard or waste paper. And he would put this into his press to make bales. His press was Electric; electricity made it work; he must never

put his hand inside, even if it jammed. Instead he had to fetch Mr Hin-gall-ee.

'*Don't put your hands inside, Walter.*'

'No, Mr Hin-gall-ee.'

When the Stock Room was clean, he would push a large basket into the lift, and take it to the shop floor to collect all the rubbish from behind the counters. If the shop was full, he would have to keep shouting, 'Excuse me. Excuse me, please.' He must shout politely, not loudly. Once Mr Richards, the Manager, had told him not to shout so loudly. 'Shout quietly, Walter,' he said. Then he laughed.

'*It's a joke, Walter.*'

So then I laughed. Mr Richards laughed, and then I laughed. You have to laugh at jokes, don't you?

2

*If he didn't mend his ways she would go a long
way away where he would never find her*

Walter opened his eyes slowly, and tried to focus them on the
chair beside the chest-of-drawers in which his mother always sat,
waiting to shake him until he woke. It took some time for him to
realize that the chair was empty. Slowly he lifted his head from
the pillow, and supported himself on one elbow. He looked round
the room and, not finding her, closed his eyes again. It was too
soon. He had woken too early.

But the amount of light coming through the summer curtains
told him that it was not early. The sound of traffic from outside
told him that it was not too early.

The silence inside the room worried him. There were no sounds
coming from downstairs. Where was she?

Walter pushed the bedclothes back slowly. If he were to get out
of bed before it was time to do so, she would be angry. He would
be under her feet. He listened again for any sound which would
tell him what was happening. Nothing. He swung his own feet to
the floor. Usually his mother would do that. He was performing
actions which were hers; that was dangerous. The lino was cold,
and so was the room. It was summer, but the sun had not been
strong enough this year to warm the people, some of whom still
had fires. He moved to the door, listened, then went out onto the
landing. He was creeping like a burglar, half-expecting his mother
to jump out at him, and shout. He moved slowly to the door of
his mother's bedroom, and listened. He had never been in there,
at least not that he could remember.

He knocked on the door, and waited, expecting to hear her shout at him, wanting to know what he was at, wandering about before she had woken him. No shout came. He waited, and knocked a little louder. No answer.

'Mother?' His voice was shaky. Something was wrong. If she had been up, she would have heard him by now, even though he had walked on his toes; she knew every creak and knock the house made. He remembered times she had looked up from the evening paper, and said, 'Subsidence!' and when he had asked what that was, she had replied, still reading the paper, 'That noise. It means the house is sinking.'

Walter trod on each of the sixteen stairs down to the hall, and studied the pattern of the carpet on each as he descended. The carpet in the hall was red, without a pattern. On the rug by the front door lay a brown envelope. Walter bent to look at the name on it, 'Mrs Sarah Williams, 23 Bancroft St, Bamber Bridge, near Preston, Lancs.' It was an address he knew well, having been made to memorize it, in case he should ever get lost.

There was nobody in the living-room, parlour or kitchen. Out in the yard, his pigeons were making their 'Why haven't we been fed?' noise. It was late, then; they never called to him like that until he had had his own breakfast. The table in the living-room had been laid ready; she always did that the night before, to save time. Once she had said, 'I don't know why I do things to save time. I have too much of it as it is.'

Walter went back into the hall, and put on his macintosh over his pyjamas. He returned to the kitchen, and placed wellingtons on his bare feet. Then he unlocked the back door, and went into the yard to the Pigeon Loft.

'It's alright. You haven't been forgotten.' In the shed beside the loft, Walter used the old pair of grocery scales to weigh out the right quantities of rape, niger, linseed, hemp, millet, groats, maple peas and tares. His father had taught him to recognize the different seeds and grain, and which iron weights he should put on the scales for what. But since hemp was what they seemed to like best, picking out the small grey pellets so quickly that they seemed to be appearing in a speeded-up film, Walter cheated and gave them more than the ration, using the four-ounce weight instead of the two-ounce. As he mixed the ingredients, he talked to the birds continually as his father had done, 'Who's a pretty bird, then? Who's going to have a nice breakfast? Yes, then. There you are,' opening the door of the Loft carefully so that no bird flew out, and bending low while the tumblers and tipplers flew about his head, wing-flapping each other to get at the food. Sometimes birds landed on Walter's head, arms and shoulders. Since in the past this had led to Walter's having to wash his hair or change his jacket before leaving for work, he now wore an old overall and one of his father's caps to do the feeding. But this morning was different.

This morning he was late. The birds showed their disapproval of his lateness by pecking at each other, and making the grunting sound which pigeons make to show they are not pleased. Walter poured the food into the feeding-trough, and changed the drinking-water. The trough was immediately covered by hungry and angry pigeons.

Before Sarah had put a stop to the hatching of any more eggs, Walter had taken down the partitions which kept each variety of bird separate, so that he could sit on his stool in the Loft, and watch all the birds at the same time. The Long-Faced English Tumblers, who were his favourites because of the long flip-flop feathers on their feet, and the silly diving, rolling and tumbling they did in the air when they were let out, had now interbred with the Russian High-Fliers, so that now their offspring tumbled high among the clouds and out of sight, and the only tumbling still to be seen was of the pure-bred birds. The cross between the White-Lace Fantails and the Russian High-Fliers was not interesting, and their cross with the Tumblers merely produced Parti-Coloured Fantails. As for the colourful Turbits, the White-Lace Fantails ignored them, and only one Turbit had attempted an alliance with a Russian High-Flier, but this was after a rigorous egg-collecting had started, so Walter would never know what a Russian High-Flying Turbit would look like.

The food for the pigeons was paid for out of Walter's pocket-money, and Walter's mother had warned him that if he allowed any more eggs to be hatched and squabs to be born, she would stop his pocket money altogether, so that the pigeons would starve. Even after Freda, the prize-winner, his father's favourite, Old Reliable, even after she had found a corner of the loft and sat there facing the wall, her feathers puffed out, as dying pigeons are wont to do. even after she had, during the night, fallen dead from that last perch, and been found next morning by Walter, and buried in a tiny patch of the front garden where fire-coloured nasturtiums bloomed, even then his mother had not allowed him to hatch out any more eggs. It was a waste of good money, she told him, paying all that out for fancy food. Wild pigeons eat what they can. 'As they go, they go. Next time, take the body over to the park, or into the fields somewhere away from the house. I'm not having a pigeons' cemetery under my front window.'

This morning he was pecked and wing-flapped by two sitting birds. He exchanged the real eggs under them for plastic ones, and the unsuspecting birds returned, grumbling, to their nests and attempted to hatch the hollow eggs.

The birds fed, Walter returned to the back door of the house, where he removed his wellingtons, and left them on the step until he had laid newspaper down on the kitchen floor. Then he brought in the wellingtons, and stood them on the paper. That done, he listened. No sound. Nothing.

He went back into the hall, and stood at the bottom of the stairs, looking up. She had to be somewhere. It wasn't a Sunday, so she couldn't be at Chapel.

He climbed the stairs, and knocked on the bathroom door. No answer. The door was unlocked, so he opened it, and looked in. No one inside.

He tapped again on her bedroom door. 'Mother?' No answer. He turned the handle slowly, and pushed the door open a little.

'Mother?' No answer. He was afraid to open the door any wider, and look into a room he had never seen.

'Please!' He waited, and listened to the silence. 'I'm sorry.' He was not sure for what. 'Don't play that game.' His voice cracked. He did not wish to play that game. They had not played Hide and Seek for . . . he could not remember how long for. Strictly speaking, it had not been a game at all, however called so; his mother had used it as a punishment. If Walter had done some wrong action, she would hide herself in some place he could not discover, until he had cried, and screamed for her to come out. When she had revealed herself, she had warned him that, if he didn't mend his ways, she would go a long way away where he would never find her.

She must be punishing him for something, and he could not remember what he had done wrong.

'Won't do it again. Promise.' His hand still held the door-handle, but all he could see of the room was one side of a very large and highly polished Victorian wardrobe.

'Please come out. I'm sorry.' He waited. The only sound was a clock ticking. *'What does a clock do, Walter?' 'Tells the time, miss.' 'And what else?' 'Ticks, miss.' 'Very good. Now, what does the little hand do?'*

'Can I come in?' He waited.

'Shall I?' No answer.

Slowly he opened the door, an inch at a time. With each inch, he spoke the words, 'Mother.' At any moment she would shout at him, stop his pocket money, take his plate and make him eat his food under the stairs. *'Tells us what time it is.' 'No, I'm asking about the little hand. What does it say?'*

Finally the door was open, and she had not shouted. The room was in darkness, but for a beam of sunlight, cutting through the gap between the curtains, and dividing the room into halves. The bed was very wide, and higher than his own. The eiderdown which covered it was purple, with elaborate gold embroidery of dragons breathing out scarlet and green flames.

He turned his eyes slowly towards the pillow, and saw the outline of a head. The face was in darkness, but the beam of sunlight touched the edge of his mother's hair. He had never seen her hair let down. It was white, and spread out over the eiderdown from both sides of her face. It was so long, it must have reached her waist. Where the light caught it, it glistened like frost. Years of brushing night and morning had given it that shine.

Walter moved forward one step. 'Mother?' He could see her face clearly enough now to notice that her eyes were closed. He moved closer, and put his hand into hers, feeling the wedding and engagement rings on her fingers. The hand was closed and cold. The fingers did not move in response to his own. *'Why do we need clocks, children?' 'Yes, to tell the time, of course, but why do we need time?'*

He was frightened. Certainly something was wrong. He went to the window, and pulled back the curtains, still expecting her to wake, blinded by the light, and shout at him. But even when the whole room was flooded with daylight, her eyes remained closed.

Everything in the room seemed larger than life. He sat on a stool which was set in front of a dressing-table, which had three mirrors at different angles, so that he could see three of himself at once.

On the bedside table an alarm clock ticked away the time he had learned to tell. He was going to be late for work, since he could not leave without waking her.

Walter moved to his mother's bedside, and shook her shoulder. It was curiously stiff, like wood. He had no idea how to re-set the alarm clock, so that it would ring and waken her, so instead he shouted, 'Wake up, mother!' as loud as he could. He touched her wooden shoulder again, but found himself reluctant to shake it, so instead he shouted again, this time very close to her ear.

She remained still, her eyes closed. Walter wondered what he should do next. He returned to the kitchen, found two saucepans, brought them to his mother's bedroom, and clashed them together like cymbals. Even this had no effect.

Once she had woken him from a very deep sleep by squeezing a sponge of cold water over his face. He took one of the saucepans to the bathroom, and partially filled it with cold water. Standing over her, he held the pan as high above her face as he could, and begged her yet again to wake up so that he would not have to use the water. There was no reply.

As gently as he could, he tipped the pan. Water trickled down onto his mother's forehead. It ran over her closed eyes, onto her cheeks, down the sides of her neck and under the collar of her nightie until the pan was empty.

He remained where he was, frowning and holding out the pan, until the droplets of water which were lodged in the corners of his mother's mouth had dried.

His arm ached from holding the saucepan. It was clear that his mother did not intend to wake. He placed the pan on the bedside rug, and as he did so, remembered how his father had gone to live with Jesus in Paradise. 'When you grow old, Walter, you sometimes fall asleep for a long time, and you have to stay like that until Jesus makes up his mind whether He wants you to go and live with Him.' Jesus's eventual decision, his mother had told him, would depend on how good He thought you had been up to then.

How long would he have to wait for Jesus to decide about his mother? He could not go to work until he knew. He must stay here, and wait with her until Jesus had decided. He must be here when his mother woke up.

Then there came a dreadful thought. What if Jesus did decide that Walter's mother should leave Bamber Bridge to live with him? Perhaps if Walter spoke to Jesus, and explained that he would not know what to do without his mother, that might help Jesus to come to a quick decision. Jesus would understand. His mother had always told him, 'Talk to Jesus, Walter. Don't just reel off what I've taught you as if it were a game. It's not a game. It's serious. He listens. Talk to Him as you'd talk to a friend. That's what He's there for.'

Walter knelt on the bedside rug, and placed his hands together to make the shape of a steeple. He closed his eyes, and coughed to clear his throat. He frowned, trying hard to think of what to say. The tick of the clock seemed even louder now. Time passed; nothing could stop it. Unless he spoke to Jesus quickly, he might be too late. He screwed his eyes up tighter, to help him to concentrate, and then he began:

'Gentle Jesus, meek and mild, look upon this little child. Pity my simplicity. Suffer me to...'

He had to stop. The prayer wasn't finished, but he had to stop. It wasn't right. What he was saying wasn't right. He didn't want Jesus to suffer him to come to Thee, if 'Thee' was Jesus. He didn't want to go to Jesus, not now, not yet. He wanted his mother back.

Walter thumped his fists on the side of the bed with temper. Why hadn't his mother taught him a prayer which would explain what he wanted? What was the point of 'Bless Mummy and Daddy and Grandma and the pigeons' when what he needed was to... He couldn't find the words to express exactly what was needed.

He rose to his feet, and bit at the back of his hand to stop himself bursting into tears of frustration. He rocked backwards and forwards as if ready to begin a race. He paced round the room, cursing the goldfish inside his head which wouldn't let him think. The clock ticked on, and he couldn't think of the right sort of words, the sort of words which would cause Jesus to listen. All prayers had special words in them, words you wouldn't use every day, words that you saved for only Jesus. Telling him to talk to Jesus

144

as a friend had not meant that he should use ordinary words, but that he shouldn't singsong or gabble the prayer to get it all in while he could still remember it. He covered his ears with his hands to shut out the sound of the clock's insistent tick, and lowered himself onto his knees again, his eyes screwed up tight. He could think like this. Catch one goldfish, and keep it still. With his hands to his ears, he began:

> 'Gentle Jesus meek and mild,
> Look upon this little child.
> Pity my simplicity.
> Please send my mother back to me.'

After a moment, he added the words, 'As soon as you can,' and stood up.

The prayer had pleased him. He had made it rhyme. And since his mother had told him that Jesus could see anything he did, there was no need to go into details about why he needed her more than Jesus did. Jesus would understand. He would know that Walter had to have his mother back. All Walter had to do was to wait.

He stood watching his mother's eyelids for any sign of movement. Jesus would now be considering what he had said.

Twenty minutes later, his legs were tired, so he went to his mother's pink basketwork chair, and sat down. From here he could watch her face. She would be angry to find herself damp when she woke up, but if she gave him time to explain, she would understand the necessity.

At eleven twenty by the clock on the bedside table, his stomach began to make noises to remind him that he had had no breakfast. But if he left his mother now, she might wake, and anyway, were he to go downstairs and begin eating before Jesus had come to a decision, Jesus might be offended, and think that Walter did not really want his mother back.

At half past one, he had to go to the toilet, either that or mess himself and his mother's pink basketwork chair. He had held off as long as he could, moving himself about in the chair, and now there was no help for it. He stood quickly, whispered, 'Excuse me, Jesus,' and rushed for the bathroom.

When he had done what was necessary, and washed his hands, his mind turned once again to food. Now that he had been excused and left the room, it was better to get something to eat while he was still out, than to return to the bedroom and have to ask to be excused again.

In the kitchen, Walter filled a large cardboard box with tins from his mother's well-stocked pantry. A dish and a spoon were all he would need to eat with. He put them, with a tin-opener, into the box, and carried it upstairs.

By two forty-three, he was back in the pink basketwork chair, having consumed a late lunch of baked beans, followed by peaches and evaporated milk.

His mother's eyes remained closed, and his own had become very heavy with the concentration of looking at one thing for such a long time. He forced himself to stay awake. He was in no doubt that very soon his mother would wake up, and everything would be as it had been before. All she had told him about Jesus convinced him that Jesus was not the sort of person who would leave Walter on his own. He couldn't be left on his own. Even to think about it frightened him so much that he had to close his eyes and shake his head until the thought went away.

He remembered that she had told him once that it was no good expecting miracles to happen overnight, or prayers to be answered on demand. 'It's not "Ask, and ye shall be given," not in this world, Walter; I shan't speak for the next, but not in this one, not down here. You have to wait. Waiting your turn is all part of living. Patience is a virtue. Our Lord, Jesus, has millions and millions of other people to think about besides you.'

Walter was tired. He tried not to yawn, in case he should do so at the very moment that Jesus decided to look down, and saw him.

At five twenty, he opened a tin of corned beef, and cut bits off the lump of compressed meat with his spoon. He ate as much as he could, and wrapped what was left in a page torn from a copy of Woman's Own, which he had found stacked, with several hundred other copies, on the top shelf of his mother's Victorian wardrobe. He must try to remember what it was he had wrapped in the picture of a lady in her underwear, before it went bad. 'Corned beef wrapped in lady with very little on.' He said it aloud to help him remember. He must finish the corned beef. To let good food go bad was a sin.

What would have happened at Woolworth's today when they

noticed he had not arrived for work? There was no way he could think of to let them know that he had to stay at home in order to wait for his mother to wake up.

His imagination toyed with visions of the waste paper and cardboard piling up higher and higher behind all the counters until the salesgirls were standing on it to keep it down. As it mounted, so did they. They towered up above the customers so high that the customers could see up their overalls. They held down the fronts of their skirts, and were unable to reach the tills; they could neither receive money from the customers, nor give it in change. 'Leave it on the counter,' they shouted down. 'If you've got the right money, leave it on the counter. I can't wrap anything for you. Wrap it yourself. Walter hasn't turned up for work.'

Groceries would be the worst hit by Walter's absence. So many cardboard boxes! The longer his mother slept, the more work there would be for him to catch up on when he returned. Nobody else would do his job. They didn't like getting themselves dirty. 'That's your job, Walter, not ours.'

His mother's face seemed to have grown paler, or was it just the light? Outside the pigeons were making their 'Why haven't we been fed?' noise again. They would have to wait, as he was wait-ing. He opened the window, and shouted into the back yard, 'Patience is a virtue.' Jesus would be able to hear them too. He watched over all living things, even cockroaches and worms. Perhaps if Walter were to go down and let out the Russian High-Fliers, they would be able to fly up closer to Jesus, and maybe even catch his eye and consequently his attention.

At seven thirty, when the birds had been calling to him for their food for well over an hour, he excused himself again, and went downstairs to feed them. Jesus would not approve of cruelty to animals.

After weighing the food, and placing it in the trough, he left the pigeons squabbling over it, and began carrying the heavy bags of grain and seed upstairs to his mother's room.

At the door, he studied the size of the room, and considered the amount of food still to be brought up from the shed next to the Loft. He moved the bags to the bathroom, placed the bath-plug in its hole, and tipped bag after bag of seed and grain into the bath. Hemp, millet, tares, linseed, rape, niger, maple peas and ordinary corn were mixed together. Walter stirred them up, using his hands and arms, and feeling the silkiness of the linseed as it got under his fingernails. Linseed was not the pigeons' favourite food, but it was good for them, and they ate it if they were hungry.

When the birds had eaten, and settled on their perches for the night, wondering no doubt why their supper was so late, and why they had not been let out to fly, Walter lifted each one down in turn, and placed it gently into his father's travelling-basket. The basket held six birds at a time. In all he made seven journeys, carrying the birds in the basket up to his mother's room.

It took him an hour and a half, and when the last bird had been released, and had fluttered, heavy and uncertain, round his mother's bedroom, trying to find a surface on which to land which was not already occupied, Walter looked again at his mother, and saw that her eyes were still closed.

The birds made a great deal of noise and fuss about this change in their routine. They fought for room. Since this was the moulting season, feathers floated down from the top of the wardrobe, the chest-of-drawers, and even from the shade of the overhead lamp, as each bird tried to stake its own claim. If his mother were to wake up now, she would scream the place down, but there was only one of Walter, and being only one he could not be in two places at once; she would have to understand that. He had given the matter thought, and he had come to a decision. Either he let the birds slowly starve, which would be cruel, or he released them so that they became wild, and would no longer return to the Loft for food, or he kept them with him, waiting for Jesus to make his mind up. And he had chosen the third of these solutions.

As Clarice, a White-Lace Fantail, landed on Walter's mother's chin, displayed her crop (by blowing it full out) and her tail (by spreading it as wide as she could), and strutted and cooed to claim his mother's chin for her home, Walter was sure his mother blinked, and his heart stopped for a moment. He waited, but she didn't blink again, so he lifted Clarice from his mother's chin, and placed her on top of one of the dressing-table mirrors. The bird peered down, and, seeing its own reflection in an an upside-down position, attempted to peck at it.

Lavender-scented soap was rubbed into a warm facecloth, which was then used to wipe the chin. His mother did not seem to be stiff any more. Perhaps it was a stage towards waking. While

Walter was at it, he cleaned the rest of her face. Small feathers and dust from the top of the wardrobe had settled all over the putty-coloured and wrinkled skin. Walter worked cautiously, afraid that she might wake while he was wiping her, and afraid also that she never might.

He had removed all her ornaments, combs and brushes to the safety of a drawer before letting the birds loose, and had found in that drawer a pair of glittering ear-rings shaped like Blackpool Tower. Now, noticing some pigeon droppings matted into her long white hair, he took the brush out again, and began to brush his mother's hair clean of bird-shit.

Doing so, he discovered that he liked brushing his mother's hair. It calmed him. The static electricity which the hair still contained seemed in some way to prove that she was just sleeping, and waiting, and no more than that. With each brush-stroke he laid the hair down over the colourful counterpane, and watched wisps of it rise again towards the brush, as if it were showing him that it and she were still active.

By the time he had grown tired of brushing her hair, it was dark outside and the birds had fallen quiet, some of them standing on one leg, some on two, but almost all with closed eyes. Walter drew the curtains together, and groped his way back to the bed. He did not turn on the overhead light, because Edna and William, a pair of Turbits, had managed to claim its shade as their perch. There was plenty of room beside his mother. He would sleep on top of the counterpane as he was, fully dressed. By morning Jesus would have made up his mind.

The clock continued to tick loudly, and from time to time, a pigeon would make a quiet noise of curiosity at realizing it was not where it should be at this hour. Walter lay beside his dead mother, and allowed his protuberant eyelids to come down, shutting out all but the possibility of a bad dream. He was asleep almost at once.

Something was tapping gently at the outside of his left eyelid. It had woken him. He was awake now, but his eyes remained closed. He dared not open them in case whatever it was that was tapping should tap again at his open eye.

With his eyes still closed, he slowly lifted his right arm, and brought his hands towards his nose on which, he could by now feel, the bird was standing. Then he slid his fingers under the bird, gripping its legs and using his thumb and little finger to keep its wings pinioned. He was then able to lift the pigeon away from his face, and open his eyes to see which pigeon it had been. He had decided that it would be Dora. He was right. It was Dora.

He swung his feet to the floor, wished Dora a good morning, and stroked her gently. Her eyes were brighter and more alert than his. She blinked, and then cocked her head on one side as if asking for an explanation of these new living-quarters.

Walter yawned, and looked slowly round the room. From every available surface, the eyes of pigeons were watching him. He noticed that his mother's double-fronted Victorian wardrobe was now decorated with vertical black and white lines of pigeon droppings. As well as the triple mirror of the dressing-table, his mother had a full-length mirror on a stand, and this had become tilted, and at its highest point, two English Long-Faced Tumblers, Marge and Lionel, were billing and rocking in preparation for copulation. His mother's pink basketwork chair had been taken over by Norman and Marlene. Norman was a Russian High-Flier and Marlene a Birmingham Roller, originally from quite another Loft, who had met Norman high in the air one evening, and followed him home.

On each of the four bedposts, a single male bird was circling on the spot, its crop inflated, claiming that particular perch for his own, and daring any other male to challenge and fight him for it. A lilac-coloured Turbit ran backwards and forwards along the top of the pelmet of the curtains. Two female White-Lace Fantails on the dressing-table began fighting, but the fight was confused by the triple reflections of the mirror, so that there seemed to be eight White-Lace Fantails altogether, and neither of the two birds could be sure that what she was flapping her wings and pecking at was in any real sense an adversary.

Walter clapped his hands together, and shouted, 'Linda! Enid! Stop it!' The two birds stopped fighting for a while, but continued to make low threatening noises at each other and at the reflections in the mirror. Walter decided that he had better cover the mirror, when Linda and Enid might calm down, realizing that there was room on the dressing-table for both of them, and believing that the other six birds had been seen off.

His mother had not moved. There was a faintly musty smell in the room, which was not the smell of pigeons, but might, he supposed, be his own smell. He opened the door cautiously so that none of the pigeons could escape to another part of the house, betook himself to the bathroom, and found the bath full of pigeon-food.

He had never taken a bath without the supervision of his mother. He must manage as best he could. He filled the washbasin with warm water, stripped, and stood on the bathmat, soaping himself all over. He enjoyed the feeling of the slippery lavender-scented soap all over his body. But he could not reach his back.

It was a problem. The more he thought about it, the more it worried him. Would he have to stay dirty until Jesus made his mind up, and Walter's mother woke up? His arms were long, but they would only reach around him so far. As he worried at the problem, the soap which he had spread liberally on the parts he could reach began to dry. He felt itchy. This was another cause for worry. It had never happened after a bath supervised by his mother.

He removed as much of the dry soap as he could with a towel, but still he itched. As he scratched himself, he wondered what his mother would say if she could see him. Jesus was certainly taking his time about sending her back. He began to have doubts about the everlasting love Jesus had for humanity in general and for Walter in particular; his mother had told him of it, but she might have been wrong. She had taught him to sing, 'Jesus loves me. This I know, for the Bible tells me so.' If Jesus loved him, why was He leaving Walter on his own like this? Why was He taking so long to decide?

He scratched moodily at the hair in his left armpit, and felt frustrated that he could only scratch two parts of his body at the same time, when many more than two parts itched. A positive fear then entered his mind. What if his mother had seen Heaven, and walked in Paradise with Jesus, and had liked it so much that she had asked Jesus not to send her back to Walter?

Walter looked into the bathroom mirror, and named his fear aloud. 'What if it's that? What if that's what it is, then?' One of his scratching hands ceased from scratching, and was used to hold his forehead. 'It could be, couldn't it? What if it's her, Walter? If she doesn't want to come back, then, boy? He wouldn't force her, would He? Don't suppose so. No, being Jesus, He wouldn't. Forcing's not a good thing to do. No.' He moved his hand from his forehead, and began to bite at the side of his index finger. The goldfish flicked about very fast inside his head, and he closed his eyes to stop them. His body still itched. With his free hand, he scratched it where he could. What might his mother at this moment be saying to Jesus? She had asked Heaven so many times to rescue her from her evil, wilful, disappointing son. She had spoken so many times of how much better off she would be without him, of how death was all she could look forward to and the pleasure of complaining, when she should get to Heaven, of the unfairness of her life on earth.

Within his mind, his mother's conversation with Jesus became mixed up with what she would say to him, Walter, if she could observe his present condition. 'I've earned my place. Looking after such a – stop scratching, boy. You're not a dog, are you? There could only be one reason, Lord, I should have been landed with such a burden, and that's to try me out for Heaven. Shan't tell you again! Look at him! Nobody can tell me that's not a penance.'

He was naked. He itched, and his back was unclean. This was the day he was supposed to change his underwear, and he had no idea where the clean ones were kept. Again, there was no help for it; he must step once more into the underpants he had just removed. He remembered the musty smell he had noticed in his mother's bedroom. She had told him that the customers at Woolworth's would notice if he did not change his underwear. But he had not gone to Woolworth's. The pigeons would not notice if he smelled; they had their own smell.

'Where's Walter, then, eh? Where's he got to? Don't know. What you mean, "Don't know"? Haven't seen him, have I? Got to get all this rubbidge cleared away. Go on! Look! "Clear it right away," I said. Got to get rid of it today, not next week, boy. Now! Move yourself! Girls can't sell goods if they're up to their whatsits in sticky toffee papers. What's funny about that, eh? Go and get Walter. Go on! Fetch him here. Where is he, anyway? What's he doing in the bathroom? Where's our handsome hero? Where's the housewives' favourite choice?'

He was dressed. He was standing at the top of the stairs, listening to the pigeons in the bedroom, and staring down at the front door. What would he do if they gave him the sack for staying away? Two letters were pushed through the letterbox. He watched them land on the mat, and expected his mother to walk into the hall from the kitchen, pick them up, and shout to him to hurry.

He waited, and then, remembering where she was, ran down the stairs two at a time, opened the front door, and shouted after the postman. But the postman was too far away to understand what Walter shouted, and looking back, and seeing the silly Williams boy standing at the front door waving his arms, waved back cheerfully.

The postman went on round the corner, and continued to make his deliveries, amused by the antics of Witless Walter at Number Twenty-Three. Walter went back inside, and closed the door. If he could have made the postman hear, he would have told him about his mother, and asked him to send someone to watch her while he went to Woolworth's.

No help. He picked up the letters, which were addressed to his mother, and took them up to her.

3

How could you let her go like that, covered in bird-droppings, after all the years she's cared for you?

The sound of the doorbell woke Walter, the long persistent ringing of someone who knew that the house wasn't empty, and was determined to be answered. He swung his legs off the side of his mother's bed, and felt the stickiness of fresh pigeon-droppings crushed between his stockinged feet and the bedside rug. The sticky substance clung to the wool of his socks. As he tried to scrape them clean, he collected more, and as he moved, it seeped through, and made contact with his feet. He and the pigeons and his mother had been sharing the same room for seven days, and his mother not only continued to sleep, but had begun to look far from well.

'Is your mother in?' It was the woman who came sometimes with a catalogue, and never looked at his face. Nor was she looking at it now. She had seen through the frosted glass that it was a man coming to answer the door, had known that this could only be Walter, and had directed her glance at the area where his knees would be, before the door opened.

'Yes.'

'Only, I haven't seen her for some time, and I've come to . . .' The woman's voice trailed away. The stench which was coming towards her seemed to be rushing to excuse itself from the house. It was a stench she had not encountered since childhood, when her brother had kept a lame blackbird in the outhouse for four weeks.

The woman was so surprised by the strength of the stench that she forgot her habit of never looking at Walter's face, and allowed her glance to stray from his knees, and wander slowly up his body. His shirt, shoulders, arms and hair were covered in dried black and white bird-droppings, and a streak of them had run down the side of his cheek, in front of his right ear, stopping when it had reached the sharp corner of his jawbone.

'Did you want to see her?' The woman was looking him in the face. That pleased him. 'She's . . .' He wasn't sure how to explain. 'She's not been very well. I've had to stay at home with her.'

The woman's mouth, which had been open for some time, closed, then opened again just long enough to form the words, 'What's she ill with?'

'I don't know. She won't wake up.'

The expression on the woman's face changed, and informed Walter that he had said too much. He began to worry, remembering the state of his mother's bedroom.

'Can I see her?'

'She's sleeping.'

'Yes, you said.'

His mother would have died before opening the door to anyone without at first checking to make sure the house was tidy. Walter stood, and the woman stood, neither knowing what to say next. The silence seemed to go on forever.

Then Walter said, 'I'd better go and see to her.' Before he could close the door, the woman had her foot up on the step.

'Just a minute. I'm in a bit of a mess, you see. The Mail Order Club have sent me a nasty letter about your mother missing her payments. I wasn't going to bother her, because I know how regular she is usually, but I'm sure she'd want to know. It's a mistake, bound to be, but they do have the right to reclaim the goods if the payments fall behind.'

She was thinking fast, lying in her teeth. Somewhere in this house there was an old lady with only an idiot son to look after her. Already she was writing the newspaper report in her head, 'Kind Neighbour Saves Elderly Lady from Starving'. It would be 'elderly'; they hardly ever say 'old' – 'pensioner' perhaps or 'OAP' if they were short of space; no, 'elderly' was better; it would do well. 'Idiot Son Kept Mother Locked in Cupboard'.

While she was trying to decide what she would wear when

interviewed on television, she realized Walter had spoken. He had said, 'If you like.' Not only had he spoken, he had moved to one side to let her pass. The woman hesitated. She needed time to adjust from her fantasy of overnight fame to the smell of Walter and the house. Perhaps, once he had lured her inside, he would become violent, hold her at knife-point and force her to do all sorts of disgusting things.

She stepped over the threshold, and watched him carefully as he closed the front door behind her. She would let him slit her throat open rather than allow him to touch her 'in that way', or, indeed, in any way.

Walter led the way upstairs, still worrying about the state of his mother's bedroom. He said, 'I couldn't do any cleaning. I haven't been able to leave her. Excuse the mess.' He had heard his mother say that, even when she had just finished spring cleaning. On the landing, he turned to the woman and said, 'We have to go in carefully. The birds might escape.' The woman thought it best to humour him, and nodded, 'Of course.' He opened the door just enough for her to get in sideways. At first, all she could see was the side of a large Victorian wardrobe. Then she moved in further, squeezing past the door.

Her entrance disturbed the pigeons. As if they had all at that moment decided to take part in an avian version of the Paul Jones, they began with great noise and flapping to change places. The room was filled with feathers and dust. The woman placed her hand over her mouth, and what started out as a stifled scream became protection against choking.

Then she turned, and saw Walter's mother, lying with her silvery white hair spread out over the purple bed-cover, her face the colour of old and very used plasticine, pigeon droppings in her hair, on her forehead, and almost completely covering the head-board of the bed.

'She's . . .' The woman stopped herself; it was better not to risk provoking him. 'She's sleeping very heavily, isn't she? I'll come back some other time.' And left him, standing there, as quickly as she could.

At the front door, her hand holding it open for a quick getaway, she shouted back at Walter, 'How could you let her go like that, covered in bird-droppings, after all the years she's cared for you? She's been dead for days, you great mistake of a man. It's criminal.

They'll be coming for you, don't worry! They'll know what to do to make you learn.' She slammed the front door behind her, with enough force to crack one of the panes of frosted glass.

Walter stood where he was at the top of the stairs, his head swimming with brightly-coloured goldfish. What had she meant? Perhaps she didn't believe in Jesus. Among all the other thoughts which swam in and out and darted about, was one which at least gave him the opportunity for uncomplicated action. He remembered noticing that Helen, one of the Turbits, had diarrhoea, and since he was already out of his mother's room, he might as well go down to the Loft outside and get the pigeons' first-aid box. Castor oil was what was needed.

PART FIVE

He Becomes a Charge on the State

I

*He didn't suppose it would be cold in Paradise.
Otherwise they wouldn't call it 'Paradise'*

A doctor, a policeman and a Social Worker arrived at three fifteen that afternoon. Walter opened the door to them, and led them upstairs to his mother's bedroom. Each in turn squeezed round the door, so as not to allow any pigeons to escape.

Walter watched the doctor pull the stained eiderdown over his mother's face. The Social Worker put an arm around Walter's shoulder, and asked him to show her where the kitchen was, so that she could make them all a cup of tea.

As they drank the tea (without milk, since it had gone off) there were questions, some of which Walter could not answer. No, he did not know what day it was, or remember what he had eaten for lunch. Since moving into his mother's room, he had not kept proper mealtimes, but had eaten something from a tin when he was hungry; the question bore no relation to the way he had been living, but that was too difficult to explain to these people, so he merely told them that he thought the last food he had eaten was frankfurters and baked beans, but that he could not swear to it.

He did remember the names of the people with whom he had worked at Woolworth's. The Social Worker promised that she would telephone Mr Richards to explain why Walter had not been to work.

Finally they came to the question which all three, doctor, policeman and Social Worker, considered to be most important. It was, 'Have you any relations, Walter? Someone you could go and stay with?'

Walter's answer caused all three servants of the public to sigh. They sighed in turn; then they looked at each other, and sighed again. The policeman shook his head from side to side. Walter wondered why his having no relations should upset them so. His mother had said it was a blessing. Every Christmas she had said, 'Thank God we've only ourselves to buy for. I don't know how some of these large families manage, I really don't.'

It did not seem important. The doctor had said his mother would have to be taken away. He assumed that she would be taken to hospital, but surely they would bring her back. He could look after himself until then.

Now the Social Worker was speaking. 'You can't live here on your own, Walter.'

He tried to explain that he would be alright for a few days, that now he didn't have to stay with her, he could go to work, where there were Canteen Lunches, and so he would manage until she came back.

The three public servants did not seem to understand this explanation; they did not take it in. They looked again at each other. What Walter did not know was that each was unwilling to utter a word which had not so far been uttered. After a long silence, the Social Worker said, 'I think that's your department, doctor.' The doctor took out a spotlessly clean handkerchief, and wiped his hands. 'If you'd been called to her in the first place, you'd have had to tell him then.'

The doctor coughed. Walter gave him respectful attention. The doctor wiped the corners of his mouth with the handkerchief, and said, 'Now this is not going to be easy for you to understand,' and ran down. Clearly nothing about the whole business was easy for anyone. The doctor said, 'Now, look, Walter, have you ever had a pet?'

'Pigeons.'

'Apart from pigeons. Have you ever had a dog or a pussy cat that has . . . well, grown old, and . . . I suppose even the pigeons . . .'

'Never had a dog.'

'Well, you see, your mother was quite old. And what happens to people when they get old, is . . . well, after a while, they . . . they die. It's quite natural; it happens to everyone. And that's what's happened to your mother. I'm afraid she won't be coming home.'

Walter knew what it was to die. Freda, the Favourite, the

162

White-Lace Fantail, the Prize-Winner, had looked at the wall, refused food, and died, and Walter had buried her in the garden. He had not associated death with human beings, certainly never with his mother. The goldfish in his head raced and darted about. Finally he said, 'Jesus wanted her?'

'Yes,' the doctor replied a little too eagerly. He was thrown by the question, but grateful to find that religion had its uses. 'That's exactly it, Walter. Jesus has called her to Him.'

The Social Worker, who was a card-carrying agnostic, made a small noise of disgust. Walter wondered if she were about to be sick. The policeman was following his own train of thought, which was what would happen to all the pigeons. Beautiful, some of them were. Two, or perhaps three, would make an excellent birthday present for his eight-year-old son. He would have to construct some sort of cage or box in which they would live, but the policeman was much practised in Home Improvement, and would enjoy that.

'I'm told they breed like rabbits. Is that true?'

He had uttered his thought aloud, and the other two public servants looked at him for an explanation.

'The pigeons.' He remembered his official position. 'I mean, they can't stay in that room; it's a health hazard. Rats, you know what I mean?' They did not know what he meant. 'Rats and pigeons, they go together. I mean they often do, but they shouldn't.' He was not getting through to them, and so broke off. None of the pigeons would fit into his pocket without being noticeable. Perhaps if he came back later after dark, that would be best.

The Social Worker leaned forward, and touched Walter on the hand. He was thinking, or trying to. His mother had told him when his father was taken by Jesus that, once Jesus had decided that He wanted you, nobody saw you on earth again. The Social Worker had to shake Walter's hand before she had his attention. 'We'll have to find you somewhere else to live, shan't we?' She spoke as if the somewhere else to live were to be a treat. Walter's brain could not accept any more information. He felt sleepy, and he yawned. That was what his brain made him do when it was full, and no more could be squeezed into it.

'Will you come upstairs, and help me pack a suitcase?' She still had hold of his hand, and was now standing. Walter did as he was bid. He rose, and followed her upstairs.

163

He took clean clothes into the bathroom, to change in there. The bath was still full of pigeon-food. Walter contemplated washing himself all over at the sink, but when last he had done so, as he remembered, he had itched, and he did not wish to scratch in front of strangers. So he simply changed his clothes.

While he changed, he thought about the pigeons. Perhaps if he were to leave the bedroom door and the bathroom door both open, the pigeons would find their food. He could fill the wash basin with water for them to drink. It was true that they would also bathe in it, that they would foul the water and also the seed in the bath, but at least it would last them until he returned from wherever he was being taken.

He left the wash basin full of water, and presented himself to the Social Worker on the landing. She had finished packing his case. Now she bent forward to whisper in his ear, 'Is there any loose money in the house? Perhaps in a drawer somewhere? Anything at all of value – your mother's jewellery? If there is, I'd take it now if I were you, before someone else finds it.' She tapped the side of her nose with her index finger, and closed one eye slowly.

Walter remembered the ear-rings he had seen, and took them from the drawer. He also remembered that his mother kept some money in a biscuit-tin, hidden behind the rows and rows of tinned fruit in the pantry. She called it her 'Mad' money; Walter never knew why. He removed the tin, and placed the contents, nine pounds and four shillings, in his jacket pocket.

During the time it took him to perform these actions, the gold-fish in his head slowed down a little. He realized that he was to be taken somewhere. He had assumed that he would be returning, but something in the lady's manner, its conspiratorial quality and its urgency, now caused him to question this assumption. There were other questions which still darted about, like what would happen to his job in Woolworth's, why Jesus had kept his mother and left him on his own, and where did the lady intend to take him and why, and there was the uncomfortable and growing certainty that he himself had no choice in determining what was to be done with him, but these were secondary to what was now the most important question, was he to return or no. If he were not, there was something he had to do.

'Will I be coming back?'

She did not answer. He persisted. 'Will I?'

The Social Worker sighed. 'No, Walter, I don't think you'll ever come back here. I'm sorry.'

Walter grabbed a saucepan from the kitchen, and ran up the stairs, two at a time. He filled it full of pigeon-food from the bath, opened the bathroom window, and poured the food out to land in the back yard. When the bath was empty, even to the last handful, he rushed into his mother's bedroom, opened the windows as wide as they would go, and shooed the pigeons out.

Like aeroplanes leaving for a night mission, they took off in twos from the wardrobe, the dressing-table, the overhead light and Walter's mother's pink basketwork chair, each pair stopping for a moment on the window-ledge and looking about, before descending to the grain spread out for them in the yard beneath.

The wind came in through the window, and blew the stained purple eiderdown away from his mother's face. She was still here. The silver-white hair was caught by the wind, and rose into the air. Walter watched. His face set itself into a mask. He could not cry, not now. He closed his eyes, and remembered his mother's hair as he had always seen it, pulled tight into a roll behind her head. Why had Jesus not taken his mother's body, when He had taken the rest of her? Could she and Jesus see him now? He turned, and looked out of the window, up into the sky. He would leave the windows open. His mother's hands had been cold for some days; she wouldn't mind. He didn't suppose it was cold in Paradise. Otherwise they wouldn't call it 'Paradise'. He was leaving the window open for the pigeons. They would get frightened when it started to get dark. They needed somewhere high to perch.

The Social Worker called to Walter from the hall, asking him to hurry. He put the saucepan on the bed beside his mother's feet. He was frozen. He couldn't move. He shivered from the cold of the open window, from fear and from sadness. His knees sank to the floor, and he put his hand over his mouth to hold in a scream. His throat ached from being stretched so wide; he had to release it, and let the noise come out. With the noise came tears. He gripped his mother's feet with one large hand, and said, 'I will be alright, though, won't I? Tell me I'll be alright.'

People he couldn't see made sounds of reassurance, and pulled him to his feet. He was helped downstairs by the policeman, and he sat at the front in the Social Worker's car. But by then he had stopped screaming, stopping crying; he was quite silent.

Women with folded arms were leaning out from doorways, not wishing to be seen, but wishing to see. To Walter they looked like a spread-out hand of picture-cards. He would not scream now, even though they watched and waited. If they had not seen him fighting with the policeman, and trying to get back into his mother's house, they had missed that sight. It would not happen again. He had promised. And they in their turn, all three, the servants of the public, had made Walter a promise. They had promised him he would be alright. He had asked, and they had told him, 'You'll be alright.'

He was shaking again now, frightened and sad, but he would not scream. He had given his promise.

2

One sulky subnormal, handed over and signed for

'What's this?' A man in a white coat was holding some of Walter's hair.

'Pigeon-shit.' The Social Worker answered without looking up from the report she was writing. 'He had about a hundred of them shut up in his mother's bedroom with him.'

'Why's that?'

The man was asking Walter. Walter didn't want to talk. He didn't answer.

They had promised him he would be alright. He had sat beside the Social Worker in the front seat of her car, and she had told him that it was a nice place she was taking him to, but she had lied.

The man in the white coat was asking him more questions. Some of them were questions the Social Worker had already asked. Did he know his date of birth? When was his birthday? How old was he? What school had he attended?

They had driven past the large double gates, and she had waved to a man in uniform, standing outside the lodge. Walter had heard the gravel of a long driveway crunching beneath the tyres of the car, and for a moment he had felt important.

Had he ever run away from school? What had he eaten for his last meal? When had he eaten last?

They were going to look after him. They had told him so; they had promised. They were going to take care of him. That is what they had said, and he had believed them.

What day was it? What time of day? Did he realize where he was?

The ride in a car, the gate with the man in uniform, the way the Social Worker had spoken to him as she drove, all this had reassured him. She had called him Walter, and asked him about the pigeons. Then the car had stopped, and he had looked out, and seen the size of the building. As she had turned off the engine, and pulled at the handbrake, she had said, 'Built as a Workhouse in 1839. You wouldn't know what a Workhouse is. I expect you would have done then.'

It was grey. Grey stone, with six stories and far too many windows for Walter to count. He had never seen so frightening a building. He had wanted to run, to hide in the bushes, to do anything but go inside.

And they had promised.

Did he always know when he wanted to use the lavatory? Did he use it properly? Could he count? Add? Subtract? Multiply?

For a while he had refused to get out of the car. The Social Worker had grown impatient. She had said, 'It's not as bad as it looks from outside.' She had pulled at his arm, and he had resisted.

Could he write his own name? His address? The man was reading the questions from a printed sheet of paper and, as Walter gave answer to none of them, the man made a stroke with his pen against each question as it went unanswered.

Finally he had realized that he could not sit in the Social Worker's car forever. He had placed one foot out of the car onto the gravel. The goldfish in his head had told him to run, but while he was still looking about, trying to decide which way he should go, two men in white jackets had come quickly from the entrance of the hospital and taken hold of his arms, pushing him forwards towards the large double doors.

Once they were inside the hospital, the Social Worker had told the two men that Walter would be alright now, and they had backed away, and then gone inside a small room. Before the door closed, Walter had heard one of them say, 'Your deal,' and seen that they sat down and resumed their game of cards.

The Social Worker had smiled, but Walter had sensed that this to carry it, since she was tired, and they had almost a quarter of a mile of corridor to walk. The quarter of a mile was wide and high, as well as long. It echoed with the sound of Walter's squeaking boots and the steady measured step of the Social Worker's sensible shoes. It echoed with the sound of iron doors being banged, of large keys being turned, with shouts and screams, sobs and moans. It echoed with the sound of a voice as high and shrill as a seagull, with the conversation of old and not-so-old men, who stood at the corners where smaller corridors crossed this large one, and whose conversation was not with each other but with themselves. The voices of these old and not-so-old men had been low and confidential, but still they had echoed. Walter had passed the men, glancing nervously at them from the corners of his eyes (since it was rude to stare), and had seen that some scratched themselves, some picked their noses, and some hugged their arms to their chests, smiling or giggling at private and pleasurable thoughts. Who were these men? What was this place?

Do you know where you are? Can you tell me when you last . . . if you last . . . have you ever . . .? Do you know . . .?

One man had repeated the word, 'Hullo,' over and over again. Walter had answered, 'Hullo,' and this had caused the man to say the word more quickly, repeating it, each time using a different inflection, 'Hullo! Hullo? *Hull-o. Hull-o. Huh-lo,*' on and on, even when they were well past him, with the 'Hullo' slower again, sad and flat and disappointed, as if he had wanted Walter to answer each 'Hullo' with another, and had been rejected when this did not happen. Walter had turned his head, and shouted another 'Hullo' back at the man, hearing it echo more than once, but the Social Worker had said, 'Don't encourage him,' as if the man had been a dog, begging for food from a guest's plate. The only word of hers which Walter had heard echo was the word 'him', which he had heard twice, 'him, him'. She was not a woman of any great resonance.

The corridor had smelled of boiled cabbage. The walls had been painted dark green up to the height a man could reach. Above this, they were a yellowing cream.

Do you know where you are?

At the next corner, an old man had been pacing backwards and forwards, flicking his hands vigorously as if he wished them to drop off from the ends of his arms. Walter had wondered what the man's hands could have done that he wished so desperately to lose them.

All the men he had seen wore stained clothes which didn't fit

169

them, trousers without buttons but with elasticated tops. Some had pulled the trousers high up onto their chests, leaving large gaps between their trouser turnups and the tops of their shoes or (more often) slippers. The heads of all the men had been shaved at the sides and back, with the hair on the top left short and of equal length, as though a pudding-basin had been used to support the barber's hand while he trimmed round it.

The shortness of the men's hair had reminded Walter of his father, whose own hair had never been as short as that. He wondered whether his father and mother had yet met in Paradise. If they had, and could see down to him, he begged them to ask Jesus to take him quickly from this place.

The man in the white coat was now writing on another sheet of paper. 'Religion? C of E, I suppose?'

The Social Worker said, 'I'm not sure. There was nobody to ask. Do you know your religion, Walter?'

Walter knew well enough that he was Chapel, but he would not answer; he would not speak. The man in the white coat shrugged, and wrote down 'C of E' while the Social Worker continued to scribble at her report with a ball-point pen.

As they had approached yet another thick iron door, Walter had heard a man behind it screaming the word, 'No,' over and over again, and thought he could hear also the sound of fighting, of blows being struck and heads hitting the wall and the door itself, and all the time this hysterical voice pleading, 'No... No... No... Please...' Walter had ceased walking at this point, and had said as firmly as he could, 'Can I go home?' He had stopped so suddenly that the Social Worker, deep in her own thoughts, had not noticed, and had gone on ahead.

Walter had remained where he was near the iron door. He knew that he had turned no corners. He could find his way out. If he were to run fast enough, he could get past the men who were playing cards. If it were done, it had to be done at once and quickly. Walter had half turned, and looked back the way they had come. But if he were caught, what would be done to him in this place?

The Social Worker had noticed he was no longer by her side, and had walked back to him slowly. 'What did you say?' She had made it sound as though what he had said was in some way most extraordinary.

Walter had repeated what he had said.

The Social Worker had smiled, but Walter had sensed that this was not a smile of pleasure. 'This is your home now, Walter.' She had paused, allowing time for the words to sink in. 'You need looking after, and that's what this place is for. It's what the people here are for. To look after you.'

Walter had wondered if the people who were to look after him were like the old men he had already passed in the corridor, and who had not seemed capable of looking after themselves. There was also the matter of the iron door, against which at that moment he had seemed to hear the sound of some person being thrown. So he had pointed at it, and said, 'I'm frightened.'

'Oh, you are silly, Walter. That's nothing to do with you. They're probably just playing a game. They could be kicking a ball about. You like football, don't you?'

Walter knew the difference between the sound of a ball being kicked at a door and that of a head suffering the same fate. He had said, 'I don't like it here. You told me it was nice.'

Once again the Social Worker had smiled her patient and pleasureless smile. 'How do you know what it's like until you've tried it? I happen to think that it is nice – for someone like you. What would you do out in the town, all on your own? The Corporation wouldn't let you stay in that house; you'd have to walk the streets.'

She had removed the gloves from her hands, and placed them in her handbag. She had taken Walter's free hand in hers, and once again they had begun to walk. As they had walked together along the great corridor, Walter had felt all will, all hope, all happiness and all energy drain away from him.

And so they had come to this room, where a man in a white coat asked him questions, most of which he could answer, and none of which he would, while the Social Worker wrote on an official form with a ballpoint pen.

'He's sulking. He's decided he doesn't like it here.' The Social Worker had finished her report. She took her gloves from her handbag, and began to put them on. She had done with physical contact for the day.

The man in the white coat said, 'Hey! Don't forget to sign for the hand-over.' He handed her a printed form with a carbon copy attached.

171

'Just like me to forget the most important bit.'

She signed, and the man tore off the top copy, and gave it to her, saying, 'One sulky subnormal, handed over and signed for.' Then they both laughed, and the Social Worker held out a gloved hand to the white-coated man, and he shook it.

Walter watched from the glass booth of an office, as the man and woman walked together to the thick iron door. The man lifted his white coat, examined a large bunch of keys which hung at his waist, chose one, and unlocked the door with it. The Social Worker stepped through into the long corridor, and the door was locked again behind her.

Walter sat in a small hip-bath. Lukewarm grey water just covered his genitals. A man in a faded beige coat scrubbed at his back with a stiff brush and carbolic soap.

Suddenly the man forced Walter's head down between his knees, so as to wet Walter's hair and the pigeon-droppings which were matted in it. Walter swallowed some of the grey waters, and began to choke, and the man slapped him on the back with such force that he bit his tongue. Then the man continued his work, rubbing carbolic soap liberally into Walter's hair, pulling out the pigeon-droppings together with a little hair, and massaging Walter's scalp until it stung.

Thereafter Walter's pubic hair was given the same treatment, although it contained no pigeon-droppings. At this point of a bath, Walter's mother had always handed the soap and flannel to him, saying, 'You can do that,' and Walter attempted to explain this to the man. 'I . . . I do that . . . I can do that,' he said, but the man in the coat of faded beige took no notice, continued with his work, and never spoke.

The man was strong. Walter was pulled from the bath as if he had no legs of his own. The man had gained this strength from years of pulling from baths patients whose legs were of no use to them.

Walter stood shivering on the cold linoleum, while the man rubbed him all over with a small rough white towel, which bore the name of the hospital as a sign that it was the hospital's property. Walter's own property, the clothes in which he had arrived and his suitcase with its contents, had been taken away from him. The money he had rescued from his mother's biscuit tin was in the pocket of his jacket with her Eiffel Tower ear-rings. He should have asked to keep them, but since he had been taking off his clothes to have a bath, there would have been nowhere he could have put them for safety. Perhaps they would be given back to him when he was allowed to wear proper clothes again.

The man held Walter's privates cupped in his hand as he combed Walter's pubic hair. Clearly he was looking for something. With each stroke, he held the comb up to the light and close to his eyes. The same process of combing and searching was applied to the hair on Walter's head.

After the combing and searching came a searching without combing. First the man turned Walter round on the spot, scanning his body for bruises. Then he forced Walter to bend over, prised his buttocks apart, and examined what he saw before him. Then he turned Walter again, grasped his penis and squeezed it, squinting at the hole for any sign of a discharge.

Walter did not know what the man was searching for. He did not know why any of this was being done. At no time did the man explain to Walter the reason for his actions.

Next the man led Walter into another room, in which there was a weighing-machine smaller than the one which stood by the door at Woolworth's, on which customers might weigh themselves by putting a penny in the slot. The man weighed Walter (the machine did not require a penny) and made a note of Walter's weight on a card; it was eleven stone, four ounces. Then he took Walter's wrist in his hand, consulted his own wristwatch for what seemed to be a long time, and made another note. He examined the teeth in Walter's mouth, holding the mouth open with his fingers, and pulled a face. Walter took the face to mean that the man was not pleased with what he saw.

A large stiff white nightshirt was placed over Walter's head, and pulled down. Walter noticed that it had been darned and patched in a great many places. To wear over it, he was given a dressing-gown, which felt greasy. Old foodstains decorated the lapels and front. It stank of stale urine. There was no belt or cord with which to tie it, and so it stayed open at the front unless held. Walter held it. If his mother and father really were looking down at him from Paradise, they would be surprised to see him dressed like this.

He was given bedroom slippers which had been fouled several times, and felt damp. His own, which his mother had bought for him, remained in his suitcase. Wherever that was.

Walter was allocated a bed in a dormitory containing sixty-nine other beds, all of them occupied. The man in the faded beige coat directed him to his bed, and gave him two pills to swallow. He then spoke to Walter for the first time, and for the first time explained an action. He told Walter that the pills were to help him get off to sleep in the strange bed, and that they were only given on the first night. After that, he told Walter with what could only be described as a twisted smile, Walter would have to use what other methods were to hand in order to get off to sleep.

The time was seven thirty. All lights except the one in the glass booth at the end of the ward, which was occupied by the Staff Nurse, were turned out.

At eight o'clock, the Night Staff arrived, and the Day Staff went home. Walter was still awake, in spite of the two pills, and heard someone say, 'We've got a new one. Might be a bit of trouble. If he kicks up, give him the needle.'

The man in the bed to Walter's right was crying into his pillow. Between sobs, he whispered words. Walter thought that the words were meant for him to hear, so he leaned closer to the man, but what he heard was,

> 'Lord, who lives in everlasting light,
> I love thee ever with heart and hand,
> That has made me to see this sight,
> First out of all the people of my land.
> Here shall I be born, King of Bliss.
> I shall not want or wish for aught.
> God of all Gods, I await them to recognize me.
> Please, please, let it be soon.'

He looked up into the darkness above his head, and tried to stop himself from thinking about what might have happened to Lydia, Stella, Lionel, the Muffed Tumblers and the Fantails, and all the other birds he had set free. Being free to them wasn't what it was to people. They had all been born in the Loft; they were used to a routine, and, as far as Walter knew, they liked it. Free, they would be frightened. There would be cats and rats. And the rats would be real rats, not those smiling rats who followed the Pied Piper in his jigsaw.

Without proper shelter and food, the pigeons would get depressed, and become ill. They were not used to being out late at night.

Anything might happen. Turbits were not practical birds.

He thought he heard something move swiftly across the floor to the left of his bed. Then he felt a tug at the bed-cover (which also bore the name of the hospital). He became still, wondering what could be tugging at his bedclothes.

A moment later something which he took to be a large hairy dog jumped up onto the bed on top of him. He was frightened of dogs. He slid further down into the bed, and covered his head, so that if the dog bit, it would only bite the blankets.

The hairy thing pulled the covers away from Walter's head, as a dog might dig to bury a bone. He felt its hair against his face. It gave off a sweet sickly smell, not just from its breath, but also from its sweat. Walter was not to know that what he smelled was digested paraldehyde. They were arms he was fighting, human arms; it was not a hairy dog but an old hairy man. The hairy man's face was touching Walter's face. He was breathing heavily. His arms were stronger than Walter's arms, thin, bony and strong. They had pulled the covers down as far as Walter's waist, and were now trying to pull the nightshirt up.

Walter was almost suffocated by the foul sickly breath and the rough beard which its owner was rubbing all over his face. With the breath came words, sibilant hissing whispers, as the old hairy man said, 'Here! You're new. Give us a bit of a feel. Give us a bit. Excite an old man. Go on, kid; let's have a bit of fun.' With these words, Walter felt sharp nails on the end of bony fingers groping between his legs. He tried to roll himself into a ball, and to protect his privates with his hands, pulling the bony fingers away.

Walter struggled in silence, not wishing to disturb the other patients and the Night Staff, who sat drinking coffee in the illuminated glass booth at the end of the ward. Then he realized that what the old hairy man was doing to him was what Elaine had done so long ago in the Park. The sticky stuff which she had drawn from him was about to burst out again. It was too late; he couldn't prevent it. He could feel it building up inside him, ready

175

to gush forth onto the clean sheets he had only been lying between for an hour.

Then it happened. The sticky stuff shot from him into the old man's hands and into his own hands. As it did so, Walter let out a loud involuntary sound, half pleasure and half shame.

Immediately all the lights were switched on. The old hairy man jumped from Walter's bed as a dog might jump from a chair, and scuttled halfway across the ward. A window in the nurses' booth was opened, and a voice shouted, 'Go back to your own bed, Ben Gunn. He's much too young for you, you dirty old sod.'

The old hairy man crouched in the space between the two rows of disturbed patients, and growled back at the two night nurses, 'Gyah! Pig Shit! I got him first.' Then he laughed, a gurgling asthmatic laugh, and said, 'He's a virgin. Shot his bolt.' Then, still in the same crouching position, he started to make his way back to his own bed, cackling like a pantomime witch, 'I got him. I got him first.' When he had reached his own bed at the other end of the ward, and jumped into it, again very much like a dog, the lights were extinguished, the glass panel in the nurses' booth slid closed, and the coffee-drinking was resumed.

Walter's thoughts moved backwards over what had happened to him in so short a time, reliving the time when they had dragged him, screaming, from his mother's bedside to the Social Worker's car, his promise to be a good boy (which he had kept) and their promise that he would be alright (which they had not kept), and all the prolonged ceremony of his entrance to this hospital.

He pulled his nightshirt down over what his own mother had refused to touch, and closed his eyes. He wished his mother had taken him with her to be with Jesus in Paradise.

The man in the next bed was talking again:

> 'You sleep, brethren, yet I see.
> Sleep on now, all of ye.
> My time is come, to taken be;
> From you I must away.
> He that hath betrayed me,
> This night from him will I not flee.
> In a sorry time, born was he.'

In spite of the sleeping pills he had been given, Walter spent the next four hours wide awake. The sticky stuff dried on his thighs and nightshirt and on the top sheet of the bed, a patch of which now felt stiff to the touch. This worried him. In the morning, someone might notice, and make fun of him. Walter did not know exactly what had happened on this occasion any more than on the last, but the conversation at Woolworth's had taught him that anything emanating from the place his mother would not touch was bound to be a subject for ribaldry.

At two in the morning, he fell asleep.

Four hours later, he was woken up.

3

What are you staring at, Cinderella? Lost your slipper?

The words which woke Walter were, 'Got any bacca? Got a farthing? Bollocks!' The old man asking the questions did not wait for answers. He had asked the questions so many times, and always received a negative response, that he knew that to wait was a waste of time.

Walter's eyes had not yet focused. He assumed that the old man's words were still part of his dream. He was waking from a dream (or rather a nightmare) in which his mother had gone to join Jesus, and he had been tricked into entering a Lunatic Asylum, where he had been poked and prodded and made to stand naked while his private parts were pulled apart and squeezed.

He closed his eyes again, and then opened them, expecting his mother to rise from the chair in which she always sat, and to come towards him, reminding him to thank the Lord for safe deliverance through the night. But instead of his mother's face, there was now a large round black shiny face with very white teeth, grinning not more than six inches away from the end of Walter's nose.

The mouth which contained the teeth moved, forming words. It was speaking. Talking. Talking to him, to Walter. And what it said was, 'Get out of that wanking pit, young man. It says here in your notes that you can stand, and even walk. Well, that's very lucky, 'cos that's what you're about to do.'

Walter blinked at the face, hoping it would go away, but it stayed where it was, and slowly the details of what he had thought to be a nightmare came back to him, and he realized where he was and how he had got there, and that the nightmare was real.

'Come on, man. This ain't no Health Farm you at. We got work to do.' The black face moved, and Walter's bedclothes were pulled off him.

Walter raised himself up on one elbow, and tried to take in his surroundings. There was noise. A lot of it. All kinds of noise. The black man who had woken Walter wore a white coat. A small bald-headed man with over-large hands had grabbed one arm of this white coat, and was trying to communicate with it by using a series of subdued shrieks. The bald man reminded Walter of a Toby Jug without its hat. The black nurse appeared to understand the meaning of the shrieks, for he replied, 'Yes, Harry. I will in a minute. We have a new friend. Have you not seen him?' The Toby Jug man shook his head, and approached Walter, holding out hot spongey fingers to be shaken in friendship. Walter shook the fingers. Then the Toby Jug man turned to the black nurse again, and made a further series of shrieks, pointing at Walter, and the black nurse said, 'Yes, alright then; you show him. But don't take all day.'

Walter was not sure that he wished to be shown whatever it was the Toby Jug man had been instructed to show him, but all that at first happened was that the Toby Jug man took Walter's arm, and helped him off the bed. Then he and the Toby Jug man stood side by side on the bare floorboards between Walter's bed and the bed of the man who had cried, and spoken God's name in the night. There was only just enough room for the two of them. Then the Toby Jug man stretched out his arm, and pointed all round the room, making a noise which Walter knew must have a meaning, which he was unable to guess.

A completely naked man was propelling himself along the floor in a sitting-down position. By moving his heels, then his bottom, and then his hands, he was able to travel extremely fast. This posture was also most convenient for undertaking the activity on which his heart seemed to be set, which was the gathering up of any piece of dirt he could find, and popping it into his mouth quickly like a hungry bird. Walter watched the naked man scrape up seven pieces of dirt with his thumbnail and pop them into his mouth before he forced himself to look away.

Not all the men in the ward wore stiff white nightshirts as

Walter did. Some wore pyjamas, the trousers of which were now being removed and thrown into a trolley. All the pyjama trousers handled in this way had been wet or soiled during the night. The trolley was almost full, and Walter realized why the windows were all being opened so hurriedly, and why it was so cold.

The window-opener used a long thick pole. He wore a coat of faded beige, like the man who had given Walter a bath, but he was not that man; his hair was red as carrots. Even when he had opened all the windows of the ward, the stench of soiled pyjamas was still overpowering.

Walter was aware that he should be doing something, but did not know what, and rather than do something wrong and be either punished for it, or scorned, or both, he thought it wiser to do nothing. The black nurse who had woken him was now at the other end of the ward, and the Toby Jug man had held out his bunch of fingers to be shaken a second time, and then moved away. Walter looked about for Ben Gunn, with the hope of not seeing him, and because there were sixty-nine other men in the room, not counting the Staff, his hope was realized.

Everyone looked physically odd in some way. Some of the men had heads too large for their bodies, and some had heads too small. Many had bodies which were twisted, with elbows permanently bent, and fingers splayed out, unable to grasp or grip. Some walked with a strutting gait on the balls of their feet, leaning forward with chests out. These men reminded Walter of a male pigeon strutting in pursuit of a hen, who must run in front of him to avoid having her tail trodden on.

A young black patient hopped around the ward, holding his left leg by the ankle.

Not all the men communicated in grunts or noises, but the only actual words Walter could understand were those spoken (or more frequently shouted) by the two men in white coats and the carrot-haired man in faded beige.

'God, it stinks like a sewer in here. What was it you had for your dinners yesterday? Was it brussel sprouts again, was it?'

Walter had not realized that he had been noticed, but now the carrot-haired Irish ward orderly was speaking to him. It seemed safer to concentrate his gaze on the floor.

'What are you staring at, Cinderella? Lost your slipper?'

Walter grinned, thinking that the safest thing to do.

'Oh, he's got a sense of humour. Well now, that's a precious thing in a place like this. Let's hope it lasts. Meanwhile, if you can stand, you can walk, and if you can walk, you can help some of these poor paraplegics to get out of their beds, and you can start ripping their filthy pants off them.'

Walter had no idea what the word 'paraplegic' meant, but the orderly had nodded towards a man in the bed opposite. This man was sitting up in his bed, shaking all over as if he were about to freeze to death.

Walter made a tentative move towards the shaking man, not at all sure what he was going to do or what had been asked of him. The carrot-haired orderly said, 'Yes, get that one. Do our Clifford first.'

The shaking man stank of excreted brussel sprouts. Walter placed a hand under each of the man's armpits, then turned and looked for guidance to the orderly.

'Well, pull the bedclothes back first, you great twopence half-farthing. How do you expect him to get his feet to the floor? He's not the Great Houdini.' Walter left the shaking man's armpits alone for the moment, and rolled the tightly tucked-in bedclothes down towards the shaking man's feet. When the man's trunk was uncovered, the full impact of the digested brussel sprouts hit Walter hard in the face. He closed his eyes in some faint hope that, by shutting off his vision, he might succeed also in impairing his sense of smell.

Slowly and with excessive care Walter pulled the bedclothes away from the man's feet, and then began the even more difficult manoeuvre of taking the feet from the bed to the floor without allowing the top half of the shaking man to fall backwards off the other side of the bed. Where the shaking man's feet landed, Walter found a pair of soiled bedroom slippers, much like the ones he himself had been made to wear. His own, he remembered, were still under his bed.

As Walter began to place the shaking man's shaking feet into his slippers, the orderly shouted, 'Pants off first, you great lump. Get his pants off, and wipe his bum clean with them.'

Walter looked up at the face of the shaking man, who was now sitting on the side of the bed. The man's mouth was so large that it covered a third of his face. His lips were thick and shiny, and they were wide open. Wide open. Walter marvelled at the size of the man's tongue, which hung out of his mouth, dripping warm saliva onto Walter's hands.

The man's eyes were small and almost closed, but they moved, and watched Walter's eyes. Walter stood, supporting the heavy shaking man, so that he too was standing. Their faces were so close that they almost touched. The shaking man belched, and Walter smelled the wind as it was released. The enormous open mouth lifted a little at each corner.

'That's right, Clifford. Start the day with a smile, and get it over with.' The carrot-haired orderly worked with amazing speed, stripping, cleaning and redressing one patient after another, operating for most of the time by touch, since his eyes were on Walter and Clifford.

Walter smiled back at the shaking man, just to show him that there was no ill feeling. The man was larger than Walter, and heavier. As he leaned against Walter, with his head hanging loosely to one side over Walter's shoulder, it became possible to untie the cord of his pyjama trousers, which, aided by the weight of what had been deposited inside them, dropped to the floor.

Walter had to strain to support the shaking man's weight, and was not at all sure how much longer he could bear the strain. He had reached the point at which he needed further instructions. Slowly he managed to turn his head in the direction of the orderly.

'It's alright; I'm watching you. Now, don't go falling in love with Clifford before breakfast. Just you get his sodding bum wiped.'

There was no way that Walter could reach the fouled pyjamas, which he had been told to use for wiping, without lowering Clifford onto the bed. He began to bend down, Clifford's body bending with his, but seeing this, the orderly shouted, 'Don't you dare let his bum stain that sheet, if it hasn't already done so.' Walter managed to hold Clifford in suspension, his bottom some three inches from the sheet, while he groped for and eventually touched the pyjama trousers. Instantly he became aware of a further problem. Clifford's feet were still inside them. He lifted one foot out, rested, then lifted the other. Then he pulled Clifford a few more inches away from the bed, and managed to hold him there while he reached round with the soiled trousers and gave Clifford's bottom a perfunctory wipe. In any case, he noticed, the sheet was already stained.

'Puts you right off brussel sprouts, doesn't it?' It came to Walter that perhaps he had found, in all this place, someone whose disposition was fundamentally friendly. 'Clifford's your job every morning from now on. When you get a bit quicker, I'll give you the pleasure of Maurice and Albert. Tuesdays are worst. They've usually had cabbage the night before, and there's so much ill wind farting about in here, you have to hold onto the bedposts to retain your dignity. Now find yourself some nice pretty clothes from that pile over there, and get yourself dressed.'

In the pile of pretty clothes were trousers with elastic waistbands, no fly-buttons and no flies. (Walter remembered how long he and his mother had struggled before he had accomplished the undoing and doing up of buttons.) There were no underpants and no vests. The shirts were all stained and collarless, and the jackets were creased and rumpled, and so either too large or too small. All the clothes were slip-on clothes; their construction held no difficulties for the dresser, their appearance no pleasure for the watcher. Everything was dark brown, lovat or dark grey. He did not wish to wear anything he found. His mother would certainly have burned everything in the pile.

'Come on! Get a move on. What's your name?' This time a man in a white coat was shouting at him; the white coats seemed to be superior to the beige. Walter looked at the floor. He did not like to be shouted at when he had done nothing wrong.

'I said, "What's your name?"'

Walter told the man quietly that his name was Walter.

'Say "sir" when you speak to me, Walter. I'm the Staff Nurse on this duty, understand?'

Walter nodded, so as to avoid the necessity of saying 'sir' immediately.

'You're new.' The Staff Nurse informed Walter of this fact in a manner which suggested that Walter did not already know it.

'Yes, sir. I know, sir.' There; he had got it over. He remembered that he had not cleaned himself since handling Clifford's pyjama trousers. 'Please, sir, can I wash my hands?'

'What for?'

'They're dirty, sir.' He held them out in proof.

'Alright. In there.' The man pointed to the Wash Room. 'And don't take so long choosing your wardrobe. It's not Friday, and we're not expecting the Queen.' The beige-coloured orderly

183

laughed at this last remark, though Walter could not tell why. And the significance of Friday was only revealed to him later.

He washed his hands, and returned to the pile of clothes. The orderly told him to bring Clifford some clothes. 'Nice big ones. He's a hell of a big man is our Clifford.' He patted Clifford under the chin. 'Aren't you, lovely?' Clifford sat on the side of his bed, wearing only his pyjama jacket, and shaking, partly from his ailment and partly from the cold. 'And don't take all day about it,' the orderly said. 'It's so cold in here with the windows open, the brass monkeys will be after knitting themseves fur-lined jockstraps.'

Walter dressed as quickly as he could in the first things that came to hand. Then he took the largest shirt, jacket and trousers he could find in the pile, and helped Clifford to get into them.

'Now bring his wheelchair from the Recreation Room.' The orderly pointed to a room on the other side of the nurses' booth. 'It's got "Number Twenty-Six" painted in blue on the handlebars. Can you recognize a two and a six when you see them?' Walter nodded. 'Well, that's a blessing, I'm sure. We'll be entering you for the Brain of Britain before we're through. Go along now, and get it. Then you can push him down to breakfast. Am I not spoiling you, Walter, with all these treats?'

The Recreation Room was almost as large as the room in which Walter had slept. It was bare, except for the chairs which surrounded the room, their backs to the walls. Some of the chairs could at one time have been described as 'easy chairs' but few of them were likely to give much ease now, the kapok stuffing having been removed by patients whose condition caused them to pick and pluck. Among them were twenty-four wheelchairs, with painted numbers on the handlebars which went up to the fifties. They seemed to be haphazardly scattered among the other chairs. Walter was later to discover that the placing was not at all haphazard, but invariable, each wheelchair patient having his own favourite place to sit.

On the window-ledge there was a radio. Its knobs had been removed. Walter was later also to discover the secrets of this radio, which had long ago been tuned to the Light Programme with a pair of pliers, on which station it permanently remained, and which could only be switched off (an operation which took place on Friday afternoons and at bedtime) by pulling its plug out of the wall-socket. The orderly who had long ago tuned the set had also permanently adjusted its volume, so that only by sitting with an ear pressed against it could one make out what was being said. What the BBC said was not relevant to the lives of the men who lived in Ward C3, and the faint persistent music of the Top Ten acted as Muzak, neither demanding nor getting attention.

Breakfast was served in the Dining Room, which was used by patients from all three wards of C Wing. C1 housed fifty patients, C2 sixty, and C3, Walter's ward, seventy. The patients were graded by the hospital authorities according to their capabilities, and C3 contained the lowest grade. It was also used as a Punishment Ward. To be sent down to C3 from either of the other wards meant that a patient had been violent, or anti-social, or a persistent irritant to other patients or to the Staff, or that the patient had regressed. A small room off C3 was used to isolate very violent patients. There was nothing in this room which could be used as a weapon, the mattress was on the floor, and shutters across the windows prevented the glass from being broken or the white enamelled chamberpot from being emptied out of it onto heads below. The floorboards near the radiator were stained where isolated patients had pissed on the radiator to make steam when the chamberpot was full.

Walter had not been graded as of low capabilities by the authorities; he had not yet been graded at all. All newcomers to the hospital were first put into C3 as part of the process of assessment. This assessment was more sophisticated than might at first appear. Even if a newcomer should prove himself to be capable, if he should also prove himself helpful to the nursing staff, he might be kept in C3 nevertheless, otherwise the proportion of three Staff to seventy patients would have been unworkable.

Unaware of this, Walter was being helpful. He had wheeled Clifford to the Dining Hall, where one hundred and eighty handicapped male persons sat at twelve very long tables. Only forty-one of these persons were capable of using a knife and fork. Walter sat on a chair next to Clifford's wheelchair, and looked at the spoon before him. He thought again of his mother, watching from Paradise, and knew that she would wish him to ask for a knife and fork. A *good boy eats with a knife and fork, Walter, not a spoon.*

185

A Staff Nurse asked those gathered here today to thank God for the blessings they were about to receive. Walter wished that he were about to receive a knife and fork. Perhaps his mother would mention it to Jesus. What he did receive, as did the other hundred and seventy-nine persons gathered there that day, was a plastic bowl containing powdered egg which had been scrambled and allowed to cool, along with a thick slice of white bread, spread sparingly with margarine. This was almost thrown onto the dining tables by the Staff, there being, at each place, a round rubber placemat coloured grey, put there to stop the plastic bowls from sliding across the tables. Each of these hundred and eighty grey rubber placemats had a pattern of raised rubber circles on the top, intended not for ornament but as a further precaution against sliding bowls. In the grooves between the raised circles were re-minders of meals long past.

Walter looked across at the long line of faces at the other side of the table. Some of the men held the plastic bowls up to their mouths, almost drinking the scrambled egg. Others shovelled it into their mouths with their spoons, and if it fell onto the front of their clothes, they rubbed at the wasted egg with their sleeves.

There were eleven men at Walter's table who wore plastic bibs, each having a trough at the bottom of the bib to catch spilled food, so as to give it a second chance of reaching its target. Most of them could not achieve the physical action of spooning the egg from its bowl and getting it to a mouth, not even their own. Six of the eleven sat like Clifford, not even trying to eat, but shaking and staring at the food in front of them. These men seemed to have bent and twisted hands and bodies, as if their bones were the wrong shape or size. One of them leaned forward above his bowl, opening and shutting his mouth as if willing the egg up into it.

Walter saw a nurse spoon-feeding a man who could not feed himself, and when he had finished his own meal, which did not take long, he got up from his chair, and began to feed Clifford. Clifford, who was used to waiting his turn to be fed, dropped his head back as far as it would go, and watched Walter through the narrow slits behind which were his eyes.

Automatically, without even thinking about it, Walter fed Clifford in the way in which his own mother had taught him to feed himself. The nurse, who was now feeding his third patient, merely used his own hands, and spooned each spoonful into the patient's mouth, but Walter placed Clifford's right hand on the spoon, and pressing his own fingers around it, guided Clifford's hand to Clifford's mouth.

Feeding Clifford in this way was exhausting, since it required much of Walter's strength to prevent Clifford's hand from shaking and spilling the food, and it took much longer than the method of feeding practised by the Staff, but Walter thought that, if he were to show the Staff what he was capable of, they would realize that they had made a mistake, and allow him to go home. The Indian nurse meanwhile had begun feeding his fifth patient. He observed Walter's novel and exhausting method of feeding Clifford, but let him get on with it.

Those of the patients who could both walk and be trusted with cups, left the table after finishing their egg and bread, and were given watered milk to take back to their places and drink. Watered milk was brought to others by the Staff in cups with spouts, and they were assisted to drink. Walter had been used to tea with his breakfast, but in its absence, even watered milk would have been welcome. However, just as Clifford swallowed his last spoonful, the same Staff Nurse who had asked him to thank God for what he was to receive, lifted a handbell, and shook it. Those patients who could stand, did. Others waited in the wheelchairs for some-one to push them back to the ward. A few chairbound patients used their own arms to turn the wheels. As swiftly as breakfast had been given, its remains were cleared away. There could be no doubt that it was over.

Walter assumed that it was now his job to push Clifford back to the ward. As he turned the wheelchair, he felt a hand on his shoulder, and the Indian nurse said, 'Are you going to feed Clifford from now on?' Walter, not being sure what the right answer to that question might be, decided that a nod was the reply which would commit him least. To his relief, the Indian nurse said, 'Good boy! That will be very nice. Save me trouble.' Walter, prodded to it by a sudden mental picture of his mother's disapproval at seeing so much of her teaching (on buttons . . . on spoons) destroyed in this place, seized his chance, and asked the nurse if he might have a knife and fork next time.

'Yes, certainly. What you do is to go see that man over there.' He pointed to a beige-coated man standing behind a food-trolley, scraping left-over scrambled egg into a bucket. 'Ask him for a knife and fork before each meal. Then remember to take it back to him when you are finished. They all have to be counted, see? Knives and forks can be dangerous. You understand? Someone I once saw a fork pushed right into his eye. Blinded. Very dangerous. You understand?'

Walter nodded.

Back at Ward C3, Walter and Clifford were counted in, just as, when the door had been unlocked for them to go down to the Dining Hall, they had been counted out. This happened at every mealtime.

No patient was permitted to leave the ward without being escorted by a member of Staff, and since there were rarely more than three members of Staff on duty in Ward C3, a reason for leaving the ward had to be important.

Visitors were not encouraged. They caused work. Visiting was allowed on Wednesday and Saturday afternoons, and anyone wishing to visit had to apply in writing at least one full week before arriving. It was extremely inconvenient for Staff to take time out from their other duties in order to make sure that a patient being visited was given a special shave and put into his own clothes. Then, since visitors were not, of course, permitted to visit the ward (which could never have been brought into any condition which visitors might regard as being even minimally suited for human habitation), more time had to be taken in escorting the patient to the Visitors' Room. Fortunately for the Staff on Ward C3, very few patients ever had visitors. Walter himself did not expect anyone to come and see him. Nobody except the doctor, policeman and Social Worker knew where he was, and although the Social Worker had promised to inform Mr Richards, the manager of Woolworth's, he was in no doubt that she had broken that promise as she had the promise that he would be alright. Besides, Mr Richards was a busy man. It was unlikely that he would take half a day off work to visit Walter.

Occasionally a patient from C3 would have to be escorted to the hospital dentist. But very few of the patients had their own teeth. Most had dentures. They owned dentures, but seldom wore them, since most, at some time or other, had had their teeth con-fiscated, either for biting other patients or for forgetting to take

188

the teeth out at night and falling into the danger of swallowing them, or even for simply leaving the teeth around, by which they might become lost or misused, when confiscating them was safer, since at least the Staff (if not the patient) then knew where the teeth were.

Where they were would be in a large bowl. Whenever a nurse saw a patient sleeping with his teeth in, those teeth would be removed, rinsed meticulously in water and Milton, and placed in that bowl, which already contained more than a hundred pairs of National Health dentures, most of them belonging to patients who had died. Then if later the relatives of that patient were to write (allowing a full week) that they wished to visit, a simple process of trial and error would provide that patient with teeth, perhaps as many as a hundred and thirty pairs from the bowl being tried before a pair was found which would fit, was not too stained, and would not fall out when he smiled. If he smiled.

It was altogether more convenient for the Staff if the patients were without teeth. One of the patients in Ward C3, whose teeth had been in such excellent condition that they drew blood every time they met in a white-coated arm, had been escorted to the dentist and spent much of one day there, emerging with nothing in his mouth but his tongue, some raw and badly cut gums, and a great deal of blood. National Health teeth had thereafter been provided for him, and were kept in the large bowl.

The red-haired orderly showed Walter where, in the Recreation Room, to place Clifford's chair. There was a straight hardbacked chair against the wall next to where Clifford liked his chair to be, and Walter sat on that.

'Now, don't you be getting yourself too comfortable there, me boy. You'll be standing in line for your shave any minute now. Harold will sort you out.'

Walter looked at the Irish orderly with absolute incomprehension.

'You'll soon pick up these little rituals we have.'

Walter, who had never heard the word 'ritual' in his life before, became convinced that it meant something unpleasant and almost certainly painful. In this he was not very far from the truth.

It seemed that the men in the beds on the lefthand side of the ward were shaved on Mondays, Wednesdays and Fridays, the others on Tuesdays, Thursdays, and Fridays. The reason why everyone

189

had to be shaved on a Friday was because that was the day when the Chief Staff Nurse made his weekly inspection. No shaving was done on Saturdays or Sundays unless one of the patients should be inconsiderate enough to have a Saturday afternoon visitor.

Walter looked round at the other patients. He was now in a different world from the one which had contained his father, mother and the pigeons. It seemed very close to what his mother had told him of Hell, except that it manifestly lacked heat. Deformed demons, half man, half animal, moved around him, some looking at him, some through him. All seemed to be waiting for something, but he could not even guess at what it was. This was their ward, not his. Some of them must have been born here, sent as children, been here so long that they had forgotten the world outside. Why were they all waiting? What were they expecting?

Ben Gunn stood in the centre of the room, shouting obscenities at anyone who brushed or touched him. In the lefthand pocket of his jacket, there was an unused toilet roll, in the right a plastic cup. The cup was of dual use. It was an ashtray (for the hospital was not a prison; the patients were given a small amount of pocket money for cigarettes or sweets, and were allowed to smoke in the Recreation Room) and also a spittoon. Sometimes it was emptied.

When Walter saw Ben Gunn, he turned to Clifford, and pretended to be talking to him. Too late! Ben Gunn had spotted him, and although he had seen Walter only briefly the night before when Walter had been brought into the ward and put to bed, and not at all during the sexual assault because the lights had been out, Ben knew all the patients of C3 by sight and, knowing Walter's to be a fresh face, realized that this was the person he had attacked. He came to Walter, and stood close to him, his short legs almost touching Walter's knees.

Walter had stopped pretending to talk to Clifford, and was looking down at the polished floor. The sweet sickly stench of paraldehyde, which Ben Gunn always carried about with him, just as he carried his toilet roll and plastic cup, filled the little space there was between them, and grew even stronger as he opened his mouth, and cackled, 'Gawd, you're ugly! An ugly virgin! Cor!' Then he walked away, and the stench went with him.

Walter sat up straight, as his mother had taught him, in a hardbacked chair next to a man whose body he had handled as intimately as if it were his own. It was a different world. Hairy stinky old men touched him in the dark, and laughed at him before others. Walter looked at the screwed-up faces of the men about him. Jesus had made these men, as he had made all men. These were Jesus's mistakes, and for each He would get a cross. In the world Walter had left, there were people who could dance, sing, play musical instruments, paint, be leaders of men, like Mr Richards. There were people who looked nice, like Mrs Silver on Cosmetics or the filmstars he had seen in the papers. All those people were Jesus's successes, and for each of them He would get a tick. But if Jesus were perfect, as Walter's mother had insisted that He was, why had He not got ten out of ten? Why had He made so many mistakes?

And what were they waiting for, these mistakes, who paced up and down, or leaned against the wall, or shook, or dangled to one side over the arms of their wheelchairs, like marionettes whose strings have been cut? What did they want, these mistakes, who hugged themselves and made wordless noises – screams, gasps, screeches, grunts, mumbles, moans, whines? Some of the sounds the mistakes made seemed to be sounds of pleasure. How could they enjoy themelves in here, when all their bits had been so badly put together by Jesus?

As Walter looked at the other men in the Recreation Room, and saw how many different mistakes had been made by Jesus, a hand gripped his upper arm, and pulled him to his feet. Walter let out a small cry of surprise, but when he saw the face that went with the hands, he gave no resistance to the man's pull. The man's head was too big, and his eyes seemed unfocused and were directed either to the ground or to the sky, so that the pupils almost totally disappeared under the slanted eyelids. And the man mumbled, asking questions without waiting for answers, since he himself provided both question and answer.

'Which side you sleep? Right, innit? Yes, right. That'll be it. Must be right. Jack's bed, that was. Died last week, dinnee? Tuesday, wossit? Think it was. Might not, though. Might been after that.'

During all this, the man maintained a tight grip on Walter's arm, and pulled him towards a queue he was organizing. Starting at the entrance to the Wash Room, it curled into the Recreation Room, and ran along one wall.

'Get you shaved today, see? Jack got shaved Tuesday. Thassit. I remember. Tuesday Jack died; he'd had a shave. Here, you! You stand there and don't move. Got to learn. Learn you, when you're new. I learn you. Me. I'm Harold. How d'you do?'

Harold held his hand to be shaken, and Walter shook it. Then he patted Walter on the shoulder, his eyes squinting upwards, and said, 'There's a good lad. Got to learn.' It seemed to Walter that there was a great deal of shaking hands in this hospital. He wondered if it were a practice in all hospitals. Meanwhile, he was in for a wait. There were sixteen men in the queue before him and others round the corner whom he could not see. Harold had also disappeared round the corner into the Wash Room, and later Walter was to find out why.

The queue moved forward slowly, and Harold returned from the direction of the Wash Room to make hurried trips round the Recreation Room, each time bringing back a patient whose day this was for shaving, and placing him in the line behind Walter. Then he would move up and down the line, pushing at the waiting men, demanding that they keep the line straight, and pulling at the shoulders of those who stooped.

With ten men before him and twelve behind him, Walter's feeling of aloneness became absolute. He had carried it around all morning. For moments when he had been helping Clifford, it had been pushed into the background, but it was still there. Now it was full, complete, all there was. This was their world, not his. When his father and mother had been alive, he had never thought about the future. Now there seemed not to be one, no point in it, not here, not in here, not in this place, not like this. Not queueing for a shave, not cleaning and feeding Clifford, not being attacked and then laughed at by Ben Gunn. Not here in this room, not locked up, not in here, not as a helpless watcher of pacing, hearer of screaming, of shouting, of anger. Not as a smeller of perpetual stenches... Not as an unwilling witness of the mistakes, the smelly angry mistakes that Jesus had made. His crosses. Walter wouldn't be a cross. He wouldn't wait for Paradise here, not as a cross, not as a mistake; he wouldn't be that. His mother had taught him to be good, to do things; he could do things. He had a job. She had said to him, 'Are you going to do well, and make me

proud of you?' and he had. They had liked his work at Woolworth's, and his mother had received a letter from Mr Richards.
She had read it out aloud to Walter and his father. Mr Richards
had written, 'Dear Mrs Williams, Your son, Walter, is working
so hard, and doing his job as well as any normal person could do it.
I am very pleased to inform you that we wish to keep him on, at
a wage of three pounds and ten shillings per week. Walter is a
good boy, whom we here think you should be proud of. Sincerely,
R. H. Richards, Manager.'

His mother had cried, and hugged him. He had made her proud.
She had looked at him with tears on her face, and said, 'Now
there's nothing wrong with you. Don't let anyone ever say there
is. Anyone who has a letter like this to show has nothing to worry
about. Three pounds ten! They're not exactly putting a strain on
the Woolworth millions, but it could be a lot worse. You have a
job. A job for life, I should think, if you want it. Good boy!
I'm very very proud of you. So is your dad.'

And his father had put his paper down, and said, 'Aye, lad.
Keep up the good work.'

Walter could remember that.

4

*It was impossible to give every patient a straight
parting without the application of a great
deal of lavender-scented brilliantine*

Six months later, when Harold was moved to Ward C2, and
Walter had proved to the Staff what he was capable of, Walter
was given the responsibility of Harold's old job.

Six chairs had to be placed in a line before the six wash basins
in the Wash Room. A patient had to be placed in each of the six
chairs, and each patient had to have lather applied to the area of
his face which was to be shaved. This enabled the nurses to move
from one patient to the next with a razor containing an extremely
blunt Seven O'Clock blade, and scrape off the lather without
stopping or putting down the razor.

The nurse worked quickly, and Walter had to dash about, as
Harold had done, to keep up with him. Having now lived in
Ward C3 for six months, he knew which patients were on which
side of the ward. He rushed from the Wash Room to the
Recreation Room, picking out the men whose day it was to be
shaved, as Harold had done, and then back into the Wash Room
to use the shaving brush and stick of shaving soap to make a
lather and apply it to the faces of the waiting patients.

Unlike Harold, Walter did not insist that the line of men be
straight, nor did he pull back stooping shoulders, nor did he lather
all six faces one after the other, since his own experience of
Harold's method had taught him that, by the time the nurse
reached the third face, the soap on the remaining three would
have dried and. be beginning to itch, which, taken with the

bluntness of the razorblade, had caused several of the patients to develop rashes. The bluntness of the blade was not due to any intention of causing pain by the nurses. They themselves suspected that the hospital administration, for reasons of economy, bought razorblades in bulk, and that these blades were 'seconds' – rejects which were sold off cheaply. Also they were bound by Standing Orders which laid down that one blade should be made to last for fifty shaves.

Walter watched the nurse carefully and calculated the speed at which each nurse worked. By spending less time in forming the men into line, which, under his regime, was no longer as long or as straight as it had been, he was able always to keep two chins ahead.

However, in spite of Walter's improvements in the routine of shaving, there was one incident of violence, caused by the tender and painful rash of an extremely large patient, and the bluntness of the razorblade in use on that particular morning.

Walter was working up a creamy foam on a patient whose head always had to be held while the nurse shaved him, since the usual state of that head was to be in perpetual motion. Meanwhile the nurse applied his razor to the chin of the very large man in the next chair.

At the moment of contact between razor and chin, the large patient shot his arms up into the air, and stood. His sudden movement sent the nurse staggering backwards and the razor flying through the air. The chair was overturned, as the large patient made for the door, and the bristles of Walter's shaving brush blocked the shaking-headed patient's nasal passages.

Before Walter and the nurse had time to collect their thoughts, the large patient was back in the Wash Room, blood dripping from his chin, and a heavy chair held above his head. It seemed both to Walter and the nurse that the intentions of this patient were not peaceable. It took the nurse only the fraction of a second to come to this conclusion, and only another fraction of a second to get himself inside one of the toilet cubicles, where (the cubicles having, of course, no locks) he placed his back against the door, his feet against the base of the WC, and leaned at a thirty-degree angle. There he would be safe, at least for a short while, and if the large patient should attempt to climb over the door, he must relinquish his hold on the chair to do so.

Unwilling to be parties to what might happen, the other patients in the Wash Room ran quickly out of it, leaving Walter and the shaking-headed man, who alone among them all was unaware of what was happening.

Thwarted by the speed of the nurse, the large patient turned his attention towards Walter, who backed away, shaving brush in one hand, stick of shaving soap in the other. Neither seemed to be an adequate weapon with which to take on a man of six foot three, holding a chair over his head. The large patient advanced and Walter retreated. Then the shaking-headed man, who had soap up his nose, sneezed. The sneeze was so loud that it sounded like a threat, and the large man turned sharply to see who was attacking him from the rear.

It was only a moment, but Walter used it to its full advantage, and dashed out of the Wash Room, disappearing into the crowd outside, to find the other nurses on duty and tell them what had happened.

But the nurses made excuses. They were busy. It was up to the nurse doing the shaving to control his patient.

Walter gave up trying to persuade the other nurses to do anything. He stood at a distance from the Wash Room at a point where he could observe both the entrance and the exit.

He stood listening, surrounded by noise and chatter. The constant background buzz of jabbering and gibberish continued, but inside his head there was silence. He was waiting for a sound which he knew would come, which would cut through both the silence inside his head and the jabber outside.

When it came, it was not as he had imagined it. He had not thought that it would sound like an animal, like the breathless pathetic scream of a rabbit. Four sounds. Four animal noises, and then nothing.

The buzz of chatter did not stop. The patients of Ward C3 were well used to the noises caused by pain and to the meaningless sounds of hysteria. Only Walter knew. Only Walter waited and watched. But not for long.

The large patient reappeared from the Wash Room, looked about him, puzzled, and then moved into the crowd of jabbering voices. He was no longer holding a chair.

Walter went into the Wash Room.

The man up whose nose he had inadvertently applied shaving

soap, now had no nose. He had no skull or teeth; he had no longer a chin to be shaved. His ears remained. Between them there was a concave of the different kinds of matter which had, a few minutes earlier, made up a face, lathered with shaving soap.

Three weeks later, there was an Inquiry, at which Walter was asked to identify the large man who had held the chair.

Walter did so. He told the Inquiry what all three nurses who had been on duty at the time of the incident had instructed him to say. He said that the patient who had been killed had been irritating the larger man, who had rushed out and come back with a chair. He said that he and the nurse in charge had tried to disarm the large man, but had been pushed aside.

Nobody cross-examined Walter; he was not subjected to harsh questioning. What he said was written down. Nobody asked him whether either he or the nurse had sustained cuts or bruises while struggling with the violent patient. The Inquiry did not inquire how the shaking-headed patient, who had never spoken one word to anybody during his sixteen years in the hospital, had been able to irritate the large man into such extreme and passionate violence.

The large man was not asked for his own version of what had happened. He was sent to another hospital.

Walter was thanked, and praised for his bravery.

A word much used by the nurses and orderlies was the word 'condemned'. They would say, 'I'm condemning these trousers,' and proceed to tear them into two halves. Or they might say, 'This jacket needs condemning,' and pull a sleeve off it. The only way their requests for new clothes, bedding, shoes, or any article of necessary equipment could be met, was if they had first 'condemned' the article in such a way as to render it unusable.

Once a month, 'condemned' articles were replaced. (Most condemnations took place at the end of the month.) Brooms, buckets, shoe-brushes, facecloths, soap, toilet rolls, all had to be accounted for, and the accounts audited.

Every Friday was a day of pomp and ceremony. Much work and speed were necessary if all were to be made ready for the Chief Staff Nurse's Friday afternoon inspection.

The open ends of all pillowslips had to face away from the door of the ward, so that the Chief Staff Nurse would not see a pillow (grey and white striped, usually stained) protruding from

197

its slip. All the taps had to be polished, and a responsible patient set to stand guard over them to make sure that nobody used them after they had been made to shine.

The bare boards of both Recreation Room and Dormitory had to be polished. One patient would carry a large tin of wax polish and a stick, with which to scoop it out and dollop it onto the floor-boards at regular intervals. Four other patients would work with bumpers, pushing and pulling them to work the polish into the wood until the floor had a shine which would gain the approval of the Chief Staff Nurse. These bumpers were like doormats with bristles, which faced down, and which had on top a heavy cast-iron square, the same size as the mat. Attached to the square was a large and heavy pole with which to push the bumper backwards and forwards. Polishing the floor was tiring, and required strength. No patient liked doing it, and those who were picked had to be strictly supervised.

Since mentally handicapped patients come, like the human beings whom they in certain respects resemble, in different sizes (these sizes being, if anything, even more varied than the sizes of the human beings whom, etc, some being abnormally large, both wide and high, and some abnormally childlike), the beds in which they were to spend most of their lives were also of different sizes. Such differences would not do for the Chief Staff Nurse. Whatever size the bed might be, on Friday afternoons the iron rail at its foot had to be in line with all the other beds, so that some of the smaller beds, and the lockers beside them, might be anything up to two feet away from the wall, with consequent discomfort to the smaller patients and inconvenience for the orderlies. After the inspection, they would all be pushed back.

Since seventy chins had to be shaved on Friday mornings, Walter was excused from any of the cleaning jobs, but during the six months before Harold had left the ward, Walter had pushed and pulled the heavy bumpers back and forwards, had polished the taps, helped to make beds and re-site lockers, applied Cardinal Red Polish to the tiled window-ledges, dusted the bedside lockers, cleaned the toilet bowls, scrubbed the Wash Room floor, applied brilliantine smelling of lavender to the heads of the non-ambulant patients, and combed their ill-cut hair so that every patient had a parting on the correct side of his head, and each parting was as straight as the footrails of all the beds.

The barber, who visited the ward once a week to cut thirty-five heads of hair in under two hours, referred to his work as 'sheep-shearing'. It was impossible, therefore, to give every patient a straight parting without the application of a great deal of brilliantine, the stench of which was as overpowering and even more sickly than the smell of paraldehyde. The Chief Staff Nurse never seemed to notice that several of the patients had red and sore eyes, caused by the lavender-scented brilliantine which had run down their foreheads. If the taps and the floor shone, and all the pillowslips were facing the right way, he was happy. And his happiness was what everyone hoped for.

Once a week, there was a film show, always a comedy, sometimes silent – the Keystone Kops, W. C. Fields, Chaplin, Abbott, and Costello, Laurel and Hardy; since most of the patients had poor memories, often the same film was shown two weeks running. Everyone was obliged to go to church on Sunday, which was easily arranged, since the church was inside the grounds of the hospital. Both church and hospital had been built in 1839, the hospital then being a workhouse, and its paupers had been held to be as much in need of the consolations of religion as of food and creature comforts. Religion had in those days frequently replaced both food and comforts and that it did not still do so may be accounted some form of progress.

Those patients who were allowed out for walks outside the grounds did so in an orderly crocodile, two by two like Noah's animals, except that the male patients turned right outside the hospital gates, and the female patients left; there was no intention, as Noah had, that they should increase and multiply. Neither the male nor the female patients were on wet days allowed to go out at all. This would never have done for Noah, but the drying of wet hair, clothes, and feet would have meant more work for the hospital Staff.

The days passed, and Walter gave up counting them. He knew now that 'they' would never realize that they had made a mistake, and send him home. His life had become submerged within the routine of the hospital. He became a 'trusty', a friend to the nurses and orderlies. From the day he had lied for them, they had begun to treat him as someone who was neither a patient nor a member of Staff, but as someone who just happened to be there, someone on whom they could rely to help them. Ward C3 was, of course, where they needed help most.

More and more of his time was spent in helping others, and less and less in looking back, or expecting his mother to leave Jesus in order to come and collect him.

There were moments when he heard himself sighing, or caught himself thinking about Woolworth's. Someone else would be collecting the rubbish now. That someone else would be operating his, Walter's, press. That someone else would be using Walter's wirecutters to make the bales, and would be patted on the back and praised by Mr Richards. He wondered whether anyone at Woolworth's had asked what had happened to him, whether anyone had tried to find out where he was.

There were other moments when he thought of the pigeons, usually at night, as he lay awake, listening to the man in the bed beside him talking to God. He would silently mouth their names, and see each one in flight. But as time passed, the list of names he could remember grew shorter, and the number of times he thought either of the pigeons or Woolworth's grew fewer. The natural life of a pigeon is not long, and cats may shorten it.

He was neither happy nor unhappy; he just was. His birthdays came and went, and so did Jesus's. Jesus's birthdays were celebrated with balloons, trimmings and roast chicken. Paper hats were worn by Staff and patients, and a bottle of brown ale was issued to everyone. One year a Children's Brass Band from a local school arrived (an hour later than they were expected), and the seven hundred and thirty-four male patients sang those bits of Christmas carols that they could remember, and hummed the rest. Some rocked, more excited than the children, and some cried, perhaps because they remembered happier Christmases, shared long ago with mothers, fathers, brothers, perhaps merely because of a generalized surfeit of emotion. The memories of such patients being, as is known, poor, the second explanation for their tears may be considered more likely.

Walter remembered all the words of all the carols, and sang them in a flat, tuneless, but loud and purposeful manner. He tried not to think of Christmases past; he tried not to upset himself. He sat, as always, beside Clifford, and held Clifford's hand, and if he found his thoughts drifting away out of his control towards the memory of his mother's voice singing, 'Away in a Manger',

'Silent Night', or 'Unto Us a Child is Born, Unto Us a Son is Given', he would squeeze Clifford's hand tighter, shake his own head from side to side, and try to laugh. Then he would turn to Clifford, and sing the words of the carol into Clifford's ear, as if he were trying to explain to Clifford the wonderful miracle of the Nativity.

Clifford gave no outward sign of hearing Walter or the carols or the Children's Brass Band. If Jesus existed for Clifford, He had not provided for His creation any way by which Clifford could join in the celebration of his Maker's birth.

Later a paper hat would be placed on Clifford's head, and the food Walter would put into his mouth would be special food. Brown ale would be held to his lips to drink, and he would drink it. But it might as well have been the vinegar Christ was given; it might as well have been medicine, champagne, or even bleach. Clifford was unable to take part in the joy of Christmas. He was unable to exhibit any pleasure in or gratitude for the fact that, thanks to Jesus, he, Clifford, had been saved.

5

People didn't laugh at the leader of the crocodile

'I want to go home, and be a joy to my mother. I'll be self-contented then.'

It was ten past eleven, and the man in the next bed to Walter was talking to himself.

'Even though she's over sixty, she's the most true and honest woman in the whole of Banstead or any other area to those who know her.' (The man in the next bed was himself over sixty.) 'If I had a pound note for every lie these legal and medical people have told me, I'd be a very rich man. The worst one has moved to Dorking now, but that won't help him, don't let him think so; it'd do well for them to be more honest. They'll all be crossed off the Legal Register . . . Pills for internal tension!' He made a noise of derision. 'Trying to break my mind down.'

'Pains in my head, doctor. Are you a Jew? It's as well to know. They want me in here until the land returns to certain owners. I'm not allowed to say their names. They've taken out a court order to stop me naming them.' A cry. 'I'll not be silenced.'

'There's none so chilly as our poor Willy, and he's now dead, poor thing. One worm said to his friend, "Let's go and have a piece in dead Ernest." Even a so-called madman can tell jokes, did you not know that?'

'You have your mother's eyes, Billy. That's what they always said to me. Always. Wasn't that funny? They're blue, you see, like hers. This is just a temporary assignment, being in here. Being a waiter's not a job you'd choose, now, is it? It's very depressing when you can't find the right job. I get awfully sad some days, mother. Being in here, it's not good for my health. I know you think I'm a perfectionist, but this really is not the place to spend too much time. I'm not perfect; nobody is. But I do try; it's just that I have my sad days. I can't get out of bed for being so depressed. It's the people in here depress me. I know I shouldn't say this, but there's some of them in here are more than a little odd.'

'If you come to collect me at the end of term, could you bring my cricket pads? I can't bat very well, but my knees are sore from kneeling so often to pray. If God is good, I may sleep tonight, without crying for you to touch me. I miss you so much, mummy. Please come and fetch me home.'

Muttering. 'From forth thy barren womb, shall come a child . . . Here shall I be born, King of Bliss.' The man cried, and fell asleep, and Walter fell asleep also.

Later Walter was woken by the sound of heavy snoring. Low, deep, guttural and unusual noises were coming from the man in the next bed. They sounded like snores, but in all the years he had slept next to him, Walter had never heard him snore. After considering for some time what he should do, he got out of bed, and fetched the nurse on duty.

At four a.m. on July 12th, 1967, the man in the next bed to Walter's died of a heart attack.

Ten years had passed. He was a 'trusty'. They trusted him.

He had put on weight; the hospital food was mainly stodge. He was allowed to wear his own clothes, except that now they were too tight. The orderlies gave him good second-hand clothes, and he was allowed the use of an iron to keep them pressed. It was in the Staff's own interest to keep Walter happy. They found him a beige overall to do the dirtier jobs, such as the changing of Clifford, Albert and Maurice. It was a sign that he was one of them.

While others did hand-exercises, to teach them to co-ordinate eye and hand (ten years had passed; the treatment of the mentally ill progresses), while others made a man with five matchsticks, threaded beads, wove indifferent baskets, counted with buttons, played with plasticine (which was thought to lower the incidence of masturbation), scribbled drawings which, viewed by a sympathetic eye, were really quite like those of Dubuffet, and which

203

they carried about with them all day, made round shapes of cardboard, painted shells to be stuck on the sides of plant-pots, began (but seldom completed) rugs, worked with raffia to make brightly coloured tablemats, Walter undertook no such remedial or creative occupations, but merely assisted the Staff.

While others were herded like sheep, counted in and out of the ward, made to stand naked and shivering, holding onto the wall-bar in the Wash Room while Walter or one of the Staff gave them stripped washes known as 'Under the Arches', and were allowed baths only once a month, while they had to ask for sweets and cigarettes bought with their own pocket money, but kept locked away in the office, Walter drank beer in the office, sitting down with the nurses, and chatting. Except that Walter himself did not chat; he was attentive, but silent. One of the reasons that his position of privilege was permitted to continue was that he never boasted of it, or overstepped the mark.

As long as his duties were done, he was allowed outside the ward whenever he desired to be, allowed to walk the grounds of the hospital. Had he asked, he would probably even have been allowed outside the Main Gate on his own. They knew he would return. He was a 'trusty'. They trusted him.

Many times, while leading his crocodile of twelve mistakes, mis-shaped by Jesus, he could have run away, darted up the nearest alley and hidden, or jumped onto a passing bus before anyone could catch him. But where would he go? How would he live? What would he do to get money? The money from his mother's biscuit tin, which he had brought to the hospital with him, had of course disappeared. Only her diamanté Eiffel Tower ear-rings had been left in his jacket pocket.

And if he were to run away, who would look after Clifford?

While leading the crocodile, he had noticed that those who lived in the real world, the world to which he had once belonged, wore clothes dissimilar to those he remembered. The women, in particular, looked very different. They wore more make-up on their faces, and had shorter hair. Some even showed their knees.

Walter found himself trying to remember what the naked women in the mucky books he had been shown in Woolworth's looked like. If he concentrated hard enough, he could bring into his mind a picture of Mike pressing his girlfriend against the lift gate in the yard at the back of Woolworth's, and he could perform in his mind that process known by cameramen as 'tracking' (though he had never met a cameraman, and did not know the word), by which a part of the picture is made to grow, pushing the rest out of the frame, and the part which grew would be Mike's hand as it lifted the girl's skirt until her knickers were showing, and then moved inside the knickers, so that the hand itself would be lost to sight, and only its outline could be seen, moving up and down. By this time, the outline of the hand would have increased considerably in size; it would be occupying the whole of the picture.

He looked at the women and young girls whom he saw outside the hospital grounds, and imagined for a moment that he was Mike, and that women liked him and would allow him to lift up their skirts. These thoughts worried and excited him, and he would place a hand inside his trouser pocket, and hold himself until the thoughts went away.

The men who walked behind him, holding on to one another's hands, were not interested in what they saw on their walks. They did not notice the people who stood and stared at them, or those in passing vehicles, who pointed and laughed. Walter had ceased his old habit of pointing and laughing back. It was the other men, the men behind him, at whom such people were pointing. They were the ones who were laughed at, not he. He was at the front; the people would believe him to be a member of Staff. People did not laugh at those who spent their lives looking after the sick. They did not laugh at the nurse who followed the crocodile, and would not laugh at the man who led.

Sometimes, if the weather were fine and the nurse on duty indulgent, Walter would be allowed to take Clifford on these walks, pushing his wheelchair at the front of the crocodile. Clifford liked walks. When left behind, he moved his foot up and down on the footrest of his wheelchair. It was too lethargic to be called stamping but Walter knew what it meant. Every time he was not able to take Clifford with him, he would go and sit with Clifford on his return, hold his hand, and tell him what he had seen.

His own interest in the real world, which he saw on these walks, had diminished over the years. He noticed the changes in fashion, buildings being knocked down; none of it concerned him. Some of the buildings stood, half-demolished, for years, and reminded him of houses his mother had taken him to look at during the war, with exposed wallpaper fading, fireplaces crumbling. As one year followed another, the walks outside became more and more like the film shown in the hospital on Wednesday evenings. They could distract him for a few moments, but as he returned to the hospital and entered the Lodge Gates, it was as if a hand had been held up between projector and screen to remind him that what he had been watching was only make-believe. What was real for him now was the hospital and the routine. This was his real world. It had to be. He would never get out of it.

WALTER

As when the dove
Laments her love,
All on the naked spray,
When he returns
No more she mourns,
But loves the live-long day.
Billing, cooing, panting, wooing!
Melting murmurs! Silver grove!
Melting murmurs! Lasting love!

JOHN GAY
Acis and Galatea

PART ONE

June

1

Her mother had always dressed June in yellow.
It was a colour the fast American drivers
would find easier to see.

'Are you sure you're going to be all right?'

June didn't reply. She moved around the room, sipping red wine from her glass, and picking up Christmas cards and staring at them. As each card reached eye-level, the picture on it became blurred, out of focus. She had to hold each card at arm's length in order to read who had sent it. The action of lifting and focusing became automatic.

'I said, "Are you sure you'll be all right?"' June moved the wine around the inside of her mouth with her tongue, and continued to inspect the cards.

The Heart Foundation. The National Trust. Mentally Handicapped Children. Shelter. Spastics. Autistic Children. The Canine Defence League. Cystic Fibrosis. 'Enter Ye In at the Strait Gate'. Children's Fund, Bromley. The Brain Research Trust – a picture of some Deadly Nightshade. There was even one with a poem by Patience Strong: who the hell was that from? 'And underneath it all, the promise of spring.'

'June, I asked if you . . .' Clive's voice trailed away.

She had opened a card with a picture of a fat partridge on the front, and thought she read, 'This card has helped Doctor Barnardo's to purchase another child.' That couldn't be right.

She had dropped each card after having read it, and found that she had neither the strength nor the inclination to pick them up. Clive spoke louder, determined not to be ignored. Well,

3

she would not, did not ignore him. No sooner had he pronounced the words, 'Are you –' than June had swung round on him, hurling the two-hundred-year-old rummer through the air, and smashing it into tiny glittering fragments against the chiffonier.

'For Christ's sake, stop it! Stop it! I'll go mad if you don't.'

As always she had aimed just to miss him, and as always he had stood absolutely still, flinching only at the thought of one valuable antique damaging another.

There was a silence, and also a dent in the top drawer of the chiffonier. They both noticed the dent at the same time.

Clive spoke quietly, his voice trailing off into a prolonged sigh. 'Well, that's knocked fifty pounds off the value of that.' June covered her ears, and screamed her Maker's name in the direction of the ceiling. Upstairs Baby John woke, and began to cry. Again Clive spoke quietly, 'Does blasphemy make you feel better?' June glared at him, threatening that if he didn't go, didn't move, didn't leave, didn't get out before saying another word, she would throw something else, but he stood where he was, and said just as softly as before, 'I simply asked if you were sure you'd be all right.'

They moved together, she towards the Elizabeth Frink sculpture, *Harbinger Bird IV*, he with meticulous precision towards the broom cupboard. It was a routine in which he was well practised.

Then he was back, with dustpan and brush, sweeping up the glittering splinters of what had so recently been worth twenty pounds. June sat in an armchair, covered her face with both hands, and listened to the sounds made by brush and splintered glass on bare floorboards – floorboards which she had herself stripped and polished.

He said, 'There's chicory and picking cheese in the fridge. Try not to let it go bad.' Would he never go?

He shook the glittering splinters in the dustpan, looked at them, and sighed. 'There are various tins and things in the pantry. You shouldn't starve. Try to eat something, even if only for Baby John's sake.' Then he stood, leaving the dustpan and brush where they were, and came slowly towards her.

As he drew closer to her, she thought of, and then rejected,

4

the idea of spitting in his face. It would be comic; she was out of practice.

He laid the palm of his right hand on the top of her head, as if he were a priest giving her a blessing, and said, still softly, 'Here, come on, love! It's only for a few days. I'll go up, and quiet him. Will you be all right?'

Then he waited, but, since she did not move, took the hand from her head, and began to turn away. June grabbed the hand, and held it, pressing it tightly between both her own hands, then bringing it up against her face.

Clive sank into a crouching position beside the chair, and used the index finger of his free hand to draw a line down her forehead, over her nose and lips, and round under her chin, where he gently rubbed the backs of his fingers. It was one of his more irritating displays of affection, this tracing of her profile, since he knew, if he stopped to remember, that her profile was the feature of herself which June liked least.

'Why don't you ring someone? Ask them round for a Christmas drink.' June released his hand from hers, and they both remained still and silent, listening to Baby John's crying, each waiting for the other to make the next move.

It was Clive who made it. His calves and thighs had begun to ache; he would have to stand before cramp made standing impossible. He stood. Then he went upstairs.

She sobbed silently and painfully, biting the back of her hand to prevent noise, and listening as Clive paced backwards and forwards above her head, across the new carpet which covered the creaking floorboards, cooing sweet nothings to Baby John whose own tears had now ceased.

Clive struggled to close the front door of their newly acquired house. Her house now. The recent damp spell had caused all the wood to swell. All the doors were difficult to open, and, once opened, almost impossible to close. The front door was easier to close from the inside, easier to open from the outside. The house, like June, did not like being left.

He did not hear her whisper. He pulled sharply at the knocker, taking the door by surprise. Just so he had surprised June, with

5

his announcement that he intended to spend Christmas with his wife.

The door closed. The consequent sound of the windows shaking in their frames echoed down the street, and Baby John screamed. It was one of his wolf-like gutsy screams. The respectable Jewish neighbour to the left would be lifting the receiver of her telephone to make contact with the respectable Catholic neighbour to the right. The road in which she lived, June thought, might aptly have been named 'Minority Row'.

The Jewish lady on the left had put in an appearance that very morning, picking her way cautiously down the garden path as if it were laid with landmines, holding a piece of old newspaper in hands heavy with rings. What the newspaper contained appeared to be a cross between caviar and the droppings of mice.

'Excuse me. I hope you don't mind. But you've been banging against the wall, haven't you?'

June had wondered if she had overlooked some by-law. If she had, she would soon know it. 'Yes, I was trying to move some old bookshelves.'

'I think you've disturbed some mice. They've been coming through the fireplace.' There was, June knew, a Magi-Coal Electric Fire in that fireplace. Not even mice would have braved real flames. 'I had a man from the Council round, and he asked me to ask you if you'd mind putting this down. Mind you don't touch it. Not with bare flesh. It's terribly poisonous.'

The urge to pick up a handful and place it in her mouth while the woman watched, had lasted only a moment. Instead June had taken the two sides of the newspaper into her own hands, and had thanked the woman for her trouble. Then she had watched her glancing down at the litter in the front garden. Theirs was not a dirty street, but every piece of paper dropped in it seemed to find its way into this garden. This was because the foundations of the garden wall had collapsed, and the wall leaned in towards the house, so that the gate had to be propped permanently open.

Now Clive gave a tug at the permanently open gate, and glanced up at the window behind which Baby John was screaming his wolf-scream.

6

June remained where she was, watching him unlock the car door. At every step of his progress from the front door to the car, she had said to herself, 'If he goes any further, I will do it. If he moves another inch, it will prove that I must. It will confirm that I'm right.'

He sat in the driver's seat, and turned the key to start the engine, and with it, the car radio. She thought, 'He's doing everything in slow motion to make me squirm.'

What she persisted in calling 'the theme from *Elvira Madigan*' and Clive called the Second Movement of Mozart's Piano Concerto Number – well, what the hell did it matter what Clive called it? – that music floated through the window of the car. It was another sign, another proof. They had driven around Winderton in that car, listening to that music, while she had huddled in the passenger seat, pressing herself against the door in her dirty white mac, feeling like an inmate from the Local Asylum, being taken out for the day. She had sat with her fingers interlocked, the tips of both index fingers touching and pointing like the steeple of a church. *Here's the church; here's the steeple. Look inside, and – look! no people.*

Of course, in *Elvira Madigan*, they had both done it; they had done it together.

The cat's-eyes in the middle of the road had floated towards them, giving the impression that she was being taken somewhere, and the need to keep her own eyes open and her body still had seemed acute. Movement was vulnerability – any movement; it suggested progression. It implied that one was moving through time, not standing still in it. She did not accept the progression. There was none.

Clive's car pulled away from the kerb, and was gone.

In the hall, she moved her hand slowly over the rail of the banister, and felt its roughness. The caustic soda she had used to strip off the old paint had hidden in the joints, only to reappear after she had applied three coats of polyurethane. Its reappearance took the form of little white bubbles, rough to touch, which made the rails look as if old paint had been left on them. Weeks of careful work marred by a poison which hides, only to reappear after everything had been glossed over.

7

The gas fire hissed in time to the wind outside, and more grit dropped from the ventilator onto the newly painted white hearth. Stupid to paint a hearth white. Defying the laws of nature again.

She turned on the radio to drown out the sound of crying from upstairs. 'This is *Nightline* on M.B.C., and you're talking to Tony Fox. Now let's see who the next caller is going to be, and remember, please remember: first names only, please.'

The wind also slid through the Vent-Axia in the kitchen, and blew out the pilot light of the water heater. North Sea Gas floated around the house, reminding her that it couldn't kill her, but was prepared, unless she turned it off, to make what was left of her life as unpleasant as possible. Therefore June refused to turn it off. Life *should* smell as it was – stale, arid, sickly and expensive.

The North-West Gas Board could whistle for its money. She would not be here to pay for misspent, free-floating, high-speed North Sea Gas. The Board could whistle as its faulty equipment whistled. It could whistle to the moon, if it so wished. June would not be heading in that direction.

She looked at the line of coffee mugs. '*I have measured out my life with coffee spoons.*' She had no favourite among the mugs, but always used the same spoon, a mass-produced Woolworth's apostle-spoon, apt for the measurement of such a useless life.

'*Good morning, madam. I am conducting a Survey on the Meaning of Life. How do you see yourself as using life? How do you occupy its measured hours?*' '*I empty full ashtrays into a pedal-bin.*' June emptied a full ashtray into the pedal-bin in the kitchen, and wondered how it would be to climb inside the black plastic bag which lined her dustbin. Would she be able to manage the operation, while holding a glass of water in one hand and the sixty-nine pills she had saved in the other? Would she then be able to swallow the pills, throw away the glass, and just have time, before blessed unconsciousness supervened, to replace the lid of the dustbin from the inside? Perhaps she might be able to close the plastic bag, by pulling in the top and securing it from below with an elastic band.

By Wednesday she would certainly be ready for collection, more than ready. She tried to imagine the expression which would creep over the black dustman's face, as he watched what he had thrown into the cart making its way between the teeth and rollers of its mechanism.

No flowers by request. Mourners should make their own way to the Municipal Rubbish Dump, Green Lanes, Didsbury. Ashes to ashes, carpet-sweepings to dust, non-returnable bottles to un-burnable plastics.

June found the sixty-nine pills she had hidden, and counted them. Once upon a time, she couldn't now remember when, but at some time, Clive had said, 'You can't begrudge her the odd day or two. You really can't, love, be sexually jealous.' And now, time having passed and memory blurred, not thirty minutes ago, in this house, decorated by her, paid for by him, he had said, 'Myra's pregnant. I can't afford to upset her.' They must have been odd days indeed, if Myra had been receiving visits from the Archangel Gabriel.

He had tried his best not to show his pleasure. He had tried to make the pregnancy sound like an irritating mistake, just another vexing trap which life had laid for him, but the tiny horizontal lines at the corners of his eyes had gained small upward-pointing additions, as if he had marked his own handiwork and given himself alpha for effort – the effort he claimed he had never made.

June lifted bastard Baby John from his cot, and placed her cheek against his soft lolling head. She and Clive had invested in an extra-wide double bed, because of the restless nights they would suffer with Baby John. Now she had the restless nights with Baby John, while Clive had them with . . . She imagined Myra sitting up in the centre of the bed, reeking of Johnson's Baby Powder and Boot's Lavender Water. The woman from next door (Number Twenty-Six: June knew the front of the house well) would have been in to do Myra's hair. All over the country, Friday night was a Myra night. In every village, town, and city, in isolated farmhouses, in crofts and bothies, pink brushed-nylon bedjackets were sitting up in bed, squeezing their plump mottled thighs together to hold back a secret, and to keep in the rolled-up Marriage Licences they were using as Tampaxes.

Downstairs on the glass-topped table, among those Christmas cards which were not littering the floor, there were sixty-nine

9

pieces of a jigsaw which needed bringing together. She had hoarded them like a miser. They were of different sizes, different shapes and colours, some tablets, small and white, some capsules, some spansules, green and black, black and red, yellow and black, the colour of hornets, always black somewhere. They were like sweets; she had saved up her sweeties. There were sixty-nine.

Sixty-nine ways out.

She rocked unwanted Baby John in her arms, and began to sing:

> There was a man
> Went round the town,
> To hunt a supper up and dow-how-hown.
> He feels his cash
> To count his pence,
> And all he had was just six cents.
>
> He finds at last
> A right cheap place,
> And stealeth in with bashful fa-hay-hace.
> The bill of fare
> He runneth through
> To see what his six cents would do.
>
> The waiter he
> To him doth call,
> And whispers softly, 'One fish ba-haw-hall.'
> The waiter roars
> It through the hall.
> The guests then start at, 'One fish ball!'
>
> The scantness of
> The fare he sees.
> 'A piece of bread now, if you plea-hee-hease.'

'You get no bread,' she said. 'You get no bread, Baby John, with one fish ball.'

'What's wrong with your marriage, Mrs Jephcott?' The woman

10

had rested her right elbow on her right knee, and leaned forward, and June had seen her glance at the tiny gold watch on her thin fragile wrist four times in the last five minutes. The wrist carried no scars. Only the mark made by the watch.

'I want to know what you think is wrong with it, not what you say your husband thinks.' God, she was careful! 'What you say your husband thinks'! Why couldn't she admit that she didn't believe a word of it, that she had guessed that June wasn't a 'Mrs' anybody, that June had a husband, it was true, but that he was someone else's husband? What June had was a lover of seven years' standing. At which thought, June had summoned up a picture of Clive, standing to attention like a schoolboy in a corner of the bedroom, and then another of him standing naked with all his bodily parts at attention, and she had smiled at the picture, and then, without thinking, said aloud, 'A seven-year erection,' and had heard her own voice saying it in that quiet dark room, and seen the expression on the face of the woman sitting opposite.

'How many more minutes have I got?'

The woman had then looked at her watch properly for the first time, without any attempt at deceit, and replied, 'Well, I think we could usefully spend the last ten minutes summing up, and work out where we might start from next time.'

June had laughed, and then stood, looking down at the woman. 'There won't be a next time. I'm afraid I'm not very good at sums.'

The woman had shown no surprise. Clearly this had happened to her often. 'That's up to you, of course, but aren't you being a little unfair? I did mention that Marriage Guidance is an ongoing thing, not an instant remedy. We have to end this interview in ten . . . well, in eight minutes now, because someone else is waiting,' but June had reached the door, and turned, and said, 'Please don't concern yourself. I've decided what to do.'

'May I know what it is?'

June had looked at the brown linoleum. 'There isn't the time to tell you.' She had opened the door, and stepped out into the corridor, where there had, indeed, been another woman waiting. The woman had looked up at June, and then at her watch, and

June had said, 'I hope you're good at arithmetic,' and moved on out into the street before the waiting woman could answer.

Baby John had been unable to make his choice known, and so she had chosen for him; she had given birth to him. If she had made the opposite choice, and had aborted him, she would now be free to carry out her plan without having to worry about his safety.

It was Christmas Eve. To do it now would be best. No one would come near for three days, and, since Boxing Day fell on a Sunday, Monday was also a holiday. To do it now would mean that she was as sure as she could be of not being interrupted. Ever.

There was still the problem of Baby John, however. She had no way of knowing how long a two-month-old baby could last without nourishment. It was too late to ring up *The Daily Telegraph* Information Service, and, strangely enough, it was something they had never mentioned at the Dame Alice Harkness School for Girls. Nor could she remember that Doctor Spock had offered the information as part of what every mother should know.

If she attempted to leave him on the doorstep of one of her respectable neighbours, with a note of his feeding times pinned to his bedjacket, she would almost certainly be noted and invited in for tea and ginger-nuts. If not that, then they would come battering at the door when they found him, phone the Police and the Ambulance Service; they were not people who could leave well alone. Nor would simple honesty serve her. She could not say, 'Excuse me, Mrs Goldberg, but since you don't celebrate Christmas, I wondered if you'd mind looking after Baby John until the Festivities are over, after which he will be taken into Care or claimed by his father. I've decided to end it all, but I don't want to take him with me, because he hasn't really had time to find out whether he likes it here or not.'

Baby John was a problem. But all problems have their solutions. She had decided on her own, which was the final one. She should be able first to decide on his.

June walked about the house, touching things – things she had

12

spent so much time and energy on, not to mention money. How could she be absolutely sure that Baby John would be all right? She sat on the stairs, trying to clear her head of every thought except the problem, and feeling with her hands the new thick bitter-chocolate-coloured carpet, and the smoothness of the Brilliant White gloss paint on either side of it, the paint which had taken her so long to apply, because her hand shook and she had been afraid of painting the carpet.

It wasn't wasted, not completely; someone else would probably live here. Clive would probably sell the house fully furnished, and someone, whosoever, would enjoy what she had done.

In the living-room, she stroked her hand up and down the long curtains. She had searched for weeks for material she liked, and then had found this at The Designers' Guild, and then waited more weeks while the friend of a friend made up and lined the curtains, and had then allowed one of her many cats to stain them. But they had been cleaned; she could not see the stain now, only the heavy beige cotton, with wild flowers, mostly bluebells and buttercups, embroidered with brightly coloured wool. She felt the texture of the thick rough embroidered bluebells and buttercups. She liked them, would always like them (for as long as always would now be), liked wild flowers by far the best. She had been born in a house, semi-detached but with a long garden and in a quiet road, and beyond the garden had been a hill which was climbed to reach a wood and bluebells.

She wanted bluebells now, wanted to watch the juice trickle from their stems and see it hang suspended like saliva round a dog's mouth, wanted to be five years old again, and to sit in the sandpit just outside the front gate of that quiet house, watching large lorries full of American soldiers pass by, the quietness disturbed for a few moments while they waved and shouted and threw down chewing-gum to her.

Even the brief glimpses she had caught of those GIs had created in her mind the misconception that American men were more exciting, more physically attractive than other men. She was, it was true, only five years old, and they were, it was true, better nourished than the people of her village. They filled their uniforms, which had been tailored to fit tightly and display the

13

nourishment therein. It had all been propaganda. To a little girl of five, those gum-chewing faces couldn't ever be on the losing side. June had known, long before Churchill or anyone else, that Britain would pull through.

Death had seemed terrible then.

If only her green three-wheeler bicycle could have carried her under one of those large conveyors of confident well-nourished GIs, and if those handsome faces, some white, others black, could have been the last faces at which she'd had to look! She would have lain there, pressed like a buttercup between the pages of a Bible, her green bicycle representing the green twisted stem. Her mother had described it to her like that, the danger, had threatened her with that death, pressed flat by wheels which were at least twice her own size, if ever she were to take her bicycle outside the gates, and had shown her the Bible, with a pressed buttercup covering Matthew, Chapter Five, Verse Four. She had always dressed June in yellow, always yellow. She had explained that it was a colour which the fast American drivers would find it easiest to see.

That was before her mother had lost interest in life.

June pushed the pram containing Baby John into the Casualty Department of the hospital nearest her home, and sat next to a young Irishman, who slept with his arms folded, his head and reddened face lolling forward onto his chest. His cheap pale green lightweight suit was creased from having been slept in, and the lapels were stained with recent vomit. June could smell the exhaled bitter and the remnants of the vomit. Poor old Paddy! Poor Paddy, the Next Best Thing, so far away from home, so lonely and so innocent! When would religion pay back its debt to society?

She counted five other casualties waiting, including a middle-aged couple, both of whom looked so unhappy that she could not tell which was the one in pain.

There seemed to be three very young doctors on duty, one black, one white, and one khaki. All three moved with backs erect and shoulders tight with self-importance, their white coats

14

open and flapping, displaying their suits and ties, the trappings of professional status.

She would tell them that Baby John (who now slept) had coughed up blood. It was difficult to disprove. She would show them his bib with the bloodstains on it. (She had cut her finger, and mixed the blood with some of her own spit, before wiping her fingers on the bib.)

She would be fearful, and would weep, and they would wake Baby John, and most likely be greeted by his wolf-like scream. All three looked to be young, inexperienced, new doctors; they would be worried by the scream, at the sound of which strong men had been known to weep. They would do tests, find nothing wrong, and offer to keep him in overnight.

As far as she could tell, there was no one there, no one at work behind the moveable screen, who knew her, no one to recognize her, no older doctor whose suspicions might be aroused by a middle-class mother with hair which had not been washed for some time, and fingernails which were broken and dirty. The bags under June's eyes were full and violet, but these young boys would put that down to stress over the baby. She was already getting inside her role as a distraught mother, leaning over the sleeping Baby John, and working herself up towards tears. They were young; they wouldn't dare to take risks with a baby, neglect of which might lead to exposure in the Sunday papers. She would tell them that she had heard of babies dying of internal haemorrhages, that she had never before heard Baby John scream like that, and that it was the screaming and the blood coming together which had so frightened her. They would do tests, keep him in overnight, and feed him. Overnight. That was all she needed. Tomorrow, when she didn't turn up to collect him, they would inform the police, but they would probably wait until the evening before doing that. Then the police would have to find her. There would be time.

The sound of an ambulance siren suddenly galvanized the three strutting young doctors and the disinfected nurses into swifter motion. Screens were hurriedly moved, revealing half-dressed patients to those who still waited. These looked round, in some surprise and disarray to find that their semi-nudity now

15

had a larger and unprofessional audience. A thin old man with a bony sunken chest backed, forgetting his ailment, away from these untrained eyes, and collided with a steel trolley loaded with surgical instruments.

White robes and masks were hurriedly donned, and disposable gloves unwrapped. The black, white and khaki doctors moved as if in a speeded-up film. This was drama, the rest, routine. A nurse announced to those waiting, 'I'm very sorry, dears, but we have a real emergency now. An accident. You're going to have to wait.'

The real emergency (as opposed to the unreal ones, who sat around June, sleeping or enduring their pain in silence) was wheeled in on a stretcher, the saline drip already connected, the fight for a life already begun.

June got a brief look at the face on the stretcher before it was pushed hastily into the Intensive Care Unit. It was that of a young man. It wouldn't see the New Year in, not that face. June didn't know how she knew, but she did. She was sure, sure of the waste, sure of her wish to change places, sure that the expression on the young man's face was one of relief.

Without planning, or even thinking about it, she had, after standing to see that face, begun to walk. She kept on walking out into the yard of the hospital, without even looking back, without Baby John and his pram.

He would be all right; he would be safe there. If she hadn't seen that young man's face, she might have weakened, changed her mind as so often before, or simply taken enough booze and pills to knock her out for the two days of the holiday, and then returned for him.

But she had seen the face, and its expression of relief. She was convinced that the expression on the young man's face meant, 'Please don't bother me. I'm all right. Please leave me alone. I'm not going to jump back into life crippled, just to please you.'

She felt a sense of purpose. It gladdened her, and was expressed in her stride. Now she could just go, leave, get out, quit, and Baby John would be taken care of. She had the means, the opportunity, and, most important of all, she had the will. She was determined and committed.

Rather than wake Baby John and a great many neighbours

by tugging and banging it, she had left the front door ajar. It was not a night for burglars, not Christmas Eve. They would all be home, filling their children's stockings. Any chimneys down which they climbed tonight, would be their own.

She took her coat off in the hall, having managed to close and lock the front door quietly. She draped the coat over the banister. It fell to the floor. She stood, looking down at it, unable to decide whether to pick it up. The decision seemed important. She must get everything right this time, and the coat reminded her of the mistakes she had made in the past. So many things could go wrong. She left the coat on the floor, to remind herself how easy it was to fail.

On the glass-topped table, she set out three glass tumblers, and poured what was left of the red wine into them. Then she made herself three mugs of coffee.

The main problem would be to swallow as many of the sixty-nine pills as she could before she became unconscious, and unable to finish the job. With the help of coffee and wine she must fit together inside her stomach the brightly coloured parts of the jigsaw.

Throwing up was another problem. It had happened before. The throat seems to close, rejecting any more, or a capsule breaks in the mouth, leaving an acid taste, and causing nausea.

She went back into the hall, and regarded the coat on the floor. It reminded her of the danger of negative thinking. That had also happened before. One tiny doubt, one hesitation, or just half a second thought, one break in will-power, and the careful acquisition of the means would have been wasted, and the pain endured for nothing.

Back at the glass-topped table, she saw that everything she needed was in front of her. The pills and spansules would be easier to pick up if they were in a bowl or dish than spread out on the table as they were now. Such small details should not be overlooked. She placed the pills in a mixing-bowl, and walked about the room, tidying the Christmas cards. She would not draw the curtains together. If she did, some nosy-parker might notice them closed on Christmas Day, and decide to investigate. But

17

what if the same or a different parker should look in through opened curtains, and see her body on the floor? She would do better to take it all upstairs.

June lifted the glass-topped coffee table carefully, so as to spill neither drink nor pills, and carried it into the hall. Then she saw again her coat lying on the floor.

She didn't like upstairs, didn't like being upstairs alone. And dying in the middle of an extra-wide double bed was so . . . so . . . She couldn't at that particular moment think what it was so, but she knew it wasn't her.

She took the glass-topped table and its contents back to the living-room. She began to tidy up. She was too busy tidying to work out why dying like that wasn't her. She discovered herself to be wiping the stains of red wine from the wall above the chiffonier. She discovered that she was in the kitchen, wiping away the wet rings the coffee mugs had made on the white formica work-surface. Her hands (she discovered) had become damp. She wiped her hands on a tea-towel. They must be steady, her hands, clean and steady.

What she was doing was putting off the moment of starting, and every moment she wasted in putting it off was a moment needed. She needed all the moments she had, to be sure of success.

Sitting on the sofa, with everything laid out in front of her and within reach (she had changed the positions of the red wine and coffee twice), she tried to think of a suitable last thought. A thought for the day, Christmas Day, a thought with which to say, Goodbye. There would be no notes. Notes were not June either. Then she had it. This was her thought: 'Now I lay me down to sleep, I pray the Lord my soul to keep – His hands off.'

The first handful of pills was easy. None got broken; none stuck. There was no retching; there were no half-second-thoughts. Clearly it was wise not to attempt too many at once.

The second handful she swallowed with red wine, and the third with cold coffee. A spansule stuck, and it took a whole mug of coffee to dislodge it. A whole mug of coffee. And time, precious time.

Then there were still at least half the pieces of her jigsaw left

18

on the table, and it was as she reached out for them that the room started to move.

Her arm was heavy, and a little girl's chubby hand came up to meet her lips, crushing brightly coloured flowers between her fingers as saliva dripped from June's mouth.

Then she was pacing about, couldn't stop, backwards and forwards. She knew that something was wrong. Pacing was what kept you alive, if that was what you wanted to be. Did she want to be alive?

The gaps between her teeth became tight. It was as if layers of fine wire had been wound in and out between each tooth, pulling them all together. She put her fingers inside her mouth, and pulled out bunch after bunch of what she knew to be peacock feathers. The feathers were long, meant for display. Each had small silver jointed brackets in the stem.

She smoothed out each feather by pressing it down hard against the glass-topped table with her hand, and left it there to dry.

After a few more tours of the room, the tightness returned, and the process was repeated. More pacing, more feathers. The pacing grew quicker, and the feathers became larger, taller, thicker. Then there was pain.

Her fingernails were scratching at the back of her throat, trying to dislodge something which had stuck there, and was burning, scorching her throat as it melted. She was frightened, terrified, panic-stricken. Her fingernails wouldn't reach.

She was holding her head face upwards under the cold-water tap, her mouth wide open. She felt the full force of the water hit her, hit her, hit her. She swallowed and swallowed, desperately, extravagantly, ravenously, filling herself, feeling her stomach stretch, bloated with water.

The scorching which had started in her gullet was now spreading outwards and downwards inside her chest.

Then she was pulling at all the doors of the house to get out. But the doors were damp and swollen; they kept her in. She was trapped and choking.

Breaking a window with her bare arms, she noticed how dark and ruby-coloured the blood was. She heard her baby cry, heard

19

it scream its wolf-scream. The Social Services had come to take him into Care. They wore a white beard and the red robe of Father Christmas. Beneath the synthetic beard of the Social Services, her baby was fighting for breath and spitting blood.

She was running, falling down and crawling on hands and knees along pavements fouled with dog shit. The stench of it made her vomit, as Paddy the Next Best Thing, the young Irishman in the crumpled green suit, had vomited.

Poor Paddy!

The vomit tasted of acid – anti-depressing, tranquillizing, sleep-inducing acid.

She lay on her back, resting for a moment, just a moment. Then she began to move again. Now the dark Christmas morning sky was below her, cutting and nicking her body like sharp new razor-blades as she crawled. Above her back, the dog-stained pavement bore down on her, crushing her. so that she crawled on her belly while the Christmas stars beneath made sharp clean hairline cuts in her knees, belly and elbows, where she had broken the window and pushed herself through it.

Cat's-eyes winked at her, and ran away. Why did sleek black cats have all the luck, and where's the fucking Guiding Star that's supposed to lead me to the child? Which of the bastards is it? She could smell the sodding shepherds and their scabby dogs, but where the hell were the Wise Men. 'Sorry, dear. Wise Men are off. They've all gone. Can't afford them nowadays.' So where was the gold? The frankincense? The baa-lamb?

Then she was up again, and running. Time was important, every moment of it. Turning a corner, she steadied her balance by touching some curved iron railings.

Something, which might have been an electric current, shot up her right arm, and tightened around her chest in stinging bands. Bells were ringing in the roots of her teeth. They were hollow, and they were ringing.

She continued to move forward.

She was there, lying on the steps of the Casualty Department. She had arrived. She was now a real emergency. A real unreal emergency.

The words 'Pheno Barb' were whispered to her with enormous pleasure.

Then the feeling of movement in her stomach. Starting very small, it grew. Eventually the whole Irish Labour Force was inside her, building yet another bloody motorway. If only a betting shop or a pub would open to give her ease.

Poor Paddy!

Above her, the sound of heavy breathing and the smell of stale tobacco. Someone who smoked heavily had just run up several flights of stairs.

'Boring cow!'

They handled her roughly, and asked her why she had never thought of her child.

Never?

Among antiseptic tiles and squeaking highly polished shoes, could be no talk of peacocks' feathers and none of reasons. The grunting cursing Irishmen walked down her throat in heavy boots; she felt the tips of their picks in her pharynx. She groaned, cursing all immigrant labour. This was the fifth scraping and dredging job they had performed on her. Her groans would give pleasure to her rescuers. Pain was a necessary part of the ritual.

They kept her waiting for news of her child. She dared not ask, and the faces which drifted past her bed were tight and dull. The child might be 'as well as can be expected under the circumstances' or 'No change in his condition'. What condition? Had she left the bib, with its prepared bloodstain, in his pram?

No change. That's what it's all about, Baby John, isn't it? No change? After all . . . all *that* . . . here we are again, happy as can be, could be, or ever will be. For ever and ever. No, *please!*

'How do you feel?' The question needed thought. She thought. She answered the questions.

'Like a small grey mouse . . .
in a very large cage . . .
Running round and round
and in and out . . .
through a maze.'

He made a noise of encouragement, a noise that meant, 'Go

21

on.' She saw no point in going on, but the words would come out anyway. They were the words of her vocation and his trade, of patient and psychiatrist, the dialogue of her life, untidy piles of nouns and pronouns, verbs and adverbs, conjunctions and disjunctions. She saw herself rummaging through the whole world's rubbish-heap of words, looking for those she had lost, the real ones, the important ones, not those she used but those which meant something, the words worth saying.

'Go on.' This time he had used the words themselves instead of the noise which meant the words. But she was still watching herself picking up words which wouldn't do, and casting them aside (so that the rubbish-heap never grew smaller). They wouldn't do; they were overused, they oversimplified what she wished to say.

'Go on.' His words had reached her inner ear, causing her to feel unbalanced. She reponded automatically, still sifting through the rubbish.

'Go on what?'

'About the maze. You said you felt . . .' He was one of those who left his sentences unfinished.

'Yes. I know what I said.'

He waited. That was his job, most of the time, to wait, and listen, and perhaps to record. Case-notes.

She allowed him to wait. Then she said, 'I told you about the maze?'

He made another noise. This noise meant, 'Yes.'

'Well, the object is to find the exit, right?'

He had nodded when he made the noise, and now nodded again, but without a noise, so that she was reminded of a toy dog looking out of the back window of a Ford Cortina. Then he nodded yet again, and said, 'Yes. If there is an exit. So what's the mouse doing about it?'

'Squeaking blue bloody murder.'

'Instead of?'

'I don't know. You're the expert. You tell me.'

'No one's the expert. There aren't any.'

He paused. June felt tired. Her work on the rubbish-mountain of words had exhausted her. He said, 'So what do you think the mouse should do?'

'Lie down, and go to sleep. Except that it can't sleep. If it tries, it's given a mild electric shock, just enough to make it squirm.'

Both of them waited, each willing the other to speak. Then he gave way. That also was part of his job. 'Let's talk about your depressions. What causes them, do you think?'

He actually had the nerve to ask her what he was being paid by the National Health Service to find out. He waited. She didn't answer.

'The fact that psychiatry has failed to help you in the past needn't preclude your having another go, need it?'

She shrugged her shoulders, thinking, 'Come on! Let's see you earn your money.'

'Despair is fairly common nowadays, particularly in women of your intelligence. Haven't you noticed that?'

'No, I don't find other people's problems very exciting.'

He gestured. He had changed from noises to gestures. What words were represented by the gesture? The only interpretation she felt able to give was that the gesture meant 'San Fairy Ann.' However, words followed it.

'There's no such thing as a totally destructive personality, Mrs Jephcott. I think you're trying to overdramatize your situation by saying that. Wouldn't you agree?' Why not? Yes, of course. Right! Sure! O.K. Fine! Great! Now what? She considered correcting the 'Mrs' to 'Miss', but it was too obvious, and might even be expected. Better to maintain silence.

'There must have been a time when you and Clive were happy together. What caused that happiness? Shall we try to concentrate for a moment on that?'

'Why do you try to justify everything you say by turning it into a question?' No answer. 'Go on, doctor. Make a simple statement, just for the hell of it. I shan't hold you to it; I don't expect you to be God. If you were, you'd have a lot to answer for, and I'd be the first to put the questions.'

He looked at her for what seemed to be a long time. The moment of suspense excited her. Perhaps he would drop her, shrug her off as manipulative and beyond help, pass her on to some poor

23

junior shrink, with ideas and ideals both still bright, who would take one look at her records, and shit himself at the challenge.

He said, 'Have you really set your heart on being the most unhappy person in the world? There are no prizes, you know.'

Now, suddenly she was angry. With the anger, she found energy. 'My heart was "set", as you put it, by someone else. The seed from which it grew was carefully planted in a womb of rotten eggs. The sowing was done between stiffly starched sheets. Unhappily, neither of the parties present on that occasion could have known that, ahead of that tiny bead of spermatozoa, would be thirty-five years of almost total unhappiness. I don't suppose they lay back, panting and thinking to themselves, "Well, there's a right load of misery, to spread gloom and despondency when we've gone. All we have to do now is to make sure it has a really awful childhood, and in no time at all, it'll be wishing you hadn't uncrossed your legs tonight, mother." My mother always had something crossed. Her legs or her fingers. Or her eyes.' She paused. He was watching her show off. She said. 'I don't suppose that conversation really did happen, do you?'

He shook his head. Well, then, he had made her angry. Score for him! Since she had started, she might as well go on, and let the words come whence they might. She leaned back, and looked at the ceiling.

'I was eight when I first wanted to die. Do you know how many times I've tried?'

'Yes, it's all down here.'

'No. Double that figure. At least, double it. I've tried more times than there are days in the month, and I don't mean February. And if I fail until I'm seventy, I shall have tried at least once for every year of my life. I'm committed, you see. Unsuccessful, but committed. For three months after each attempt, I've felt a little better. Told myself it wouldn't happen again. By the fourth month, I'm planning it. I can't see ahead; I can only feel from moment to moment. And what I feel like now is a long continuous weep. The whole of my body is aching from the effort of suppressing waterless tears. You said, "despair". It's like wanting desperately to be sick, and not being able to. It tightens on me like a corset, contracting slowly until it pushes my heart up into

24

my mouth. How can my baby survive having a mother like that?'

He didn't answer the question, but said instead, 'Tell me about when you were seven.'

'I've told you.'

'No. Someone else, perhaps. Not me. I want to know.'

'It'll be in the notes.'

He continued to wait, doing what he was paid to do. Then he said, 'Tell me about the people who adopted you.'

'They were perfectly ordinary middle-class people, who never did a thing wrong in their lives, except in allowing me to grow up.'

'How old were you when they adopted you?'

'Eight.'

'And your real parents?'

'It's in the notes.'

'Yes?'

'I remember her, not him. By the time I was four, he'd gone. I just remember damp soft hands, very soft for a man. That's all. Not much, is it?'

'No.'

'Then there were just the two of us. And she was like me. Couldn't cope. I probably come from a long line of non-copers. Oh, hell!'

He waited. He was paid to wait.

'I suppose it was depression, only they called it Tired Blood in those days, and Iron Tonic was the cure-all. Or Horlicks. No one dished out tranquillizers or anti-depressants where we lived; it was, "Go and get yourself a tonic, girl. You're looking run-down." I remember one or two of them, shouting that to her from the front gate when they saw her in the garden.' She stopped, remembering the Bluebell Wood, the heavy pleasing scent of it, and her own small chubby hand gripping the stems of the flowers so tightly that they wilted before reaching home and water. 'And Wincarnis,' she said.

'Them? Who were "them"?'

'The neighbours. Almost nobody came in through the gate. It was a small village, and I think they sensed that there was more to it than being run-down. Anyway, she wouldn't talk to anybody who did come, so they weren't encouraged to call again.

25

She didn't even talk to me very much, not my mother. She didn't need anybody, or want anybody. As I grew older, and able to look after myself, she just became less and less . . . less tidy. By the time I was seven, she'd taken to sitting on the doorstep in her nightdress. Day in, day out, she just sat there, resting her chin on her hands, and staring at the lupins. She'd given up Horlicks by that time. The garden was overgrown, but the weeds weren't high enough to stop the neighbours from seeing her over the fence . . . I missed a lot of school. She didn't seem to bother, and you can imagine what it was like with the other children, when your mother's the woman who sits on the doorstep in her nightie. The School Inspectors came round a few times, and had a good look. They couldn't get any sense out of her, and they saw the state of the house, so they sent someone from the Council. She cried, I remember. I didn't. Couldn't. Not then; I've made up for it since. Anyway, I thought it was going to be for a short holiday – that's what they said, "We're taking you off for a short holiday, June, while your mummy has a rest." There were no relatives, it seemed, or anyway, none near enough. I don't think there were any – no aunties, no uncles, no gran. So the holiday was to be with a foster-mother. The adoption came later.'

He was listening, doing his job, the job he was paid to do. Would it be by the hour? For a hospital consultant, perhaps not. At least he hadn't looked at his watch. 'It's all in the notes,' she said. As listeners go, he was fair to average. She had met many listeners, watched them for their reactions as she dug into her dust-mountains of words, picking them out and releasing them like hot-air balloons to be carried who knows where, each one a bubble with the word 'thinks' printed neatly on it in lower-case type.

'Would you like to go back to your mother now?' He was speaking, asking questions, earning his hourly rate. June rubbed her eyes.

'Yes . . . Well . . . That's just what I did, didn't I? Four times. That must be in the notes. I ran away, got a bus back to the village. It was nine or ten miles, must have been; I can't remember; I know it seemed a hell of a long way. They were trying

26

to get her into a hospital – loony-bin, I suppose – shrink-tank. But they couldn't find a place for her right away, so they'd persuaded someone from the village to pop in from time to time to check up on her. The fourth time I went, she wasn't there, and nobody would tell me where she'd gone.'

She stared at the wall in front of her, searching for the words which came next. But she had finished. Surely? 'Finished,' she said, 'It's in the notes.'

But he was waiting, as was his job. So there was more. Something left out. She couldn't have forgotten. He had his living to earn. Something left out. She tried to speak. Perhaps they would come to her, the right words.

'I . . . I . . .' It was then she remembered, and with the memory came anger and tears. The floodgates had opened, and she shouted.

'I . . . I . . . couldn't get her up the bloody stairs; I just couldn't. She wouldn't let me, not until it had gone dark, and then I had to wrap her in a blanket . . . wrap it round her. She was waiting for him, all the time for him. The sodding arsehole of a wet-handed creep! It was for him.' June's face contorted as she tried to control herself. 'We'd have been all right if they'd left us alone.'

She covered her face, and sobbed. He waited. He was paid to wait.

After that the anger was gone, and she was limp, limp and tired, and could speak flatly, factually, pick the words and place them out, flatly, on a board, for his inspection. She had shouted, but there was no justification for such anger after thirty-one years, none whatsoever. To cling so long to anger was obsessive; the past was past.

'The last time I ran away, and went back to her – I mean the last time she was there – the third time, she was . . . she was lying on the bed, wrapped in an old grey blanket, very still. I thought she was dead. And all I could feel was relief that she hadn't . . . that they hadn't taken her away. Then I kissed her, and she moved. She'd no idea who I was. She just stared. I couldn't stand it, couldn't . . . meet her eyes. So I moved round to the other side of her, and lay down on the bed. I was cold,

27

but I couldn't get under her blanket. I just lay there, shivering, with my arms round her . . . I was eight years old.'

He was crying. Poor sod! She had never made a shrink cry before, except for the one who had wanted to take her to bed. What a way to earn a living!

PART TWO

Walter and June Confined

I

From the moment the first load of depressed women arrived, Walter no longer felt brave enough to inspect his path.

Walter had spent hours watching the new building rise, brick by brick. He had seen the ground cleared and levelled, and trenches dug for sewage pipes and drains, had watched hardcore brought in lorries, which tipped it into piles for the bulldozer to spread out evenly, had seen the bricklayers arrive with their spirit-levels and diamond-shaped trowels, had watched them chip, and scrape, and pat the bricks into place. And the man who shovelled sand and cement into the noisy concrete-mixer had noticed Walter's interest, and had called him over.

The man had lent Walter his shovel, and had told him how much of each ingredient to throw into the circulating tub. Walter had made concrete. The man had smoked a cigarette and watched, as Walter made concrete, and then together Walter and the man had shovelled Walter's concrete onto the hardcore, and had then patted it level with the edge of a plank.

It was a path. Walter had made part of a concrete path. The workman had said, 'That's your stretch of path. You made that.' And he had smiled at Walter, and Walter had smiled at him; they had been friendly together. The man had said, 'That'll still be here when you and I are gone.' Then the man had marked the stretch of path made by Walter, by painting two thin green lines on the red brick wall.

After that, he had visited his stretch of path twice a day, just to look down at it, slide his hand over it, and test its firmness with his foot, and the painters, carpenters and plumbers had laughed and waved to him, for they all knew it was Walter's piece of path.

Walter had asked members of Staff (more than one, since he wished to be certain) the purpose of this new building, and had been told that it was for mothers with small babies who were depressed and unhappy. At first he had thought that the babies would be depressed and unhappy, but when he had watched the first ambulances of mothers arrive, and had seen their faces and heard some of them crying, he had known that these, the mothers, were the unhappy ones.

What had once been called a Workhouse, and had then become an Asylum, and was now called a Mental Hospital, but which had never changed its outward appearance with all these changes of name, now contained in its grounds a new two-storey building of red brick, with an interior of clean surfaces, many of wood, with furniture of a light appearance and in bright colours, and the name of this building, which was so at odds with the solidly depressing Victorian exterior of the Mental Hospital, was The Mother and Baby Unit. Severe post-natal depression was what had brought most of these mothers with their babies to the Unit. The severity of the depressions endured by these mothers ranged from the extreme depression which had induced them to wish to kill both themselves and their babies to the comparatively modest depression of those who were merely unable to cope with any part of the daily routine of feeding, changing and sterilizing bottles.

From the moment that the first load of depressed women arrived, Walter no longer felt brave enough to go close to the building and inspect his path. He was therefore forced to content himself with admiring it from a distance, and even then only on alternate days when he marched a crocodile of what had been known as 'inmates' when Walter had entered the hospital, but were now called 'patients', past the new Unit and out of the main gate for a walk. Always when passing the Unit, he slowed his pace until he was almost marching on the spot, causing those behind him to run into each other and become momentarily confused. This was not responsible behaviour in Walter, who had

32

been placed in charge of the crocodile because he was a patient of long standing, and trusted by the Staff.

Two months after the first depressed mothers had arrived, and Walter was returning from one ·such walk, pushing Clifford, his own special charge (who could not speak, could not do anything for himself, for whom everything was done by Walter), he saw someone standing on his path. A woman was standing there. Previously he had seen people walking over it, seen a woman pace up and down over it, covering it several times, had seen a woman pause on it to light a cigarette, but he had never seen anyone remain on it for any length of time. This woman was standing still, doing nothing but stand. Her head faced downwards. She was looking at the path Walter had made.

Walter stopped pushing Clifford. He tried to see what about his path was engaging the attention of the woman, but he was too far away from her to make out such detail. Meanwhile the patients behind Walter, those whom he privately thought of as 'Jesus's mistakes', broke ranks, and began to push at each other, to giggle and to swear, so that Walter felt bound to continue.

Perhaps it had cracked. The workmen had told him that cracking had to be watched for, with paths. 'Too much of one thing, not enough of the other, or a bad frost before she's settled down, and she'll crack before the month's out.' There had been no bad frost. If Walter's path was cracking, it would be because he had put in too much of one thing, or not enough of the other.

That night he lay awake, imagining the cracks in his path getting wider. So deep were they, that people fell through, screaming as they fell, the sound and echo and re-echo of their screams filling the hospital grounds, announcing that it was Walter who was to blame, Walter who had neglected to put in enough of the other, Walter who had doomed them to this long agony of falling. Walter would be called to account, the friendly workman would be sacked, and the husbands of the depressed women who had fallen through the cracks would hang about outside the hospital gates, carrying long knives, athirst for Walter's blood.

The following day was not one on which the crocodile went for its walk, and Walter's duties on the Ward kept him too busy to get out. But if there had been accidents at the Mother and Baby

33

Unit, the Staff would know, and would speak of it amongst themselves, as Walter listened, and since they did not, the depressed mothers could not yet have been swallowed by cracks.

Next day Walter led his crocodile very slowly past the Unit. The woman was still there, standing on the same spot, still gazing at the path. Walter kept the walk short, and found on his return that the woman was there again, or perhaps had never moved. Yet still that night there was no mention in all the conversation and gossip of the staff of any cracks in the paths which surrounded the Mother and Baby Unit.

Were they keeping it from him?

It was Thursday. No walk to be taken until Friday. But he found five free minutes, and used them to run from his Ward (for Walter had great freedom in the Hospital) to a point from which he could see the new Unit, and his path, and the woman standing on it. But he was still not close enough to see for himself whether there were cracks.

She was still there on Friday when the crocodile went out for its walk, still there when it returned. He was desperate now. He could not wait until the next walk on Monday, and anyway, as long as he was with the crocodile, he still would not be able to get any closer.

But Walter had freedom; he was a trusty; he was trusted. He might go almost anywhere he wished, within the grounds of the Hospital. Outside the Main Gate was another matter, but his path was not outside the Main Gate. On Sunday, he would have some respite from his duties in the Ward; he could find time. He could see for himself on Sunday that all was still right with his path, and he would.

Each day, she had stood as she was standing now, with her back against the wall, her fingers feeling the bricks and the mortar on either side of her, stroking the roughness of the orderly bricks, and running her forefingers along the straight lines of mortar, knowing the lines to be true, but testing them. Whatever the weather or people did, no matter how topsy-turvy, uncertain, illogical or bent her own mind, these truly horizontal lines comforted her.

34

Well, he had approached, and was standing some four feet away from her. She had noticed him on the very first day she had been allowed out into the air. He had been leading a crocodile of twitching, misshapen, swearing patients from the Hospital. He had led his crocodile out of the gate, and, later, back in again, and both times he had slowed the procession, and had stared at her. He had a beak of a nose in a long face, and wore a flat cap; though he had appeared to be the leader, he must be one of them. After the first time, there had been others, and always he had slowed the crocodile as he came level with her, staring across, and causing his followers to change step or collide.

Yes, he was the leader, no doubt of that. Had he been alone, June felt sure, his arms would have swung in time to *Colonel Bogey*, but in fact they were taken up in pushing a wheelchair containing a man with an enormous head and gaping mouth. Even at that distance, the mouth could be seen to be gaping, the enormous head to be lolling; the man who watched her must care for that gaping mouth and head. He had stared at her. She had grown interested – not that she considered it a possibility that she should have any real interest in another human being, but the pattern of behaviour was interesting; it interested her. She began to time the duration of the crocodile's walk by the clock on the central tower of the Hospital, and noticed that it grew shorter and shorter.

Now it was Sunday. There was no crocodile. He had come alone, and was standing near her. Close as he was, he continued to stare at her, but he did not speak. Therefore June spoke. She said, 'I could stand here all day.'

Though she spoke to him, she did not look directly at him. Nor did the man reply. Since she had not asked a question, perhaps he did not consider a reply to be necessary. She asked a question.

'This patch of concrete we're standing on is level, isn't it?' That was a personal, private question though he could not know it, and it would not be personal to him. But June had made him privy to a private concern of her own that all lines should be straight, all true, all comforting. She had offered him the chance

35

to reassure and comfort her by confirming the straightness of the path. Would he now do so?

Walter looked at the narrow strip of path they were standing on. He had been right; there was something about his path which worried her. He could see no cracks. What had she been looking at?

'They level the ground, and put hardcore down. Then they level the hardcore, and pour on concrete. Then they level that with something, don't they? They level everything.'

Walter had shovelled the concrete on, not poured.

'What's it called, what they use for that, the levelling?' She squinted up at the sky, trying to bring the name to mind. Again she had offered him a question. If he himself had a store of words, different from her own, now was a time for him to use it.

Walter shook his head. The workman had shown him how to smooth the concrete by using the edge of a piece of plank. It had had no special name, and had, earlier on, also been used for scaffolding.

'They pat the concrete with something like the edge of the plank.' June's gaze had dropped a little from the sky to the clock on the central tower. Long ago, when the Hospital had still been a Workhouse, and had grown all its own food on its own farm, tilled by the sweated labour of the unpaid inmates, the tower had been used for water. Now the sometime farm had become Grounds, in which the new Unit stood and mains water had been brought in, so that there was little use for the tower but to hold a clock, reminding the inmates, the patients, those living dead, that there was always time. Time the Healer, Time in which miracles might yet be performed if one waited long enough. The clock was permanently twelve minutes slow. Perhaps Time's first act of healing should be on its own innards. June said, 'The plank makes ripples in the concrete, which flatten out later. Maybe that's all it's called – a plank.' She lowered her glance further, and studied the path. She did not care to look too long at the exterior of the Hospital, which, for some reason, frightened her. 'It's not completely smooth, though, is it?' she said.

Walter drew his right foot across the path, feeling the unsmoothed-out ripples. If this was a fault, it was not his. It was as the workman had told him to do it, and the workman had said it was well done.

'If it were completely smooth, it would get slippery in the rain.'

Walter nodded. The workman had said much the same.

'Hardcore is the most important ingredient, do you agree? Without that, the concrete would sink into the ground, or spread about so thinly that it would crack under pressure. It's very important to have a firm base on which to build one's ...' Her words faded away into thoughts, old, tired, much-used thoughts of knocking everything over, letting it all topple, and starting again.

Frost was what would crack it. The workman had told him.

'Don't you agree?'

She was not looking at him, but at the path. Then she turned her head slowly, and looked directly at him for the first time during this encounter. 'It's not a good day you've chosen for making new acquaintances. Why has it taken you so long to approach me?' She laughed, a short involuntary laugh, which came up suddenly from nowhere, like a burp or a hiccup, so that she excused herself and let go of the wall for a moment to cover her mouth with her hand, before remembering the security of straight lines, and returning her hand quickly to the reassuring mortar.

A silence followed. Walter was used to being silent, and preferred it. In the silence bird-song could be heard, and an aeroplane droning somewhere in the distance. June smiled at him, patted the wall beside her, and said, 'Welcome to my wall.'

It might be her wall, in some way, though Walter knew well enough that she had not made it, having watched those who had. He himself had physically made the patch of path. He wished to tell her so, pointed to the path, and opened his mouth, but no words emerged. He did not know why this should be, and so he turned what should have been a speech into a smile, and leaned against the wall just as she was leaning.

They stood in silence for a long time, both with their backs against the brick wall of the Mother and Baby Unit, to which June had been sent with Baby John from the hospital at which her stomach had been pumped out. She had been told that she

37

would be better here for a while, should not go home, that her baby would be at risk, while here people would help her to care for him, and she herself could be given Tests. What tests? Well, they would try new pills, a different psychiatrist, an altogether new approach. E.C.T.? Well, that was a possibility certainly; that might be something to try. The really important thing was not to give up. All this, June remembered while she stood next to the watching man, her back against the wall, and Walter did not think of anything in particular except that there was, after all, nothing wrong with his path, and that it was pleasant to be in the company of someone who was not Staff, yet who neither twitched, grizzled or dribbled, and who had smiled at him.

This place was to be a halfway house, a stepping-stone, except that no one seemed able or willing to tell her where her feet might land next. Here she was to be under observation; that was all they would say. 'We'd like to try one or two new things, and keep you under observation.' Well, she was certainly being observed, if only by this inmate, who had observed her on the very first day they had allowed her out into the fresh air, and was now leaning on the wall some four feet away.

A man in pyjamas, dressing-gown and bedroom slippers walked past, supported on either side by a nurse. The man's head hung forward, his chin pressing into his Adam's apple, his feet dragging along the ground. A slipper came off his left foot, and was left behind. A few yards further on, the other came off also, and was also left behind. The nurses had noticed the loss of the slippers, but had decided to keep hold of the man and continue walking, thereafter taking a short cut across some gravel, against which the man's bare feet were lightly cut.

Normally Walter would have retrieved the slippers, running after the nurses, and being thanked. But today wasn't a normal day, not for Walter.

June said, 'I'll bet he wishes they'd finish him off.'

This was not a statement fully understood by Walter, but he did not expect all, or even many statements to be fully understandable. Instead he counted the number of bricks between himself and June. Today he had found the courage to approach her, to walk slowly along the narrow concrete path, and then to stop near her, so that now they leaned against the same wall, six bricks apart. She had not screamed, or run away, or even asked him what he wanted. She had not complained about cracks in the path, because there were none. She had remained still, feeling the wall with her hands, and looking at the concrete he himself had made. She had talked to him, and smiled, had patted the wall beside her, inviting him to lean on it. And he had leaned, as she was leaning, and she had talked to him, had asked him why it had taken him so long to come and see her, had known that he had been watching her, and had not minded that.

He could hear the sound of a baby crying. She must have a baby; that would be why she was here. She must be unhappy, must be a mother, must be depressed and unhappy.

It was hard for Walter to believe that anyone who had given birth to a baby could be unhappy. He had seen babies on his walks at the head of his crocodile of Jesus's mistakes. The babies had been in prams, and people had stopped to look at them, and to talk to them in a funny way, with much repetition. The mothers of such babies had seemed proud; they had told their babies' ages, and wiped their mouths, and not appeared at all unhappy. Jesus had made those babies. Jesus had made people, just as he had made pigeons, and both pigeons and people had made more of their kind.

Fifteen years ago, four years after Walter had been taken to the Mental Hospital, but when he was already trusted, and would lead out his crocodile on walks, Walter, thirty-one years old, had returned from one of those walks, on which he had observed prams and the contents of those prams, and the proud mothers who had pushed the prams, and he had said to the Irish Orderly with carrot-red hair, 'I want to make a baby.'

The orderly had looked up from what he was doing, and had seen the seriousness sitting on Walter's face, and had bitten back what would have been a cruel and witty remark, and instead had thought for a while, and then said, 'Well now, Walter! Me, as a man, I understand your feelings, and as a comparatively good Catholic, I should say it's me bounden duty to do likewise. But frankly, Walter, I could not stomach it at all. I have sixty-nine babies to look after in here as it is, you being me only grown-up child, and a blessing you may say on that account. I tell you frankly, Walter, the Blessed Virgin short-changed me in this department, for she gave me the equipment, but forgot to add the desire. Now I have a dog, and if it died or got its poor little self run into, why I'd cry meself out of this Hospital all the way to the Irish Sea, but I wouldn't flutter me eyelids twice to look at a baby in a pram. Think now, Walter. Just think on this for a minute. How many human beings of both the male and female kind are there in this very Hospital – for, sure, I'll not call them men and women, which they are not, Walter, and will never be, saving your own self. Now, will you think how many?' Walter had thought how many. Very many, more than he could count, unless they were all to stand still for a long time. 'And will you think of all the parents of the people in here? Now that must be the real tragedy, mustn't it, to have your beautiful bouncing baby end up in a place like this?'

Walter's expression had been thoughtful. It was true that Jesus's mistakes must begin life in a pram. Perhaps the mothers did not know that Jesus was to get a cross and not a tick for their offspring. The Irish orderly had misread the thoughtfulness, and had added quickly, 'Now, I can say a thing like that to you, Walter, because by rights you shouldn't be in here, and if your parents were still alive, no doubt you wouldn't be. Babies are overrated, Walter. The world's overcrowded as it is, and that's me, a Catholic, speaking. If me life-style doesn't get me Eternal Damnation, to be sure me tongue will.'

He was long gone now from the Hospital, the friendly Irish Orderly with the carrot-red hair. He had been arrested in a Gentlemen's Toilet by an *agent provocateur* in plain clothes, pleaded guilty (on police advice), was sentenced to six months in prison, and lost his job.

Walter had not thought of the Irish orderly for many years. Only the thought of babies had brought back the memory of him. After his disappearance, he had not been much spoken of among the Staff, or not before Walter, who did not know where or why he had gone, but only grieved for him a while, and then forgot. He would like to speak of him to this sad mother – if she was sad; she must be sad, or she would not be here. He would like to speak

40

on many subjects, but it seemed that he could not, since no words emerged when he opened his mouth. In any case, someone had once compared Walter's speech to a fart in a bath of soapy water; it was better that he should not speak. Let her speak, and he would listen.

Two other women came out of the Mother and Baby Unit, carrying their babies and jigging them up and down in their arms as they walked about on the grass. Then a black nurse appeared, and told June that she must go inside; it was time for Baby's feed. The nurse clasped June's arm. Leading her away; and talking to her as if to a child, she said, 'Come on, now, June. Don't you start to be difficult now. Be a good girl.'

Now he knew her name. She had allowed herself to be led away, and had not turned or said, 'Goodbye,' but he knew her name now. Her name was June.

The segregation of the sexes at the Hospital had been discontinued eleven years earlier. The large cast-iron doors dividing one wing from another had been opened. Male patients had, for the first time, been allowed to meet and even to talk to female patients. Female nurses worked on the Men's Wards. Social intercourse was positively encouraged. Every Saturday evening, a Social and Dance would be held in the Main Hall.

A branch of the Gateway Club, which has members in Mental Hospitals all over the country, was started. Walter paid his subscription and received a membership card, which proved that he was a bona fide member and permitted to take part in the Club's Activities.

He had visited every Saturday Night Dance since they began. He had sat and watched male and female patients dancing together, had watched wheelchairs pushed out onto the dance floor, to whirl and spin gravely about in time to the music. But he himself had never attempted to do this with Clifford's chair.

On the stage, a cardboard disc in which were set differently coloured circles of cellophane rotated in front of a spotlight, so that coloured circles of light moved over the walls and ceiling of the Main Hall. Loud music from a record-player with extra large speakers filled the Hall with sound, encouraging the ambulant patients to dance either alone or with a partner.

But Walter never danced. He sat, listening to the music and watching the coloured lights move about. He watched the faces of the dancing patients change colour, from blue to green, from green to pink, from pink to amber, from amber to yellow, and so back to blue.

Every week, he would be approached by female patients, asking him to dance. Usually they came two or three at a time, pushing each other forward, not wishing to be the first to ask. Often the request would be made by a third party, 'Here, will you dance with her?', and the third party would point to 'her', who usually cringed and giggled. Always Walter shook his head. 'How about her, then? Will you dance with her?' Again the shaken head, grave and firm, but not dismissive, since there would be no intention in Walter to give offence. 'Me, then? What about me? Come on! Dance with me.'

Then Walter would say, 'Sorry. I can't dance.'

'What? Can't do *that*?' The spokeswoman for the group would point to the dancers, astonished that Walter should be unable to move clumsily to the music, which was all that she required of him. But Walter was too self-conscious to move in public to music, clumsily or daintily, with or without a partner.

Once he had danced, but that was many years ago, at the Woolworth's Annual Dinner and Dance, held each year in Blackpool. That was when his mother and father were alive, and his father's pigeons lived happily in their Loft in the Yard and mated every spring and throughout the summer, and Walter had worked in the Stock Room at Woolworth's, sweeping up litter, baling paper, and being often praised for the thoroughness of his work. They had gone to Blackpool for the day, all the Staff in a coach, and the dance had been held in the evening. Jean, who looked after the shelves of soap-powders, detergents, pan-scourers, bleach and lavatory cleaners, had pulled him bodily from his place at a table with trainee floorwalkers, who had been trying to get him drunk. Having had some drink herself, she had jumped up and down, holding tightly to Walter's hand, and he had stood, bent forward, with Jean and the Ball Room going round and round him, the red textured wallpaper and the gilt wall-lights turning and spinning, until Jean had realized that he was either going to fall over or to be sick, and perhaps both. So she had taken him away to the table next to her own, away from the trainee floorwalkers, in order to look after him, and she had sat beside him on the coach when they went home, with an arm round his shoulder while he slept.

That was the nearest Walter had ever come to dancing, and the memory of it made him want to laugh and cry, both at the same time. Jean would be almost sixty by now, and would never know what had happened to him.

'I'll tell you one thing, Pop. We certainly landed in the shit when they brought us here. When I look around, I wonder what I fought and survived two world wars for.'

Walter remembered Pop and his friend Rubber Face, to whom this remark had been made many times more than once, in Walter's hearing. He remembered Rubber Face for his facial contortions, and Dominoes for the blackness of his skin and the whiteness of his round eyes. He remembered Dopey, Sneezy and an Indian patient whom they had christened 'Bombay Curry'. He remembered Ben Gunn, a hairy, thin but strong old man, who had jumped on Walter's bed like a dog, and sexually assaulted him on his first night at the Hospital.

He remembered Maurice and Albert, whom he had washed and dressed every day of the week, right up to and even on the days they had died, Maurice having outlived Albert by three months. He remembered Adrian, who would never allow his body to be clothed, and propelled himself along the floor on knees and elbows, picking up dirt and eating it, and Noddy, who walked round all day in his nightshirt, sucking at a baby's feeding bottle, and Ernest, who drank his own urine, because he liked to make people laugh and hear them call him, 'Dirty bugger!'

He remembered a winter's day in 1960, when all the patients in the ward who could walk were ushered out into the freezing yard, and hosed down with cold water, because one of the nurses had mislaid a pound note. And he remembered Reggie, who had

43

shouted, 'If you can't treat me with kindness, don't treat me at all.'

Walter remembered how the Social Worker, policeman and doctor had dragged him away from the bedside of his dead mother, where he had been waiting for Jesus to decide whether she was to go to Him or not, since if the decision were negative, she might reasonably be expected to return to her own son, who needed her. He remembered the promises they had made to him that they were taking him to a nice place, where he need not stay if he did not like it, and that they had lied. He remembered Bernard, who had once said to him, 'They told me I'd be here for two weeks, just for the rest, and that was forty years ago.' Bernard had been sixty-eight when he had told this to Walter. It was his birthday, and he was crying. He had never had a visitor. He had been sitting beside Walter, sticking labels onto rubber bones for dogs to play with, and the tears had rolled down his sallow wrinkled face, and dropped onto the pile of rubber bones.

And Walter, remembering, was now forty-six. And he had never had a visitor. Nobody had come from Woolworth's to see him, and he had never had any conversation with anyone who was not either Staff or one of Jesus's Mistakes. Until the sad lady in the Mother and Baby Unit had allowed him to approach her, and had spoken to him freely, though he had not been able to reply.

Her name was June.

Bernard had leaned forward over the rubber bones one day in the spring which followed his sixty-eighth birthday, resting his head on the bones, and snoring loudly. The other patients had giggled, and left him alone, thinking that he had fallen asleep, but he had never woken from that sleep, and no one came to claim his body.

Had Bernard been one of Jesus's Mistakes? If so, he had not been a very large Mistake, not one which was immediately clear to see. Walter knew that he himself was not a Mistake at all; in his case, mistakes had been made by others. But perhaps Bernard had thought this also, and perhaps he had been right to think so. During his nineteen years at the Hospital, Walter had been given various tests, but no action seemed to follow them, and whether he was a failure or a success was never divulged to him. They were just 'Tests', part of the Hospital Routine, and he applied himself to them, as to the rest of that routine, as best he could. One test had involved the soldering of four wires of different colours to the correct terminals of an eight-pin television plug, another was the assembly of a bicycle pump, in which nine different operations had to be performed in a certain order, or the pump would not work.

They were just Tests; they were not the same as Work. For much had changed at the Hospital in nineteen years. A swimming pool had been built in what had once been a side-ward, and Walter held a Certificate to prove that he had once swum a width of heavily chlorinated water without his feet ever having touched the bottom. There were, as has been said, social activities. And in the general cause of giving the patients human dignity, there was Work. Walter had stuck purple satin hearts onto Valentine Cards. He had packed dolls' Vanity Sets into boxes. In the Carpentry Shop, he had made bookshelves and boxes for cutlery. On the Hospital Farm, he had dug manure into the ground, and seen the orderly lines of peas and beans he had sown sprout into life and grow. He had learned how to repair boots and shoes.

For Work, Walter was paid; human dignity had to do with money. For a week's work, Walter might be paid – sometimes had been paid – as much as one pound and fifty pence, the money to be spent in the Canteen on sweets or cigarettes (though Walter did not smoke), all his other needs being, of course, provided for. Work was different from Hobbies, which were sometimes called Occupational Therapy, which was not paid. Walter was not good at Hobbies. He had tried to make pottery, and failed; nor could he draw or paint. He was an indifferent performer with a needle, either at embroidery or plain sewing, and all the raffia mats he made had to be unpicked or thrown away. In any case, though time might have to be allowed for Work, and the financial rewards of Work, Walter could not often be spared for Hobbies. Most of his nineteen years at the Hospital continued to be spent in the faded beige overalls he had been given in his first year, and

45

in assisting the Staff to feed, clean, shave, dress and undress the non-ambulant patients. Particularly Clifford.

Once a month, Drama was organized in the Main Hall of the Hospital. The organizer was a large lady with hair of a pepper-and-salt colour, roughly the texture of wire wool, pulled well back and disciplined into a bun at the back. She brought with her five disciples from her Studio in the town, and together they acted out 'situations' with the more tractable ambulant patients.

The situations acted out were simple, even childish to Walter's mind, so that he was unwilling to take part in them, but the large lady regarded them with such seriousness that not to participate would have been impolite, and if what was acted out together rarely had much relevance to life in a Mental Hospital, perhaps it did reflect the reality of life outside the gates.

They had, for instance, to rescue a baby from a tree. In this situation, the five disciples stood in the centre of the Main Hall, holding above their heads a sheet, on which a doll had been placed. The Lady Organizer informed Walter and his colleagues that this doll was her baby, and that the tree had taken it from her. The trees in the Hospital Grounds were common elms and sycamores, which did not go about snatching babies – except that in those days before the building of the Unit, there were no babies inside the Main Gate, so perhaps the trees might have snatched them had there been any to snatch. In any case, Walter and others were enlisted to rescue the doll-baby from the snarling, hissing tree. They were not to go straight in, wasting their lives in a useless unplanned attack. They must first make a plan to cut down the tree, before a strong wind came, and blew the baby out. It seemed to Walter that getting the baby out of the tree was what *he* was being required to do, and if a wind would do it for him, why bother? But the baby, he was told, would break if blown out of the tree by wind, but would be safe if only the tree were chopped down instead by Walter and his companions.

Walter worked away with an imaginary axe, chopping at the kicking legs of the disciples. Other patients mimed sawing the tree down. A patient named Roger, who could read, and did read children's comics (donated and brought round once a week on a trolley), set about planting dynamite in the roots of the tree, and laid a long fuse across the hall to a place of safety from which he could blow the tree, baby and all the rescuers at once to smithereens. The baby had, therefore, to be rescued quickly by non-violent means, which was to charm the tree by the use of music. All the patients present, and the Organizer, *and* her disciples joined together to sing 'Rock-a-Bye, Baby, on the Tree-Top', at which the tree quivered for a while, and then lowered the doll on its sheet gently to the ground, to be reclaimed tearfully by its mother, and the patients thanked. Walter had moved his lips, but did not sing.

Then the Lady Organizer had called for silence. In the general buzz of mutual congratulation, she had to call more than once, but she was a woman of strong personality, and silence was obtained. In that silence, she looked at each patient in turn directly, to compel attention, and then said, very quietly, 'Have you ever thought what would happen to the world, if all the patients all over the country, who are in Mental Hospitals like this one, were suddenly to decide to go on strike, or just walk out?' There was a pause. None of them had ever had that thought. Those who were capable of reason, applied reason to it. The single member of Staff present in case of emergencies, cleared his throat.

The Lady Organizer, who had been sitting cross-legged, still holding the doll, now stood, and gave the doll to a disciple. 'About sixty thousand people live and die in Hospitals like this one,' she said. 'Did you know that?' The disciples began to gather up their props. Drama was over for that month.

Walter remembered the lady's question for a long time, and thought about it often. He knew what a strike was; though he had never taken part in one, strikes had been spoken of when he worked at Woolworth's. But his imagination would not stretch to the concept of sixty thousand people walking out of hospitals all over the country at some prearranged signal. Where would they go, where would they live? He knew well enough that he was not the only patient with no family and no home; most of his fellows in the Hospital were in the same condition, and there were others whose families would not have them at home, because

47

they were too much trouble. The Hospital was their home. Perhaps the Lady Organizer had not thought of that.

Nevertheless the question worried him. It would not have been put if it had not been thought important. Was there, in fact, some provision made for people like Walter, even for Jesus's Mistakes, outside the Hospital, where they could go if they were ever to strike or for any other reason, and was the knowledge of this place being deliberately kept from them?

2

A young man sat cutting his arm with a rusty razor-blade. He said he just wanted to know what it felt like.

In the Mother and Baby Unit, there was a small lounge, with armchairs, a settee, a television set, a radio and a very large supply of back numbers of *Woman* and *Woman's Own*. There was a small kitchen, used mainly by the nurses, and a dining-room with ten chairs set round a central table. Behind each of the ten chairs, pushed against the wall, there was a baby's high chair.

Upstairs there were two bedrooms of three beds, and two of two beds. There were two bathrooms and three W.C.s.

In the corridor between the kitchen and the lounge (where the television set was left on all the time, even when there was only a test card to look at), a tall girl paced backwards and forwards. She was seventeen years old. She was chain-smoking, dragging on each cigarette with exaggerated energy. Every time she reached the door of the lounge, she stopped for a moment, and looked towards her child, who was bouncing up and down in a walking-frame. The child was happy and pretty. Her seventeen-year-old mother had so far made two attempts to kill her.

'Fetch her a nappy.' A young nurse was speaking.

'No. She's all right.' The young mother turned away.

'I said, "Fetch her a nappy." ' The nurse stood, blocking the girl's way.

'I've just changed her.' The young mother dropped her cigarette

49

butt onto the linoleum, and twisted the pad of her carpet-slippered foot on top of it.

'She's damp.'

'So what? She dribbles.' The young mother searched her pocket for matches.

'I'll wait here until you fetch her a clean nappy.'

'You'll wait a fucking long time, then.'

The conversation was about the state of the baby's nappy, but its sub-text was about authority and ownership. Since the young mother's attempts at infanticide, the child had become the property of the State, or rather of the Social Services, whom the nurse was now representing. The baby could be kept if the mother would accept help and treatment, or it could be given away if the mother were, over an acceptable period of trial, to prove to be unfit to keep it. What it could not be was thrown away; what it must not be was abandoned in the Ladies' Waiting-Room of a bus station.

'I left it there because I knew, if I kept it, I'd try to kill it again. I haven't had a moment's happiness since it came. Nobody cares about me any more; it's all her.'

They had made allowances for the mother's youth, and for the fact that the father was already married. No member of the Social Services would easily consent to separating a child from its mother; that was a drastic measure, and should only be undertaken when all else failed. Anyway there is the legal position to consider. Remove a child too readily for fostering and within a month, the mother may demand and receive it back. Time is needed for the mother to consider her position in all its aspects.

While that time is taken, anyone representing the Social Services may expect to have to endure some friction.

Having been unable to find a light for her cigarette, the young mother pushed past the nurse, and went to look for matches. She returned with a box of matches and a clean nappy, and held the nappy out to the nurse. The nurse said, 'You do it.'

'Fuck off, black self-righteous cow ! You're the one who says she's wet. You get paid for this, so you do it; you change her.'

The nappy was thrown at the nurse, who took it, lifted the child from its walking-frame, and talked to it as she changed its nappy.

The young mother watched, drawing even more deeply on her cigarette.

Her name was Kathy. She shared a bedroom with June.

June, watching from the bedroom window, saw Clive's car pull up outside, and watched him as he methodically locked it and went round, checking all the doors. Did he suppose that someone in the Mother and Baby Unit might steal it to make a quick getaway?

She looked beyond the car to the enormous old Mental Hospital, and realized for the first time what they had meant when they had told her that this place was to be a stepping-stone, and why they had avoided saying where next she would go. However, they would not, could not, send Baby John with her to that place. As long as Baby John was with her, she could expect to remain on the stepping-stone.

She debated with herself whether to go down and see her visitor, her very first visitor, her baby's father. But she knew that if she did not go down, the nurses would come upstairs and nag at her until she did. As long as the Victorian hell-hole across the way remained a threat, it would be better to play the nurses' game.

He wanted to kiss her. She turned her face to one side, and allowed him to hug her to him. It would make him feel better, would release some of the emotion he felt and perhaps just a tiny bit of the guilt as well.

She said, 'My hair's falling out. Had you noticed?'

'No.'

'Well, it is.'

The nurses had watched the embrace, and watched while she led him towards the lounge.

'Two handfuls yesterday. I didn't comb it this morning. I think my mind is pushing it out from underneath.'

'Have you been getting headaches?'

'It feels as though it's bursting sometimes. Soon grey jelly will start seeping through my eye-sockets. Not long after, it'll all be over, thank God.'

'I'm afraid I didn't bring anything. Grapes or anything.' The only other occupant of the lounge was Kathy's little girl in her walking-frame.

51

'I don't know what's going on. There is something going on. Something strange, but I can't describe it.' They were still standing. 'Do you want to sit down? Take your coat off? How long can you stay?'

He took off his coat, and sat down, but avoided answering her third question, knowing that whatever he said would not please her.

She sat beside him. She had become thoughtful and serious. Now there would be no playing games with herself and him; he knew them all. To her own surprise, she realized that she wanted him to like her. But that was too much to expect, after seven misspent years.

'I'm the only one who knows what goes on inside my head, and I can't describe it to them, so how can they make me better?'

Kathy's baby girl pointed her chubby fingers at Clive, and made gurgling noises.

'All the others know why they're here. Andrea wants to give her baby away. Kathy thinks she may kill hers. Janice's mother wouldn't stop touching her baby, so Janice screamed until someone took notice, and brought her here. Rita has the mind of a seven-year-old, and was raped in the back of a car. All the others have simple post-natal depression, cured by the passing of time, and simple doses of pills. I'm the only one they can't help, because I can't explain. They think I'm not trying.' She was twisting a strand of Rita's knitting wool round and round her right index finger, pulling it tight to make the finger change colour.

'God's the only other person who knows what's going on inside my head. Why does He let people go insane? Why does He allow places like this?'

Clive didn't know. He shook his head.

'The vicar was here. He doesn't count as a visitor. He comes to see us all. I asked him. I said, 'Why does God allow it?'

'What did he answer?'

'I can't remember.'

'It couldn't have been very enlightening.' He was not used to her new-found interest in religion. 'Anyway, I thought you didn't believe in God.'

She frowned. Either she had not heard him, or had not understood. She said, 'I don't see why people shouldn't be allowed just to be put to sleep, do you? What's the point of Mental Hospitals?'

'Some people get well.' There was no conviction in his voice.

She thought he looked fatter. He looked well. Myra must be looking after him. He must be sleeping, living a restful uneventful unhysterical quiet life.

It was time. While with her, he had lost weight, developed bags under his eyes from lack of sleep, had always looked shell-shocked, always waiting for the next attack, mental or physical. He had never hit back. Never. Not even once. With her, he had been perpetually off balance, from dodging the missiles she threw. The screaming! crying! sulking! She remembered her own guilt, and the aftertaste of pointlessness, and the numbing calm before the next attack. One psychiatrist had called it 'psychic numbing'. So much of psychiatry seemed to her to be more to do with the giving of names than of curing.

Yes, he looked well. She had spoiled and wasted seven years of his life. She owed him an explanation.

'I never knew, you see. I never realized that people could know they were going mad, and not be able to do anything about it. I'd always thought it just happened, without one's knowing, that one went on believing that one was just the same and it was the others who'd changed. Everyone out of step but me. Do you understand what I mean?'

He nodded.

'It's cruel, isn't it? When you know it's happening?' Again he nodded. 'How can they help me, if I can't tell them what's wrong?' She saw that he was wary, unsure as to whether she were playing one of her little games with him. He wasn't used to her being serious, not about something as important as this. But she was sure, as sure as she could ever be about anything. She was sure. She was serious.

His bewildered expression told her that he couldn't help. He looked well and prosperous, he had put on weight, but he couldn't help.

'The other day was good. I knew that the voices on the radio were real, and that the lawn outside was real; I walked on it. I

53

have been outside; I am allowed. We could go for a walk now if we wanted.'

He held her look for a moment. It was a moment that seemed to contain all those other moments when they had been physically close, and she almost cried out for the comfort in those moments. Then he looked down at his wrist, and June noticed his watch, and realized that the comfort of those physically close moments was all in the past.

She had cried 'Wolf!' too often. It was unfair even to consider that he might help her. She would let him off the hook gently. She owed him that, at least.

'But then that meant that up until that time, I couldn't have known that the voices on the radio and the lawn outside were real.'

There, she had done it, had admitted that she was not well, suffered hallucinations, could be considered mad. Therefore he had been right to leave her; he was not a psychiatrist, and could not have helped. She watched the muscles in his face relax. He was no longer responsible for her.

A thought: 'June needs help' does not mean, 'June requires support and assistance from those who love her,' but, 'June has no right to expect anything, even love, from those who say they love her, but must seek assistance from the place authorized to give it, which is the Bin.'

Kathy's little girl had managed to move the walking-frame, and was standing close to Clive, with a sticky hand held out, patting his knee. The child's face looked up at him, bright and alive with hope. Kathy paced the corridor, and stopped each time at the door to look at her child, as if she were trying to come to a decision.

Clive touched the fine blonde hair of Kathy's little girl. He said, 'Who are you, then? Who do you belong to?' The baby made gurgling noises of laughter, and patted harder at this unfamiliar knee covered with fawn cavalry twill.

June said, 'Do you want to see Baby John?'

'Yes, of course. Where is he?'

'Sleeping. I'll get him in a moment.' He reached for her hand, and took it inside his. 'Now he feels secure,' she thought. 'He knows there isn't going to be a scene. No demands, no threats. Poor love! he's so transparent.'

54

Her hand was cold and dry, and the skin hard. Difficult to believe it could ever had been sensitive to touch. The knuckles were hard, like knots in oak. He didn't remember her hands like this. These were the hands of a stranger, not the hands which once had been able to arouse him. These were dead hands. Perhaps that was where death started, at the extremities. It couldn't be far away from her; he had seen it in her face. She had often said that death was what she had always wanted. But what would happen to the child – his child?

'Today isn't a normal day.'

'Why not?'

'It just isn't.'

'Is it better or worse?'

'Both.' Kathy had stopped pacing, and stood just outside the door, looking at her child, and scowling. Clive moved his hand away from the child's head.

'I'd give anything not to be here. I made a pact with God. He can have all my hair and teeth if He'll give me my mind back.'

'I thought it was your mind you were trying to get away from.' She thought, 'If only he wouldn't preface every remark by saying "I thought" in that way! Doesn't he know how it provokes me?' There was nothing for him here. Why bother to come? She was not his wife. They had pretended; that was all. Myra had the ring. the licence, and now what went with them, her husband. He was back. He had just been away for a rather long holiday, a seven-year sabbatical. Soon Myra would be presenting him with a legitimate baby. Why had he come?

'Why did you come?'

'To see you.'

'Why?'

'You've no one else.'

'Is that a good enough reason?'

'I think so.'

'Does Myra know?'

'Yes, of course she does.'

He was lying. Childishly he had allowed himself to be led into a trap. He had given himself away, and the likelihood was that, when he got home to Myra, she would also know that he was lying about where he'd been. The idea almost made June laugh, but she forbore. Instead she thought, 'If I feel nothing, then death is not taking place.'

A young man had arrived to see one of the other women. The two of them sat holding hands in the opposite corner of the lounge, and talked in whispers. She was called Enid. She was about to be sent home.

'Are you sure you want to see Baby John? You don't have to, just to be polite.'

'I want to see him.'

She released her dead hand from his, and stood up. 'I'll see if he's awake.'

She did not come back, and, after waiting fifteen minutes, Clive asked one of the nurses to make sure that June was all right. The nurse returned to tell Clive that June was in the bath. And so he left.

The sun shone directly through the window. She lay in the bath, hands on either side of her nose, eyes not quite fully closed, and felt the ache of disappointment well up from the base of her stomach.

What she saw were the translucent gossamer wings of butterflies, made in collaboration by the strong sun and her lowered eyelashes. What she felt was disappointment enough to make her cry, to break her heart, all that. (Her heart, she decided. was pumping a little faster than usual.) It was the injustice of her disappointment which was unbearable, like heartburn which never went away, and could not be alleviated by Bisodol. Had anyone died of a continuous heartburn?

She looked down at her body. It was hers, but she did not wish to have it.

'It's yourself you're trying to punish, not me. Your anger's directed towards you really, not me. It's you whom you wish to harm, not me. Why?'

She didn't know why. Of all the people she had ever known, only Clive used the word 'whom'. And she used it sometimes.

'That's why you had asthma as a child.' Was that Clive? No, it was the therapist. Therefore, recast the phrasing. Therapists ask

56

questions; they rarely make statements. '*Was that why you had asthma as a child?*' Better. '*Self-inflicted hysteria, do you think? Isn't your anger really fear? So where does that leave us?*'

Surely he meant, where did it leave her? She had thought about the question, stretching her mind to pull it free from the numbing effects of Valium and anti-depressants, and had spoken slowly, hearing her words slur. 'I'm angry with myself, and the anger is really fear?' The shrink had nodded, pleased that she had it right. It had seemed to June that she was like Frankenstein's Monster, slowly repeating well-rehearsed sentences to prove it was human. 'You're saying that I'm frightened of myself, and not of life?'

A pause. Then, 'What do *you* think?'

She thought. 'I think you're sitting in the wrong chair, doctor.'

Puzzled. 'What makes you say that?'

'Nothing makes me; I just chose to. I'd disproved all that Freudian "self-fear" crap before I was twenty. Where have you been, doctor?'

He had swallowed. Score! She had thrown him. Then, 'I'm quite aware of your intellectual – '

'Then, don't insult it, for Christ's sake.'

Blinked. Reached for a prop to occupy his hands. It had been a gold propelling-pencil. 'Why do you write something off, just because it seems simplistic?' Still strong with the questions.

She had brought his face into as sharp a focus as the drugs would allow, and studied it. Did he really believe what he had said, or was he just treading water while he sought for something more convincing?

She had tried to help him. 'Couldn't we at least start from the point where I blame myself for what happened to my mother, so it's not just myself that I'm angry at stroke frightened of; it's my performance. Or to put it more simply, doctor, it's what I do that makes me angry and frightened, not what I am. I know how an intelligent woman ought to behave, but I don't wish to "behave"; it bores me. And boredom frightens me. The blank pointlessness of one day following another without change. The daily routine, that's what sends me flying to the aspirin bottle.' He had continued to watch her, his fingers twisting the propelling-pencil. 'I once tried one of those Therapeutic Communities; you know the sort of

57

thing – "Growth through shared living"; we were going to discuss and question some common assumptions. Sounded like an excuse for several days of free groping and a bit of tripping the light fanego – "Ego-trips round the lighthouse, and home for a Cream Tea." Well, it was a mess, of course, but not in the way I'd expected. Most of that happy group were so bored that they couldn't even bear being awake. One young man sat cutting his arm with a rusty razor-blade; he said he just wanted to know what it felt like. Well, that's me, doctor; I'm him. Except that I'm a physical coward.'

He had not reacted, and his expression had been similar to expressions June had very often seen before, and which had usually meant, 'Don't ring us. We'll ring you.'

The bath water was cold, and a nurse was banging at the door. There were no locks on the door, for obvious reasons. The nurse came in.

'Get out of that bath, you selfish person. We only got two baths up here, and you lie there for over an hour like Lady Muck. Three more minutes, then I pull you out by the hair myself, OK?'

June leaned forward, and pulled the plug out. Stepping-stone or no, she did not have to step, and would not, not to there, not to that piece of Victorian ugliness, not to any Mental Hospital. The black, brown, Irish, Scottish, Welsh and yellow sods in white coats who had fucked up her plans, and forced her to live, taken away her positive wish to die and left only a hole where once it was, could go and screw themselves.

Next time she would make sure, do it quickly, use a bread knife. Surely it was only like cutting a finger, over in a minute, and no comeback. She certainly wouldn't use pills again. Most of them were bloody placebos anyway. And gas had lost its lethal effectiveness. Thanks to the bloody North Sea, one could no longer either commit suicide or simmer a stew; everything burned on North Sea Gas except the human soul. A double-barrelled shotgun up through the mouth would be quick, providing one's arms were long enough to reach the trigger. Perhaps she should fall onto a bread knife, as people in Shakespeare fell on their swords. *Hold here this bread knife, Rufio, while I run upon it.*

Slit wrists in a warm bath might be colourful and noble, but

58

some sod would be bound to want to borrow a cup of sugar, or sell you an Encyclopedia before the water had time to cool.

The water in her own bath had meanwhile run away, down the plughole.

3

If she were to compete, she knew, she would lose him completely.

They met every day, leaned against the same bricks in the same wall, and looked down at Walter's stretch of concrete. He would have told her that it was he who had made what they were standing on, and that it was level and safe, without cracks, but he dared not speak. She talked; he listened. Sometimes he would nod, sometimes shake his head, but he never spoke, for he remembered, 'Your voice sounds like a fart in a bath of soapy water.'

The second time they had met, she had asked him what his name was, and he had produced a pencil from his pocket, and printed 'WALTER' on one of the new red bricks. Then she had said his name, and told him hers was June (which he knew), printing it on the brick next to the one he had used. Then she had asked him why he never spoke, and he had not answered. She had waited, and then asked gently if it was because he couldn't speak. He had looked at the ground, unable to lie and unable to tell the truth. She had nodded slowly, and touched his hand, and Walter guessed that she had taken his lack of a reply to mean that he wasn't able. She had said, 'What can't speak, can't lie. What isn't a lie must be true, Walter. True; straight; level, like this wall. You must have your own built-in spirit-level, set into your head.'

He had nothing set into his head, though one of the inmates of his Ward had a metal plate, the result of an attack by boys while he was still Outside. But he would not contradict her.

June thought it ironic that truth should be found here, not locked

60

in, but confined, all the same, by ignorance, that she should bump up against truth by accident in a Mental Home, where more lies are told by the minute than in any other human institution, save perhaps the House of Commons.

Time passed, and nothing changed but the cloud formations, and they changed slowly. She did not talk all the time, nor did he listen. She was thirty-eight years old, with a wealth of experience (most of which she would have been happier without) and he was forty-six with very little experience of the world outside those large wrought-iron gates, towards which she would often look. When this happened, Walter felt cold, shut out, empty, as he had on the day his father died. He wanted to say something to distract her attention from the gates, but dared not speak now, or she would be angry with him for deceiving her.

He was aware that, since he had begun to come and stand here beside her, his mind had slowly changed, and that he now believed that the real world began outside the Hospital gates, not inside. His world inside the gates was real too, but it was different, a different world for people who were different, who were too sad, too odd, too old, too handicapped to look after themselves, or for violent people who might harm others and themselves. June was not part of this world. Neither was he. If June was sad, that was something which passed. (For Walter, sadness was something which always passed.) He and June were not there because they were mistakes made by Jesus. They were there because of mistakes made by people outside the main gates.

She was looking outside. He scraped the side of his shoe across the ripples in the concrete to distract her, and she turned, and looked at him. She said, 'What are you thinking?'

He tried to smile without showing his teeth. She would not be pleased by their colour.

'Did you never learn Sign Language?' He shook his head.

'Not that it would help us, unless I learned it too.'

He wanted to know why she was here, why she was unhappy; he wanted to see her baby. He took out his pencil, and printed 'BOY OR GRIL?' on one of the bricks. Then he pointed to the door of the Mother and Baby Unit.

'It's a boy. Baby John. Don't ask me why I call him "Baby"; I

61

don't know. Except perhaps to remind myself that he *is* a baby, and helpless.' She had never thought of it until now.

'Babies survive, though, most of them at least. There are a lot of people looking after their interests. It's the grown-up babies like me who need help. My baby eats, sleeps, cries, breaks wind, and smiles. They tell me the first three months is the most important time for him. If I give him enough affection, and make him feel secure, he'll grow into a healthy normal upright boring citizen, and resent visiting me at Christmas. But how do you give affection if fear is a regular part of your day, and you can't even fight it, because you don't know where it's come from, or why it's there?'

She had lost him. He was looking at the Main Gate. Their relationship was based on simple thoughts, simply transmitted, and received in a simple way. It was one-sided, since she spoke and he wrote misspelled words on bricks or made primitive signs, but she welcomed it, and found it relaxing. No performance, no games, no need to compete or to pretend. If she did, she was sure she would lose him completely, scare him away, and she needed him, needed his truth, needed someone who couldn't, wouldn't judge her. He stood there, with his flat cap above his beak of a nose, and received all she said without evaluation. She had arrived in Hell, and found a soulmate.

'Will you hold my hand?' She held a hand out towards Walter, and he looked down at it. Slowly he lifted his own arm, and took her small fingers into his.

'Thank you. It's more reassuring than holding the wall.' Her fingers tightened their grasp on his. The dry hardness of her hand surprised him.

Four days later, he brought her a present.

He had made a small box out of cardboard and Sellotape. He had stolen a piece of purple satin, used in the making of Valentines. He had placed the piece of satin (which had the words 'My Valentine' printed on it in gold) inside the box, and placed on top of it his mother's diamanté ear-rings. Of the objects which he had brought with him to the Hospital, they were the only ones still in his possession.

Bright red tissue paper, left over from the previous Christmas, had been used to wrap the box, and silver tinsel tied in a bow which it had taken him thirty minutes to perfect.

Then he had carried the beautifully wrapped present around in his pocket for six days, unable to find the right moment to give it to her.

Now he held out the present. She took it from his outstretched hand, and began slowly to unwrap it, frequently pausing to look up at him and show her pleasure.

'You've wrapped it beautifully. It must have taken hours.' She removed the lid of the home-made box.

'Ear-rings! They're lovely.' She held them up to the sun, and they glittered. 'It's the Eiffel Tower, isn't it?' Walter nodded.

'But where did you get them?' Walter printed 'M.U.M.' on one of the bricks. Soon they would have to leave his patch of concrete path in order to reach clean bricks on which to write. Nothing was ever rubbed out or written over.

'Are you sure you really want me to have them?' Walter nodded vigorously.

'I need my hair done properly now, to show them off.' Walter smiled, hiding his teeth. It had been all right. She had not laughed at him.

By now Walter had begun to neglect the jobs he did for the Staff on the wards. From some he excused himself, some he delegated to other patients, and some he did at twice his normal speed. Fortunately, the job which, up to five years ago, had taken most of his time, was now automated. No longer had he to marshal his charges outside the Wash Room for shaving, run in to soap six chins, run out again to reorganize those waiting, while an orderly scraped at chins on which the soap was already drying with a blunt Seven O'Clock blade. There were two electric shavers fastened to the wall in each of the wards for men, and Walter lined up those to be shaved in short lines, as far as the flex would reach, allowing them to lean against the wall like puppets some of whose strings have been cut, and when they were shaved it was without cuts or irritating rashes.

Members of Staff, nurses in white coats, orderlies in brown, noticed Walter's new neglect of his duties, and resented it. He was a trusty; they trusted him. Once he had lied for them – or had, at least, not told the truth – had covered up neglect, the murder of one patient by another in the Wash Room, but few of those members of Staff whom he had protected now remained; the episode was forgotten, except by Walter. What members of Staff knew now was that someone who had felt pleasure and pride in being at their beck and call, now spent all the time he could make in leaning against the wall of the Mother and Baby Unit, holding the hand of a female patient. They became jocular with him. 'Here's our Casanova. Here's our sexy Walter. Got the ring yet, Walter? Has she proposed to you yet? Going steady? Got a ready-made family there, Walter. Has she given you your oats yet? Shown you how it's done? Have to keep your pencil sharp, Walter.'

Just so, long ago, before he ever entered the bounds of the Hospital, mock had been made of Walter by the bus-conductor and his friendly passengers, and by the trainee floorwalkers of Woolworth's. *I laugh. He laughs. They laugh.*

'How old are you, Walter?'

Walter scribbled on a brick, first the number four, then the number six. He did not feel forty-six, or even twenty-six, had no real notion of age, which was to do with birthdays which were not celebrated in the Hospital. Nineteen years he had been here. Nineteen years spent, quite gone; they would not be given back to him for good service. He couldn't even begin to add up the number of mornings he had woken up in the same bed, or the number of meals he had fed to Clifford, or the number of faces on which he had spread shaving-soap.

Ben Gunn had died long ago, eleven years. He would not have been allowed into Paradise. Jesus would not have wished Ben Gunn to live with Him for ever. Even a short visit was unlikely. The Devil would have taken Benn Gunn in. Perhaps Ben Gunn had known this, and his behaviour in the Ward had merely been practice for Hell.

Clifford remained. Walter tried to imagine Clifford wearing long white flowing robes. He would stain them, and if he continued to stink as he stank now, Paradise would cease to be paradisal. Yet, as far as anyone was able to tell, Clifford was good, not evil. Speechless and confined, as he was, in a wheelchair, his opportunities for

64

evil-doing were not many. Also, as far as could be guessed, he suffered, and it was only fair that he should at last experience bliss.

As Walter watched the clouds moving slowly, he thought of meeting his parents again in Paradise, of being above those slow-moving clouds. Would there be pigeons? His father, he knew, would wish them. The Russian High-Fliers which had been kept in the Loft at the end of the yard had, even in this life, often ventured above the clouds, and had to be brought down again by the shaking of a food tin or the sending out of Freda, the dove, best-loved, as a decoy.

He was alone, and no thinking of a Paradise full of pigeons and of parents (though his mother had never liked them) could make him less so. Only holding June's hand, and listening to her talk, made him less alone. But now, although he was with her, she was leaning back against the wall, with her head turned towards the Main Gate, and his sense of aloneness was as complete as it had ever been.

His mother had told him that Jesus had given him his body to look after. It was his, but only on loan until he died, and he had a duty to keep it well, and clean at all times, ready for Judgement Day, when Jesus was to decide who should live with Him and who must go elsewhere. And yet his mother herself had gone to Jesus with pigeon droppings in her hair, and He had not sent her back to brush them out.

He had more than his own body to look after now. Maurice and Albert, he had cared for them more intimately than his own mother had cared for him, touching and cleaning parts his mother would not touch. Clifford ... it was a long losing battle he had with Clifford's body, perpetually renewed; it would never end. What would happen to Clifford – her head was still turned towards the Main Gate – what would happen to Clifford if Walter were ever to leave the Hospital?

June had not slept, had lain awake all night wondering which of her memories the current of electricity would blot out, had made a list in her head of priorities, which should go first, had contemplated the uniqueness of human memory, no two minds recalling the same incident in the same way, had forgotten totally the many

65

times she had wished to be without those memories which were now in danger and which she had now begun to cherish.

She had laughed when they had said to her, 'It leaves no lasting deficit,' which made it sound like an overdraft at the Midland Bank. She had laughed, imagining old Thanatos, the death-wish, in unarmed combat with tiddly little Eros, the libido, the life-wish. 'Watch out, Eros. Your loincloth's slipping.'

Now she was watching the light grow through the gap in the curtains. It must be six o'clock, or maybe seven. She never wore a watch.

At ten thirty, they were coming to collect her, and take her over to the 'treatment' room.

The Sister had said, 'There's nothing whatsoever to be frightened of,' and June had replied, 'I give you full permission to finish me off. I'll put it in writing if you like. I'm not afraid of death, only pain.' The Sister had made a sound with her tongue and teeth, signifying that she had lost all patience.

Oh, Sister, you have lost all patients. That would be the day.

June lay on her bed, on top of the covers, staring at the lampshade, patterned with flowers. There were no bluebells, no snowdrops, no wild flowers. The flowers were not identifiable at all; they were an unimaginative designer's impression of flowers, simple lines and unnatural colours, confected to be mass-produced, as untruthful as people. Except, of course, for Walter.

What was she doing, still in this world, filling up space and breathing air, both of which might be put to a more productive use?

At ten twenty-four, two nurses came for her. They were the same two who had walked the man over the gravel in his bare feet. They smiled, and nodded towards her, and said, 'How are we this morning?' without desiring a reply, but she had had her answer ready, 'Ready to lose our head.' Then they had both laughed, without conviction, and one of them had said, 'Your boyfriend's outside. You'd better comb your hair.'

It was true; Walter was outside, leaning against the wall. He had been there since nine o'clock. When the nurses appeared, holding June by the arms, he stood almost to attention, and gave a half-hearted wave.

June didn't see the wave. She was concentrating on what her feet were doing. She did not wish to lose her slippers. One of the nurses shouted to Walter, 'She'll be all right tomorrow. Come and see her then.' Walter's mouth opened, and he was about to shout his thanks, but he remembered in time that he was dumb, closed his mouth again, and put his hand over it to keep it shut.

'You're early. I haven't done this one yet.' A man in a white coat spoke to the two nurses.

'We'll wait.' Along the wall was a line of chairs, and the two nurses sat down, leaving a chair between them on which June was to sit. June sat.

'This one' was a woman in her fifties, who lay on a high bed. She was quite conscious, and she turned her head towards June, opening her toothless mouth, and saying, 'You'll not want to watch this, love. Get them to walk you outside for a bit.' June noticed that the woman's false teeth and brooch were on top of the cabinet next to the high bed.

The man in the white coat, who now held a syringe, said, 'You stop being bossy, Mary, or I'll change this sharp needle for a blunt one.'

'Well, look at 'um. Lazy so-and-so's!' She referred to the two nurses.

After the injection, the man cleaned Mary's hair with spirit, and applied a white lotion to her forehead. The nurses made no move to take June away. One of them had picked up a magazine, and was reading how to mask unsightly spots or acne. The man looked at the nurses from time to time, and clearly would have preferred June not to watch, but only when he was standing with the E.C.T. machine switched on, and the headphone-like contraption in his hands did he say, 'Well, if you're not going to take her away, you'd better bring the screens.' The nurse who was not reading sighed noisily as she crossed the room and brought one hospital screen of tubular frame and green cloth, which she placed in front of June instead of around the woman in bed. The other nurse stopped reading in order to laugh.

'I don't know why you're so sensitive about her feelings. You should see her card. This one's tried to kill herself more times than you've had hot dinners.'

June could see almost as much through the gap between the steel frame and the green cloth as she could before the screen had been placed round her. It was almost as if the nurses wanted her to see what was going to happen to her.

The man placed the headphones on the front of Mary's head, each round piece covering a temple, and Mary's body went into convulsions, her legs kicking out wildly and her arms swinging and thumping the bed. The limbs came down so hard that June felt sure one of them would break. Then white foam appeared at the corner of the woman's mouth; she looked like a dog in the throes of distemper. Mickey had looked like that.

June closed her eyes, and thought of the memories she might lose, thought of her list of priorities, of her mother sitting on the doorstep in her nightdress, her mother lying on the bed looking up at her without seeing her, of the grey blanket she couldn't get under, of walking and running miles back to see her, of her not being there, and of crying for days thereafter without stopping. She thought of the children's shrink who had told her, told a child who could not have been capable of understanding such a thought, that her tears were a protest, and that after them would come mourning, mourning for the lost object, and then – had he predicted Thanatos, the death wish? No, he could not have done that, would never have made such a prediction to a child, would have told her (*had* he?) that after a proper period of mourning the 'process of healing' could begin. But it had not begun, because all too soon came Mickey, and the woman's flying limbs now brought back the feeling and smell of Mickey so strongly that June leaned back and banged her head against the wall to stop the flow of moving pictures in her mind.

Mickey had looked like that, just like that, the last time she had seen him. They had shared a bedroom. Both were foster-children, fostered by a woman they had called 'Auntie Eva.' Mickey was a year and three months younger than June, and, as well as a room, they had shared a feeling of separateness, both being in mourning for the loss of their love. They shared each other's secrets and brushed each other's hair, whenever either of them felt the need for tears, since they had forbidden themselves tears.

Someone was holding June's head, to prevent her banging it

against the wall. The teeth of the two nurses were clenched with the effort of keeping June's head still.

Mickey had clenched his teeth; he had looked like these two faces, one on each side of her. He had galloped along the path through the field in front of her, pretending to be a horse, and she had galloped behind, holding on to the end of his school tie, pretending to be his charioteer. Then he had fallen in front of her, and she had stumbled over him, laughing, believing that he had fallen on purpose in order to wrestle with her on the ground. He had done that before.

Only, this time he didn't laugh with her, or lunge at her, rolling with her over and over in the grass. This time he shook, his limbs jerking and thumping the ground, as if he were a shot rabbit, except that a shot rabbit squeals, and Mickey made no sound at all but the sound of his limbs thrashing the ground. He had looked at her, and she had seen from his face that he was terrified, and noticed for the first time how green his eyes were, pale green like the colour of unripe apples.

Froth had come from Mickey's mouth, just as it came now from the mouth of the woman on the high bed. And June had run home, screaming – no, not home; she had never called it that – had run to Auntie Eva's house, screaming and crying and trying to get the words out to tell what had happened. They had run back together to where Mickey lay, but he had stopped struggling and kicking by the time they reached him, and lay still, with his school tie draped across his chalk-white face and covering his left eye.

She had watched Auntie Eva undo Mickey's tie and some of his shirt buttons, and lift him in her arms, pressing him against her purple cardigan, and talk to him as if he were still alive. 'Come on home, Mickey darling. Come on home for your tea. What did you do today? Did you eat your dinner? Were you a good boy?'

Auntie Eva had carried Mickey home in her arms, and June had remained where she was, looking down at the trodden grass.

She had never seen him again. She had never asked about him, and his name was never mentioned again in Aunt Eva's house. She was now Auntie Eva's only child – her only foster-child. She and Uncle Phil never asked for another.

Four weeks later at school, another boy had told her that he knew where Mickey the Mouse was buried. He said he had seen men digging a new hole, a small one, and had later watched them filling the hole in again, after people in their best clothes had walked away from it. The boy had asked her whether she had seen Mickey die, and what a dead person looked like. She had told the boy that it was just as if they'd gone to sleep, and the boy had said he did not believe her.

But Mickey had looked like that. In the end.

Her eyes opened, and she tried to focus them. She saw a lampshade, with artificial flowers painted on it. She had been asleep, but for how long? She could tell by the amount of light coming through the gap in the curtains that it must be either early evening or early morning. But which? And at what time of year?

She lifted her head from the pillow, and a sharp pain shot through her left temple. She felt heavy, too heavy to lift herself up onto an elbow. Her head ached.

There was another bed in the room, unmade. June smiled. Mickey had never made his bed. Why did she feel so heavy, so large? Was this the day she had planned to go home? Had they guessed that she intended to run away again, and had given her something to make her heavy so that she could not run?

Someone was arguing downstairs. Shouting. She could not make out the words. A woman's voice was screaming hysterically. Was it her mother? Had her mother come to take her home? Auntie Eva never shouted like that. She must get up quickly, go downstairs, see her mother, persuade her mother to take her away from here. That was why they had given her something to make her sleep.

June rolled onto her side, and reached for the floor with her left hand. The pain in her head grew worse. Someone was tugging her hair out by the roots. With her hand on the floor, she lowered her left leg to the ground, then her right hand, and finally her right leg. She was out of bed, but could not truthfully be called 'up'. Why did every action take so long?

She crawled on hands and knees towards the door. The carpet was new. There had been no carpet before; she remembered boards, dark oak-stained floorboards surrounding a square of blue lino.

There were toys too on the floor. She could not recognize them. They were not hers or Mickey's; they were for a baby.

At the door, she reached up for the handle, and used it to pull herself to her feet, but her legs buckled, and she slid to the floor again.

If only she could get downstairs where they were arguing ! Even if it wasn't her mother's voice she could hear, but the voice of a stranger, she would still be able to sneak out by the back way, and run to the railway line. Then all she would have to do would be to follow it. She had not been that way before. They would not think of it. Why did her head hurt so much?

'You stupid fucking cow, I'll knock your teeth out if you don't shut up. You put her down.' Kathy was pacing the Television Lounge, the veins in her neck standing out, as she screamed at the woman who sat holding her little girl. The other woman tried to ignore Kathy, and to watch the television.

'Put her down. She's sodding well mine.'

The woman holding Kathy's little girl remained absolutely still, her right hand pressing the child's head against her chest.

'Please do as she says. Put her baby down.' A nurse, who had up until now watched in silence, was speaking.

'Not until she finds the manners to say "Please". She's not fit to have a lovely little baby like you, is she, my love?'

Kathy darted across the room, pulled the baby from the woman's arms, and flung it to the floor. It screamed, and the nurse rushed forwards. As the woman started to rise, Kathy grabbed her hair, and smashed her head against the television screen. The whole of one side of the woman's face oozed blood, where it had been torn by the jagged glass of the screen.

June had managed to get the bedroom door open and had slithered downstairs in a sitting position. She had almost reached the bottom when she heard more screams, as women ran out of the Television Lounge.

'Fucking stupid silly cow ! Wouldn't listen. I warned her.' Two nurses were struggling to hold Kathy's arms. Nobody would spare time and effort to attend to the woman with the cut face. Kathy broke free of the nurses, caught her little girl up in her arms, and ran past June and up the stairs.

June, who could make out only that a woman carrying something was rushing past her, shouted, 'Where are you going, Mummy? I'm here. Don't go. What are you carrying? I don't want another doll. *Please! Take me home!*' Up above, a bedroom door could be heard to slam.

When June reached the door of the Television Lounge, she saw two nurses leaning over a woman in a purple cardigan, whose face was covered in blood. The nurses were picking pieces of broken glass out of the face, and the woman sobbed as they did so. This woman was Kathy's mother.

June said, 'Why does she never talk about Mickey? Can you tell me?'

4

Let's go over to the dead elm, and watch its nerve-ends drop to the ground.

'A blow-fly's brain weighs only point eight four milligrams. Yet its behaviour may be richly complex.' She waited for a response. The day was cold.

'What do you think about that?' Since, even if he had been capable of any positive response, it could hardly have been written on a brick, Walter shrugged his shoulders, and smiled.

'It was in *The Reader's Digest*. All human life is there.' Walter frowned. Her voice sounded different. Louder. Sharper. She was leaning against the wall as usual, but rubbing her knuckles over the bricks, and bruising them. He held out his hand, and she took it. 'Yes, hold my hand. I was so frightened yesterday. I almost came to look for you.' He placed both his hands round her bruised hand, and held it tight.

'Why do you never talk to me? Why won't you? Why do I have to talk for both of us?'

Walter looked at her, puzzled and wary. She knew he could talk. How? He took the pencil from his pocket, and searched for a clean brick on which to write, but she took hold of the hand which held the pencil, and said, 'No, don't do that. Please! Say anything, anything at all. I know you can speak. You have a past; tell me about that. What happened to your parents?'

She knew he could speak. Consequently he was not able to speak.

Slowly he returned the pencil to his pocket. She watched. She was upsetting him, making him anxious; he might walk away, and leave her on her own. She must be careful.

'Please, Walter.' It was unfair that he should not speak, when she had told him she knew he could. She wished to be diverted from her own life, did not wish to talk or even think about that; she had spoken to him at length about her own life, her fears, her hates, her desire for death, and now she required diversion, and his life would do. He owed her that. He had deceived her, had allowed her to believe him dumb, allowed her to say silly things while he had listened. At least, she supposed he had listened; he had usually responded in some way – a smile, a frown, a shake or a nod of the head, a word on a brick.

They had shared an unspoken understanding, unspoken because he never spoke. But if he could speak, did that not destroy the understanding? He had visited her every day, and lately they had held hands, and he had looked at her. The penetration of his stare had at first unnerved her, but now she welcomed it, needed it, needed his listening since no one else seemed to listen to her any more, needed his truth.

But if he was deceiving her, where was the truth?

Even now, he did not speak. Why not?

Other people, when she spoke, wore a mask of interest, but behind it would be busy with thoughts of their own. Even when they made notes of what she said, their attention would be given more to the making of notes than to her, than to June.

'What are you thinking about?'

Walter shrugged.

'Until the year 1770, long before you and I were born, visitors were allowed to enter a Loony Bin called Bethel for a penny a time, just to watch the antics of the lunatics. I doubt if they'd pay anything just to watch you and me standing here.'

Walter had never had a visitor, of a paying or any other sort. Why did she want him to talk?

From where they stood, they could see the bare branches of a tree. It was an elm; it was dying of Dutch Elm Disease, dead twigs still clinging to a branch, the trunk held still by its roots. Perhaps even the roots, deep underground, were decaying, but the fine delicate twigs still moved in the wind, brushed against each other, touched and momentarily held, waiting for leaves, waiting for life, which would never return to them.

'I'm a tree with Dutch Elm Disease. My nerve-ends are like twigs.

They protrude in delicate bunches, and if a strong wind comes along, they'll snap off. Meanwhile I wait.' She sighed. 'I'm thinking aloud, and expecting you to listen. It's better that you don't understand what I say. They don't in there, so why should you? The rooms inside there are too small, and the world outside here is too big. Have you noticed how I cling to this wall? Or to you?' He nodded. 'I never cross a room now; I walk round it, holding on to the furniture. I have to hold onto something, or I notice myself shaking, and that frightens me. I never used to be like that; it must be the drugs. And now there's the E.C.T.' She attempted a smile, and Walter, relieved that she seemed no longer to desire any other response, squeezed the hand he was holding.

Again she fell silent, and watched the comings and goings of nurses and patients. The nurses walked decisively, the patients less so. She watched the decisive nurses, and reminded herself that what she stood on was a stepping-stone. Soon she would be forced to take the next step. Kathy had given her little girl away for adoption, and agreed to be sterilized. This done, they had sent her home. More women had arrived, and left, and the rumour was of a short-age of beds in the Mother and Baby Unit. June now shared a bedroom with Rita, physically thirty-one, mentally and emotion-ally a child, who had nightmares, and kept June awake. Also the room seemed to be full of dolls and the prams of dolls and scrap-books containing coloured pictures of the Royal Family and a general abundance of toys.

Walter was looking beyond her, wondering what, if she should insist on his speaking, he would find to say. He could see trees behind her, and grass, and a sky of blue-grey, and then a bird. It was a pigeon.

'What are you looking at?'

He pointed. 'Oh, a bird.' He was still holding her hand. 'Let's go over to the dead elm, and watch its nerve-ends drop to the ground.' Walter was uncertain. 'It's all right; I'm allowed out as far as that. I just need something to hold onto.'

Still holding her hand, he walked with her. She was a woman. He was holding her hand, and walking with her, across grass. His knowledge of women was small. He remembered the pictures of naked ladies he had been shown at Woolworth's. Those pictures had been mucky, he knew, because the word had been used to describe them, but in some way desirable. A flash of memory brought back to him what had been (though he had not known then that it was) his only sexual experience, when his willy had been stroked by a girl with whom he had been playing hide-and-seek, and he had . . . it had . . . he shivered. That had been on grass behind a bush. He was walking across the grass, holding June's hand. He remembered one of the trainee floorwalkers at Woolworth's, rogering his young lady against the wall of the yard, while Walter swept up litter. He was forty-six years old, and for the last ten weeks his private thoughts had been of June, with whom, hand in hand, he now walked across grass towards a dead elm.

'I can read you like a book, my lad. Nothing you think is hidden from me.'

That was his mother. She had always been right. In every way.

They reached the dead tree, and walked round its thick trunk so that they were hidden from the Hospital. June loosed his hand, and leaned against the tree, looking out first across the open country, then above her at the dead branches. She smiled, and said, 'Are you happy, Walter?'

Was she teasing him? Had she read his thoughts?

'You're not mad, are you?'

He shook his head.

'But is it O.K., being you?'

He thought for a while, then nodded.

'Don't you ever have complicated thoughts, or are they all simple unworried ones?'

Again he frowned, trying to guess what the right answer was, the answer which would please her. Though if he should find it, how could he utter it?

'I know you can talk. I've asked my nurses, and they've spoken to your nurses.'

There! It was out! She did know. He had not told a lie. He had never said he couldn't talk. But he had allowed her to think so.

'Most of the time you look happy – for someone in here, anyway. At least not tormented.' She was tormenting him now, and his face showed the strain of it.

She could not know about the goldfish which were darting about

76

inside Walter's head, all the questions without answers, the thoughts interrupted by other thoughts, none of them finished, none giving him a clue as to what she wanted him to say. There was always a right answer to every question, hidden behind all the wrong answers. There was always one right answer; his mother had taught him that. All you had to do was look for it. But how could he even begin to look when his thoughts would not keep still, but flickered like fishes in a glass bowl?

'Why don't you speak to me, now that we both know you can? Is it because I'm bonkers, and you're not?'

He smiled, couldn't help doing so; for a moment the fish were still. 'Bonkers'. He liked the word. It rhymed with 'conkers'. Which were the colour of her eyes.

It was cold. The cold wind crept its way into her open-knit cardigan. She had been pulling it round herself, but now she let it go, and began instead slowly to undo the top button of her blouse. Walter's eyes moved away from her to the dead twigs of the elm beneath their feet, but he knew what she was doing.

'Give me your hand.' She took his hand, and slid it between the opening of her blouse and the inside of her bra. His hand had been inside his trouser pocket, and was warm, rough, and very large. He discovered that his hand was cupping her left breast, supporting it from beneath, while his forefinger found the nipple, and moved it from side to side.

'Don't be surprised if it leaks on you a bit. Baby John rejected his mother this morning in preference for a bottle. Sometimes they hurt when they get so full.'

June closed her eyes, and leaned back against the tree again. As she moved, Walter attempted to withdraw his hand, but she gripped his wrist, and placed the hand back where it had been. Walter glanced about him, worried that someone might see them. June said, 'Please don't look so worried. This is doing us both some good. Only a baby has been near that for many a long day. They're not the best pair of knockers in the world, but considering their neglected state, they're not too bad. What do you say?'

Walter opened his mouth, formed the words 'Thank you,' and withdrew his hand slowly.

He had spoken.

'I'm sorry if I've shocked you.'

'You were warm.'

'Inside. Yes.' A silence followed. His eyes were turned towards the ground, hers on him, watching and willing him to look at her. And when he did, she smiled, and said, 'Hello, Walter.'

'Hello . . . June.'

She had not laughed at the sound his voice made.

Another silence, broken when June said, 'Now you've made *me* silent. Some would call that a miracle. It's up to you to talk now.'

'Your . . .' He could not bring himself to say the word, but gestured towards the blouse.

'Breasts?'

'Like pigeons. Doves. Touching . . . your . . . Like smoothness. They . . .' He tapped his fingers against his heart to illustrate his meaning. 'Heart . . . beat.' If you wished to lift a pigeon, the left hand must be placed in the air some way above its head to attract its attention, while the right was slid underneath, touching the warm softness of the pigeon's breast. And at those moments you could feel its heart. All this, Walter knew, but his attempt to put it into words succeeded only partially.

'Thank you, Walter.'

She was serious. What he had said had pleased her. She leaned back against the trunk of the tree, her head tilted up to study the sky. It was cold, but it was clear. There was silence in her head. All those prompting, clever, destructive voices which roamed the caverns and corridors of her mind had been struck dumb by one small compliment. No witty venomous toads dropped from her tongue. It was peaceful; she enjoyed the peace, which must, of course, soon end, since it was not in the nature of peace to persist.

'Do you know about doves?'

He did; that knowledge had not gone away, during the long years at the Mental Hospital. There by the tree, grass and dead twigs below their feet, bare branches above, he told her of his father's pigeons, in all their several kinds, the White-Lace Fantails, the Russian High-Fliers, the Long-Faced English Tumblers and the Turbits, of Freda, the dropper, sent up as a decoy to bring the Russians down, who had won a prize, and of the death of Freda, her face turned to the wall and her feathers fluffed out. As they

78

walked back across the grass to the Mother and Baby Unit, holding hands again, he looking down at her, her face turned up to his, he told her of being taken by his father to the Harrogate Show, when Amy, the Tumbler, had come third in her class, of how a small boy had tried to run away with a Black-Lace Fantail, knocked over a whole row of cages, and sent a flight of Antwerp Smerles to roost in the rafters. He told her how, after his father had been taken to Jesus, he himself had looked after the pigeons, fed them, and controlled their breeding by taking their eggs, how then Jesus had taken his mother also, and while Walter had waited to see whether Jesus would keep her or send her back, he had only been able to look after the pigeons by moving them into his mother's bedroom, where Linda and Enid, Fantails, had done battle with their own reflections in the dressing-room mirror, Norman, a Russian, had occupied the pink basketwork chair, Edna and William, Turbits, had used the lampshade as a swing, Marge and Lionel, Tumblers, had copulated on the full-length mirror, and all had shat profusely on his mother's hair.

He had brushed his mother's hair, and tried to keep it free of pigeon droppings, and she had lain for days beneath a purple counterpane on which had been embroidered a gold dragon breathing out green and scarlet flames, and in the end Jesus had made no decision at all, or at least none which he had communicated to Walter, but a Social Worker, a doctor and a policeman had come, and taken Walter away from his mother and from the pigeons, so that he had not seen any of them again since, but assumed that his mother must, after all, be with Jesus, since otherwise she would not have left him in this place.

He talked, and she listened. They walked round the Mother and Baby Unit five times. Words spilled out of Walter's mouth, one memory following another, as if they had been locked up for too long. Then Walter noticed the clock on the central tower, and said that he would be late; he had to help with the handing out of tea. And June said, 'Will you come and see me again?' knowing that he would, and Walter asked whether it was all right for him to come at the same time tomorrow, knowing that it was, and June smiled and nodded, and Walter ran off across the grass, leaving her standing on the concrete he had laid, one hand against the line of bricks in the wall behind her, the other touching the buttons of her blouse.

His voice, if she allowed herself to think of it, was rather like a fart in a bath of soapy water, but there was a comfort in him. He brought peace.

5

A man in a white car stopped and asked me if I knew the way to Oidham

'Will you come with me? Tonight?' She had turned her head to face him, and he could see his own reflection in each of the dark shiny brown conkers which were her eyes.

They were going to move her into the main building. The Mother and Baby Unit was not intended to deal with the problems of long-stay patients. Most of its mothers, if not positively elated, at least less depressed than when they came, were returned to what was called 'the home environment', to be visited by Social Workers; they became out-patients, and attended an Out-Patients' Clinic. Some few, who did not respond to treatment at the Mother and Baby Unit, would require to be separated for a while, for just a while, from the babies with which they could not cope, and would receive more intensive treatment in a hospital environment. This would be for their own good and for their babies' good. The babies would be well looked after while the mothers were receiving this more intensive treatment, and in the end, when the mothers were well again, they would be reunited.

June was, of course, quite free to refuse this treatment. She was not free to remain forever at the Mother and Baby Unit, to break its rules and become its first long-stay patient, but she was free to leave it and to return home. She was free to go wherever she wished, but not (again each freedom brings its own curtailment), not to take Baby John with her. They were sure at the Mother and Baby Unit that June, as an intelligent and responsible woman, would agree that she could not be allowed to take Baby John with her,

81

since, in her present disturbed and depressed state, she might harm him. She had abandoned him once, and attempted suicide. They must assume that, lacking the benefits of more intensive treatment, she would be likely to do so again.

So?

So, if she were to refuse the more intensive treatment and discharge herself, she would not be allowed to keep the baby. The Social Services would apply for a Court Order, to take Baby John into care.

'Will you come with me? I can't do it on my own. I need you to help me.'

She was not stupid; she knew a trick worth two of theirs. They might apply for a Court Order, but if she did not appear, the case could not come to Court; it must be adjourned. Adjourned and adjourned. No magistrate would take a child from its mother without at least hearing what its mother had to say. The Social Services would have the care of Baby John while she was gone; that could not be avoided, whichever choice she made, but it would not be official, it would not be Care, not the subject of a Court Order; they could not, as they had done to June herself, place him with foster-parents or into a Home; he would still be hers.

Only she could not do it alone. She must have help. Walter must help her.

'I've got to get away. Will you come with me? I can't do it on my own.'

Minutes passed. He wanted to tell her that the forbidding Victorian building in which he himself had lived for nineteen years wasn't as frightening as she thought, but though the regime had changed much since he had entered it nineteen years ago, though one grew used to it, she was no more one of Jesus's Mistakes than he was; he knew that; it would not do for her.

He wanted to help her. They had talked together, as he had talked to nobody else. They had held hands, and were holding hands now. His hand had held her breast. But he had responsibilities. Also, during all his time there, he had never broken one of the Hospital's rules, and did not know what would happen if he did. He was a trusty. They trusted him.

82

Her neck was so fine, like a female dove's. He could have made her a necklace of his thumbs and forefingers.

'I . . . can't. Sorry.'

Her lips were dark and dry from the cold, and puckered where the mouth-drying properties of anti-depressant drugs had caused them to split and then heal. She held his hand against her skirt, so that his warm palm was against her body, and the tips of his fingers just touched the mount of Venus. He closed his eyes, and attempted to stop the goldfish darting about inside his head. Mixed with the flashing gold were the coloured lights which moved over the faces of the jigging patients and over the face of Clifford, turning his large open mouth, with its thick lips and suspended saliva, purple. And overlapping with Clifford and the lights and the goldfish there was Mike, the trainee floorwalker, moving his hand up and down inside the knickers of the girlfriend whom he pressed against the wall of Woolworth's yard, while Walter swept up toffee papers and empty cigarette packets and dirt.

'I've got to look after Clifford.'

Beyond the wrought-iron spears of the Main Gate was the road, which led to the world he only saw during walks. In that world there were buses, cars, lorries, people who ate with knives and forks instead of spoons, and wore trousers with buttons and flies for which they were themselves responsible. People in that world slept alone or in pairs, as his parents had done, in small rooms which didn't stink of piss and shit. People in that world made babies as freely as pigeons did, instead of exciting themselves into handker-chiefs or toilet paper and hiding the evidence in their pockets to be flushed down the W.C. later, flushing away what had been given by Jesus to make babies.

'They'll find someone else to look after Clifford.'

'And the others. I help them.'

'They'll find someone else to look after the others. You've done your share. What if Clifford died soon? You'd have wasted your life for nothing. What would your mother say if she knew you'd wasted your life?'

His mother could see him now. She would be looking down at him, with Jesus. She knew what he did with the body he was supposed to be keeping clean for Judgement Day.

83

He moved his hand slowly away from her stomach. He wanted above all else to help her. If they ran away, they would be caught, he supposed, and punished. He could not bear that she should be punished alone.

'Please help me.'

'I . . . can't.'

He knew he would have to help her. And she knew he would.

Since it was Saturday evening, Walter washed, and put on his best clothes to go to the dance in the Main Hall as usual. He had been lucky enough to have found two plastic carrier bags in Sister's office, and had filled them with his belongings. He had tied the bags to the underside of Clifford's wheelchair, and draped a blanket over the chair while he had bathed and dressed Clifford ready for the dance. Clifford's eyes had followed Walter's, as Walter had applied Brylcreem to Clifford's hair, and experimented with five different partings. While Walter cut Clifford's fingernails, Clifford watched. On most days, Clifford seemed uninterested in what was done to him for his own cleanliness and comfort. On most days, his eyes only made contact with Walter's at the moment of waking, when it seemed that he required reassurance that Walter was still there. Once, when Walter had been placed in another ward because of flu, tales of Clifford's misdeeds and lack of cooperation had filtered through to Walter, and Walter had been pleased.

Walter had become expert at interpreting the tiny changes of expression which flickered across Clifford's face. He knew what he could expect to see if he were about to lead some of the other patients out on a walk, and leave Clifford behind. He knew the expression in Clifford's eyes when Clifford wished to thank him.

Most of the time, what Walter did for Clifford was taken for granted, since he did so much. What Clifford most liked was physical contact, his hands rubbed, or, as Walter always did when drying them, his feet gently stroked. He liked toffees or chocolates, but took them as part of his rations, without thanks or acknowledgement. He liked food and sleep. Many people might be able to recognize pleasure or displeasure in Clifford, but only Walter was able to mark degrees of feeling, and where others might see only physical expressions having to do with the breaking of wind or

84

with the motor reaction to a scratch, itch or tickle, only Walter knew that such physical expressions also contained – and even communicated to those who could read the code – thoughts. Walter knew that Clifford was capable of something else besides thought, and if he had known its name might have called it by that name, 'intuition'. It was because of this something else that he was unable to make contact with Clifford's eyes this Saturday evening; he was afraid of what might be communicated by that contact. If Clifford were to sense what was going to happen, he might start to play up, make noises, stamp his feet on the footrest of the chair, and so draw attention to them both. Partly for this reason, and partly in order to clear his own thoughts, Walter did what he had often done when alone with Clifford. He spoke his thought aloud.

'I don't have to. I can always change my mind. I don't have to do what she said.' He knew, even as he said it, that he was not convincing himself, but hoped that it would convince Clifford and forestall tantrums.

At the door of the Main Hall, he showed his and Clifford's membership cards, took five pence out of his own pocket and five pence out of Clifford's hand, and gave it to the man on the door. Even though they had been coming here for many years, it was important to show their cards and do things right. This was the only Club of which he and Clifford were members. Outside the Hospital gates, he would not be a member of anything.

He wheeled Clifford over to their usual place, and sat down. They were early, as always; the music had not begun, and some of the abler patients played skittles in the centre of the hall. Clifford's eyes still watched him. He forced himself to look into those eyes and to speak to Clifford. He touched Clifford's hand, and, smiling, said, 'Are you all right?' The eyes stared back. 'We've come to the Dance, see?' He gestured perfunctorily towards some of the other club members, and Clifford's eyelids flickered for a moment, but he did not look away from Walter.

When all membership cards had been examined, and sufficient time allowed for the accommodation of latecomers, the man on the door would leave his post, and would join in the dancing. Then the members would be allowed to come and go as they wished. Some might even leave as couples, to hide in dark corners of the hospital, and kiss. Walter had never done so, but he knew that it was done.

From the beginning of that period of freedom to the ending of the Dance, when freedom would also end, and the members return to being patients, there was a time during which he must act. It would be dark outside. He would be able to push Clifford in his wheelchair over the neatly trimmed grass to the Special Activities Unit, where there was a room with a mattress laid out on the floor, kept for violent or self-mutilating patients who required calming music and observation. The spare key for the Special Activities Unit was kept hidden behind a loose brick; this practice had obtained ever since three members of staff had left the hospital, all forgetting to hand in their keys to the Unit, which had resulted in the Unit's being locked, with no key available to release a trainee therapist and four large and disturbed patients. Walter knew the hiding-place because he was a trusty, and one of his many duties was to escort difficult patients from their wards to the Special Activities Unit.

Here he was a trusty. Outside he would not be anything. This was not a thought to be spoken aloud.

Clifford would be safe in the Special Activities Unit. He would sleep on a mattress, and be discovered in the morning. He would miss breakfast, but it would be made up to him.

Walter would allow half an hour after the main lights of the Hall had been turned off, and only the circles of coloured lights illuminated the dancers' faces. There would be less chance then of anyone's seeing them leave. Also he wanted to watch for the last time the faces changing from pink to amber to green and back to blue.

He listened to the loud music. His thoughts danced, not confusingly, but in alarming order. What was the real nature of the world outside the gates? Here he was liked, had a place, and was given privileges. Outside he would have nothing except what was in the two plastic carrier bags tied to the underside of Clifford's wheelchair.

For nineteen years he had concentrated on doing well whatever he had been asked to do, first in the hope that they would realize their mistake, and let him go, and later because it had become a habit. Out there, what would they ask him to do, and how well would he be able to do it?

June had asked him to help her get away. She could not manage without his help.

The time for leaving was growing nearer. He would allow ten more minutes, just to be sure. He was afraid.

June paced the room she shared with Rita. Both babies, her own Baby John and Rita's Robin Christopher, were asleep. Her suitcase had been packed all day. She had explained four times to Rita that she was to be transferred to another part of the hospital. It had to work.

Rita sat on her bed, cutting pictures of animals out of women's magazines and sticking them into a scrapbook with flour-and-water paste. Since she had lost the brush, she applied the paste with two fingers, wiping them clean on her Winceyette nightdress. Although she was thirty years old, Rita still wore white ankle-socks and a hair-slide in the shape of a butterfly.

Downstairs, at a desk near the door, reading the latest Denise Robins, there was a Staff Nurse. To use the fire-escape, one had to break a glass panel and pull a handle which caused alarm bells to sound all over the building. No way out there.

June could hear dance music. Of course – it was Saturday night. Would Walter have gone to the Dance? She opened her suitcase, and stared down at her trousseau for this elopement. What was there was all she owned now.

'Do you like ducks?'

'Yes, with orange sauce.'

Rita made a noise and also a face, both intended to signify repulsion of eating meat and fruit at the same time. Rita's mother had kept her in the clothes she had been wearing as a girl of sixteen, simply letting them out with patches of different materials as Rita grew larger. Since she was a skilful sempstress, these patches had always seemed somehow to be part of the dress, but Rita's pregnancy (which she would in any case not accept as a fact) defeated her, so that she had simply let in a large piece of scarlet taffeta to the front of all Rita's still wearable dresses, so that now Rita seemed always to be wearing a bloodstained apron over the offending spot.

It was dark outside. June rested the side of her face against the cold window, and looked towards the lights of the Main Hall. Surely he would have left by now.

'What are you looking at?'

'Fairies at the bottom of the garden.'

'Are they dancing in a ring?'

'No, they're drinking Guinness, and telling dirty stories.'

'When Mummy worked at the Mill, the old lady next door let me do this every day.'

'What?'

'Cut out pictures, and paint.' Rita watched the white sticky paste roll from her fingertips to her wrist, and recited, 'Pretty girl. Box of paints. Sucked her brush. Joined the saints.' The point of her tongue jabbed tentatively at the white gook. Noticing the expression on June's face, she said, 'It's only flour and water. I like it.'

Rita had a mental age of seven and a half. Since her father's death, when she was six, she had lived with her mother in a cottage between Rawtenstall and Birtle. Rita's mother had worked on the same six old-fashioned looms for twenty-five years until the introduction of automatic looms had led to early retirement. Her belief was that the decline of the Lancashire cotton industry was directly due to automation. Her life with Rita had been one of peace and routine. Neither she nor Rita would accept the fact that physically Rita had grown into womanhood.

When would the dratted girl stop cutting, sticking and sucking, and go to sleep? The other women in the Unit had already begun to complain about the holes in *Woman* and *Woman's Own*.

'Do you want to know how I came to get Robin Christopher?'

'No. Go to sleep.' She wished she could be certain Walter would come.

Clifford's wheelchair had started to squeak, and Walter was conscious that the wheels and his own best shoes were leaving marks on the trim lawn. He wished he could be certain that what he was doing was right.

The key was where he had expected to find it, and the door opened without too much noise. But what should he do about the light? If he switched it on, it might be noticed. If he left it off, Clifford might become alarmed at being undressed in the dark.

Walter stood in the darkness, his hands on Clifford's shoulders, and tried to remember the lay-out of the Special Activities Unit. When his eyes had adjusted to the darkness, he pushed the wheelchair towards the corner where screens surrounded the mattresses on the floor.

He found a mattress by feeling for it, and began to remove first Clifford's jacket, then his tie and shirt. Clifford mustn't be allowed to sleep in his best suit.

There was just enough light for Walter to see Clifford's eyes, still watching him in everything he did. He had forgotten to bring pyjamas, and in the nineteen years he had dressed and undressed Clifford he had not known him to possess underclothes. The room was warm enough, but the feel of woollen blankets next to his skin would be yet another strange experience for Clifford, and might induce perturbation.

Shoes and socks off. Walter lifted Clifford's upper body from the wheelchair, and supported it with one shoulder while he undid the loose-fitting trousers and manoeuvred them to the floor. This was the moment Clifford chose (if choice came into it) to urinate. The warm piss splashed down onto Walter's hands and the sleeves of his jacket, onto the trousers round Clifford's feet, the cheap hair-cord carpet and the edge of the mattress on which Walter was about to place him. Walter withdrew his hands quickly, and placed them on Clifford's hips above the line of fire.

Like two Saturday night drunks, the two men leaned against each other, as they waited for Clifford's bladder to empty. How could he have forgotten? Clifford was always taken to the lavatory before being put to bed.

Walter lowered his right hand, and shook out the last few drops as instinctively and habitually as he would shake his own penis so as to avoid stains on his underpants. It was just one of the many physical actions he performed for Clifford without thinking about them. Only now he was thinking about them, because today wasn't like the other six thousand, nine hundred and thirty-five days he had held Clifford's 'private thing' in his hand.

Why, after all those hundreds of times, should he feel strange

89

now about touching Clifford? Clifford wasn't watching him any longer, couldn't see Walter's face; he was leaning over, waiting for the pyjamas which Walter had forgotten to bring to be placed upon him. He was staring through the darkness to the mattress, and adding saliva to the already wet trousers around his feet.

Walter's feelings were too complicated to be sorted out. He did not wish to remember that this would be the last time he would see Clifford. He must not allow himself to become sad. He had made a promise to June; it must be kept. His mother and Jesus would be watching to make sure he kept it.

The thought which pushed him into further action was that Clifford might assume that Walter was waiting for him to relieve himself more fully, and might, if he were not laid quickly down upon the mattress, present him with a going-away present he did not wish.

Clifford lay on his side on the sheetless mattress, and allowed Walter to place two blankets over him, tucking them under the mattress for warmth. He was again watching, but showed no other sign that matters were not as they had always been.

Walter fussed around the mattress on his knees, unable to accept that all he had to do here was now done. His next task, which was to locate a ladder, would be more difficult.

He looked into the watching eyes, and sighing said, 'I've got to go.' And then, knowing that what he hoped was impossible, waited for Clifford by some miracle to reply, to tell him that what he was doing was right, perhaps even to smile. He wondered if he should find Clifford's hand under the blanket, and shake it, or touch his face. He waited, unable to decide, feeling the sadness he had promised himself not to feel until slowly, more slowly than Walter had ever seen him do so before, Clifford closed his eyes and their glimmer of white could no longer be seen in the dark.

Walter stood, and walked out of the Special Activities Unit.

'A man in a white car stopped, and asked me if I knew the way to Oldham. I said I didn't. I was picking flowers. It was very hot. I remember that.'

If Walter came while Rita was still awake, they would have to bind and gag her.

'What are you listening for?'

'Nothing. Go to sleep.' June continued to walk, and to touch the wall.

'He bought me some cashew nuts and brown ale. I never had beer before. It's very nice, isn't it?'

She had pointed out the window. She had said slowly, spelling it out, 'Third window from the left.' She had not asked whether he knew left from right, but he couldn't have climbed up to the wrong one; she'd been watching.

'He said he'd drive me home. Then he stopped. He said it was hot. He took off his jacket. It wasn't a proper road he stopped on. It was a track.'

He had promised. Given his word. He had said, 'I promise,' and his voice had sounded like a fart in a bath of soapy water.

'He started tickling me. I'm very ticklish. We were giggling, and tickling each other all over.'

He had given her his dead mother's diamanté ear-rings, vulgar replicas of the Eiffel Tower.

'The door was locked. I tried to climb over the back seat to get away from him. He was being naughty. It hurt. Like what dogs do to lady dogs. He had his hands up here, squeezing my chest. I had to cry. Then suddenly he made ever such a funny grunting noise, and just stopped.'

His oily hair stank of lavender brilliantine. She had no idea men still used it.

'Then we listened to music on the car radio. The second time, it didn't hurt at all.'

Even if she could climb from the window without a ladder, she was frightened of the fields.

'But that was outside on the grass. We'd gone outside because it was hot. We laid on the grass, and he stroked me all over, and put his hand between my legs.'

'You really must go to sleep, Rita. Think of what your Mummy will say if I tell her you stayed awake all night telling me about the travelling salesman who fucked you in so many different positions until you were sore.'

91

'That's a rude word. Only nasty people say it.'

'Well, I am nasty. Nasty and desperate, so go to sleep.' He wouldn't come at all now. She'd been wrong. He would be too frightened of the world outside, too scared of what he believed 'they' might do to him if he were caught.

Perhaps he had been unable to find a ladder.

'Tell me a story.'

'No. Go to sleep.'

'How did you get Baby John?'

'I advertised in *Exchange and Mart*.'

'Read to me.'

'No, it's too late.'

'Shall we play Snakes and Ladders? Just one game.' June beat her clenched fist against her thigh, and let out a gasp of frustration.

'Mummy said I should have taken down his car number. The police would have beaten him up.'

Then she heard it. Just a noise. Her heart skipped a beat. Suddenly she was scared, scared and excited. The noise happened again. It was, it must be, the sound of a ladder being rested on a window-ledge.

'What's that?'

'What?'

'Noise.' Rita was pointing to the window.

'It's nothing.' Rita was getting out of bed. June grabbed her. 'Yes, well, it is something actually.' She was thinking fast, holding onto Rita with one hand and reaching for a pillow from her own bed with the other. 'It's a game.' She hoped she was sounding joky and relaxed; she certainly didn't feel so. 'A surprise for you, Rita.' Rita's expression was more of suspicion than of surprise. 'A secret game I'm going to teach you.'

Rita was backing away as far as the length of June's arm would allow. 'You're hurting my arm.'

'I'll bet you've never heard of this game, have you?'

Rita moved her head very slowly from side to side. June had released her arm, and was ripping the pillowcase down its seams. There were more noises from outside. Walter was climbing the ladder, which had squeaky rungs. The two women watched each other. June knew that Rita might scream at any minute, and would certainly do so if she saw Walter's face pressed against the other side of the window.

Holding the pieces of pillowcase, June advanced slowly on Rita. As she advanced, she smiled in what she hoped was a reassuring manner.

'What's that noise?'

'That's a friend, come to collect me.'

'Why?'

'I'm doing what all those girls do in the school stories. I'm running away.' June was close now. She had twisted one piece of the pillowcase to make a gag.

'I can't read long story books, only comics.'

At this moment, Walter's face appeared at the window. Rita's pointing finger shot out, and her mouth dropped open to form a scream. June pounced. The piece of pillowcase was stuffed into the middle of that mouth, and Rita's head forced down, so that the ends of the cloth could be tied at the back of her neck. Rita was a well-developed thirty-year-old, and sticky with paste. June was reminded of women wrestling in mud, and wondered how the travelling salesman in the white car had got away with his balls still hanging where they should.

She had left the window slightly open. She dared not release Rita, but signalled to Walter to come in. Together they tied Rita's hands with the rest of the pillowcase, then her legs with the cord of her dressing-gown, and strapped a leather belt round her knees. Though Walter could not understand why all this was being done, he was much more adept at doing it, having had plenty of experience in the restraint of agitated patients.

Rita would be found in time. She would not choke, or if she did, that could not be helped. A moment's hesitation. Would she, in fact, choke? No, she would not; she was a survivor. June picked up her case. Walter preceded her down the ladder. She switched the light out. The elopement had begun.

When they were both on the ground, she helped him lift the ladder away from the wall and lay it on the grass where it would be less conspicuous. He was no more burdened by worldly goods than she. Less so; all he had was in two carrier bags. She took his

93

hand in hers, and said, 'I was beginning to get worried, but you kept your promise. I shan't forget.'

They staggered hand in hand over the clayey wet furrows of a field, she carrying her suitcase, he his carrier bags. When they reached the other side, they stood for a moment by the hedge, trying to get breath back and to decide which way would lead them to a gap or gate. Walter took June's suitcase, realizing that he should have offered to carry it from the beginning, for she was clearly exhausted, bent double taking in deep gasps of air, and holding onto his arm for support.

'I'm sorry.'

'What for?'

'Not carrying your suitcase. It's heavy.'

June stretched herself up on her toes, and kissed the side of his face. 'It's all I've got in the world now.' She could just make out the outline of his beaky nose and the long jaw and the flat cap he always wore. 'It's all I have in the world now, except you.' She stroked the cheek she had just kissed, using the back of her mud-covered fingers, and was sure it was wet. His cheeks were wet. He was crying. Walter was crying.

For once in her life, she had made someone happy. Usually she had the opposite effect on people. (It never occurred to her that these might not be tears of joy.) They started walking again, he with the suitcases now balancing the carrier bags. They had chosen to walk to the right out of instinct.

Walter was now hers, and she was his, a heavy responsibility for them both.

PART THREE

Walter and June Liberated

I

Whatever happened from now on, as long as he could be with her, he would remain happy

It was September. They would go south with the migrating birds. To the north there was nothing except rough country, depressed towns and Scotland. Scotland wouldn't welcome them.

To the west there was very little land before one reached the coast. Fleetwood, Southport and Morecambe would all be counting the season's takings, covering the turnstiles, pulling down the shutters on the Bingo stalls, and sweeping up the last few grains of sand from the floors of Guest House bedrooms. Only Blackpool, with its flickering illuminations, would be making a last attempt to squeeze a few more pence from the weekend motorists and cut-rate coach-trippers, jammed together and overheating, on the Golden Mile to see the Lights. Blackpool wouldn't welcome them.

South. It would be easy to navigate. June looked at the sky, and made arbitrary identifications of the Pole Star, the Plough and the Bear. They would turn left at the next crossroads.

They walked, counting the telegraph poles. At every tenth pole, they rested for the time it took June to count a hundred. They turned and turned again, lost the telegraph poles, and counted cat's-eyes, resting after each hundred pairs. Then, finding a road too narrow for cat's-eyes, counted strides, resting after each hundred and fifty. Since June's strides were shorter than Walter's, he had to skip from time to time so as to match her.

The moon raced along, always keeping just ahead of them, as if it were their own very personal usherette's torch, leading them closer and closer to the large Cinemascope screen, before which they would sit, heads back, necks aching, holding hands and

97

watching the garishly coloured world in which no one was ever really hurt, and the failures always came out on top. Meanwhile, in order to continue to hold June's hand as he walked, Walter was forced to cross behind her every time he needed to change her heavy suitcase from one hand to the other. June carried his two plastic bags, which were considerably lighter.

June felt high, light-headed, enjoying her new-found freedom. She had brought no tranquillizers. Who needed them? She knew from experience that anti-depressants took nine or ten days before they began to make any effect. Logically, therefore, they should be effective for nine or ten days after she had ceased to take them. Anyway, to be walking along a road under a sky full of stars, with any and every possibility open to her, was too pleasant, too exciting to be spoiled by caution or logic. 'Logic!' she shouted towards the sky. 'Logic is what you make it.' Walter, who was embarrassed by this loud shouting, and fearful that it might attract attention and pursuit, ran quickly behind her, changing the suitcase to his other hand and using his free hand to hold as still as he could at least one of the two hands with which she was swinging the plastic bags which contained all his worldly goods.

'Logic is for fools who need their foolishness explained to them.' The carrier bags were safe now, but June's voice remained loud and shrill. This was not an aspect of her personality which she had previously shown to Walter, and he was worried by it.

'Logic could never begin to explain why I feel like bursting with happiness, because my feet are blistered, and I'm cold and wet, nor why I'm here on this particular bit of road with you to hold onto.' Happiness filled her to overflowing, and she skipped along the road for a hundred yards, leaving Walter behind to pick up the knife, fork, spoon and shoe-cleaning brush which fell from the carrier bags as she twirled them.

Then she was standing still in the middle of the road, head back, watching the wisps of grey cloud rush past, between her and the moon. Her voice was soft and gentle, as if singing to a sleeping child.

> 'There was a man
> Went round the town,
> To hunt a supper up and down.

98

The bill of fare
He runneth through
To see what his six cents would do.'

Walter reached her. He stood beside her, with one arm around her shoulder. She turned her face to him, and he saw that her face was wet. 'Why did you come with me? Why did you lumber yourself with a stretcher-case like me?' No answer. Walter pressed his lips against her forehead. 'It's all illogical. Logic has been ill for some time, requiring rest and quiet and no questions asked of it.'

They began to walk on again slowly, Walter's arm still around her shoulder. 'I love the night-time, as long as I'm not alone. I love the thought that all these fields and bushes are teeming with night-life, just like the West End of London. Foxes, stoats and weasels, preening themselves to go out and dazzle the punters. Badgers trying desperately to remember their kerb-drill, as they dodge the hooting taxis in the Charing Cross Road. You've never been to our lovely old capital, have you?' Walter shook his head. 'We'll go. That's where we're going. I haven't seen much of it either, not since I was a student. We'll see it properly – not one of your quick dashes round the Tate, and being groped front and rear by Persian teenagers in Madame Tussaud's. No rush for us. No expensive tourists' rip-offs. We'll sit and stare. Ships, towers, domes, theatres and temples lie, open unto the fields and to the sky; all bright and glittering in the smokeless air.'

Then it hit them. The heavens opened, and heavy raindrops almost the size of hailstones struck the tops of their heads with such force that for a few seconds they were stunned. Then they began to run, not knowing where they were running to. 'Sodding Wordsworth!' June shouted. 'He's watering his sodding daffodils. Sod doesn't realize it's the wrong time of year.'

Twenty minutes later, they were running breathlessly between the gravestones of a churchyard. June twisted and pushed at the heavy iron ring which opened the grey weathered oak door. It opened, and they were out of the drenching rain. 'God!' June wrang out the edge of her coat, and watched the rainwater pour from it onto the stone floor.

'Pity it's not a Catholic church. We could light all the candles,

99

and get some warmth.' The echo of their footfalls on the stone floor and the sound of June's voice ringing round the church brought into Walter's mind his first day at the Hospital, and his walk with the Social Worker down the half mile of corridor, in which old men and some less old stood at corners, waiting, hugging themselves and talking to themselves. Waiting, all waiting. Much later, when Walter had thought it all over, he had realized that the only possible eventuality for which the men could be waiting must be death. Churches reminded Walter of death. His mother had said, 'They're the nearest we can get to Jesus while we're on this earth.'

He watched June slip off both her wet shoes and hang them on two posts at the end of a pew. She was thirsty. She went to look at the font, but all it contained was dust and fallen plaster.

'They haven't christened anyone here for years. Either they're all barren or on the pill.' Walter was sure they would be heard. At any moment, a door would open, and they would be told to leave. The flowers on the altar table were fresh; the large brass eagle which supported the lectern shone like gold. Certainly it had been polished this week. Walter knew about brass and the polishing of it.

'Don't suppose they keep the sacramental wine on the premises.' Walter's clothes and boots had formed a puddle on the short stretch of threadbare carpet between the pews. 'No? Ah, well, thanks a lot. Big G. I'll do the same for you some day.'

When June stopped shouting, it was not a silence which followed, but the quietness in which the ticking of a clock seemed exaggeratedly loud. 'Did I do that. Did I start the clock?' She pointed at a bright red fire extinguisher hanging on the wall. 'Hey! What do they want with a fire extinguisher? Maybe they think Satan will drop in to sign the Visitors' Book.' She laid her wet coat flat, supported by the backs of three pews.

Walter knew that his mother would have said that the loud ticking of the clock was to remind the congregation that their days were numbered. He wished to unlace his boots, which had walked and run a long way, but instead he stared upwards towards the dark rafters. At any moment, Jesus and his mother would see them. They would have heard June shouting in God's House. There would need to be a great many trumpets in Heaven to drown out June's voice.

June had taken off some of her wet clothing, and was pacing about, trying to find something with which to dry herself. Walter waited. His feet were wet. He and June had run through deep puddles without noticing them, while rain had run down their backs, beneath their collars. He had never been out in rain so heavy, and now he stood in a church, soaked and waiting to know what he should do. In the Hospital, he had known what to do; the range of permissible activities was not large, was easily learned, and did not change. Here, in the real world, things happened so much more quickly and could not be predicted. He was forty-six. How much time would it take him to learn how to be like the people of the real world? Would he always be waiting, forever waiting for someone to tell him what to do? He would stand out, look odd. It was a mistake. He had made it. A mistake.

June had found a long red velvet curtain hanging near the organ, and was busy unhooking the brass curtain rings.

It would not be as simple as leading a crocodile of Jesus's Mistakes through the town, and remembering where it was safe to take them. Now there would be hundreds of decisions to make every day. He had not been away from the Hospital more than three hours, and already he was frightened, cold, shivering and wet. His boots might just as well have been made from cheap cardboard for all the protection they had given to his feet. And they were muddy, soiling the floor of God's House.

June now had the curtain down from its rail, and was using it as a beach-robe. She undressed beneath it, removing all her wet clothes, and hanging them to dry where the curtain had been.

Walter's boots looked like two large dollops of over-broiled pig's liver, and as he moved his feet inside them, water squelched through the seams. It was no good; he had made a mistake, and would have to go back. He had let Clifford and the rest down for nothing. In the real world, he couldn't take care of himself.

'Hey! Come on, love. Get out of that wet suit.' June stood before him, naked beneath the red velvet curtain, which trailed on the floor behind her. She lifted her arms to rub Walter's hair, releasing the scent of lavender brilliantine like incense into the air of the holy place. Walter kept his eyes focused on a piece of the floor.

'What's made you so sad?' She waited, wiping his face, neck and ears dry. 'Come on. Tell me.' She wiped, and waited. 'Is it me? Have I upset you? I'm overexcited and happy. I don't mean to be silly. Is it that?'

Walter kept his eyes down, and shook his head.

'Well, what is it, then?' She undid his tie, and top button of his shirt. 'Give me your jacket.' She slid the lapels of his jacket back over his shoulders, and undid the three buttons. Then she moved behind him to pull at the sleeves until it was off, and she draped it over the back of a pew.

'Do you know much of the Bible, Walter?' It seemed easier to shake his head. 'There's a bit that says, "In my Father's house are many mansions. There have I prepared a place for you". I think he knew we were coming, don't you?' No reply. 'Might have turned the heating on, though.'

Walter stood like a dray horse, pawing the ground while its owner removes harness, bridle and reins. He allowed June to unlace each of his boots, and lifted each foot in turn while she pulled the boots off. 'Aren't you going to tell me what's wrong?' His shirt and vest were now off, and she wiped his torso and arms slowly with the velvet curtain, so that Walter must have seen her nakedness if his eyes had not been tightly shut.

She placed her hand on the buckle of his belt, the backs of her fingers against the skin of his stomach. Walter did not move. She shivered, then stood on her toes, pressing her dry chapped lips first against his forehead, then against his left ear, into which she whispered, 'Please put your arms around me. We're both cold.'

Walter did as he was asked, sliding his arms slowly beneath the velvet curtain and under June's arms to touch her naked back. His eyes remained closed.

'May I take these off?' She waited, and after a moment, he nodded slowly. She undid the buckle of the belt and the top button of his trousers, and slowly lowered the zip, placing her hand inside.

At the moment June touched what his mother would never touch, almost the whole of Walter's weight came forward onto her, and sinking his face against her right shoulder, he sobbed and blubbered, making sounds she had never heard before, and amongst all those gasps and groans and cries and wails which seemed to come from low down in his chest, she understood three words, 'Don't ... know ... how.'

He had only ever seen pigeons making love, and his mother had said it would never happen to him. The pigeons had billed, the female putting her beak into the male's mouth, their heads moving from side to side, rocking each other in a shared pleasure. Perhaps tongues were to be used as beaks. He had never seen pigeons do what Mike at Woolworth's had done.

Now he felt warm breath against his mouth, and small dry lips were pressed against his own lips, and cold fingers moved the hair on the back of his neck up and down and round, twisting it into little curls. His neck tingled, and his spine shivered.

'I'll show you.' She reached for his hands, and drew him down onto the stone floor beside her.

Parted from the rocking kiss, the female bird crouched low, tapping one of her wings rhythmically, while the male circled and strutted, with his chest out and his tail lowered, scraping the ground, then stopping to preen the crouching female's neck feathers, ruffling them gently with his beak as the crouching bird's eyelids moved upwards, covering her eyes from below, signifying an extreme enjoyment.

June moved the tips of her fingers over Walter's face, lifting his chin. His eyes were still closed. June said, 'Look at me, Walter. Don't pretend it's not happening.'

He looked into her eyes. They were dark like conkers. He saw himself reflected in them, saw his own face, his own ugliness, saw what had caused children and adults to laugh. But June had never laughed at his face, never stifled her giggles with one hand over her mouth, while she pointed at him with the other. Now her hands were moving over his face, neck and ears, exciting him.

The male bird had strutted round its mate yet again, drawing out his anticipation of what was to come, before carefully standing on the crouching bird's back, flapping his wings, partly to balance himself and partly to make himself lighter.

June was pulling Walter on top of her, lifting and spreading

103

her legs. She was small, and he was heavy, and had no wings to lighten him. He would crush her.

Walter placed his hands on the cold stone floor of the church, supporting most of his own weight, while June held his private thing in her bony fingers, feeling the size and weight of it, then slithered towards it, lifting her hips to meet it.

She gasped, and bit her lower lip, as the knob of it entered her, digging her fingernails into the sides of his buttocks to stop him going any deeper. She slowed down her breathing in order to relax her body, then, after a few such breaths, leaned her head back, smiled to reassure him, and whispered the word, 'Gently.'

Supporting himself with one arm, he placed his right hand over the breast she had made him touch as they had stood beneath the dead elm. Now he could see as well as feel it, and he repeated what he had done before, cupping his hand underneath it, as he would if it were really a dove. So he felt the heart-beat, the life-pulse, faint but there. She was so small, so delicate; he must take care.

By now she had relaxed, and pulled him further inside her. Her insides had closed around his private thing. They were wet now, opening and closing, pulling and sucking at him, exciting him to go further, inciting him to go harder, higher and deeper.

There was no care now for him to take. Walter was lost; there was no Walter to care, no witless Walter with beak nose and flat cap and stained protruding teeth. There was only pleasure, so complete that it blotted out both past and future. There was only this moment of pleasure, then the next of more pleasure, pleasure building with each moment and each movement, each total within itself as he, Walter, was totally inside her. And she was holding him there, grasping at him to pull him deeper into her, then releasing him to make a sound of pleasure. *Her* pleasure. *He* made it. She was holding his buttocks and pulling him higher, then pushing him back, then squirming, whispering his name, and pulling him forward again. *His* name. Walter.

Then there was a moment more complete than all before it, and for the seconds (minutes? hours?) that it lasted, Walter moved even further away from himself and from any idea he had ever held of himself. He was not Walter; he was not anybody; he was a

104

sensation. It was not his seed that left him. Nothing left him. He himself, the sensation, expanded to fill June and the world.

He had seen pigeons transfer their sperm in but the blinking of an eye, and both birds, satisfied that the job was well done, had strutted and circled each other, with chests out and tails down, before suddenly taking off into a flight of triumph, making wide circles in the sky together, dropping and climbing, playing tricks on each other, diving, sometimes tumbling, threatening to leave with a sudden extra burst of speed, then slowing down to be caught. Then they would return, staidly, keeping each other's pace and height, showing the world that they were married, paired for life.

Walter imagined himself up there in the sky on a clear day, diving, swooping, climbing over the house tops. From that height, he looked down on the church. The wind changed as he rose even higher. He planed on the air-currents, June beside him, as they glided together on the friendly wind, with no fear of falling. They had fed extensively on hemp, rape, tares, niger, maize, linseed and maple peas. They could fly for ever.

'You're heavy, Walter.' June used her elbows to draw herself backwards so that she and Walter were face to face. He was crying silently, tears of happiness and gratitude, of pleasure and achievement. She wiped the tears away with the tips of her fingers, and, between silent sobs, Walter said, 'I did it,' and June replied, 'Yes, you did it very well.'

Walter opened his eyes, and saw patches of coloured light projected on to a whitewashed wall. These would be the rotating coloured lights of the dance in the Main Hall. He must have dozed off. He reached out a hand, expecting to make contact with Clifford, but the lights were not rotating, and outside he could hear bird-song, and there was a body beside him which was not Clifford. The body had a name. Its name was June.

The coloured light on the wall was the morning, filtered through stained glass. Walter turned his head to look at the window. In the centre pane, Jesus stood with his right arm raised, pointing to his halo. The woman who knelt at his feet was clearly being reminded who the boss was. Walter's own mother was close to

Jesus at this very moment, but he did not think she would be kneeling at his feet.

June was still asleep. Her hair had dried during the night, and had become wavy; feather-like wisps framed the sides of her face. The skin on her face was pale, almost white, her eyelashes dark, almost black. A nerve or small vein at the outside corner of her left eye beat out its pulse just under the surface of smooth skin.

Walter watched the jumping pulse, and wondered if June were dreaming, and if so, of what. After they had made love, he had watched her dress, taking dry clothes from the heavy suitcase. She had laughed, and said she had nothing that would fit him. He had held the red velvet curtain around himself, still in a maze at what had happened, moony with it.

The pew benches had not been wide enough for two bodies to lie side by side, so they had collected ten hassocks and placed them side by side in the narrow aisle between the pews, covering them with narrow strips of threadbare blue carpet taken from the pew seats. Walter had lain down on the hassock-bed, waiting for her, and she had laughed and said, 'I'm coming inside that curtain too,' and as he had opened the curtain, exposing himself, she had thrown some silk underwear, two sweaters and a tweed skirt on top of him for extra warmth.

Then they had both laughed, and she had lain down beside him, and he had wrapped the red velvet curtain round them both.

They had lain close together, keeping each other warm. She had taken both his arms, and wrapped them around her. His hands had hung limply behind her back, and although he felt awkward, he had waited. She was so close to him that he could both hear and feel her breath on his face, and he had waited, happy, afraid to make any move that might spoil his happiness, hearing and feeling her breath and trying to match his breathing to hers, until at last he had fallen asleep.

By now they would have found Clifford, lying on a mattress in the Special Activities Unit, and the woman in June's bedroom, bound and gagged. By now the Night Duty Staff would have noticed that two of the beds in Ward 3 C were unoccupied, and would have begun a search. By now they would have called the police. Every policeman in the district would have been supplied with June's description and his own, and men and dogs would be walking in lines across muddy fields. (Walter did not know that both he and June might have left the Hospital at any time they had positively announced a wish to do so.)

The decision as to whether he should wake June in case the policemen and dogs were already near the village was too difficult for him to make. She needed sleep. They had walked a long way. She might be angry with him if he woke her, and he knew that he would not be able to bear her anger, to see her now sleeping face screwed up as it had been when she had shouted at him for not talking to her.

And at that moment, when he knew how he would feel to see her unhappy, that was the moment at which he realized that the feeling he had for her, this woman sleeping so close to him, was stronger than any feeling he had felt for anyone and that it made him happier than he could ever remember being. Whatever happened hereafter, as long as he could be with June, he would remain happy. Even if they had to walk all the way to London.

At seven forty-six by the clock with the loud tick, Walter heard a woman's voice singing and the iron ring on the church door being turned and pushed. Pulling as much of the red velvet curtain as he could retrieve from June around his nakedness, he watched the door open inwards, and a huge bunch of chrysanthemums and a pair of female legs appear. 'Jesus wants me for a sunbeam, to shine for him each day.' The woman's contralto voice was a little impaired by her absence of teeth.

'In every way to please him – ' Walter ducked his head, and tried not to move, hoping that June would not move either. Almost at once, the back of his throat tickled, and a wish to cough had to be suppressed. The chrysanthemum legs announced that they wished to please Jesus at home, at school and at play. June rolled over onto her back, and pulled at the red velvet curtain. Parts of Walter were revealed which he did not wish even chrysanthemums to observe. Moreover June seemed to be about to wake. He placed a hand over her mouth, and her eyes opened.

'A sunbeam! A sunbeam! Good morning, Sir.' The woman had

stopped singing, and an arm, only just visible behind the flowers, was waving towards the altar.

To whom could she be speaking?

'And a beautiful morning it is, Sir, after all that rain You showered down on us last night. Another drop, and we'd all have been lost at sea.'

One of June's shoes was perched on the knob at the end of the choir stall, and the woman's waving hand touched it. 'Whose is this?' She lowered the flowers, so that her face could now be seen. She was looking towards the altar, and her manner suggested that she expected an answer, that she was, indeed, in the habit of getting replies to her questions straight from the Almighty. June lifted Walter's hand away from her mouth.

'It's a woman's.' Suddenly the woman let out a loud asthmatic cackle of a laugh, and rocked backwards and forwards on her heels, the large bunch of chrysanthemums rocking backwards and forwards with her.

'Have you been having a fancy woman in here, Sir? Have you?' The cackle turned into a bronchitic cough, and the woman thumped herself pleasantly on the chest.

Walter's efforts to breathe normally in spite of the tickle in his throat had caused his eyes to water.

'If you've been seeing other women, I'll not stand for it.' The woman's gaze roamed round the church. Walter covered his head with the red velvet curtain. Perhaps, if he could not see the woman, she would not be able to see him. Perhaps she would mistake him for a pile of rags.

'You emptied your bath-water, and then got your young lady drenched in it. You don't deserve fresh flowers. I'm in a good mind to take them home. Randy old Goat!'

Walter could hardly believe his ears. He remembered that his mother had told him to say his prayers to Jesus as if he were talking to a friend, and not to reel them off as if they were multiplication tables, but there was a difference between respectful friendship and gross familiarity. This woman talked to Jesus as if she were His wife.

Walter and June peeped over the top of the pew, and watched the woman's back moving, as she pulled old flowers from the vase before the altar, and replaced them with her chrysanthemums. Her hands worked away, breaking stalks and arranging blooms, while she continued laughing and talking.

'Come out, come out, whoever you are!' She must know they were still in the church. She lifted her head towards the cross above the altar. 'Don't you complain! These are all I've got left in the garden.' The flowers were white, red, yellow and bronze. 'If you don't like the colours, you know what you can do, don't you? You can do the other. Like as not, you were doing a bit of the other in here last night. And don't you forget, I want a nice sunny day from you, a week tomorrow, for Gladys Earnshaw's wedding. I booked you for it two weeks ago, but you've a head like a sieve ... You owe it to her. She's been unlucky in love more than enough times, and never laid eyes on a good whist-hand.'

The woman had finished her arrangement, and, using the altar rail to get to her feet, she groaned, 'One of these days, I want a few quiet words with you about my knees. It's no joke having knees like these two. A bee wouldn't be seen dead with them.' The church was filled again with the sound of her wheezing laughter, as she climbed up onto the organ seat. When the laughter and its echo had both ended, she said, 'And those not a million miles away from this organ who've made off with my red velvet curtain can put it back from whence it came.' And again laughed. Walter looked at June, and June at Walter, and Walter cleared his throat.

The woman's hands were poised over the keys of the organ, and she once again addressed the cross above the altar, but this time in a serious voice. 'Are you ready, Lord?' She paused for the length of time it would take Him to answer. 'This is the nearest to a service this village can give you, sharing our vicar with so many other parishes, but at least we have two more in the congregation than usual. I hope they'll stay to the end.'

At first the sound which came out of the organ was not unlike the woman's own wheezing breath, but when the pipes had cleared themselves of the week's dust, the music swelled nobly out. Walter and June sat still and listened. What was being played was not a Sunday School hymn, but a prelude and fugue by J. S. Bach, and it was played delicately and surely and with such controlled emotion that no one could have left before the end.

109

Walter was reminded of the School Band which came to the Hospital every year just before Christmas to play carols to the patients, and of the nineteen times he had sat next to Clifford, holding Clifford's hand and gripping it hard every time one of the tunes made him feel both full and empty, reminding him of his mother's voice, singing to him. It was at those times he had felt most secure. And June was reminded of some time, not to be fixed in her memory, when she had heard a young boy with a clear unbroken voice, singing his well-rehearsed solo for the Nativity. That high pure voice, giving its witness to the joy of living, had tricked her for a few moments into a sense of belonging to something, perhaps even to someone. But it had been only a trick then, was only a trick now. There were far too many shopping days left before Christmas.

The music stopped. The woman removed her fingers from the keyboard, and lowered her head as the vibration died away. Then she turned to face them.

'Thank you for staying. I played as well as I can today. I'm pleased you heard it.'

June said, 'It was beautiful. I'm sorry about the curtain. We got rather wet.'

'There's a man with you, isn't there?'

June said, 'Yes, this is Walter. I'm June.' And as she spoke, she realized that the woman's eyes were opaque, and that she wasn't looking at them after all, because she couldn't.

2

Haven't you noticed how many of the pigeons have deformed feet

It was the hub of Empire. June had told him so. 'Hub' was the centre, the dead centre of the British Empire. They were sitting together at the hub of Empire in Jubilee Year, resting their feet.

'This is where it's all happening. Look.' Walter looked. He had done little else over the past four days. He had walked and looked. He had waited by the roadside for lifts from lorry drivers, and looked. He had looked at the stained-glass windows of churches, at the Shopping Centres of provincial towns (all of which looked very much like one another), at the formica-topped tables of Transport Cafes; he had sat down by the bank of a canal, and looked at the water. June had said, 'I'll show you the Thames. It moves like oil at night.'

They had eaten seldom and badly. Walter's stomach, which was used to three meals a day of starch and calories, had started and was continuing to complain. He said nothing of this to June, for he knew that they had only thirty-two pence left between them. His amazement at what things cost in the real world had still not left him.

It was the hub of Empire. Eros pointed his arrow towards a large poster close to the Clydesdale Bank, which depicted an enormous naked girl, whose name was Emmanuelle. The naked girl smiled back at Eros. One hand, in obedience to the 1973 Obscenity Act, modestly covered a mount of Venus only slightly smaller than Ben Nevis. The poster was in two parts. One part announced that *Emmanuelle Discovers America*, the other that *Emmanuelle Goes Kinky*. 'She certainly gets around,' said June.

'Look.' Walter had looked. He continued to look. June had read to him the legend inscribed on the statue of Eros, from which it appeared that the boy with the arrow was also a certain Anthony Ashley Cooper, who was to be ever remembered for the strong sympathies of his heart and the great power of his mind, and who had (June said) taken children from the coal mines, in which they were being worked to death by their starving parents.

There were children all about them at the hub of Empire, sitting with them, resting their feet. Well, perhaps not children, though some were young, some not so young, all distinguished by chalk-white faces and long unkempt hair. Some sat on the island on which Eros stood, surrounded by traffic; others seemed to wish to get closer to Boot's, the all-night chemists, so that they should be first in the queue at midnight when their prescriptions became valid. The Right Honourable Anthony Ashley Cooper had allevia-ted the plight of boy chimney-sweeps, and ensured that children under the age of eleven should not be employed in the textile industry. Drug abuse in his day, June told Walter, had been strictly the prerogative of the rich.

They were at the hub of Empire. They had passed a shop named Cuddly Dudley's, in which customers could see themselves on closed-circuit television, and buy T-shirts on which by some magic photographs of those very faces, frozen by the television camera, had been printed. 'Everybody wants to be famous and remembered, 'cept thee and me.' June prodded at Walter's ribs, which had already become sore from such prodding. Her Lancashire accent had broadened from the moment they had approached Watford.

Walter watched the water which spurted from the mouths of the intertwined fish and the cherubs which surrounded Eros, and which made pools on the pavement and steps before running away down the nearest gutter. It was beginning to grow dark. Three black youths rollerskated through the pools of water, making damp wheelmarks on the pavement. It seemed to him that he had begun to be surrounded by coloured lights, and since he knew that this could not be so, and that hunger and weakness must have carried his mind back to the dances at the Main Hall of the Hospital, he concentrated harder on simply watching the damp wheelmarks fade from the pavement, and hoped that this attack would go away, and that he would not faint, and disgrace June at the hub of Empire. It did not go away. The coloured lights persisted and were joined by a high squeaking noise, as if millions of rubber soles were skipping over highly polished linoleum. The goldfish which had once inhabited his head, in order to confuse him by their darting about, had now been replaced by flickering Christmas Lights, and thousands of tiny children Country Dancing in black plimsolls. He closed his eyes. If he could sleep, even for a little while, they would go away.

'Look, Walter!'

Walter opened his eyes, and looked. The lights and noises were not inside his head; they were outside and all around him. Strips of light in every colour flickered on and off, some forming words, others shapes or pictures. The lights moved, danced, cascaded into patterns, and then were gone, only to begin the dance again the moment after. And the noise came from starlings, thousands of them, drowning out the traffic, as they swarmed on all the ledges of all the buildings, from Swan and Edgar's to Lillywhites, from the Piccadilly Theatre (where the lights advertised a production of *Wild Oats* by the Royal Shakespeare Company) to the Criterion Theatre, outside which there was a picture of the actor Leslie Phillips, holding up a pair of knickers. It was the hub of Empire.

Starlings covered the ledges, the windows, the columns, the arches, even the supports of the very coloured lights which seemed to be the cause of their chatter. They lined up like disorderly soldiers, forever fighting amongst themselves, breaking ranks and reforming. Suddenly a whole kit (larger, so much larger than any kit of pigeons) would take off together, swerving and swooping over tourists and traffic, before fighting for places on a building very similar to the one they had just left. Only the London Pavilion remained untouched. It had been newly painted, and Walter thought it a delicacy in the starlings to avoid a building which was still clean and refurbished.

'They paint the building with something which burns the birds' feet. Haven't you noticed how many pigeons have deformed feet?' Walter had noticed, and had wondered why.

It was the hub of Empire, but the great wheel of that Empire was much diminished now. The wheel would no longer turn.

Enormous sections of it had fallen away, and the hub was all barnacled over with Sex Shops and Souvenir Shops, amusement arcades at which the youth of Empire gambled away its pennies while waiting to be accosted by punters, and cinemas showing X-certificate films.

The Souvenir Shops sold patriotic dolls in Welsh, Scottish or Irish national costume and Fun Dolls in busby hats. They sold keyrings, Jubilee mugs, teacloths, back-scratchers and egg-warmers, cowboy boots and hats, fringed shirts of leatherette, multi-pocketed jackets and jeans, jeans and still more jeans. They sold pub mirrors, on which had been superimposed the faces of Marilyn Monroe, Starsky and Hutch, Elvis Presley, Humphrey Bogart, James Dean and Laurel and Hardy, plastic belts advertising Coca-Cola, Kit-Kat or Cinzano, belts which were also tape-measures and hessian shopping bags advertising Guinness or the Sex Pistols.

The Sex Shops sold, not sex itself, but Aids to Sex. Some of these aids were magazines and books, neatly covered in transparent plastic so as to avoid their being marked by the sweaty hands of punters. Some were mechanical (The Non-Doctor Vibrator), some medicinal (Libido Tablets and Orgasm Cream). One frivolous Sex Shop sold Jubilee Knickers with a Union Jack. Another sold the Oriental Duotonal Balls. June had left Walter standing outside the shop while she went in to inquire what was the function of these balls. At first the assistant had refused to believe that she did not already know, and guessed from her accent that she was one of a coach-party of ladies from the north and had been sent in by the other ladies to embarrass him. But since there were no other ladies, but only Walter, outside the window of the shop looking in, he relented and explained that the Duotonal Balls were not intended as replacements to be used by men who had carelessly mislaid their own, but were for the pleasuring of lonely or at least unsatisfied ladies. Placed in the vagina, the Duotonal Balls aroused excitement, and the string which connected them was not merely a useful device to allow them to be recovered; of itself, it massaged the clitoris. The housewife without a man, or whose husband was much away during the daytime and overtired at night, might, by the simple insertion of Duotonal Balls, obtain sexual relief, while doing the

114

housework, and actually achieve an orgasm while Hoovering under the bed.

June had left the shop without buying a pair of Oriental Duo-tonal Balls. She had not liked to tell the assistant that she and Walter had only thirty-two pence between them.

'Are you hungry?' Walter nodded. 'You should tell me.'

They should both go down below Eros to the Piccadilly Under-ground Station, where there were toilets. June would visit the Ladies, Walter the Gents, and they would both wash their faces and comb their hair, because they were about to eat in a restaurant, where people notice such things. 'Come back, and wait for me here when you're ready,' June said, and she picked up her suitcase, and moved away from him. 'I won't be long. Yours is over there, down those steps.'

Walter looked where she pointed, and, when he turned back, discovered that he had already lost sight of her in the crowd of people on the other side of the road.

Since leaving the Hospital, the only times they had been sepa-rated were when Nature called, and even then, since Nature had seemed to call most often when they were in the countryside, only by a bush or a hedge; they had still been within shouting distance. Here shouts would not be heard. There were no bushes, hedges or even trees, save those they had passed in Leicester Square, which had electric cables nailed to their trunks and floodlights secured to their branches. Even dogs were forbidden by a public notice from answering a call of Nature against those trees.

Walter waited for the lights to change so that he could cross the four lanes of traffic which separated him from the stairs to which June had pointed. He wondered how, with only thirty-two pence, they were to eat in a restaurant where people would notice whether he had combed his hair. They had started with six pounds and thirty-two, of which sixty pence had been his. He had been unable to draw out the twenty-five pounds and eleven pence he had saved at the Hospital, because there had not been time to do so, and in any case Walter was known not to take money out, but to put it in, and taking it out would have aroused suspicion. Walter had never been able to understand why he had saved, except that clearly it was an activity his mother would have approved, and there was very little on which to spend the one pound fifty which might be the reward of a week's digging. He had never needed to buy food (except for sweets) or clothes. His mother had done that for him until she had gone to stay with Jesus, and then the Hospital had done it.

He stood pissing into the urinal, and wondered why the Gents here was so crowded, and why everyone seemed to be looking (or avoiding looking) at everybody else. It was the hub of Empire, but that was hardly an explanation. Three men, who had finished at the urinal, stood combing their hair; this grooming seemed to take them some considerable time. Another rubbed his hands in a current of warm air, and every time the current appeared to be about to stop, he pressed a button, and started it again. Another leaned against the white-tiled wall beneath a notice which read, 'No loitering', and blew smoke rings from his cigarette. Others stood at the urinals, not pissing at all, but shaking and rubbing their private things, their heads turning from left to right, as though looking for someone or expecting to meet a friend. Walter became convinced that he had found his way into a place where criminals collected. He had heard that London was full of crooks, and they must meet somewhere.

It cost Walter five pence to wash his face and hands, and even in the Wash Room, men looked at each other's faces reflected in the mirrors. He stood at the washbasin, supporting his two plastic carrier bags between his legs for fear that one of the crooks should make a grab for them.

He shaved, using the cheap safety razor and blades June had purchased for him on their second day of freedom. The soap he had brought with him from the Hospital would have to last a long time, so he used the soap provided by the Wash Room. After all, he had paid for it.

Then he removed his cap, and tried to comb his hair. It was matted, and there were knots; it needed washing. He had forgotten to bring any lavender brilliantine, so his hair stuck up where he had lain on it, and would not lie down. He would be bound to have to remove his cap in a restaurant in which appearances were noticed. He had better wash his hair.

He refilled the basin with warm water, and dipped his head in it, pressing the carrier bags between his legs in a vice-like grip. Someone tapped at his right shoulder. This sudden contact so surprised Walter that he straightened his back, and turned round so quickly that water from his hair sprayed round the room, and particularly across the face of the man who had done the tapping.

Walter drew back the wet hair from his eyes, and blinked in order to focus on his assailant. It was the Wash Room attendant, who now stood in front of him, and with deliberate slowness removed a spotlessly clean handkerchief from his trouser pocket, raising it to dry his closed eyes and dripping chin.

'Don't do that.' The attendant's eyes were still closed.

'Sorry.' Walter bent down quickly to retrieve the pullover and stained underpants which had fallen from one of the carrier bags. The attendant explained that the nearest Public Baths were in Marshall Street. These basins were for the washing of faces and hands, but not hair. Hair clogged the pipes and plughole. There are men who lose hair during the washing of it. Anyone who has experienced the removal of large quantities of hair of various colours, textures and shapes from plugholes already in receipt of the natural oils and greases of the body, to say nothing of the soap-scum caused by the hard water of London, does not wish to repeat the experience.

The Wash Room attendant had started by simply addressing his remarks to Walter, but as his recollections grew and his anger with them at the injustice of fate which had brought him to this profession and his revulsion at handling the world's redundant hair, he addressed his remarks to a wider audience, spreading them around the Wash Room and out into the room in which men both old and young stood at urinals pretending to piss.

Walter listened. Water ran from his hair into his eyes. It dripped onto the collar and lapels of his jacket. As it ran between the soaking collar of his none-too-clean shirt and made its way from vertebra to vertebra, it cooled. After some time, the attendant discovered that he had expressed his anger and frustration as fully as he had the energy to do, and ceased. The silent disassociation by the men young and old, waiting about in the underground toilet, of themselves from the attendant's unhappiness could almost be felt. Only Walter gave attention, and that attention, hang-dog, pathetic, gaping, was entire. 'Better rinse out the soap now you've started,' the attendant said, and Walter, who knew well that no soap had yet been added to his hair or the water, let the discoloured water out, and seeing that the attendant had been right, and that three long hairs had indeed come out of his head, removed them from the plughole, and refilled the basin with clean water.

'I'll get you a towel.' Walter took the towel, and rubbed at his head, thinking it better not to mention his own towel, which was in one of the carrier bags. 'Where have you come from?' Walter considered, and decided that it was safe to answer, 'Hospital.' The attendant nodded wisely. 'And I don't suppose you've got another five pence for the use of the towel?' Walter stopped rubbing his head, and shook it. The attendant, wishing no longer to be reminded of his excess of emotion, said, 'All right, we'll pretend you didn't use it. Now off you go.'

Since even Walter could see that the towel was now dirty as well as extremely wet, he did not think that anyone would accept it as an unused towel. 'Now off you go' had been intended as friendly appeasement by the attendant, but Walter interpreted it as an order, and left the Wash Room at once, as he was, his hair still damp and frizzy from the rubbing, his cap and carrier bags in his hands, backing away before anything else went wrong, or the gang of crooks for whom all the other men were clearly waiting, turned up, and shot up the joint.

'I would like a Dover Sole with French-fried potatoes and peas, and my companion will have the Jumbo Mixed Grill, with rump steak, chips, etc. We'll both have Mixed Salads, followed by Vanilla Ice Cream with Hot Chocolate Sauce, two large white coffees, and a bottle of Tavel as soon as you can, please, since I see by your Wine List that you don't have Cendré.'

They were sitting in Hennekey's Grill and Griddle. Their table was near the door.

'Are these your bags, madam?' The waiter looked timidly at the now muddy suitcase and plastic carrier-bags.

'Yes. Why. Are they in the way?'

'No, madam, but we have to be careful of bombs.'

'Yes, one would have to be careful of those, but not in my

luggage. As you can see from its rather muddy state, a porter dropped it in a puddle, but I was the only thing to explode.'

'Very good, madam.' The waiter left them, and June turned to Walter, who sat opposite her, and smiled. She had changed her clothes, and now wore make-up. Not as much as Mrs Silver, who had supervised the Cosmetics Counter at Woolworth's, but enough to fascinate Walter. He had never seen her looking so much like a film star and so happy.

'Feeling better?' Walter smiled and nodded. She had been waiting for him, as anxious as a parent who has lost its child or a child who has lost its parent. She almost cried with relief when she had seen him approaching, his hair all damp and frizzy. She had hugged him to her, smelling of make-up and perfume. He had tried to tell her why he had taken so long, and they had sat together on the steps below Eros, while she had combed his hair gently, unravelling the knots, and used the same comb to clean his fingernails.

Then they had walked arm in arm across the street, and now here they were in an expensive restaurant where appearances were noticed. He had not changed his shirt, which was still wet and dirty, but the lights were set against the wall, and covered with dark-red shades which matched the textured wallpaper. There was not enough light in this restaurant where appearances were noticed for anyone to see the dirt on his shirt-collar. It was warm here. His hair would dry flat, as June had combed it. Perhaps steam would be rising from it even now. He touched his head, feeling and flattening his hair.

June reached across the table for his hand, and he gave it to her.

'Don't be nervous.' Somehow she must have found some money to pay for the meal.

'When we've finished the wine and the coffee, all you have to do is what I tell you. All right?' Walter nodded.

The bill amounted to nine pounds forty, including service, and arrived with the coffee. June made a point of adding it up, and searching her pockets for her purse. She placed the closed purse on the plate next to the bill, and told Walter to take his time drinking his coffee. There was no need to rush.

Their next project, June said, involved another long walk.

When she and Walter had both finished their second cups of coffee, June spoke to Walter in a quiet voice, her lips hidden by the now empty coffee cup.

'I'm going to take the bill and my purse, and stand up. When I've done this, you pick up the suitcase and the bags, and get out of that door. Don't rush, and don't stop or look back. Just keep walking. Turn right outside the door, and keep walking. I'll meet you by the City Guide in Leicester Square – you remember that large map we stopped and looked at? Just keep walking in a straight line, and you'll come to it. All right?' Walter nodded.

'Here goes.' June stood, and moved slowly towards the back of the restaurant, peering closely at the bill as if she were short-sighted. Walter also stood, and picked up the luggage as he had been told. Luckily, customers about to enter the restaurant held the door wide open for him, so that he was soon out in the street and heading towards Leicester Square.

The waiter approached June. He smiled over her shoulder at the incoming customers. 'A table for four? Certainly, sir. I'll be with you in a moment.' He said to June, 'Is there some trouble, madam?' and she squinted at the bill, holding it even closer to her eyes, and said, 'Yes, I don't seem to be able to bring it into focus.'

Then suddenly, with an expression which any drama students would be delighted to have in their repertoires, she clutched at her chest, and bent double. This was followed by noisy and hysterical inhalations of breath and by wild gestures towards the door. The waiter backed away a little, and the customers at the nearest table pretended to be blind and deaf. More gulps of air, and between each gulp, painful words. 'Pills ... he ... he's got ... pills ... heart ... heart pills ... must ...' June turned, and began an unsteady walk towards the door. The turn concealed from the waiter her next action, which was to push one finger of the hand already covering her mouth well down into her throat, touching the back. June retched convincingly. More customers had entered, and, in some concern for themselves and their clothes, leaned backwards over the already seated diners, so that the way to the door was clear and any pursuit impeded.

Once outside the door, June continued her performance for only a short time, not wishing to attract too much attention. Then she began to run.

Walter waited as he had been told, and June appeared, skipping over the flagstones.

'Old gags are best.' She placed her warm and somewhat sweaty hand into Walter's, picked up both plastic carrier bags with the other, and began to walk. Walter, as usual, carried the suitcase, which never seemed to get lighter. He wondered why he had been sent on ahead and where she had found money to pay the bill. He stroked the palm of her clammy hand with his thumb. Her hands had never been like this before. He said, 'You were frightened.'

June stopped and looked at him, surprised by his intuition. Then she said, 'Yes. That's half the fun.' She smiled, lifted his hand to her mouth, and kissed the back of it. 'Anyway, it's a very long time since I did anything like that. Clive would never let me.' Her smile turned into a giggle. 'He was always afraid there might be someone in the restaurant who knew him.' She began to walk again, and Walter concentrated on keeping up, and hoped he would not soon have to change hands. 'Since he always cheated the Income Tax, by claiming every meal out as a business expense, he said it wasn't worth the risks. Clive took more foreigners out to meals than the American Ambassador, and most of them were really me, and most of the time I didn't really enjoy it.'

She paused again to study the bust of Shakespeare, which stood on a pedestal roughly in the middle of Leicester Square. In the four corners were busts of Joshua Reynolds, Isaac Newton, William Hogarth and John Hunter, and since it was Jubilee Year, each of these famous men had recently been cleaned, and the cleaner had placed a transparent plastic bag over each of the famous heads. The London pigeons had ignored the plastic bags; there was clearly no pleasure to be found in shitting on plastic. Consequently Shakespeare, who had not yet been cleaned and had no bag, had received more than his fair share of their attention. Walter was reminded ·of his dead mother's hair, all matted with pigeon droppings.

They were so close still, Walter and June, to the hub of Empire. Someone had discarded a large fish-head, together with some of the fish's skin, and near it a Japanese boy sat, reading a tiny book held very close to his face. His spectacles reflected the floodlights set in the trees of the Square. Next to him was a fat man with a shaven head and dirty overcoat. As Walter watched, the fat man rose from the bench and felt in all his pockets several times over for a key which, in fact, was dangling from his thick belt on a long chain, striking against the paving stones each time the fat man moved his hands from one pocket to another.

No one was in a hurry. If the people in the Square had places to go, they also had the time to get there.

An elderly man in a greasy raincoat rose from another of the benches, and, with the aid of his steel elbow-crutch, made three strides before the crutch slipped, and the man fell backwards, his legs and arms in the air, and lay there like a dog which is hoping for its stomach to be rubbed.

June and Walter moved to help, but were beaten to it by two younger men.

'Look at the poor fucker. He's pissed isself.'

'Got a bottle in his pocket. Lucky you didn't break your bottle, mate, as well as your water.'

They had lifted the man to his feet, and he stood there, looking down in disbelief at the front of his wet trousers. The two young men moved on, laughing.

The elderly man's eyes focused on no one in particular, and his remarks were addressed generally to his surroundings. 'Crutch slipped,' he said, his eyes opaque and blinking like a bird's. 'Didn't you see it? Crutch slipped.' He looked again at his stained trousers. 'Surprised me. I was going . . .' he gestured vaguely towards the Gentlemen's Toilet which is at one corner of the Square. 'I was on my way.' His small features crumpled, and his eyes shed water, and his lips were trembling. 'What's the point?'

June ceased altogether to feel gay. Her high spirits were replaced by a generalized sadness, which caused her to cry both with and for the elderly man, who never saw her tears, but walked away, wiping his face with the back of his free hand, walking unsteadily, his trousers wet, his pride injured.

'If a child in Tasmania itches, I scratch. If the man in the moon pricks his finger, I feel the pain, and self-pity leaks from me at every pore.' June drew in a deep breath. 'Waterloo, Walter; that's

122

where we're bound. You'll see the river at night, the bridges lighted up and the water moving like oil to ease the hinges of this once-great city.' Her mascara was running, and the make-up on her face felt thick and heavy. She would wash it off.

Her hand touched the handle of the drinking fountain, but it was out of order. No water spurted up to cool and cleanse her face. 'Nothing works for long, does it?' She looked up at Walter, who was watching the two black lines run down her cheeks. She said, 'Wrap yourself around me for a minute, and tell me I'll be all right.'

Walter stood with his arms around June, the right side of his face resting on the top of her head, and wondered where and when they were going to sleep. But all he said was, 'You'll be all right, June. We'll both be all right.'

He wanted to add that he loved her, which was what people in films said to each other. Laurel and Hardy did not say it, but it was said by some, particularly those in the position in which he now found himself, holding each other, standing up, perhaps in some public place. But Walter could not say it, couldn't form the words. Instead he said, 'Will you show me the river now, please?'

3

She wondered if there were a rule in the Police Manual that they should continue to give the kiss of life until the ambulance arrived.

The river at night moved like oil, just as June had promised. If Walter concentrated on a small area, it almost comforted him. There were even ducks swimming around the SS *Hispaniola*, which was now a floating restaurant. They waited for bread.

But it was hard to narrow his concentration down to the comforting ducks. The width of the river, the length of the bridge, the towering buildings on each side, some illuminated, some in darkness, with only the thousands of windows reflecting the lights of the river and the streets, these were altogether outside his range of comprehension. The Royal Festival Hall, the Shell Building, the National Film Theatre threatened him from across the water, and the enormous concrete slabs of the National Theatre looked like a crouched and frozen animal. On his own side, Cleopatra's Needle and the distant floodlit dome of St Paul's, set among the tower blocks of the Barbican, said to him, 'There is no home for you here, Walter. You are too small; you are nothing.' To be alone here, to be lost, would be terrifying.

Walter was not lost, was not alone. June was with him.

The people here moved fast, looking down or straight ahead. They moved past Walter like buses one has just missed. Even if he were brave enough to shout after them, they would not turn round; he would have to wait for the next. The people who lived in London must all be like Mike, the Trainee Floorwalker in the Stock Room at Woolworth's, intelligent, quick-talking, moving, always moving, on the move, on the way to somewhere. '*Come on, Walter, move your arse!*' If you didn't, you'd soon get knocked over, trodden on, lying there under the feet of the quick-talking, fast-moving people. It would be hard to be old here. No wonder there were benches in Leicester Square.

The coloured lights of the SS *Hispaniola*, reflected in the thick black oil of the Thames, reminded him of a taffeta dress his mother had once worn. He allowed his mind to be drawn into them, pulled down into warm sleep (for oil was always warm). He could forget his cold feet and face, forget the rubbish and beer cans floating in the river, forget that they only had thirty-two pence and nowhere to sleep. He closed his eyes, and imagined that he was being rocked, wrapped in warm taffeta, in time to the soft rhythmical tapping of the river against the wall. Soon June would want to move on.

But June began to hum. She would not take him away yet. She was humming to herself, and he knew the song, could remember some of the words, sung so often by his mother in the days before the Hospital. Walter lowered his head onto the backs of his hands, saying the words silently inside his head.

> 'We shall gather at the river,
> The beautiful, beautiful river,
> Gather with the Saints by the river
> That flows by the hand of God.'

It was cold, very cold. They had reached the Arches, close to what the student June had once known as Charing Cross Underground Station, but had now been renamed Embankment.

It was 1977, the year of the Queen's Jubilee, and fifty-seven bodies were lying on the pavement under the arches down by the river. The bodies were pressed together for warmth, and because there were more bodies than space.

It was Jubilee Year. During the nineteen thirties at a time of unemployment, hunger marches and strikes, when George Orwell was living down and out, there were seldom more than two hundred people living rough in London. In 1947, the L.C.C. (as it then was) had abandoned its count, having found only six. But there had been progress, prosperity and achievement since then, twenty-five years of the New Elizabethan Age (1952-1977), and when, in 1973, the journalists of *The Sunday Times* had gone out to do a head count of those sleeping rough in London, they had found one thousand, four hundred and fifteen, not counting those sleeping in derelict buildings which had been reckoned too dangerous for the journalists of *The Sunday Times* to enter.

Her Majesty had gone walkabout all over her domain, walking through lines of prosperous and progressive citizens of the New Elizabethan Age, waving Union Jacks. Walter and June stood looking down at the lines of horizontal bodies under the Arches, fifty-seven of them with another four (June had done her own head count) sleeping on the steps of a building appropriately announcing itself as the 'B.B.C. Layhouse'. One of the bodies on the Layhouse steps was that of a woman who had crammed herself into a blue plastic milk-crate for warmth.

The bodies lay on flattened cardboard boxes, some with newspaper wrapped and tied around their legs, others with a covering of black polythene. One man had made a tube of cardboard boxes like a coffin and wrapped polythene round it; only the top of his head was visible. Some had their feet inside boxes; most had piled rags on top of them and wore several layers of clothing. Above them could be seen an official notice: 'THE DEPARTMENT OF PUBLIC HEALTH. ACTION WILL BE TAKEN WITHOUT PRIOR NOTICE AGAINST ANY UNAUTHORIZED PERSON PARKING, TRESPASSING OR DUMPING RUBBISH ON THESE PREMISES.'

It was 1977, Her Majesty's Jubilee Year, less than a mile from the Hub of Empire. Walter picked up a bottle which had once contained Mellow Brown Full Sweet South African Sherry, and now lay in the gutter, where it would break and puncture the wheels of passing cars. In a corner nearby were at least a dozen similar bottles, which had severally contained Dulcet Cream, Full Rich Tarragona from Yates's Wine Lodge and Maryland Sweet White. He placed the bottle from the gutter with these others, and hoped it would stay.

It was so very cold. He grasped June's hand. Surely this couldn't be where she had intended them to stay the night? Yet she stood, gripping his hand tightly, and staring down at the bodies huddled together.

He had learned much about June since they had met, some of it contradictory. He knew that it would not be beyond her to lie down with these people, simply in order to add her own body-warmth to theirs.

Walter tugged at June's hand. She pulled him closer to her. 'It's all right. We'll go soon. Never let me get as cold as they must be.' And then, after a moment, 'There isn't a God. There can't be.'

The homeless heads, sixty-one of them, counted by June, slept in snatches. There was always noise, always coughing. The sleep-less listened to the coughing, wondering whether each cough would be the cougher's last. Even dead, the cougher could not be colder. *The Sunday Times* had quoted Colonel McAllister of the Salvation Army, who had attributed the enormous increase in the number of those sleeping rough to the Mental Health Act of 1960, which had allowed Mental Hospitals to release long-stay patients back into the Community – 'the Community', that is, the Arches at Charing Cross, the B.B.C. Layhouse steps, the Bull-Ring in Birmingham, St Peter's Square in Manchester, Leeds Railway Station, various spikes (but never enough) in Peckham and points north; that is the Com-munity. And since a newspaper must be fair, and seen to be so, *The Sunday Times* had also quoted a consultant psychiatrist (anony-mous, because the medical profession must not advertise) who had defended the Mental Health Act, 1960, which had freed the Hos-pitals from acting as mere Asylums and protecting totally useless people who cannot and will not learn, and who only want to be kept, although they are not mentally ill.

Two policemen were sitting in the front of a dark-blue van waiting for trouble. They told each other jokes, and chuckled. One of them looked down the long line of cardboard, polythene and rags. The street lamps were reflected in his rimless spectacles, as he watched urine trickling from the bodies of the counted heads, and running along the pavement to join and mix with the other rubbish in the gutter.

Would he move from the warmth of his cab to pull the body of a counted head to its feet? Would he order it into the back of the van? Would he tell it to move on? If he did, where would it go?

No. Not tonight. Not on such a cold night of Her Majesty's Jubilee Year. The dark-blue van began very slowly to back away from the lines of bodies, crunching plastic cups beneath its wheels.

On the other side of the road, another van had stopped. This was a much older van, containing not policemen, but young people, four of them, who jumped briskly from it. Two of them lifted out a large container of stainless steel. It was a quarter to midnight. The soup had arrived.

Only three of the sixty-one heads looked out from under their coverings. None moved quickly. The three lookers became three standers, and arranged their paper and polythene to indicate that they would be coming back.

One of the four young people sported an Afro haircut. He carried round a large pan of soup, pouring it into plastic cups for those who did not wish to unwrap themselves from their coverings.

A woman sitting upright beside a pram loaded with carrier bags and cases was muttering something, some complaint which, since her voice was hoarse, did not carry to the young people. She wore a child's blue gabardine macintosh and lace-up boots. What she was saying was, 'Tell him to come over here. Tell him to bring some here.' A strip of once white net had been tucked under her headscarf. This was a veil. It hung over her forehead, and shielded her eyes from the street lamps. No one was allowed to see her eyes.

One of the young people noticed that her lips were moving, and went over to see what she wanted. The veiled woman waved her arms angrily at the girl, and mouthed complaints. Why couldn't she ask politely? Why did she snarl?

Now she was asking for more bread, and sliding what she had already been given beneath the lapels of her threadbare gabardine mac.

Two of the young people carried walkie-talkie radios. They held them to an ear to listen, to a mouth to speak. They were reporting back to headquarters, letting it be known where they were, in case they should be somewhere else. If medical help were needed – an ambulance, perhaps a coffin – here under the Arches, they would be able to say so to headquarters, and headquarters would dispatch it. These walkie-talkie radios had been bought with money subscribed by the public.

Twenty-five years of progress and achievement in the New Elizabethan Age. Mount Everest had been climbed, the first Morris Mini launched and the first hovercraft. Roger Bannister had run a mile in four minutes; the first steerable radio-telescope had been installed at Jodrell Bank; Sir Francis Chichester had sailed a thirty-foot ketch around the world, and Concorde had made a flight faster than sound. The youth with the Afro hairstyle held a pocket mirror to the mouths of those counted heads which had not moved.

'ANGELA RICHARDS WON'T DROP HER STANDARDS FOR ANYONE.' A weakness in the neon sign had dimmed the important 'D'. London Transport and British Rail maintain a careful, almost puritanical censorship over the advertising material they are prepared to display to their customers and employees, but had not yet been able to have the sign repaired. Below Angela's undroppable standards another advertisement asked, 'Is This the Right Time to Invest in Gold?' Neither June or Walter felt disposed to give an answer. They were sitting on a bench on Waterloo Station, waiting for time to pass, sharing tea from a plastic cup, sipping it slowly in turns, trying to make it last. It had cost them ten pence.

'No, I wouldn't tell you a lie; don't believe in it. I'm an Alk...
Alk... an Alko Holic. Can't even say it.' Michael smiles, and takes another sip from his quarter bottle of Teacher's. He is in his mid-thirties, clean-shaven, Irish. He is sitting on the same bench as Walter and June, watching the late-night travellers arrive and depart.

'I drink, but I work for it.' He takes another sip. At the Destination Board in front of them, names revolve and are replaced by other names: it happens of itself, to Walter's puzzlement. 'Andover. Salisbury. Winchester. Southampton. Weymouth.' He cannot read these names, and would not know where the places are, but he knows they are different from the names which they have replaced.

'What at? I suppose you'll ask.' They have not asked. Michael taps the side of his nose with a finger. 'Ah, well, I know that. Would you like some of this in your tea?'

June shakes her head. There has been music from hidden loud-speakers, but it has stopped. Walter has turned his attention to a man with bandaged feet, who has placed his two walking sticks against a bench, and is resting his feet by leaning on the bench and lifting one foot at a time. This man is a Regular at Waterloo Station, there being nowhere else in particular for him to go and nothing else in particular for him to do. He can hardly walk, yet if he were to sit, he would be unable to get up again, and the police have moved him once already tonight.

'No, I never lie. Where do I work, then? Ah, well, I'm a landscape gardener. Would you like one of these?' Michael has taken a handful of pills from his inside pocket and holds them out towards June.

'What are they?'

'Mog. Modger. Mon.'

'Mogadon?'

'That's the one. You know them?' June nods. 'Will you have one with me?' June smiles, but shakes her head.

June says, 'You don't have any Valium, I suppose?'

This time, Michael shakes his head. 'Slow you down, them things. Stop you thinking.'

'That's what I need.'

Michael considers this, then leans closer to June, staring into her eyes. 'You're needing them now?' June nods. The top of the whisky bottle is found and replaced. Michael stands unsteadily, shoves the bottle into the pocket of his jacket, says, 'Wait there.'

June watches, as he weaves his way to another bench, and whispers to three of its occupants. They turn to look at her, and shake their heads. One of them, a woman, points to the other end of the Concourse. Michael gives June the thumbs-up sign, and tries to walk in a straight line to where the woman has pointed.

Two more men have joined the man with bandaged feet, one leaning on the other for support. The supporting man asks Walter for a cigarette in a thick Glaswegian accent, which Walter doesn't understand, so he smiles and shakes his head. The man with bandaged feet is complaining to the others that the police have warned him off sleeping on the trains, and have told the porters to prevent him, should he try to pass through the barrier. He tells them that he is convinced that he will die tonight because of the cold. It is a simple statement, simply stated, and he adds another, that he hopes it will happen quickly, so that he will no longer have to wait about on this fucking station.

'George is bringing you some.' Michael has returned.

'Thank you. That's very kind.' The euphoria achieved with Mogadon and whisky causes Michael to sway and grin.

'Don't you know George? He has the pills. All sorts. Where did you sleep last night?' Michael does not require an answer to any of his questions. 'Didn't you see me go through that gate over there? You have to get on the right train; you have to know how to do it. They don't move Number Six till nine in the morning. The police never move me on, hardly at all. You have to look smart, though. Does he want a shave?'

Michael is pointing at Walter, who, feeling threatened, has passed June what is left of the tea, and taken hold of her free hand.

'He had one earlier.'

Michael is disappointed. His help in this respect has been refused. His loneliness returns, breaking through the comfort of whisky and Mogadon. He sways, and looks round the Station Concourse like a child on its first day at school.

June pats the bench beside her. 'Come and sit down.'

'George is coming.' This statement is more to reassure himself than her. 'Florrie!' He waves to a woman on another bench, and beckons to her to come over, before carefully sitting down again next to June.

'He can have a shave, if he wants one. Here.' Michael brings from his pocket a sponge-bag, and shows its contents to June – a razor, a bar of Knight's Castile soap, a toothbrush and toothpaste containing fluoride for the protection of both teeth and gums, even a pocket-sized deodorant spray. 'Here! Smell this.' Michael takes June's fingers gently in his, and squirts deodorant onto the back of her hand, the two hands, his and hers, touching each other, then shaking her hand and sniffing it before releasing it, as if sampling expensive perfume.

'Good, isn't it?'

June agrees, and Michael is happy again. 'Did I tell you I worked?'

Time passes.

131

It is twelve forty-five, and an Indian porter is giving a display of his ability to control an electric cleaner, steering it round and round in ever decreasing circles with one hand, then revving up and speeding towards the Bookstall, only to swerve aside at the last moment and skim past a notice warning passengers not to feed the pigeons, the large rotating brush at the front of the vehicle sweeping plastic cups, empty crisp bags and cigarette ends under the wheels to be sucked up inside.

Pigeons. They would be asleep.

'Eee! I've got more scarves than money.' This is Florrie, the lady who came over from the other bench, and now sits between June and Michael, whom she insists on calling 'Paddy'. Michael greeted Florrie like a long-lost relation, with a kiss and a hug, but in fact, as it seems, they have only met twice before.

Florrie twists and untwists her headscarf. 'No, don't grease me coat, Paddy. Tell me without touching me. Get your fingers off; they're covered with soup or something. I've got to make this coat last. He gets silly when he's drunk. Only time these blokes can talk is when they've had too much. I was sixty last week. I want to see George mesel; I've gorra toothache.'

In fact, Florrie is toothless, except for one tiny monument which stands, misshapen but defiant, like a relic of Stonehenge, guarding her lower jaw from any further attack by National Health dentistry.

'Anybody got a smoke?' Michael obliges with a small Silk Cut cigarette.

'He works, does this one. In the Parks for the Corporation. Hey! You haven't bought me for a cigarette, you know. I don't go behind the wall for a low-tar fag.' Florrie opens her mouth wide to laugh and let the smoke out. Her face is pinched and drawn, but her eyes are lively, missing nothing. As she speaks, she looks about her with quick jerks of her head, and at roughly three-minute intervals she ties and unties her brown chiffon headscarf. It is now one fifteen a.m.

'Ahm back up north after Christmas to live wi' me son. He said I could, now ahm over sixty. He's asked Council, and they've said it's all right, as long as ahm sixty. That's nice, intit? I don't like London, do you? Haven't I seen you down the Webber Street

132

Mission?' June shakes her head. 'I've been in every hostel in London. Some of them are all right. He doesn't know I come here, you know, me son. He thinks I'm booked in to a hostel. Well, I will be tomorrow – or Tuesday. If it gets any colder. Have you seen Kathy? You must know her. She comes on the trains here. Big tall woman, wi' one eye, just the one. She's sixty-two, and still works, has done all her life. She cleans down the Blackfriars Road.'

Michael's head is resting on her shoulder. 'When's George coming, eh, Paddy?'

'Don't call me "Paddy". Here, give us a kiss.'

'Hey up! I don't think I can be bothered. They don't bother me, you know, men. I can talk to them all right – be civil – but I've been on me own twenty years now. I don't need a man. Stop leaning over me like that, Paddy. If they see you like that, they'll not let you through barrier. They don't want sick all over their trains. Cleaners don't like it.'

Time passes. Long lines of trolleys, piled high with mailbags and thick wedges of the day's newsprint, begin to twist and curl around the Concourse like snakes.

It is almost one forty-five a.m. 'God, I feel awful. Thought I was going to die.' George has arrived. George is having a coughing fit. Slumped down next to Walter, his head lowered between his knees, he almost chokes on the phlegm he coughs up. He grips Walter's arm tightly, gasps for breath, and tries to speak.

'Sitting ... in the ... lavatory, I was. Come on all ... of a sudden. Feel like ripping me chest open ... Getting better ... Some bloke asked if ... wanted a hand ... get up the stairs ... Couldn't answer ... Making it worse.'

The others wait for George to recover. The fit subsides. George looks round to make sure that he is not being watched. 'Now, who needs the neurotic little comforters?' His dirty fingers delve in and out of the many patchwork pockets that he has sewn on the inside of his torn and threadbare overcoat. Seven different containers of various types of pills are brought out and held very close to his eyes for him to read the labels.

'Some of these dates are difficult to make out. Don't want to give you heap bad medicine.'

And then the eighth container. 'Valium. Five milligrams. One

133

to be taken three times a day. Mrs Eastwood. Fourth of the third, seventy-six. Last year's. A good year for Happies. Had them before?'

June nods. 'I've nothing to give you for them.'

'Did I ask?' June shakes her head. 'My life! She thinks I'm a pusher.' George looks at the others, and laughs, and the laughter starts him coughing again.

'No, sweetheart. Here, take them in health! Oh, hell! Don't make me laugh.'

The last of the tea in the plastic cup has gone long ago, and June sucks at the inside of her mouth to fill it with saliva with which to swallow one of the pills.

'Have you nothing for your chest?' Florrie has brought herself to George's attention. Soon she will speak of her toothache.

'Lost ... prescription. Five ... five weeks ago. Ooooh, Jesus! Can't find ... another bronchitic to rob.' George laughs and coughs, holding his chest and spitting at Walter's feet.

'You sound dreadful. I'd go to the hospital.'

'What can they do? ... They're not miracle workers ... Least ... least that's what they tell you. Prison ... best place for medical treatment ... Look after you there ... Three months for shoplifting ... Recommend it for anyone with an ailment.'

'Are they any good with teeth?'

'Only if you want your gold fillings removed in a hurry.' George seems to be able to laugh now without coughing.

'I've got a toothache. Right at the back.' Florrie has opened her mouth wide, and is pointing an index finger down her throat. George leans across Walter to peer into Florrie's mouth.

'Shut it quickly, woman, before they start posting letters.' He hands her something from one of his inside pockets.

'What are they?'

'Aspirin. I've run out of general anaesthetics. Here! Your mouth just reminded me; I was told a joke. There was this chap nearly drowned himself off Brighton beach, and when they got him out, a crowd gathered, and two men took it in turns to administer the Kiss of Life up his arse. Then the ambulance arrived, all flashing lights and smelling of Dettol, and the doctor came rushing over, and shouted, "Hey! What are you doing?" "Giving him the Kiss

134

of Life," they said. "You don't give it there." "We know," they said, "but have you smelt his breath?" '

Time passes. At two fifteen, Florrie wakes Michael up, and says she is getting on a train. She has been watching the movements of the porters for some time, and has seen her opportunity. The regular porters are no danger; they know what goes on. But if Florrie were spotted by a new porter, or by the police, she would be turned away, and would have to spend the rest of the night on the bench, which has become very cold now.

Michael waits until Florrie is safely in the train at Platform Six, and then follows her, giving June a nod.

Five minutes later, June stands, and, holding hands, suitcases in Walter's right hand, two carrier bags in June's left, they walk to and past the barrier of Platform Six. Nobody stops them or shouts at them. They walk to the middle of the stationary train, and climb into a First Class carriage.

'Speak, Roger! Speak!'

June and Walter had not slept well, nothing like as well on the comfortable seats of a First Class carriage as on the hassocks of the village church in which they had spent their first night of freedom. They had expected to be discovered by a porter, marched away by Transport Police, accused of trespassing: June had determined to say nothing except in the presence of her solicitor. That would be Clive's solicitor, of course. It would be a long way for him to come from Preston.

At twelve minutes past seven, they had begun to leave the train still standing on Platform Six, looking forward to becoming again part of the anonymity of the Concourse. From the barrier, June could see their bench. An enormous Alsatian police dog was resting its front paws on George's chest, its steaming breath arising in clouds from its panting mouth.

'Speak, Roger!'

The dog stretched back its lips, displaying a set of Ivory Castles which might have earned it a Best-in-Show at Cruft's.

George had woken as the dog's paws landed on his chest. His eyes had opened inches away from the long cold nose, the slavering red tongue and the glinting amber eyes which stared into his with the concentrated alertness which deserved a more dangerous object.

Roger spoke. First there was a growl, deep-throated and long-drawn-out. Then he lifted his head, pointed his nose towards the soiled girders of the Concourse, and achieved the top note of his snarling bark. The sound echoed back from concrete and metal. Behind the line of trailers containing mailbags, three policemen hid their laughter behind cupped hands.

George's right hand went across his heart, covering his chest. The dog, in response, took the cuff of George's raincoat between his teeth, and wrenched George's hand and arm upwards, where it remained, pointing upwards, as if George were making an appeal for help to the gods of the Concourse.

One of the three policemen, Roger's handler, ran forward three paces from his hiding place, and then stopped. Roger still held George's arm in the air, growling disappointedly, since it seemed that there was not to be a fight.

'Back! Back! Back, Roger! Heel, boy!' There was something wrong. The handler's voice sounded almost hysterical.

Roger released the cuff of George's raincoat, and the arm dropped limply back across George's chest. The dog-handler started to run.

'Come back, you stupid bloody dog!' Roger backed away, and sat, while his handler fumbled to get George's tie undone. Three buttons from George's shirt came away and rolled under the bench, as the dog-handler ripped the shirt open, and pressed an ear to George's chest. The dog's ears pricked up as he heard the buttons hit the ground. He was still on duty.

'Oh, Christ! Ambulance! Quick! Get a fucking ambulance.' There was no 'almost' now to the dog-handler's hysteria; the hysteria was positive. He had ripped the tie and collar from around George's neck, and with his mouth over George's mouth, inhaled and exhaled with desperate purpose.

June stood, at a little distance, watching. Others watched, but from a greater distance. The regulars did not care to place themselves too close to the police.

The second policeman, who had used his walkie-talkie to summon an ambulance, took over the task of giving George the Kiss of Life, and the third placed the palm of one hand on George's chest and thumped on the back of that hand with the clenched fist of the other. The first policeman was now leaning on a truck loaded with mail bags, and looking as if he were about to be sick. He didn't look to be more than twenty-three years old, and June supposed that this might be the first time his dog had killed anyone. Was there some instruction in the Police Manual that they should continue to give the Kiss of Life until the ambulance arrived?

Perhaps there was. It was fourteen minutes before the ambulance could be heard arriving, and the attempts at resuscitation continued for all that time.

The dog-handler had not been sick, and now rejoined his colleagues. 'Stupid bugger didn't stand a chance.'

'How do you know he hadn't already snuffed it?' This was the policeman with the walkie-talkie. Clearly it would be more convenient for everyone if George had already snuffed it.

'He moved his arm, didn't he?'

'I didn't see that. Did you?' Both the older policemen agreed that they had not seen George move his arm, and the one with the walkie-talkie added, 'Get yourself together, lad. He wasn't going to last long anyway.'

At this point, the third policeman noticed June and Walter. 'What are you staring at?'

'A dead friend. A dog. And three servants of the public, who all wear numbers.'

The three policemen stared at her. The young one wiped his eyes, and said, 'Jesus fucking Christ!'

June said, 'Not possible. If he existed at all, there's no evidence that he was a contortionist.' The two older policemen looked at each other. They had a right one here, but although they knew well enough how to deal with right ones of her sort in the usual course of events, this right one had the advantage of them.

'Would you like my official statement now, or shall we do that at the station?'

'We don't need it, thanks all the same.' The walkie-talkie policeman turned away, dismissing her.

'Your need wasn't uppermost in my mind. Now, the dead man's name was George. He was fifty-four. He liked alcohol, jokes, dogs and honesty, not necessarily in that order.' It came to Walter that June was enjoying herself, though the smell of danger was very strong around them. Perhaps she could not smell it. 'He told us only a few hours ago that he knew he was safe, sleeping there, as long as he moved on when required by the police to do so. I'm sure he felt confident that this request would be made by a human being, and not a dog.'

The white-coated ambulance men were carrying George's body away, covered by a blanket. 'It's a bit late for any of you to ask him now. Which station are you from?'

The young dog-handler was sitting where George had lately lain, his hands covering his face. He mumbled something, and was told to close his mouth. June waited. None of the three policemen told her what station they were from, and she did not know enough about the organization of the Force to know that the station would be Waterloo; they would be Transport Police.

'Perhaps Roger will tell me. Speak, Roger. Come on, nice little doggy. Save the lady time by telling her where to take her complaint.'

The policemen remained silent. June said, 'She doesn't wish to be unfriendly, and blab to the newspapers.' The policemen remained silent.

June waited. The three policemen waited. It was silent all around them. The whole of Waterloo station was silent. Even the pigeons were quiet, and Roger, instead of howling as the dogs in stories do when death is near, sat twitching his tail.

June made a pretence of rummaging in one of the carrier bags.

'What do you want?'

'Ten p. There's always somebody on duty in a newspaper office, and it's bound to be a long call.'

The oldest of the three policemen said, 'What do you really want?' and the walkie-talkie policeman added, 'You can say what you like. It won't do you any good or us any harm.'

'You're wrong on both counts. It will do me good, because if I don't report what really happened rather than the version you might be tempted to give, I shall feel bad for quite some time. And as for the harm to you, well, that's still for you to decide. If I make a statement to your superior officer, that may mean a small black mark on your record, a tiny hindrance to promotion. Whereas an article in Monday's *Guardian* about three policemen and a dog terrorizing an elderly bronchitic, and then trying to cover up the fact that the man died as a result, that might be really quite serious. It might mean you joining the millions of unemployed, some of whom have nowhere to sleep.'

'You really are a vindictive cow, aren't you?' said the walkie-talkie policeman.

'That has been said of me before, yes.'

June made her statement in a small office, reached by a door marked, 'Private. No admittance to the Public'. Walter waited outside, but was not moved on.

The Superintendent explained to June what a difficult job it was his men had to do. June said to the Superintendent that since the matter was now on record, she did not intend to take it further. The Superintendent applauded that decision. Speaking entirely in a friendly and unofficial way, he advised June not to frequent the railway termini of London for a while. A story of this kind was bound to get passed around, and British Transport policemen, like anyone else, were sensitive to criticism.

4

I've got a wanker on the line, who can't wait for Susan

They were asked to give their names, and their names were entered in a book, before the large blonde woman with the face of a Grand National winner, who sat behind a telephone switchboard, said, 'Would you like to go on through? Jenny will make you some coffee.' Then they were led by Jenny through a narrow passage, over the entrance to which a grubby slab of white polystyrene had been hung, so as to save the skulls of those clients who were in such distress that they failed to notice the equally grubby sign instructing them to mind their heads.

'Angela, love, can you take a call on seven? She's not still on Nine Thousand, is she? Oh, bollocks! I'll have to do it myself.' As June turned into the passage, the large woman's hands moved expertly over the switchboard, picked up the telephone attached to it, and in a voice from which almost all trace of horsiness had mysteriously disappeared said, 'Samaritans. Can I help you?'

'Through' turned out to be a central area in need of fresh white-wash and something quite radical done about the armchairs and what was left of the haircord carpet. The smell of cats was strong, and there were also many small cardboard boxes, which lined the edges of the floor, the words 'Rentokil. Poison. Handle With Care' written on their sides.

'I thought we'd come to the Samaritans, not an abattoir for mice.'

'Sorry?' Jenny's bright and smiling face held an expression composed to signify that she hadn't heard.

'Just thinking aloud.'

'Oh! Good. Yes, that's the thing to do. Do sit down.' They sat. 'Do you both take sugar?' Jenny was using her very best R.A.D.A.-trained toneful voice. She had discovered that the low arched ceiling of the crypt in which this branch of the Samaritans operated really made all those hours of practice with her diaphragm and head-resonators worthwhile. Her words sounded as if they were coming from a very expensive record-player with the bass control turned on full.

'Won't be a moment.' Jenny was peeping from behind the lid of a large urn; the steam rising from it was enough to straighten the waves in her hair. June took hold of Walter's hand, and gently applied pressure. Doors leading off this central part of the crypt had names painted on them – 'Geoffrey', 'Dorothy', 'Piers'. Were these the names of the people who sat behind the doors? Each of the doors had a little light beside it. The orange lights were all lit. She was not sure, but it was possible that from behind the door of Piers came sobbing. To which of these person-doors would she be confiding the reason for her and Walter's being here? One thing June had decided was that it would not be to this spinning Jenny, who now approached, slopping their coffee onto the blue stained haircord.

'You can tell I'm new to this. I can't even master Samaritan Rule Number One. "Make a good cup of coffee." ' Jenny smiled the smile she had practised and produced so often to those of the theatrical profession who might give her work. The smile said, 'Please like me,' and so many times they had liked her, told her so, had said in a genuine way, 'We like you. We really do,' so that her heart had leapt with joy. Then they had added, 'But not for this part,' and her heart had sunk. And they had thanked her ever so sincerely for having come to see them, and told her that she had made an impact they really would remember. 'Better luck next time.' But somehow, next time it was always the same, from panto in Carlisle to truly serious and original deodorant commercials: Jenny had improvised and done group work for the Royal Court Theatre, coming back day after day for three days, and at the end all they could say was that they really liked her and she had a quality. Meanwhile she had plenty of time to come in to the Samaritans two mornings a week.

141

'I should have asked if you preferred tea. We do have some bags. Will you be all right for a few minutes until someone more experienced can come and talk to you?' June nodded.

Jenny backed away towards the Reception Area, smiling as she went, and the voice of the horse-faced lady could be heard. 'Oh, you're just in time. I've got a wanker on this line, who can't wait for Susan. Sounds in a right state, poor love. It's no good me trying to cope out in the open like this; it'd scare off anyone who came in. Can you give him five minutes? You'll find he keeps losing his erection, which is making life even more complicated. See what you can do for him, there's a sweetie.'

June and Walter waited. The few minutes stretched out to more than a few. Ten minutes, then twenty, then thirty. Had they been forgotten? No Piers, no Dorothy came from behind the closed doors to speak with them. Two more people arrived, and were given coffee by smiling Jenny. One was a weeping black woman, who was also given a box of Kleenex, the other a gentleman in a dark suit, who refused the proffered coffee, and sat with his back to the rest of them, pretending to read *The Financial Times*.

More time passed. Walter and June were on their third cup. Opposite them was an old sofa, lying on it a pile of old rags and a dirty raincoat. Suddenly the raincoat and the rags moved, and a pair of feet appeared, wrapped in brown paper tied with string. Toes protruded from the brown paper, grey and bloodless, the long toenails black and curled downwards like the talons of a predatory giant bird.

At the other end of the rags there was movement. There was a nose, which had clearly lived, and above it two blue eyes, below it a pair of chapped lips at the corners of which a whitish creamy substance had dried. These features were surrounded with matted crinkly grey hair, the hairs, both of the head and the beard, seeming to be of more or less equal length.

The blue eyes blinked, then came to rest on Walter. The mouth opened with difficulty, as if the white creamy glue had been used to seal it shut.

'Where am I, Jack?' The voice was hoarse, the intonation accusing. Walter could tell that the question had been directed at him, but since his name was not Jack, turned to June for guidance.

June spoke. Loudly. 'This is the Samaritans. They say they want to help you, but I wouldn't wait if you're in any kind of hurry.'

The face winked. 'I only come here to wait in the warm. They're not supposed to let me in any more. Disbarred, I am, for disruptive behaviour, and pissing on the floor. But it's easy to get by if there's somebody new on.' His head retreated beneath the rags, and his voice was muffled. 'You'll get no money out of them.'

Jenny arrived to make an announcement, using her lower register to stress the serious and apologetic nature of her message.

'I'm terribly sorry, everyone, but we're very short of volunteers today, and it's been extra busy on the switchboard. Someone will see you as soon as possible.'

The door marked 'Piers' opened, and a man dressed as a woman appeared. He wore a short black plastic skirt, rose-pink blouse, high-heeled shoes and over-long false eyelashes, and dabbed at the make-up below his eyes with a small lace hankie held in a large muscular hand.

Could this be Piers?

'I wouldn't have minded, but I took time off work, and came all the way from Leeds, and all he says is that I'm doing it to draw attention to myself.'

An elderly lady had followed the man-woman out of the room. She had white hair, rinsed purple, and wore a twin-set and real pearls. She said, 'I know, Rosemary dear. They can be very brusque at Charing Cross Hospital, but you just have to press on, and convince him you mean business.' This lady must be Piers. As she escorted her client to the door, she said, 'Please do mind your head.' The man-woman ducked, bending almost double to make room for his beehive of a wig. The woman who must be Piers said, 'Do pluck up courage to see them at your local branch, and keep in touch.' Rosemary wobbled unsteadily up the steps in the shoes which had been purchased specially for his trip from Leeds to the Transexual Unit at Charing Cross Hospital, and then took in three very deep breaths, before opening the door and stepping out into the street.

Walter and June waited. They could hear phones ringing, and being answered. The people who answered the phones were saving lives, no doubt, but for whom?

A loud cry came from the Grand National winner on the switch-

143

board. 'Can one of you hurry your client up, and come and take over? If I don't go to the loo in the next thirty seconds, there'll be a nasty accident.'

The black woman sobbed intermittently, and the pages of *The Financial Times* were turned. From a distance, there was a susurration of voices as the hidden Samaritans talked into telephones, talking and listening – listening sometimes to silence, sometimes to complaint, to despair, joke calls, hoax calls, silent calls, breathers and wankers, the lonely, the depressed, the schizophrenic, the fearful, pregnant, deviant, children and barren persons wanting children and other persons who had battered their children, the old and those bearing the burden of the old, the mad, the perplexed – talking sometimes easily of where to lodge or squat or to obtain legal advice or of Clubs – Clubs for agoraphobics, homosexuals, the widowed – 'Have you tried the Gay Switchboard?' 'Have you tried the D.H.S.S?' 'Have you thought of Evening Classes?' – talking sometimes uneasily of life and whether it is worth living, empathizing, always empathizing, a constant drip of empathy along the telephone wires. They came in various sizes, and sexes, and religions. They came sometimes for mornings, for afternoons, for evenings, or stayed all night, sleeping fitfully by the telephone. More were white than black, more middle-class than working-class. They made many mistakes, failed often, never knew when they had succeeded. For June, who despised so many people, they were particularly easy to despise, but it is doubtful whether she could despise them more than often they despised themselves.

'John, sweetie, do be an angel, and keep an eye on the switchboard for a moment.' The loud-voiced lady was back, refreshed, from the loo. 'We're up to our armpits in clients, and someone who shall be nameless has made a balls-up of the Rota again. Oh, and don't let Deirdre see that odd-looking couple from the north; she's not in any way right for them. Give them to Simon, and tell him to turf that old tramp out. He's not really allowed in, but it's my morning for turning a blind eye.'

The door of Dorothy opened, and a young couple with a baby came out, and were escorted to Reception by a young man with long hair, rimless spectacles and a cardboard disc marked 'Simon' pinned to his army surplus camouflage jacket. There was the sound of mumbled thanks, and the Grand National winner, who seemed to have two personae, one for her fellow-volunteers, the other for clients, could be heard comfortingly giving directions for reaching a hostel, and money for the fare. A few moments later Simon had returned, and was prodding the bundle of old rags. 'All right, Shadrach. You've had a good kip. Now on your way.' Then, looking towards Walter and June, 'I'll be with you in a minute.'

The minute turned into four, which was as long as it took to persuade Shadrach that his only likely means of coming into contact with money was to pay a visit to Social Security. Then Simon turned to June. 'You haven't been to us before, have you?'

June shook her head.

'Would you like to talk out here? Or if it's private, we could go into a room.'

So they went into Dorothy, and remained there some time.

5

Shall I put 'co-habiting', then?

'Why can't you tell me where you've come from?'

'From the Samaritans. I told you.'

'I mean before that. What were you doing?'

Walter sat beside June, facing the young man to whom they were applying for Social Security. Neither answered the young man's question.

'And you're not husband and wife?' June shook her head. 'Shall I put "co-habiting", then?'

'Surely one has to have somewhere to habit before one can co-habit?' The young man put a very small white hand to his mouth, and coughed.

'You've nowhere to stay?'

'That's why we need money.' The young man already knew this, but he had been trained to ask questions so that the answers would be given in triplicate. Unreliable applicants, answering the same question more than twice, might trip themselves up, thus saving the young man the necessity of making the appropriate mark in the appropriate box on the appropriate form.

'I can't give you money or a voucher until I have some confirmation of what you've told me.' Small white-headed pimples decorated the young man's neck and chin. The blotches under his eyes were mealy. Walter knew that 'mealy' was a colour used in the description of fancy pigeons; long ago his father had shown him whole

146

classes of mealies at a greyhound track near Preston at which the Premier Show of the Fancy had that year been held. He had not come across the word since, but now it sprang, full-feathered, into his mind as he looked at the blotches under the young man's eyes, which were of a colour somewhere between fawn, grey and blue. 'Mealy,' he said.

'Pardon?'

June said, 'And if we're not prepared to give you confirmation in return for your money or your voucher?'

The young man sighed. Inarticulate Irishmen, drunken Scots, stammering Pakistanis, these were all part of the job, but a stubborn woman really got on his tits.

'Nobody arrives in that chair from Outer Space, madam. Everyone has a past.'

'Goodness! With such wit and insight, you should go far. Does the Home Secretary know where he can contact you?'

Silence. Walter wondered whether the young man's collar was too tight. June remembered that on the way they had passed a plaque commemorating Thomas Brandon, Duke of Suffolk, who had married a daughter of Henry VII, and been granted permission to mint money at Suffolk House. She stored it away neatly in that part of her mind – it was, she thought, the largest part – labelled 'Department of Utterly Useless Information'. She looked at the clock on the wall, and waited. The young man rearranged the forms in front of him, tapped his felt-tipped pen on the counter-cum-desk, and examined the length and shape of his fingernails. Finally he said, 'Would you mind taking your friend, and going to sit on the bench over there, so that someone else can use this counter?'

June smiled graciously. 'Yes, I would mind, I'm afraid. A hell of a lot. You see, I don't think you're assisting us very well with our claim for National Assistance, and so I propose to sit here with my friend until you, or perhaps someone with a little less wit, insight and arrogance and a little more experience, age and authority, helps us.' Her voice had risen in volume as she spoke, and Walter could feel the distinct sensation of unseen people listening.

The young man coughed again before he spoke, and he also allowed his voice to become louder. 'Well, *when* you've told me

147

what you've been doing, how you've been living, and where, I shall try to corroborate your story.'

'So you've said. But how?' June's acid grace was causing sweat to start up on each side of the young man's nose, and trickle down therefrom. He said, 'It's no use trying to wear me down, madam. We could sit here all day, but I'd still have to go by the book.' June wondered how many other of his female clients he addressed as 'madam'.

'Oh, come along now! You mustn't give in to paranoia. I merely want to know how you'll use any information we give you. That's not unreasonable, surely? Hello, there!'

This sudden greeting and the extra-wide flashing smile was directed past the young man and above his head. The greeting was warily returned by an older man who had appeared and been hovering behind the young man's shoulder. 'Hello! Everything O.K, Leonard?'

'Yes . . . Yes, fine, thanks.'

The young man essayed a smile, which froze as June leaned forward, and whispered, 'Oh, I *am* sorry. I didn't realize you were new here. Now, where were we? Let me help you. The past . . . yes, well the thing is, you see, we've buried it, Walter and I, and we don't want to dig it up again. And we certainly don't want the people we've left to know where we are. Now do you see?'

'Yes.'

'Good.'

'It doesn't help, though.'

'Why not?'

'Because for all I know, you might be claiming benefit somewhere else.'

This time it was June who sighed. 'And going to all this trouble to claim it twice?'

'It has been known.'

'And if we swear to you on Holy Writ that we haven't a penny, you're not prepared to take our word?'

'That's hardly the point.'

'But surely it is? There must be dozens of people come in here whose past can't be checked, and on whom you have to take a gamble.'

'Well, can you give me some kind of hint?'

Since this enjoyable game had now begun to go her way, June's smile was genuine this time. 'Certainly. What kind would you like?'

'Would I be right in thinking that the reason that neither of you has a National Insurance Number, and that you haven't been working is that you've both been ... been away somewhere?'

June's congratulatory nod meant, 'Getting warm.' Even Walter had become aware that a game was being played.

'Somewhere up north, I assume from your accent. Yorkshire maybe?'

'Not unless they've moved Pennines.'

'Sorry?'

'The Chain, luv. You're wrong side of t'ills. But you're doing very well. We're both from Lancashire.'

'But you have been away?'

'Aye.'

'At Her Majesty's pleasure, perhaps?'

June abandoned the broad Lancashire accent. 'Oh, no, dear, not that. At least I don't think she got much fun out of it. But then, of course, I'm not privy to what amuses Her Royal Highness. And in any case, if "prison" is the word you've been walking around, they don't have mixed ones, you know. No, think of our sabbatical from the world of commerce and industry as being more for medical than punitive reasons. The sentence was still custodial. Society was being saved from us. But it wasn't reckoned to be our fault.'

'Hospital,' said the young man, more in relief than triumph. 'You must have been there a long time.'

June nodded, and looked at Walter, who took his cue, and nodded also.

'And before that?'

Walter noticed that June's enjoyment of the game seemed to have ended, and that she was staring at the floor. Leadership, or at least the responsibility of giving answers, had passed to him. He said, 'Woolworth's. I worked for ... Woolworth's. Preston ... Lancashire ... Years. Nineteen years ... ago.'

Walter's way of speaking explained more to the young man than a life history from June could have done. He noticed the anxious glances from Walter towards June's glassy stare, and decided that he had asked all the questions which needed to be asked at this interview. In the silence that followed, he became aware of the buzzing noise made by the strips of fluorescent lighting. Perhaps a tube was about to burn itself out.

'Before that, I was a sort of housewife.' June's words, though spoken slowly, were unexpected. 'And a sort of mother.'

One of the long tubes of light flickered and almost seemed to split, before it blinked its last blink, and went out.

'Will you wait a moment, please?'

Walter waited. The young man rose slowly, and went to find the £23.07 he would later give them. Then Walter stood, and, taking June's head between his hands, kissed her on the forehead, and then pressed the side of her face against his overcoat.

6

I have felt the tearing of nails, and had my feet stamped on at Harrods

Between Gun Lane and Spitalfields Fruit and Vegetable Market in the City of London, they found Providence Row, a night-shelter for the homeless.

Above one of the doors were the words 'Women's Entrance' carved in stone, and on one of the five steps leading up to that door sat a woman. Her hair was matted in frizzy knots; her face was the colour of old parchment and was without expression. Her fingers played with stockings she had rolled down around her ankles. She ignored both Walter and June. Providence seemed to have made no provision in this woman's life.

From outside, the building represented a small prison or Army Barracks. The entrance for men was similar to the women's, and there was a third, cleaner and newer, marked 'Convent'. June counted the bodies waiting on the steps of the Men's Entrance. There were twenty-two. The time was four in the afternoon.

'You wait here with me, Walter. They're not splitting us up.'

By four twenty, five more women had arrived, and there were thirty-one men. All waited.

'He should be over there.' One of the waiting women addressed this advice to June, but her finger was pointing at Walter, who shuffled his feet uneasily.

'Don't worry, Rita. They won't let him sleep in your bed.' Rita's companion removed the cigarette from her mouth. This enabled her to laugh, cough and spit.

151

'Look at her, stuck up cow! It's for his own good. He won't get in.' Then, with added energy, Rita leaned towards June, and shouted, 'They only take thirty-five blokes, and there's a crowd waiting already.'

June turned on the informative Rita. 'Thank you for your concern, but he's staying with me. No one told us we'd be split up.'

'Well, I'm telling you, aren't I? I've never met a Hostel where they let you sleep with men. Not even if it's your husband.'

Walter felt as Rita did, that he should be waiting on the other steps with the men. He felt uncomfortable, surrounded by so many women. There were seventeen now, including June.

'He won't get a bed, standing there. Then you'll be split up anyway, won't you?'

'Save your wind, gal. The nuns'll sort her out.' Then, after thought, 'Ask her who sent her.'

'Who sent you here, then?' But it was at that moment that the door was opened by a small and very young nun. While the nun looked up at Walter, and smiled, and said, 'Hello!' the one woman in the queue before them rose to her feet, and, without a word or a change of expression, walked into the Refuge.

Unsurprised, the nun said, 'Hello, Margery. Have a bath, dear,' and then to Walter, 'The men are at the other door.'

June stepped forward, and attempted a smile. 'I'm afraid we're not prepared to be split up, Sister. No one warned us that we would be.'

The women behind made noises of protest, sighs, grunts, tut! tuts, and one was even driven to exclaim in a loud voice, 'Jesus Christ! Hurry up. It's fucking cold out here.' The young nun raised herself onto her toes, moved June gently to one side, and said, 'I agree, Sheila; it's very cold. If you want to bath in warm water, you'd better stop effing and blinding.' Then, lowering herself into a more comfortable stance, 'Would you mind if I let the regulars in first, and then we can talk without being barracked?'

Walter had already stood aside, and June joined him, ignoring the hostile glances from the women who filed past.

'May I see in that bag, Gertie?' Gertie opened her shopping bag, and the nun picked out of it a parcel wrapped in many layers of newspaper and tied with many yards of string. The nun untied the

152

string. 'Were you intending to knit yourself a hammock, dear?'
Gertie's reply was an expression of resigned hostility, as the newspaper layers were removed to reveal a bottle of British sherry, half full.

'I wasn't going to drink it.'

'I'll keep it safe for you until you leave.'

The nun explained to June that Providence Row was a Night Refuge, an emergency service only, that sleeping accommodation for couples was very difficult to organize, and that most couples accepted the necessity for the short time they were there. Clearly the choice was separation here or another night together on the street. And it was, as the women had said, very cold. It came to June that she was not going to win this argument, and had better give in.

They stood in the hall of the Women's Section, and waited. The young nun returned unhappily. 'We've got our thirty-five men, I'm afraid. In fact, we've turned six away. We have to turn men away most days, after five o'clock.'

June studied the lino, and said, 'I see. Well, I'm sorry.' She looked at Walter. 'You were right, and I was wrong. If I'd let you stand at the other door, you'd have got in.' Walter looked at the little nun, then back at June. He looked what he was, which was puzzled. It was true that he had thought he should be standing at the Men's Entrance, but he had never said so to June.

'Just a moment, please.' The young nun tapped Walter on the hand gently, turned, and ran down the corridor in what looked like a hop, skip and a jump.

June moved to Walter, and hugged him in affection and triumph. She had noticed the way the young nun had included Walter in the conversation, had referred to him, smiled at him, and seemed at ease with him, when most other people either ignored him or appeared embarrassed.

'Sister Rachael says we're not to abandon you to the Salvation Army. They'll only talk you to death. We're moving Reginald into a cubicle downstairs, and that'll make a bed free for you. What's your name, please?'

Walter looked to June for permission to give the nun his name, and permission was granted.

F

'Right, Walter. You come with me. And what's your wife's name?'

Walter's confusion multiplied, and June smiled. It was the only tactical error the young nun had made, and it was made so kindly that it could not be held a fault.

'June.' Walter pronounced the name with pride. He even managed a smile, being totally beguiled by this young woman of religion. If his mother should be watching, he hoped that she had taken note of how a lady of the church had spoken to him.

'Sister Rachael will be with you in a few minutes, June. I'll take Walter to his bed.'

Left alone in the hall, June heard the light tapping of fingers on the door of the Women's Entrance. She opened it, and a woman in her mid thirties, wearing a black cloak, smiled at her.

'My name is known here.' June stood aside, allowing the woman to move gracefully past her, then closed the door, and turned to find the woman's hand stretched out to her, the back uppermost, as if its owner expected that hand to be kissed. June shook the hand firmly, and the woman said reassuringly, 'There is no beginning, you know, and there never was an end. Honesty is too potent a medicine for this sick world.' Her tone was confidential, and she gave June a knowing wink, and seemed about to go, but, noticing June's worried expression, paused to ask, 'Weeping, sweet Veronica?'

'June.'

'Smile, flower child. Here are hot spices and sweet licorice, and rosemary for remembrance.'

'June,' repeated June, as she looked down at the palm of her right hand, into which the woman had pressed a piece of silver paper still sticky from the toffee it had recently covered.

The woman moved down the corridor and round a bend, humming a psalm, the upper half of her body held gracefully erect, while the lower half propelled her along with a little too much spring and a little too much bounce.

There was a shout. It was the shout of someone too pious to use profanity, but sounding so like a curse that no hearer would expect the shouter to be a nun.

'Out! No ifs ands or buts, Mildred. Just, out!' June heard the

154

quick patter of sandalled feet, as Mildred came trotting back, pushed from behind by Sister Rachael.

'Please! Let me stay. I'm not very wet. Just a little damp.'

'You smell like a Scottish Off-Licence on New Year's Eve.'

'It's for the cold. I'll tell Him.'

'Do. And give Him my regards. Don't stop at the cold. Tell Him how you broke a window, and threw up over Sister Cecilia.' As Sister Rachael released one hand from Mildred in order to open the door, Mildred seized her chance, shrugged herself free, and bolted back down the corridor, shouting as she went, 'Come, cherubim, my angels bright, we'll be in Paradise ere night.'

Sister Rachael sighed deeply. 'You realize we'll never get her out now?'

'I'm sorry, but no one else seemed interested in answering the door. I was told to wait here for Sister Rachael.'

'That's me.'

Walter was shown his bed, which was in a large room containing thirty-four other beds. Two lines of ten beds, head to head, took up most of the centre of the room, and the other fifteen beds were placed around the walls. These beds were special, being separated by hardboard partitions and curtains. Walter wondered whether one had to be ill to be allocated one of these beds, for the partitions reminded him of hospital screens. However, since none of the beds was occupied, and an ill person would be in bed sooner not later than the others, he decided that the beds were kept for privileged men.

At one end of the room was a cross, seven feet high, to which was nailed a five-feet-high Christ. Walter had seen crucifixes, but never as large as this. This Christ was only a little smaller than Walter himself, dipped in plaster of Paris, and painted.

Beside the beds there were bedside cupboards, painted white, and each bed had its own straight-backed chair. Although large 'No Smoking' notices had been erected by Fire Inspectors the men smoked openly, and some of them continuously.

The young nun walked Walter round the room, pointing out items of interest. 'That cupboard's for your valuables. It can be locked.' Walter had seen this kind of tour-of-inspection at the

Hospital. Usually it was given to a mayor (or at least a councillor), some London politician or someone collecting for a new addition to the Hospital's amenities. But he was none such. He was introduced to some of the men, shook hands, and when the desultory 'Hellos', 'Pleased to meet yous' and 'How are you?'s' lapsed into embarrassed pauses, wondered if they were waiting for him to say, 'Keep up the good work.'

Finally the young nun left him, saying, 'Will you be all right now?', and Walter nodded. It was just as though they had moved him into a strange ward.

'They'll chat to you properly, I'm sure, when I'm gone.'

They did not. There was silence. Walter looked at the men. The men looked back at Walter, wondering, no doubt, what he had done to receive the privilege of being made room for. Had some of their friends been turned away? Would someone they all knew have slept in the bed he was to occupy? With the nun present, they had said, 'Hello,' and some had said, 'Pleased to meet you,' but they had not been pleased to meet Walter, and were not now, Walter could tell by the way they stared at him. Two, he remembered, had attempted a smile, and he had smiled back. Those two seemed no longer to be in the room. Everyone had a name. The nun had spoken their names. 'This is Robert ... James ... Peter ... Leslie ... Alf ... Martin ... Joe.' He remembered some of the names, but not which names went with which faces. Christopher? Herbert? Patrick? Geoffrey? Clifford? No that was wrong. There was no Clifford. He would have remembered that name. There was no one in the least like Clifford here.

Walter discovered that he couldn't move. He knew that there was nothing physically wrong with him, but if he moved, so might they. To him. Around him.

Now they were still, waiting for him to move, but he couldn't. In the room next to this there was a television. He had been shown it, and introduced to the men who were watching it. They had said, 'Hello,' without turning round, their attention being taken up by a children's programme about a magic Fruit Machine (it paid out in fruit). He had not slept on the train, and now he would not sleep here. He would have to remain standing, so that if they moved, he could move first, away from them in some direction.

And when he had to go to bed, then he must stay awake. He mustn't sleep, not in this place.

'Didn't catch your name, squire.' The voice came from behind him. Walter turned round slowly, ready to make a run for the door.

'Walter.' He had no idea which of the men had spoken.

'Friend of Gracie Fields, eh?' The speaker was a small man with a bald head, who smiled. His voice sounded almost chummy.

Walter had heard of Gracie Fields, who was a singer, but he had never met her, and certainly did not know her as a friend.

'What you doing there? Playing statues?' Walter shook his head. The bald man approached him. 'Well, speak as you find; that's what I say. Speak as you find. Don't condemn a man until you know him. Stands to reason, don't it? Got a job?'

'No.'

'Don't surprise me. Weak chest, like me?'

Walter neither shook his head nor nodded it, for his attention had become taken up by the fact that the other men had begun to move, and they were moving away from him, not towards, to go about their own business, and ignore him. Something he had said must have pleased them.

'Government! Couldn't run a raffle. Shoot 'em. Chronic waste of good money. Haven't got a fag, I suppose?'

'Don't smoke. Sorry.'

The bald man's expression changed to that of a small child being told that Christmas has just been indefinitely postponed. 'Yeah. Waste of breath. What's the point of talking without a smoke?' Aimlessly, the bald man wandered away, muttering curses on Walter's mother, the Roman Catholic Church and the discovery of tobacco.

The bald man's name was Leslie. He wore two cardigans under his jacket.

'My thirst is sore. My thirst is sore! Vinegar and gall is not a godly drink. Where is my cocoa, Sister dear?'

'You can wait.'

Mildred jumped to her feet, and danced around the room, waving

157

her arms. 'My God, my God, why has thou forsaken me?' Her energy amazed them. She seemed never to be still.

'Hanging here like a dried-out crow! Eloi, eloi, lama sabachthani!'

'For Christ's sake, shut the row!'

She moved from a Samurai posture to one resembling an arabesque, each with equal exuberance. Her long, wavy, pre-Raphaelite hair hung down over her sore and blistered face, one moment ecstatic, the next tragic.

'It's not that you – you, my own people – don't recognize me. I can live with that. It's just that nothing changes, sisters. Nothing. They're still locking up the prostitutes of Mayfair, and playing whist for money in Church Halls. Whist Drives shall themselves be driven from the temple. How many days to Lent?'

Rita's temper, having been strained beyond endurance, broke. She had recently acquired a mug of hot cocoa, but found a more immediate use for it than to drink it. 'Fucking shit! I came here for a bit of peace.' The mug bounced off Mildred's head without breaking, but the cocoa trickled down into her wavy hair and over her forehead, reminding those present of a crown of thorns.

Silence. Then:

'With whips they shall scourge me on this body bare. Then the crown and then the cross. I have felt the tearing of nails, and had my feet stamped on in Harrods.'

Two nuns were holding Rita, and trying to pull her away, as her fist hit the sides of Mildred's face, spreading the spilt cocoa. 'Shut her up. For Christ's sake, stop her blaspheming. I'm going mad here, and you lot are laughing.' Two of the women went to help the two nuns, one taking Rita's ankles and lifting her off her feet, so that the four of them could carry her from the room. Mildred held her bruised face to the light, shook her hair back to show the other women she was smiling, and continued reciting. 'I have been made naked for all lascivious eyes to wonder at my wounds. Put to the test. Put to the fire.'

This was the point at which June emptied the bucket of cold water she had brought from the kitchen over Mildred's head, leaving the red plastic bucket covering Mildred's face.

Mildred's voice could still be heard from inside the bucket. The women laughed, and began to applaud. When the applause reached Mildred's ears inside the bucket, she removed it with a flourish, bowed, wagged her finger at the audience, laughed, and said, 'Unwise females, do not laugh at the Mad Woman of Spitalfields.'

Christopher looked as if the stuffing had been knocked out of him. His expression was one of knowing submission. He leaned against the electric storage-heater, pressed the palms of his hands to the source of warmth, and surveyed the room and its occupants with large dark sunken eyes. Everything about him was either sunken or deflated, as if the padding around his small frame, which had once filled out his clothes, was now wasted away, leaving his shirt, jacket, trousers and skin to hang, wrinkled and heavy.

He was clean. His cleanness shone. It was immediately noticeable. Christopher intended his lack of dirt not only to act as an example to others, but also as a reward for those who had put their trust in him, it being the only reward he could offer. Sister Agatha had told Christopher that the state in which he kept himself was next to godliness (he knew it), Sister Mary that he was as clean as a new pin, while Sister Rachael, who was more given to wit, had claimed that he was as clean as an old nun.

Although that Saint Christopher after whom we may suppose him to have been named was the patron saint of travellers, Christopher Considine himself never ventured further than Quaker Street to the north, Tabernacle Street to the west, Whitechapel to the east, and Cannon Street to the south. Saint Mary Axe, Bishopsgate, Worship Street, Goodman Street, Hope Place and the outside of the Stock Exchange between Threadneedle and Throgmorton Streets, where he would stand for hours, watching the faces of the stockers, jobbers and mere passers-by who came and went, made up Christopher's small world.

On cold days, he would stand with others in a Betting Shop for the warmth. It seemed to be the policy of Messrs Ladbroke, Coral, William Hill and Mecca to overheat their establishments so as to attract the cold, lonely, unemployed and homeless, not many of whom could afford to bet.

'Do you take pills?'

Walter said he didn't, for he did not imagine that the man was referring to aspirin, nor did he understand why the man should be interested in his medical history.

'Better not to.' Christopher felt someone walk over his grave, and shivered, even though he was almost sitting on the storage heater. 'You're not yourself when you're taking pills. He lives on them.' Christopher nodded to a third man, who had now joined them.

'Not any longer.'

'But you take them.'

'I don't live on them. Not now. Not at the moment, anyway.'

'You used to.'

'Yes. In the past, I have.'

'Lived on them.'

'True. I don't deny it.'

The two men talked without ever looking at each other. Walter took no part in the exchange until the second man addressed him.

'He won't eat. Says he can't bear the smell of it. Childish, isn't it?'

This second man was called Chas. He always carried a copy of *The Guardian* under his arm; a letter written by Chas had once been published in its Educational Section. He had been a teacher, would be again he hoped. He wore a brown suit and a red tie, and walked with a permanent stoop, his head down, his eyes searching the floor. A nervous breakdown was responsible for his present situation, which was the want of a situation. That and the fact that, where once there had been a shortage of teachers, there was now a glut.

'A gluttony of teachers. You wouldn't care much for the smell of them either.' He smiled. He had spoken his thoughts. It was unwise to keep everything in his head. After all, they were only words. They weren't sticks, weren't stones, but words, each with its private referents which neither Christopher nor Walter would be able to understand.

Words, as Chas knew from his reading of *The Guardian*, could explain anything away. What they seemed to be unable to do was to put him on his feet again. 'When you're back on your feet' seemed to Chas a vastly overused phrase. The nuns, who were kindness itself, said it at least once a day. His Social Worker, a girl young enough to be his daughter, said it at every visit. His doctor had said it, and even his National Health psychiatrist had said it. His actual feet, those he stood and walked on, had no difficulty whatever in supporting him. It was the other end of his body which had let him down.

'My head.'

'Pardon.'

One of the symptoms of his breakdown had been an obsessive belief that he was walking on his head, or rather on his hands, head downwards. Therefore it seemed to him that ·'when you're back on your feet' was an excessively thoughtless phrase to use.

In any case, he was now well. Chas was well, as well as could be expected for anyone out of work and living in a hardboard cubicle, six feet by eight, which he earned by keeping his bed dry and pleasing the nuns. Well, he did not really live there; he slept there. His days were spent at the Job Centre, the Public Library, and occasionally he too might be found in a Betting Shop, since he had discovered one which contained tall black plastic stools, on which he could sit and study The Guardian's Crossword Puzzle, provided he made a reasonable pretence of reading the Sports Page.

With the aid of the National Health psychiatrist, he had discovered the source of his upside-down obsession, which had consequently weakened and so died. Chas was now being encouraged to 'tail off' the tranquillizers which had enabled him to control his fears of public places, of crowds, of alcohol, Vitamin B, coffee, tea, cereals, or anything which might be eaten, drunk or inhaled to stimulate the nervous system, and particularly the brain, any stimulant, in fact, which might stimulate Chas into seeing the world as upside-down and trying to correct this view of it by standing on his head in Tesco's.

A year and eight months ago, at the age of forty-six, childless, unmarried, and seemingly unloved, he had looked up from his desk at the rows of adolescent punks who sat before him, uttered the words, 'Orwell loved shit,' and promptly burst into tears.

And the spotty punks had laughed. They had assumed it was a joke, and that his expression, which had dissolved into pain and fear, would just as quickly return to humour and confidence. It had been ten minutes before a girl had run from the room to fetch the Physical Training Instructor, ten minutes of blubbering tears and racking sobs on one side of the classroom, laughter (both hysterical and forced), elbow-jabbing, gum-chewing, shouting (wordy and wordless), missiles being thrown, pocket billiards and the stroking of after-lunch erections on the other.

Now Chas waited to be put back on his feet, to be given a chance, to be tested again before the firing-line of uninterested faces and amid the cannonade of rude noises, to stand up with a straight back and only a blackboard behind him. And not to be down and out in the City of London.

At seven forty-five, Walter stood on the steps of the Women's Entrance, waiting for June. Since he had swiftly become used to her sleeping beside him, to holding her, to waking in the morning with her there, he had slept very little, and several times he had started awake, convinced that he was still in his old bed at the Hospital, and that the happenings of the past few days had been part of a prolonged dream.

He had sat up on the side of the bed, listening to the chorus of snores and the moans of someone two beds away, who was having a nightmare, and waited for the morning, when he would return to his piece of concrete path and the wall of the Mother and Baby Unit where June would be waiting. But the morning had brought a different room, full of men who could walk, and talk, and dress themselves, unhappy men who were part of the real world, and could not be written off as Jesus's Mistakes. These men showed every reluctance to have their breakfasts and leave, even though they were free to do so. But then, they had nowhere else to go, and June wasn't waiting for them.

Walter sat down on the steps, and watched four men set fire to a wooden crate, and stand around it, staring into the smoke and flames. He watched a small boy pick up discarded cabbages, crushing them together to pack as many as he could into a string bag. Rotten fruit and vegetables of all kinds, dead flowers, paper cups, cardboard, straw and bits of wood almost covered the streets and pavements. Three women, each with a pushchair and several bags, sorted through the rubbish, picking out the best of the food. They had made an early start.

It was Her Majesty's Jubilee Year. A group of pigeons tugged and pulled at half a tomato sandwich, until a gull chased them off, its wings held high and its beak wide in a threatening screech. Behind them, a fat black woman slowly removed the pips from half a water melon she had found in the gutter.

'Let's leave what's rotten.' June laughed, as she handed Walter a pear from the ground, and found another for herself. He could tell by her eyes that she had slept, and by the way she held his hand and swung his arm backwards and forwards between them. She was happy.

Walter was delighted that she had not wanted to stay any longer in Providence Row.

From Spitalfields they walked along Commercial Street and Great Eastern Street to Old Street, along City Road to the Angel at Islington, where two pubs advertised Topless Go-Go Dancers, then along Liverpool Road, where they passed a Pie and Mash Shop selling Jellied Eels. Holding hands and singing, 'There was a man went round the town,' they walked through Barnsbury, and stopped to look at the window of a shop in which concertinas were made, then on up the Caledonian Road to Pentonville Prison, outside which a man was drilling a hole in the road. June told Walter that this was in order to assist the prisoners to escape, and he believed her. From Pentonville Prison to Holloway Prison, via Hillmarton Road, then across to Dartmouth Park, Fortess Road, until, having walked almost six miles, they came at last to the address with which the young Samaritan, Simon, had provided June, the Squatters' Advisory Centre at Tufnell Park.

There was a notice in the window, 'The Council regret that owing to the interests of Big Business, they are unable to fulfil their obligations to the homeless this year.' June read it aloud to Walter slowly, partly in order to give her time to think again. The suitcase and carrier bags did not grow lighter, and she did not wish to have to walk back to the Samaritans, who had, in any case, advised her to try the Squatters as a last resort. Perhaps the Advis-

163

ing Squatters would at least allow her and Walter to sit down while they received advice.

The door opened, and a man in a faded denim suit, who wore a beard and rimless spectacles, stood in the doorway, looking like someone holy out of Dostoevsky, but better dressed and fed. 'Just in time,' he said. 'Would you like to come along? We're about to undertake an occupation.'

June said, 'Could we sit down for a bit first?'

'I hate to ask you this, but would you mind breaking in again? Bruce didn't quite get you that time. He's having trouble with the light in here.'

The senior members of the Squatters' Advisory Service stared at the Australian holding a microphone. It was not the light with which Bruce was having trouble, but the lack of it. It was, in fact, dark. They were standing in the cellar of a one-time Guest House, now derelict, situated at the corner of a run-down Square between Queensway and Notting Hill. There were ten trainee squatters present, if one included Walter and June. They had between them, for the purpose of affecting entry, three hammers, two screwdrivers, a crowbar, and a long-handled wooden mallet which might once have been used for croquet.

'If you could break in just as you did then, Brucie would know this time where to put his pup. That's what us film types call a small lamp. We only have one, and it's dead critical, the placing. I hate to ask.'

The Senior Squatters' Adviser leaned his elbow against the damp wall, closed his eyes to indicate the degree of frustration he felt, and said patiently, 'We are not breaking in. We are entering an abandoned and derelict property in order to occupy it. Everything we do is legal.' The Senior Squatters' Adviser had practised rational argument and debate since the very beginning of his life, when, appraising the two people leaning over his pram, he had formulated the first two questions which defined his social position, 'Mummy? ... Daddy?'

'Sure, sure. Right on, man.' The interviewer/director of the two-man Australian Television Film Company sensed that diplomacy was needed. They had promised the Squatters' Advisory Service a hundred pounds for information and two interviews, and to be allowed in on an actual occupation was an unexpected bonus, for which he hoped not to be charged, since the company was already running on the overdraft of his father, a pharmaceutical chemist in Canberra. 'Not break in. Right. Did I say "break in"? No, what I meant was, if we could just see the two of you again, forcing the window, climbing in, unscrewing the locks, and then see the rest of the crowd bursting in again past that corrugated barricade some capitalist pig of a landlord has put there, it'd be great for the film and Brucie would be happy. He really thinks we're on to a winner here, don't you, Bruce?'

Bruce nodded, and said, 'Great!' The two senior members, advisers both (though they did also squat, rather comfortably, near the Tottenham Court Road), considered the request, while the actual squatters under advice – Walter, June, two students of Art from St Martin's and one from the Slade, a young man from the L.S.E., a demolition worker, two unemployed secretaries and a messenger boy who had arrived that day from Plymouth – waited. If the decision should be to do it again, they would have to climb back outside, disperse in the square into little clumps of one or two, so as not to look like a mob, and wait for a handkerchief to be waved from an upstairs window by one of the advisers, as a signal that legal entry had been effected. Then they would make their way down the cellar steps, and squeeze past the corrugated iron barricade.

'It's dangerous to go out there again. Someone may have seen us come in, and phoned the police already. I wouldn't climb through a window twice in the space of five minutes; it's asking for trouble. I mean, you can't just say to the fuzz, "It's all right, officer. I'm being filmed for an Australian documentary about the homeless in London." '

Thus the Junior Adviser. He had made a point. Both unemployed secretaries giggled and the messenger boy from Plymouth nodded gravely. The Senior Adviser scratched his beard, and considered. The promised hundred pounds had not yet been handed over.

'Couldn't we just go from the people coming through that door, and then us boarding it up? That way, they wouldn't have to go out into the street again.'

'Brucie's heart wouldn't be in it. He's set his heart on getting you breaking in – effecting legal entry, I mean – through the window, and then dismantling the locks all in one shot. It's a point of professional pride with Bruce. I mean, you can see it'd be a great way to open the film. No sound. Get it? Just you two effecting legal entry, beautifully lit.'

'Great!' This was Bruce again. 'Great' and 'Jesus' were the only two words Bruce had been heard to use on British soil. Cruel friends ascribed this paucity of Bruce's vocabulary to his mother's having been frightened by an Elocution Teacher while on holiday in Earls Court. But Bruce found that these two words, with varied intonation, expressed all he ever wanted to communicate, while also excusing his inability to remember people's names and his reluctance ever to buy a round of drinks.

The Senior Adviser nodded his head. The ten trainee squatters prepared themselves to be immortalized again, while effecting legal entrance. Bruce led Walter from the line, placed him in the corridor, and proceeded to adjust the 'pup' so that it illuminated Walter's profile.

June stepped forward. 'May one inquire what that's for?'

'Bruce wants to feature the geezer in the flat cap.'

'Why?'

'No particular reason. The face is unusual.'

'Great!'

'He's not with you, is he?'

'You see that he is. We're all "with" each other, aren't we? I thought that was my point. Also, he happens to be my lover.'

Bruce said, 'Jesus!' and June stared at him. In order to mend matters a little, the interviewer/director said, 'That's what I like about English women. You're so cruel. I mean, saying a thing like that about a bloke who's missing half his marbles, that's really cruel. I love that.'

'Great!'

Walter screwed up his eyes tightly against the glare of the 'pup'. The interviewer/director said, 'He won't do that when we're rolling, will he?'

'I wouldn't be at all surprised.'

'Can he talk?'

166

'Considerably more than Bruce, it seems. However, he's not telepathic. If Bruce wants him to stand there like that when we make our entrance, he'd better say so.'

'Would you ask him to do that? Oh, and not to blink. It's the cap.'

'Great!'

'Not to blink?'

'The light won't look that strong on film. We're dealing with illusion here.'

'You surprise me.'

They did it all again, and Bruce seemed pleased. Walter stood on his mark, and looked around without blinking, just as June had told him. He enjoyed his starring role and the attention it brought him. June had told him that this was 'acting', and he remembered the Abbot and Costello films they had shown so many times in the Hospital, and the lady who had arrived once a month to ask the patients to help her save a baby from a tree by chopping down the tree with imaginary axes.

The ten trainee squatters rushed about the building, barricading windows and securing door. No landlord, far less a policeman, must be allowed to gain entry by means of some neglected orifice, for if a person representing the owner of a property were allowed in, then the legal entry became, in some way June did not understand, illegal, and the entrants might be as legally ejected. The squat must never be left 'open'. At least one squatter must always remain in residence to allow the others in on the pronouncement of a password. All communication with such unauthorized would-be entrants as the landlord, police or the local council must be shouted from an upstairs window, or from behind the security of a barricaded door.

Hammers were brandished, large nails and planks of wood. The trainee squatters felt like City children building a tree-house. Then came let-down.

On the first floor, they discovered an interior door secured with a Yale lock. The door also contained a letterbox. This suggested to the two Advisers that they might be looking at the door of a self-contained flat. A quick squinny through the letterbox confirmed that this was so. There were the remains of unmistakable breakfast on a table within. What had seemed to be a derelict building was, in fact, occupied, and the occupant might return at any moment, to discover entrants who had, by the mere discovery of dirty breakfast dishes, become illegal.

Could a different and unorganized group of squatters be operating in the same area, without the knowledge or approval of The Squatters' Advisory Service? The two Advisers held a meeting, moving from one room to another in an attempt to avoid Brucie's persistent camera, and arguing in whispers. The two students from the St Martin's School of Art removed one of the panes of frosted glass from the offending door, and let themselves in, discovering the door to be the entrance not to a flat, but a bed-sitting room, which had not just the air but the positive aroma of being under occupation, and by someone from the Orient.

While the two Art-students replaced the frosted glass and the wooden beading which had held it in place, and while the two Senior Advisers hid in a toilet from Brucie and his partner, Len, scratching their beards and wondering how the squat could be made secure as long as someone else was living in one room of this twenty-roomed house, a key was inserted from outside into the lock of one of the side doors. But though the key was correctly turned, the door would not open, there being a large chest-of-drawers and three trainee squatters pressing against it from the inside.

Several different keys were tried in puzzlement, before one of the trainees moved the chest-of-drawers in order to speak through the letterbox.

'This house is now an official squat.'

A round male Asian face was lowered to the level of the letter-box, and brown slightly bloodshot Asian eyes blinked back at the student of Art.

'What is this, please?'

'We're squatting.'

'What is squitters?'

'Squatters. We are. Understand?'

'No, because my key is out of order. Please open the door.'

'We've blocked it. If we let you come in, you have to accept that we're legally squatting? All right?'

'No. This is my house. We buy it to let out rooms. Many, many maisonettes. You are too early. They are not ready. Much has to be done.'

'You can say that again.'

'Please tell me what you are doing in my father's house.'

Others had joined the three. The messenger boy from Plymouth had been dispatched to fetch the two Senior Advisers from the toilet. June murmured. 'In my father's house there are many maisonettes,' and was ignored.

'This is not nice behaviour after a long day's work. I shall fetch the police to boot you out.' The Asian eyes were removed from the letterbox, and Asian footsteps could be heard retreating from the door, making for the rush-hour crowds and (it had to be assumed) the police of Queensway.

Under the superintendence of the Senior Advisers, they made an orderly evacuation of the squat, and waited on the pavement outside to explain to the police. The Senior Advisers waited, the students of Art and the unemployed secretaries waited, the young man from the L.S.E., the demolition worker, the messenger boy from Plymouth, Walter and June waited; Brucie and Len waited. No policemen appeared, nor did the Asian gentleman return.

After forty-five minutes' waiting, the group was smaller. Bruce and Len explained – which is to say that Len explained while Brucie interpolated either the word 'Great' or the word 'Jesus' in support – that since they had only been able to film half a squat, they should only pay half the money, and, the pubs being open, left with their equipment. No police arrived. After an hour and a quarter, only Walter and June, the student from L.S.E. and one of the Senior Advisers remained. June was turning over in her mind the prospect of approaching the Salvation Army.

'So that's it, then, is it?'

' 'Fraid so.'

'That's all the advice you have left, is it? Squatters' Advisory Service! Jesus' '' June was not above borrowing a word from Brucie when it suited her. She took Walter by the arm. 'Well, Walter, having spent all afternoon being unpaid film stars for these people, you and I are back on the streets again.'

'Me too.' The young man from L.S.E. added his grievance to June's. 'Not very good public relations.'

'Don't you have any friends you could stay with?' The Senior Adviser kicked the kerbstone with his left sandal, and wondered if this lot were about to commit the ultimate solecism of asking for money.

'Don't know anyone in London yet. One reason I wanted to squat.'

'The Y.M.C.A. – '

' – was full last night. Full by lunchtime.'

They waited, while the Senior Adviser tried to think of words with which he could take his leave of them. Why should he always be the one left holding the baby?

The young man from L.S.E. said, 'Isn't there any room at any of the existing squats?'

The Adviser shook his head, and June realized that at any moment he would simply apologize, and leave them standing there.

'What do you usually do when something like this happens?'

'It doesn't.' The Senior Adviser smiled, and shrugged his shoulders.

'You mean, up to now everything's gone smoothly?'

'Well, no, but if there's a hitch, people usually have somewhere else to fall back on.'

The young man from L.S.E. looked at June, then at Walter, and finally at the Adviser, and said, 'Well, we three haven't. Are you just going to piss off, and leave us stranded?'

The Adviser sighed, thought, removed his hands from his pockets, looked first up, then round about, but never straight at them.

'I'll make a phone call.'

'My name's Graham,' said the young man from L.S.E. to Walter and June, and they shook hands.

They were reminded yet again that this was an Emergency Squat, a place for temporary accommodation, for one or two nights at most, a doss, no more. 'It's not fit for a pig to live in really, but it's better than a draughty doorway.'

June's thoughts went to pigs in draughty doorways, and the

170

words, 'Evenin', all,' came involuntarily to her lips. No one else saw the joke.

Inside the house was the now familiar smell of damp rotting wood, flaking plaster and musty fabric. The Senior Adviser said, not for the first time, 'I don't think the floors upstairs are safe. I'd stay down here.' Seven stair-treads were missing, and the banister rail was broken. He pushed open the door of the ground-level front room. A pair of very old tennis shoes lay on their sides in the centre of what had once been oak-stained floorboards. June said, 'Looks as if the pig left in a hurry.'

Together, Walter, Graham and June surveyed the room which would be their home, at least for one night or two.

The Senior Adviser switched on the light, and they blinked. 'Good. That's still working.'

A jagged piece of broken mirror had been propped up on the mantelpiece. They were reflected in it, looking like three prospective purchasers and a hovering and over-anxious estate agent.

'The loo's under the stairs.'

'Won't the water have been turned off?' Graham's spectacles caught the reflection of the bare sixty-watt bulb hanging from a cord in the ceiling.

'It was, but we turned it back on again. The stopcock's in the back garden. Well . . . yard really.'

June pointed at the light-bulb, and asked, 'Who pays for that?' This question amused the Senior Adviser greatly. He tittered, and toyed with his frizzy beard.

'Some questions are best not asked. We just manage to keep in dispute with them, and refuse to pay. They've had so much bad publicity lately, with old-age pensioners freezing to death, that they're reluctant to cut anyone off. But it's one reason why nobody can stay here very long.'

Around the edge of the room were five stained single mattresses. Someone had started to paint the walls tangerine, but had stopped when either paint or enthusiasm had run out. A purple poster advertised a Squatters' Benefit Bop – 'Keen and the Mustard Gang. Live!'

In one corner of the room, resting on the floor, was the frame in which the strings of a baby-grand piano were set. No other part of the piano could be seen, and June assumed that it had been burned. On top of the piano was a very old Underwood typewriter, and by it a number of white cards on which cryptic messages had been printed, one of which read, 'Beware! Savage hamster at large. Please jam door shut. Ta.' June twanged on the strings of the baby-grand with her thumbnail, and attempted to depress the keys of the typewriter, but they were all stuck. Walter sat down on a pile of bricks which had once served as a coffee table, and inspected a pub ashtray.

'If the police come, simply tell them it's a civil matter between you and the landlords, and that the landlords will have to summon you to a civil court.' The Senior Adviser had decided that Graham looked the most responsible of the three.

'Do we know who the landlords are?'

'The local Council, but it's the same thing; you're given twenty-three days on average to get out. If they don't intend to start work on the place, they don't usually hurry you. By occupying, you're keeping the rats out.'

Walter dropped the ashtray, and it broke.

'Not to worry. Plenty more where that came from.'

June found a roll of dusty faded posters, on one of which were the words, 'Re-use Paper. Save trees.'

'According to the Electricity Board's charter of eighteen ninety-three or something, they're legally bound to supply every occupier where there's an outlet. So, when you do find somewhere more permanent, don't let them come on funny with you.'

Walter had collected every piece of the broken ashtray, and was holding them in both hands, wondering what he should do with them.

'More permanent?'

'A more permanent squat. You buy a rent book from Wool-worth's, and fill a bit of it in to prove you're bona fide occupants. Then you take it to the Gas and Electricity, and ask them to re-connect you.' June made a loud *twang!* on the strings of the baby-grand. 'You'll be liable for rates, of course; there's no way round that; but you tell them you didn't realize. Those of you who aren't students' – the Adviser was looking in June's direction but not at her – 'should be eligible for a bit more Social Security, as householders. Unless, of course, you're just slumming, and have an enormous private income.'

Graham's eyes were impassive. The pieces of broken ashtray were no longer reflected in his glasses, for Walter had placed them on what was left of the mantel. The Senior Adviser realized that someone with Graham's accent might indeed have a private income; clearly Walter and June did not. 'You're at L.S.E., then?' he said.

Graham nodded. 'And you?'

'Salford Polytechnic. Used to be. I wanted to do Social Work, you see.' If Graham did see, he didn't appear to be saying. 'The Sociology Department at Salford – it's pretty well known, you know. One of the best really.'

'Really?'

'In the north.'

'Yes.'

The Senior Adviser did not know why he had begun to feel in some way inferior to Graham. He was, after all, the *Senior* Adviser; it wasn't up to him to prove anything.

There was a period of silence, during which June held the nylon net window-curtains open slightly. They felt greasy, and were the colour of the slates on the roof opposite.

Graham said, 'Well, thank you, I think we can manage now.'

'I haven't shown you the kitchen.'

'We'll find it.'

The Senior Adviser found himself being shown to the door of a squat in which he had become a visitor. Graham said. 'Oh, by the way, where do *you* live?'

'Just off Tottenham Court Road. We have the whole block of flats.'

'Good address.'

'Yes. We've been there some time, of course.' Why did he keep saying 'of course'? 'Done quite a lot to it. Painting, carpentry – you know, improvements.' Why did he feel the need to impress a trainee squatter who, properly considered, was no more than a pain in the arse? It was Graham who should be ingratiating himself if he wanted to be helped to a better squat. The Senior Adviser reverted to generalities in an effort to remind himself of his own importance. 'London's full of empty houses and flats, if you know where to look. Disorganized Councils who've bought them and can't yet afford to pull them down and rebuild. Speculators waiting for the next property boom. It's also full of people with no place to live, of course.'

'Who owns the flats you're in?'

'Some fuddy-duddy trust handles them. They're part of the estate of some old woman, who can't afford to do anything to them, and isn't allowed to pull them down.'

'Perhaps she should sell.'

'Well, that's difficult, of course, when she's got squatters.'

'Of course.' Graham smiled. The Senior Adviser found himself saying, 'If anyone should move out, I'll certainly . . .'

'Let me know? I'd be very grateful. We must have a jar very soon. Goodbye.' Graham closed the door, and the Senior Adviser shuffled down the steps, feeling like a toad who had failed to turn into a prince.

In the kitchen, June was reading the graffiti on the walls. 'DON'T SEND ANY MORE TO SHERMAN STREET. THEY'VE HAD ENOUGH,' were the words she read.

7

My hobby's a secret, girl, but I'll give you a clue.

At Eltham Street, just as in the Hospital, Walter woke at six, or just after. It was a habit, a routine he had followed for almost twenty years. Now that June was beside him, and they were in their own place (for all that they shared it with Graham), he slept as well as he had used to do in the ward, but by six thirty he was out of bed. Since he no longer had Clifford to clean and dress, or any other patients to help and organize, there was plenty of time to be used or killed before June woke. He would never wake her, and would move around slowly and carefully, knowing that she was a light and poor sleeper. Also the privacy of the time he had while she did sleep was important to him. Privacy in a hospital hardly existed; finding it was like a privilege for good conduct. Before the hospital, his mother had allowed him privacy only when he was actually sitting on the W.C. and even then he was timed. Now he was his own man – his own man and June's man – and in the early mornings, no one watched him, or even stood outside the door of the toilet, listening.

His first action on waking was to smell the air, lifting his head, and breathing it in deeply. To have done that at the Hospital, in a ward full of incontinent persons, would have been thought strange behaviour even in someone labelled as mentally handi-capped, so that Walter had saved his deep breathing for those times when he was outside the grounds of the Hospital. The first time

175

he had been allowed to be part of a crocodile of Jesus's Mistakes, the line of men had passed a group of seven rhododendron bushes, and Walter had smelled the same smell he had smelled twenty years earlier, walking through a park in the rain, his father's arm around his shoulder.

Every morning now he remembered that first walk outside the Hospital, and the earlier one with his father, and every morning he looked up, just as he had done at seven years old, and the memory of his father's face, looking down at him, owning him, accepting the fact that Walter was his, belonging to him and part of himself, gave Walter a sensation too complicated for him to be able to describe. There was happiness in it, and security, the exchange of love, and belonging, and it filled him so full and bubbled up so zestfully inside him that he had to walk about the room, smiling and hugging himself and whispering under his breath, 'Thank you, Jesus.'

That was just one of the reasons Walter needed some moments of privacy. He knew that here, in the real world, such a demonstration of so much feeling would be considered strange. He himself thought it strange, but he knew that the comfort he found in these moments was something he was meant to have. Jesus meant him to have it. He had given it to Walter in exchange for Walter's parents, and even now that Walter had June, Jesus continued to give it in proof to Walter that his mother had been right, and that Jesus did love him. Therefore Walter could not be one of His Mistakes, since mistakes are forgotten and not cherished.

Another part of Walter's morning ritual was to check and count his clothes, making sure they were all there. This had been an essential part of his routine ever since he had first been allowed to wear and be responsible for his own clothes at the Hospital. There, if anything should be missing, it had been left to him to find and chastise the guilty party. After a while, nothing ever had gone missing.

Now, if he mislaid anything, it would prey on his mind for days, and he would refer to it over and over again, telling himself and June when he had last seen it, testing his memory for any sign of weakness by recalling what they had eaten that day, to whom they had spoken, and what they had both been wearing.

After counting his clothes, Walter would examine them for stains or tears, and scrutinize each button to make sure that none was loose. To lose a button would upset him greatly. How would one go about replacing it? Finding new buttons to replace old was a hit-or-miss operation, and in Walter's experience, mostly miss. Newly bought buttons might not match, and that would be as bad as wearing a garment which was one button short. Odd buttons looked wrong. They would attract attention. People in the real world did not wear mismatched buttons.

On the fourth day at Eltham Street, one of the buttons on his jacket broke. It just split into two pieces. Walter felt as if he had lost a close friend. He sighed and worried over it all day, sometimes just standing and staring at the two pieces of button in his hand. He asked June if she had ever endured such an experience, and could she possibly explain to him why this strong and healthy-looking button should suddenly split in two? Could it have something to do with the rain? Had the wet weakened it, did she think? He had worn the jacket over eighteen years, had lived with this button, touching it and its companions several times a day on those days on which he had worn the jacket. Yet none of the other buttons had split. Could he have been wearing a faulty button all that time without knowing it?

The cleaning of his boots every morning took between twenty and twenty-five minutes. Something else he had learned at the Hospital was that if he organized his time, he never needed to rush.

He became frustrated by the fact that in London it was possible to get dirty merely by walking about. June would watch him wriggling inside his clothes, as if the grime of London had coated his skin, and was sending him mad with irritation. Skin which had been kept scrupulously clean for almost twenty years in the Hospital now seemed to attract dirt as a fly-paper attracts flies. Almost every time they passed a Gents, Walter would excuse himself, and go inside to wash his hands and face.

'Do I look all right?' Walter would ask June this question several times a day. He was afraid that he would 'let her down', and also that people would be able to tell from his appearance that he had come from the Hospital.

For some time he was reluctant to approach any of the real people of the real world in which he and June now lived. He would sweat, clear his throat, and begin to shake, if June gave him money, and asked him to buy the bus-tickets. In shops, he would stand by the door, ready to open and close it for other customers while June waited to be served. Gradually she encouraged him to stand beside her at the counter, placing an arm around his waist in moral support, and holding tightly to his jacket to prevent him from shuffling away. The way in which shop assistants would glance at him dismissively and refer automatically to her, infuriated June. Every time this happened made it harder the next time to persuade him to do the talking.

'My husband has the money,' June would say defiantly, and she would attempt to outstare the assistant until notice was taken of Walter. Sometimes this provoked knowing smirks, nods, winks, even titters, and once a heartless guttural belly-laugh from a large West Indian bus-conductress.

'If he's your husband, honey, my name's Ian Smith.' Sycophantic commuters laughed their first laughs of the day. 'That's right, children. Start the day with a laugh, and get it over with.' June wanted to punch the shiny black face, expressing so much self-confidence, to break all the gleaming white teeth and hear them drop to the floor. 'This is not colour prejudice,' she would say. 'That I feel such rage at all towards someone of your colour is the very opposite. I am treating you as an equal, you bitch, and how do you like this bunch of fives?'

What she did say was, 'Does London Transport pay you to be insulting, or is that just your hobby?'

The black head was tossed back, and the whites of the eyes flashed. 'My hobby's a secret, girl, but I give you a clue. It begins with "s" and ends in nine months, less you careful.'

More commuters laughed, and June could see that Walter had become positively frightened. She would never again pretend that they were married.

And time passed. Her Majesty's Jubilee ended, and 1978 began.

PART FOUR

Walter Alone

I

Now just holding his hand is like taking an animal to the vet's to have it put down.

'How did you get here? Where have you come from? Hospital or prison? Where have you been before that? Where did you sleep last night? Have you any money? Any possessions? None at all? How have you been living? What was your last job? Can you read? Write? Spell your own name? How much money did you say you had? Do you expect me to believe you? Do you suffer from any of the following? Epilepsy? T.B? Migraine? Asthma? Bronchitis? Piles? Dizzy spells? Gonorrhoea? Athlete's Foot? Eczema? Verrucas? Boils? Tennis Elbow? Constipation? Acute or Chronic? Alcoholism? Colour Blindness? When did you last see a doctor? How old are you? What's the colour of your eyes? What religion? Why are you arguing? Are you now or were you at any time? Having a nervous breakdown? I was. Can you drive? Type? Subtract? Tie your shoelaces? Mend roads?'

'Will you? Take any job offered? Only one you have done before? Paint white lines? Be prepared to wear a clean tie? Underwear? Promise not to pick your nose or break wind in front of customers? Be civil? Look happy? Feel happy? Be happy? Never give in to a nervous disorder? I did. Over it now. Valium is my Saviour. Lo, though it lead me into the shadow of death, I shall not fear.'

Walter's unhappiness was total. A physical thing.

'You're watching me all the time.'

181

He had moved forward, slowly placing one foot in front of another, without aim or destination. He had come to this place, the Reception Centre.

'Simply because I sit this side of the desk, and you that, doesn't mean that there is a class, cultural, intellectual gap between us. We're all on your side, you know. A desk is not a symbol; it can be moved. But then where would we put our elbows? Your cap? My forms? Biros? Worry-beads? Your identity bumf, if you had any?'

'*I can't stand being watched. Things don't always last, Walter. Feelings change.*' And he had watched her, his head lowered, and his eyes fixed on hers. '*I never plan too far ahead.*' She had waited. '*It's just not wise. Not wise for me.*' Her eyes had flickered, and she had known that he had seen the suitcases.

'My point is a simple one, Walter. I'm you; you're me. So? I'm in work; you're out. Ergo, I have a mortgage, which you have not. I'd have been a gentleman of the road, Walter, but for faulty equipment. Flat feet. Bitter disappointment. Am I putting you at your ease? I do hope so. It's what I'm here for.'

'*If you'd been able to read, I'd have left you a note. That's what people usually do when they can't face a situation.*' Once, only once, he had asked her outright, very simply, as if asking what she had had for lunch, 'Why are you so nice to me, June?' and she had laughed, and hugged him, and told him that it was because she loved him. Now she had turned her head away.

'Don't ride, I suppose? Horses, I mean. No? Daughter got onto it. Can't get her off. Sex. All that rippling dog-meat under her crutch. Where were we?'

Walter moved his mouth, and the sound of a fart in a bath of soapy water came out. Among the bubbles could be heard the words, 'I need somewhere to sleep.' Now he had spoken.

The man took off his spectacles, and held them at a distance to study the lenses. It was all right; they were still there. He spoke gently. 'Of course you do; of course you do. I'm the Prevention of Abuses Officer. I have to find out your reasons for leading an un-settled life, why you have this wanderlust. Then I point you in the right direction.' He replaced the spectacles on his nose, and picked up another sheet of paper. 'Now we come to the Warning List.

182

Haven't given me a false name, have you?' Walter shook his head. 'Not wanted by the C.I.D., are you, for any little peccadillo? Murder? Rape?' Walter said that he was not wanted by the C.I.D. 'How about constantly deserting your family? Refusing to keep them?' Walter said he had no family, and, without thinking before he spoke, the man said, 'Good.'

He had no family. He was not wanted by anyone.

'If you agree to be helped, you could become a resident. A Gate Man. For just fourteen pounds thirty-five from your Social Security, we'll arrange real security. Some of our residents have been here thirteen years. Some of them were born into institutions. It's all they know, and who's to say they're wrong? They come up to me, and say it to my face, "I wouldn't last five minutes on the outside, Mr Saunders. I'm all right for another month, aren't I?" They know where they are here. There's a TV Room, and a film show once a week. The psychiatrist visits us twice a week, and the doctor once a day. All reasonable care. Their only duty is to look after the Casuals' clothing, whereas the Casuals have to clean out the Centre before they leave. Everything has its price, Walter, even freedom. If you have a drink problem, spit it out.'

I know how you're looking at me. Your eyes watch me. It's as if you're standing on one leg hunched up, with your feathers all ruffled like one of your bloody pigeons, waiting for its neck to be wrung. My nearness is all you have to live for. The responsibility's too much for me.'

'Drink problem.'

Walter attempted to summon up what would pass for attention.

'Don't hug it to yourself. Sobriety is your best friend, more precious than rubies. Unless you can believe that, you'll never give up alcohol. We have a hundred and twenty men here at the moment with the very same problem. We have A.A. Meetings, a Sick Bay; we try to feed them up, and stop what we call "Stink Thinking".' The man became suddenly fierce. 'Why are you looking at me like that? I'll batter your head in.' Walter jumped as the man seemed to lurch across the desk towards him. 'Things like that. Remarks of such a nature.' The man relaxed, having given his performance. 'All that aggression, we have to get rid of it. I mean, take you. You're all screwed up inside, aren't you? I can tell. You need to talk to someone.' Walter nodded. 'The Catholic faith asks too much of me, Walter. My wife's a slut and my children are bastards, and I wouldn't say that to just anyone. I've been to Hell and back. I know. I've seen men with maggots in their boots.' He was wiping the sweat from his forehead with the palm of his right hand. 'It's cold and lonely out there, isn't it? Did you know that one of our Casuals was found battered to death in a derelict house near here? And there was another man, a householder, strangled in the park.'

'You make me feel bad, Walter. If I stayed with you because of that, it wouldn't be any good, would it?'

'Carry a heavy torch with me when I go out. It's the only way.'

Behind the man's head, there was a Notice Board. 'BOXING CAN CAUSE BRAIN CANCER. FILM SHOW WED 6.00. MEET-ING FOR MENTALLY HANDICAPPED CHRISTIAN FORUM NEAT APPEARANCE REQUESTED.' Below the Notice Board was a glass cabinet, in which were cups and shields awarded for success in various sports.

'If you'd left it any longer, you might not have found us here. We're supposed to be phased out by 1980. Smaller settlement units; can't see it myself. Where would they put them? Who'd want fifty or sixty assorted Jocks and Micks, pissing up against their garden wall, while they waited to be admitted to the house next door?'

'You can cope now.' He had watched her, twisting the string handles of the carrier bag between his fingers. 'Shop and cook. You're a good cook. You'll be all right, won't y_u?' Her mouth had trembled, and she had screwed her eyes up tightly. 'Hard bitches like me don't always have a soft spot. You shouldn't – Oh, Jesus fucking Christ!' She had moved to him quickly, hugging, kissing and stroking his face, her lips moving over his ears, his nose, his eyelids and eyebrows, and he had seen that her own eyes were closed, and felt the dampness of her tears, tears she had left to dry on his face.

Then she was gone, with the door left open and the room com-pletely still and strange to him. And he had stood, twisting the handles of the carrier bag, not knowing if he would ever be able to let go of those two pieces of grey string, not knowing if he would ever move.

The furniture and all the objects of the room had seemed all at once to rush into his head, fighting each other for a good place there, shouting, every object and particle of an object shouting in the spaces of his head, 'Don't go!' as he should have shouted.

But Walter had only whispered it. 'Don't go.'

'Shout! Scream! Weep!' cried the objects in his head.

He had moved quickly to the door, had been able to do so much. 'June!' One word. Too late. It had echoed round the room, and then there had been silence.

Almost silence. He had sat still, holding the carrier bag, and listened to the quiet noises the room made. At first there had only been the noises of complaint from floor and furniture, then, after much longer, he had become aware of noises from outside in the street, and he had thought of the people outside. They outside, he alone in the room, sitting there, frightened and angry that he had not touched her, hadn't reached out when he could have done, hadn't held her when she rushed to him. Then had come the realization that he had no idea where she was, and might never know, and that at some point he would have to stand up, move, walk about this room. Then he had lifted the back of his right hand to his mouth, and had wept.

He had wept.

He had walked.

He had walked as if his mother were trying to teach him to walk again, unaided, to walk as a good boy walked, not held, but with difficulty. When he had not been a good boy, his mother had said, 'You break my heart, Walter,' and he had known that a broken heart must be a painful thing. Now as Walter had walked (unaided – oh, without aid of any kind), pain had been everywhere except where he knew his heart to be.

He had walked out of the room and into the street, and pain had rung like a single church bell inside the joints of his limbs as he had moved. It had pushed at his forehead from inside, and had churned around in the base of his stomach, as though someone had been scraping the insides of his belly with a large soup-ladle.

He had moved. Unaided. Walking for the sake of it, not daring to stop. Walking would make the time pass. 'Time waits for no

G

man, Walter, and certainly not you,' his mother had said. Not for Witless Walter, dribbling and giggling Walter, Parrot-Face Williams, who had tried to pretend to be part of the real world, to feel and give love, cook, and buy goods from shop assistants. Real people, had he continued to walk in front of them, would have noticed, crowded about him, stopped the traffic, written to the newspapers.

So, although he had not been able to stop either walking or weeping, Witless Walter had, after some while, found an alley, destitute of real people, containing only dustbins, and there he had leaned his forehead against the bricks of the wall, and had continued to weep.

He had remained in the alley seventeen days. For seventeen days, he had not spoken to anyone, and came to believe that he had forgotten how.

He had told the difference between day and night by the changes in the light and in the temperature. The nights were colder. Even so, he preferred the nights, preferred darkness, as long as there had been no voices, no sounds of people talking, laughing, singing. Walter and June had sung, had held hands, and sung about the little man who had walked round the town, and got no bread with one fish-ball.

In the darkness, without human sounds, he was just like everyone else. Even the voices inside his head seemed to rest at night, as if they too were tired, and had run out of questions about June, about Walter and June, about why June had gone and where. Since his mind must know that he could not answer these questions, Walter wondered why it should ask them. His mother had told him that there was always a right answer, hidden behind all the wrong ones; he had only to reject all the wrong answers, and the right would be left. That would please her. He would get a tick and not a cross.

June had never marked or corrected his answers to questions. She had encouraged him to talk and to communicate his thoughts. As his confidence had grown, and he had discovered that he enjoyed talking, enjoyed the experience of people listening to him, giving him their full attention, he had stored up thoughts to tell June

186

when the right moment came. Working out what words he would use to express these thoughts had given him pleasure. He would wait until he saw the expression in June's eyes which meant that she was thinking unhappy thoughts about Baby John, or enduring frightening ones, and then he would start, sometimes taking her by the hand, and making her sit by him. There had been no waiting to be asked questions, no being pressed to speak, no shyness or stumbling or tripping over parts of words or forming sounds that seemed to come out wrongly. He had talked, and she had listened, often laughed, or smiled, and squeezed his hand. Walter had made words he had never used before, words he had heard and stored away in his mind. There had been no darting flickering goldfish in his head; his thoughts had been clear.

In the alley, his thoughts were not clear. He drank from an overflow pipe, and ate from dustbins, and once a dog had pissed on his broken shoe. In the alley, Walter wept and thought persistently of June.

Once she had said, 'Come here,' and he had gone to her, thinking that she was frightened and wanted him to hold her, but instead she had pointed to their two reflections in the mirror, and had said, 'Every morning we must stand here, and look at ourselves for a moment, to remind ourselves who we are. It's all there in our faces; every second we've lived so far is marked there, all those years remembered in one single expression. It's a miracle that we're both here now.'

And he had looked at her, and seen how beautiful she was. If what she said was so, the years had made her beautiful.

There passed at the end of the alley a very small boy, walking behind his father, and holding onto the hem of his father's coat, while the father carried shopping. Walter and his father. And the smell of rhododendrons strong, all about the alley.

There passed four drunken men, swaying and gliding. The shop at the end of the alley was still lighted, and sold food, and one of the men unzipped and passed water against the shop window which contained pork pies, while his companions laughed and applauded, and Walter had, for one moment, a very clear vision of the pies sitting there behind the glass, and the man's steaming water splashing on the glass which protected them.

187

He knew there were pies. He had been four times to the end of the alley, and seen them.

People passed the end of the alley, and some even walked down it. One such was the woman whose dog soiled Walter's shoe. Lovers passed, some walking hand in hand, as he and June had walked. Time passed. Walter lay on his side in a foetal position, so that the whole of him was tucked inside a small doorway. He closed his eyes, and tried to rub the world out of his mind. When he woke, he would draw it again. On a large blackboard with white chalk, he would recreate the world in sharp white lines which everyone could understand. Then he would be able to see it clearly, and fit himself into it.

Walter set himself to imagine the drawing he would make of himself, fitting into the blackboard world, but the self he saw was empty, an outline drawing of a man with a hat on.

Seventeen days of alternating light and darkness, comparative warmth and hard cold, weeping and thinking, people passing, of June, and Walter and June, and perpetual hammering questions asked by a mind which knew it could not supply the answers. *I must have food, or I die.* He had uncurled, and set himself again in movement, and walked out of the alley, and come to the Reception Centre, the Spike, and must now endure the forms and invariable procedures of the Spike, and the people of the Spike, who were so clearly of the real world.

2

We smell the same now, so don't go getting confused. June's the one over there.

Walter was told by a man in a beige overall to take off all his clothes, and did so slowly. He was to undergo the process known as 'Being Put Through'. All clients of the Spike, the lost, the lonely, the homeless, drunk or sober, clean or dirty, must be 'Put Through' on their arrival, and if, for any reason, even to buy a packet of cigarettes, they were to leave the building, on their return they would be 'Put Through' again, to strip, and shower, and stand about naked, waiting for their clothes to be fumigated. Only the Gate Men, the semi-permanent residents, were not obliged to endure this nightly ritual.

Naked, elderly and not-so-elderly men stood around Walter, hugging their sallow and sagging dugs. All were shivering. Their testicles looked ridiculous, hanging low in long-forgotten and deflated pouches like old abandoned pieces of luggage, and putting Walter in mind of untreated tripe, yellow before being bleached.

'Come on!' The man in beige had his arm out, waiting for Walter's clothes. Walter removed the last piece of his clothing, his stained underpants, and, avoiding the eyes of the shivering men, screwed them up quickly, and stuffed them into the pocket of his jacket, while the man in beige sighed a heavy sigh.

Every article of Walter's clothing, including his boots, was held up to a powerful electric light and closely examined, before being placed in a machine which looked like an oven. Once the Spike

189

had used steam, which had shrunk the clothes of its clients, who would leave in the morning with wrists and ankles protruding from shortened sleeves and trouser-legs. Time passes. Everything gets better. By the time of Her Majesty's Jubilee Year, so recently over, ten c.c.s of Ethyl Tomile had replaced the steam.

Naked, Walter discovered that his arms had grown and huge hands no longer belonged to him. If his skin had had pockets, he would have hidden them there. As matters were, they swung at his sides, as he rocked backwards and forwards, and studied the water under the duckboards beneath his feet, enduring the stares of the elderly and some not-so-elderly irregulars.

A large bar of strong-smelling soap was placed into his right hand, and he was led to one of the showers. The irregulars stood aside to let him pass. They had seen it all before, had sworn never to come here again, and here again they were.

He felt the warm water hitting the top of his head, and trickling down his body. He was forty-eight, being given a bath, as back in the Hospital, Jesus's Mistakes were given baths. Walter was not one of Jesus's Mistakes, but a person of the real world, who had loved and been loved. Yet he did not protest, for he knew that, in places such as this, it is always the sanest who seem most mad.

'Why are you so nice to me, June?' She had laughed, and hugged him. 'Because I love you.' And she had been looking at him. 'Because I love you.' She had looked at him, been able to see him clearly, what he was, and she had said, 'Because I love you,' had said it to him, Witless Walter, of whom his own mother (now with Jesus) had once said, 'You must be the ugliest person in this town, Walter, and you spent nine months inside me.'

Water. Warm water on a naked body, watched by other naked bodies, as he had watched, seen them, both of them together on a stained mattress, and the bath in the middle of the room still full of water, watched through a crack in the door, had watched Graham and June making love.

Memories. Nothing made sense.

'Sense is different things to different people, Walter. Don't let them force their sense on you. If you think something makes sense, that's all that matters.' June had told him that, but then later, 'If you'd been able to read, I'd have left you a note. Feelings change. Things don't always last.'

And she had turned her head away. 'You'll be all right, won't you? You can cope now.' What should he have answered? What was the right answer?

Once the right answer would have been to put his arms around her, and she would have hugged him to her. 'Hold onto me. It's a bad day.' But on that afternoon, as he had watched through the door, it was Graham who had held onto her in a different way from Walter, and she had laughed in a way Walter had never made her laugh, and Graham had done things to and with her which Walter would never have dreamed of doing. It had been almost as if it were not his June he was watching, not his June but a larger, stronger June, who laughed differently, moved differently, did things with Graham she had never done with him, was not the same June as she who slept with Walter, and loved him, and was good to him.

'You're very good with him.'

'Good? Goodness doesn't come into it. I took him on when I needed someone, and he was the only one there. Now he's the only person in the world who can make me feel guilty.' And Walter, looking through the crack in the door, had seen the marks and bruises around her nipples. Later, when he touched her, his June had flinched, and said, 'I'm sore, Walter.'

'Every time he uses my name, I get that heavy feeling of responsibility. Constant sidelong glances for approval! I know he's wondering why I stay with him. He still half expects to wake up, and find I've gone.' The noises she made were noises of both pain and pleasure, and the boy was biting the bruises he had already caused.

'Help Graham to empty the bath, love.'

Walter had looked down at the soapy bath-water, and then at Graham, who was tucking his shirt into the top of his trousers.

'I had a bath, and then Graham used my water.'

'Saves on the electric.' The newly dressed Graham grinned, unaware that Walter knew that they didn't pay for electricity.

'We smell the same now, so don't go getting confused. June's the

191

one over there.' It had not made sense, but June and Graham had laughed all the same.

Graham and Walter had emptied the water from the zinc bath into the back yard, and hung the bath on a nail. Then Graham had gone back to his books, and Walter had sat watching June.

'All right, love?' To his surprise, Walter had discovered that he could nod his head in the same way as he always nodded his head. What thereafter had surprised him even more was that June should have kissed him on the forehead, and ruffled his hair in the way she had always done, and that he had actually been relieved that she had done so. She was very good with him.

Walter slid the strong-smelling soap over his body as carefully as he had soaped Clifford's body every day for nineteen years. His love for June would remain a secret; in a place like this, it would help to have secrets. He would not allow himself to be sad. *'I once told him I loved him. It spoilt everything. Now, just holding his hand is like carrying an animal to the vet to be put down.'*

'That's enough.' The man in beige was shouting at Walter above the noise of the showers.

If he had banged the door or coughed, as he should have done, they would have had to stop. If he had gone into the room, they would have sat up and covered themselves. But he would not have known what to say, how to act. Instead, he had stood as still as he could, and watched.

Now, as he remembered (and had remembered so often), he saw only parts of what he must have seen then, only sections of the two bodies, which bit, licked, stroked, rubbed, twined and intertwined. Hands – Graham's, then June's – how greedy and grasping they looked. Her face, and the pleasure on it. The bruises on her breasts. Her legs, wrapped round the boy, and her blue-white ankles crossed over each other at the base of the boy's back – ankles Walter had once thought so small and fragile. The boy's bottom, pumping in and out, in and out, and June's eyes, sometimes closed, sometimes wide open as she had made a sound that had seemed almost as if she were cold, had been shuddering from the cold, yet she was not cold, but beaded with sweat all over. And lastly, as the boy withdrew himself, and lay on his back beside her, the part of him which had been inside her, resting against his left thigh, and glistening with body-fluid.

'That's *enough!*' Walter was given a towel to wrap round his waist. 'You're the first I've seen enjoy it.' He was instructed to sit on a wooden bench, and wait his turn to be examined by the doctor.

Though the doctor's manner was of total disinterest, his inspection was not perfunctory. Heart, chest and stomach were listened to, the penis squeezed, the anus stretched and peered into by the light of a small torch, and the same torch illuminated the inside of Walter's mouth and ears.

'Piles and halitosis.' A note made. 'When did you last have a bowel movement?'

Walter looked at him, and the doctor sighed. 'Shit! When did you last move your shit?'

Walter could not remember. It had not been uppermost in his mind.

'Can't remember.' A further note. Then the doctor removed from their cellophane wrapper a pair of sterile gloves made from the finest rubber, and, with the help of a lubricant, placed something up Walter's back passage. 'Now don't go to sleep until you've had a really good shit. Understand?'

Walter nodded. He did not understand why the doctor thought it necessary to speak in such a loud and distinct voice. Surely all the towel-wrapped men on the wooden bench outside the door would have heard.

'Through there! Next!'

As Walter moved past the lines of seated men, some of them looked up, but to his surprise, none of them laughed at him, or even smiled. Every one of the irregulars looked as apprehensive as Walter himself, and was so, for, apart from their extreme modesty (many clients of the Spike have run out of the building on being told that they would be required to undress) and dislike of being touched, anything the doctor might have to tell them would certainly not be good news.

The doctor made out a card for the Index, on WILLIAMS, Walter', and under the heading 'General Impression' where usually

G*

he might have written 'Poor', or 'Very Poor', or 'Critical', he printed the words, 'Not to be Bred From'.

The irregulars sat wrapped in the blankets with which they had been issued, drinking their soup and eyeing each other over the rims of their mugs.

The Officer in the white coat, whose job it was to ration out the soup, had seen it all before. He was an old man. Nothing was new to him. Bad breath, stale wind, the noisy supping of soup, eyes watching other eyes in uneasy silence, they all made up an evening which was just one among many. He had disliked most of the evenings which were past, and had no doubt that he would continue in the same frame of mind.

'Do you have a smoke on you, John?' A middle-aged Glaswegian with long hair and sideburns of the most busy and extravagant kind had posed the question. 'Come on, boy. Don't be keeping them for yourself.'

The elderly Officer's eyes were bright with anger, piss-holes in the snow of his aged skin, but he did not reply.

'Jesus!' The Glaswegian looked about him at the other irregulars, and began to sing:

'Roll out those lazy, hazy, crazy days of summer.
Roll out the soda, and pretzels, and beer.
Roll out those lazy, hazy, crazy days of summer.
I wish to fucking hell I wasn't here.'

He moved his head from side to side. 'Bloody unsociable country, this. The only person I've spoken to for over a week, and you haven't a tab for me to smoke.'

This provoked the old man into speech. 'I'd be ashamed to be in this place if I were the age of some of you. Taking charity! I was born in one war, and fought in the other.' He became lost in his own memories. His life spent in servitude was to be repaid by an old age served in solitude. He spoke to few, and was seldom spoken to. He shopped for himself, and cooked for no one else. When he listened, it was to the B.B.C. His radio licence was a prescription against insanity. 'It's all too easy. Doesn't pay to work these days.'

The Glaswegian was on his feet, and holding the old man by his white coat. 'Listen, you bugger. I used to work a fifty-two-hour shift before I started to take a dram. I had a family and five wee ones. I used to pay more income tax to your stupid government than any of this lot put together. So just you be careful when you talk to me about taking charity. I've paid for these mangey blankets and this piss you call soup.'

He dropped the old man, having shaken him so fiercely that the old man's upper plate fell from his mouth, and landed on the floor close to Walter. As the Glaswegian left the room, banging the door as he went, Walter picked up the false teeth, and handed them back to their owner, relieved to notice that they were made of a kind of plastic, and had not broken.

The old Officer took the teeth from Walter's hand, wiped them on his spotlessly clean handkerchief, placed them where they belonged, and continued to talk, as if making up for all the years he had been unable to answer the B.B.C. back. He spoke of his life between two wars, and his service in the second, and of a man named Percy, who broke wind constantly because of his nerves, and had hanged himself in a disused barn and been nibbled by rats. But the irregulars were no longer listening.

They had all been given bed tickets by the Bed Officer. These had then been exchanged for three blankets each. Some of the irregulars had asked for more blankets, and been refused, even though, of the nine hundred beds in the four blocks of the Centre, only six hundred were ever used.

In Walter's dormitory, there were forty bunks in two layers. Each was numbered, made of iron with steel springs. A rubber mattress, two inches thick, and a striped pillow, grey and greasy with dirt, covered each of the numbered bunks. The allocation of beds by numbers was important. If the police were to call during the night, to collect an irregular whose conduct had been more than usually irregular, the Duty Officer would know exactly where to find him.

Someone had removed Walter's pillow, in order to have two.

'Did you hear about the Irish G.C.E?' The relief of having got through so much in order to get here – filling in Form 3C with the Interviewing Officer, the undressing, delousing of clothing, compulsory bathing – seemed to have made one of the not-so-elderly irregulars light-headed. 'Question. England won the Second World War. Who were the runners-up?' The older tireder irregulars kept themselves apart, mumbling to themselves or to some imaginary companion.

'Question. Who's buried in Grant's Tomb?'

Walter lay on his numbered top bunk, using his hands as a pillow, and staring at a ceiling which had once been painted cream. He would not remove a pillow from another bed. He was not a Mistake, but someone in the real world, a free man in a Reception Centre into which he had freely walked in search of food, warmth and rest, which were his due.

He had never been alone before, except for that time he had spent in his mother's bedroom with the pigeons, and she lay there, unmoving and looking increasingly strange, while he waited for Jesus to make up His mind whether Walter's mother was to stay with Him or come back to Walter. He had often felt alone, but except for that once and now, had never been it. He remembered Clifford. Clifford was not like any person whom Walter had met in the real world, but he was a person, a human being, and Walter had looked after him. Was Clifford still a person, or had he been buried in the cemetery near the Hospital? Perhaps he had expected Walter to return, and had not allowed anyone else to look after him.

Here, now, Walter was looking after nobody, and nobody was looking after him. He had nobody to please except himself, and nobody had to please him. There was no need here to worry at the sound his voice made, no need to make sense, to practise sentences inside his head, to have thoughts and to express them.

He could have talked well now, if there were someone to listen, or listened well were there anyone to talk to him. June had taught him how to listen and how to talk, but since she had left him, both talking and listening were useless.

An idea came into Walter's mind, and it seemed to have sense in it, for it would explain why so many of the people he had met talked to themselves. The only reason Walter now had for talking would be to keep in practice, and not forget how, so that when he met June again, he could speak to her, ask her questions, tell her what had happened, explain. He must talk. Practice makes perfect. He must practise on the only person constantly available to him. Himself.

'*You can cope now. You'll be all right, won't you?*' That's what he would do now. He would be all right. He would cope.

He had watched her. She had said she couldn't stand it, and she had gone away. He would find her, and promise not to watch her. Ever.

'I warned her. It was him or me. I told her to choose.' The man in the bunk below was thinking aloud. He jerked himself over from his left side to his right, letting out a mirthless laugh as both the steel springs and the iron frame of the bed rattled. 'She laughed, didn't she? Thought I wouldn't go through with it, didn't she?'

Walter knew better than to proffer answers. This man also was practising talking to someone.

'Couldn't stay with the two of them there. Creep!' A moment's pause. 'Smarmy bugger too.' The man rolled over again, and Walter held tight to the sides of the bunk.

' "You'll never go. Like your comfort, don't you? You like the little comforts I give you." Comfort! Once a bloody fortnight, with the dog watching! Creep! She'll not be smiling now. He'll have left her, shouldn't wonder. One whiff of that cheesy smell behind her ears, and he'll be off. Sebaceous cysts, my toe-rag! Shouldn't wonder! Musk under her armpits and African Violets between her legs.'

Walter closed his eyes to try to block out pictures which were beginning to form, but soon the man began to practise talking again, this time in a petulant whimper. 'He'll have had her by now. Got it all the way up. Had her on the rug where we . . . had her with the dog watching.' The man was moaning and grunting quietly into his pillow, and Walter's bunk, as well as his own, was rocking backwards and forwards gently. The man was masturbating, using his free arm to rock the bunks. Walter waited for the climax. Afterwards, the man would probably sleep.

'FILTHY COW!'

'Shut your bloody noise.' Shouts from the nearby bunks, as the man below Walter gasped. 'Bet she opened like a cesspool to him.

197

Bet he never even touched the sides. Made the dog sick, shouldn't wonder.'

An angry irregular from the next bunk jumped out, slid barefoot across the adjoining tiles, and shook the man below Walter by the scruff of the hair. 'You get on with your fucking wanking, will you, and shut your filthy mouth.'

As the angry irregular returned, grumbling, to his bunk, a very old irregular in one of the bunks nearest the door began to cough, and having begun, could not stop. He climbed painfully out of his bunk, and opened a window to stand by it, gasping into the cold night air like a wizened goldfish, and clinging to the iron window to hold himself upright.

No one moved to help him. The old irregular was dying; Walter was sure of it. The other irregulars waited, not for him to close the window and return to bed, but for someone else to make a decision. Each of them knew *he* would not. The old irregular was not part of them, nor they of him. If his heart stopped, it would not spoil their sleep.

At last the coughing stopped. The old irregular's hold on the window loosened, and he fell to the floor. No one moved. Then Walter lowered his feet to the floor, and went to find someone on duty.

Two men in beige took the old irregular's body away. They would take it to the Sick Bay; he might not be dead. But Walter had no doubt that the old irregular was gone, and where. What puzzled him was why Jesus made it so painful to get there.

Five minutes later, the irregular in the bunk below had started to whimper again. 'All right in here. This is the last place she'd come looking.' Walter ignored him. He had come to a decision. He had been at fault, first hiding his tears in the alley, then coming to this place. His place was with June. He would go back to the squat, and find her.

3

Where are you pigeon ?

'Can you tell me where I am, please?'
'Coldharbour Lane.'
'I want to go to . . .' Walter searched his memory. 'Eltham Street.'
'Where's that?'
He knew he could do it. He could call up the words, and form
them. June had made him memorize the complete address during
their first days at the squat. 'W Four.'
'You'd be best on the Tube. Get the Victoria Line from Brixton,
down there. Tell them the address you want before you buy a
ticket. They'll look up what station you should get off at.'
Walter thanked the woman, and walked in the direction she had
indicated, since it would be rude to go in any other. But he could
not take a Tube, because he could not pay for a ticket. He knew
the name of the Tube Station nearest the house. It was called
Turnham Green, and was on the District Line.
He must get there before dark. At the Tube Station he would
find someone else to ask, someone who would know how to get to
Turnham Green Station. They would be more likely to know where
that was than where his road was.
But when he spoke to the man who was issuing tickets at Brixton
Station, Walter was told that he was miles out of his way. Even if
the man had known which way to point, which he hadn't, it was

too great a distance to walk, but Walter could buy a ticket which would take him there for sixty pence.

Walter thanked the man, and left his company. Studying the map outside the station, he conceived an idea. He traced the route with his finger. Not counting the one at the beginning and the one at the end, there were thirteen stations between himself and Turnham Green. If he made a list of them in order, he could walk from one to the next, and thus find his way home. Ever since he had written words on the wall of the Mother and Baby Unit for June to read, he had always carried at least one pencil in his pocket. He found an empty cigarette packet in a litter bin, turned it inside out, and wrote his list, beginning with Stockwell, Vauxhall and Pimlico, and ending with Ravenscourt Park, Stamford Brook and Turnham Green.

June would be waiting. She would be waiting for him now, pacing the floor and looking through the window. She would rush to the door, and put her arms round him. She would kiss him, covering his face with kisses. He would laugh, and she would cry, hug him and cry. *'Please put your arms round me. We're both cold.'* She had said that to him in the church, wiped his face dry, and they had made love on the stone floor. *'Look at me, Walter. Don't pretend it's not happening.'* It had happened. She had shown him how. He had seen his own reflection in each of the dark shiny brown conkers, which were her eyes. He had seen Walter. It had happened.

Walter leaned over the side of Vauxhall Bridge. He felt giddy and faint. The food he had received at the Spike had been insufficient to nourish him for such a journey, for there had been days of hunger to make up for. The muscles of his legs seemed to be pulling him down into the pavement. His knees shook. He held tight onto the parapet, knowing that if once he fell, he might not have the strength to get up again.

Then he had crossed the bridge, holding onto the wall and walking sideways, and was sitting on a bench, looking at the Thames which moved like oil, although it was not yet night. He had heard Big Ben strike noon. The sight of the moving water and his own weariness combined to drag him towards sleep. Sleep was what he did best (his mother had told him so bitterly), and his next best was laughter, when he had learned as a child so long ago to laugh first before other people laughed at him, so that they could all be laughing together.

Walter was out of practice at laughing, but to sleep now would be very easy, to lie on the bench, to float, cool oil lapping at his ears, making the sound he had once heard in a sea-shell. To lie in it, be covered by it, his eyes closed, the oil-like water carrying his weight, to drift past bright green sea-weed, where goldfish played hide and seek ! But June would not be there.

He was walking again. His legs ached, his knees wobbled, and his left foot was bleeding. He could feel the warm blood sticking to what was left of his sock. The nail in his left boot was digging deeper into his second toe. But they were his boots, moving with his feet inside them, and what was his could be commanded. Once Walter had been scared of being in charge of his whole body. No longer. He ordered his feet to walk, to go on walking; if they didn't get a move on, he would make them run.

Walter commanded, and his feet disobeyed. They slowed down. Even a child, an invalid, a cripple, a one-legged man with a wheel-barrow could walk faster. He could walk on his hands, and get to Turnham Green in half the time. Every moment he wasted in slow-ness and resting was a moment in which June might decide not to wait for him any longer.

'*I've got to get away. Will you come with me? I can't do it on my own.*'

He was crossing the Earls Court Road when he fell. The time was twenty-five to five. The rush-hour drivers hooted, and leaned out of the windows of their vehicles to shout abuse at him. This traditional greeting, given by London drivers to children, the blind, pregnant women, nuns, the halt and the lame, lasted longer than usual because Walter, having fallen, did not get up.

At St Stephen's Hospital in the Fulham Road, they gave Walter something to wake him up, cleaned and dressed his injured toe, and questioned him.

'Do you know where you are?'

'Earls Court. West Kensington next.'

'Where have you come from?'

'Gloucester Road.'
'Where were you born?'
'Baron's Court.'
'What's your job?'
'Hammersmith.'
'What did you have for lunch?'
'Ravenscourt Park.'
'What's your name?'
'Stamford Brook.'
'What are you going to do?'
'Turnham Green.'
'Can you tell me ... ? Have you ever ... ? Do you know ...?'
In so far as he did know, he told them whatever he could, and
having been told, they went away, and talked about him behind
a screen. Then they returned, and informed him that he would be
pleased to know that they had decided to allow him to stay in their
hospital overnight. They were stretching a rule, they said, since
all he really needed was rest and quiet, which they supposed he
could come by easily in Turnham Green. However, since he had
experienced a shock, and was in discomfort, they had found him
a bed.

They stood back, as if for congratulation, which was not given.

Was there, they asked, anyone he would like them to inform of
his whereabouts, anyone expecting him at home?

Walter thanked them kindly, but said he could not stay. He had
to meet someone, and that someone would be waiting. He got down
from the high bed in Casualty, and made his way unsteadily to
the door. At this, the Evening Duty in Casualty at St Stephen's
Hospital adjusted their bedside manners, and proclaimed that, if he
insisted on leaving in that condition, he would have to sign a form
relieving them of all responsibility.

Walter printed the name 'Walter' in block capitals. Then he
became agitated. He couldn't remember his surname. They were
waiting and watching him. What was it? He knew it well enough;
it began with the same letter as his first name. His initials were
'W.W.' He had already printed the second W, but what came
after that?

He was sweating, and his head was full of goldfish. If only he could stop them moving, he would be able to think properly. He screwed up his eyes tight, then opened them again, and the room was spinning, and so were the watching faces. Faces dressed in white span and merged. Six eyes of different colours, different shapes, and at different heights, whirled round above ten noses and eleven mouths, then turned to their partners, bowed, dosie-doed with three raised eyebrows, and all the time Walter's name was on the tip of his tongue, and there it remained. He must concentrate. It was Earls Court, then – was it South Kensington? no, he had passed South Kensington – was it . . . ? He visualized his list, and the words came clear. 'West Kensington': that was it.

Slowly, carefully, Walter printed ' W E S T' on the form. It was not his name, but it was a word; it began with 'W', and he could spell it; it would do.

'Right, Mr West.' Someone was talking, and he must listen. 'You do realize we'd much rather you stayed here overnight? You don't look at all well.'

Walter nodded, and said, 'It's dark. She'll be frightened.'

He stepped out into the Fulham Road, and looked at the evening traffic crawling along, bumper to bumper. The lighted lorries, buses, cars and taxis, all evacuating exhaust fumes and filling the air with noise. The lights dazzled him, and he felt sick again. He could tell it had been dark for some time. She would have closed the flimsy make-do curtains, and would be lying down, listening to music from the radio. He looked up to see whether there was a moon, and six young men wearing Chelsea scarves collided with him, stepping on his injured foot, and sending him down to the pavement.

'Mr West!'

'Sorry, mate.'

'Mr West!' He was helped to his feet.

'You all right?'

'Mr West!'

'Don't hang about, Merve. Old Bill'll think you've started something.'

Walter realized that he was walking again, but could not tell in what direction. Someone was holding his arm, and he was walking, being led. Then a door was opened for him, and he was inside. It was warm. He was back in the Entrance Hall of the Hospital.

He had only travelled twenty yards. His hand was being held by a young nurse, and she was speaking to him. What was she saying?

'There's a floodlit match at Chelsea tonight. Nobody's safe on the streets. You'd never get a taxi, even if you had the . . .' She would not say 'money'. 'Are you sure you won't stay overnight? We could phone whoever it is you're worried about.'

Walter shook his head very slowly. Such strange things were happening to him that it was not safe to try to move quickly any more.

'All right. You wait here, and we'll get an ambulance to take you home.' The young face was close to his. 'It won't get you there as fast as the Tube, but it'll be a lot safer. All right?' He could not move, even his head. 'Turnham Green, isn't it? I'll tell them at the desk. They'll come and get you when it's time, so please wait. Don't wander off again, will you?'

She was gone. He would be there before bedtime. June would wipe his face dry, and he would tell her he was sorry for having watched her. From now on, he would look at her only when she was laughing, and then she would be happy, and not mind. It would be all right. All right now. June would hold him. And she would touch him on the face with her lips.

'Are you sure this is the road? All these houses look derelict to me.'

Then they saw a light. There was a light on in the house, shining through the flimsy curtains just as Walter had imagined it.

'She's waiting up for you, then.' Walter almost fell from the ambulance in his haste to get to the front door. 'Mind how you go on that foot.'

He was giggling to himself, chuckling and giggling like a baby. Everything was as he had supposed. She had come back; she had waited. He must stop himself laughing, pull himself together, wipe that smile off his face, and remember not to stare at her. He was a man now, not the boy who had baled rubbish at Woolworth's.

Walter looked in through the window at a point where the curtains failed to meet. He was looking at their room. There were some things he remembered, others not. The furniture was the same. But there was food on one of the mattresses. He and June had never put food on the old stained matresses. They had kept it in the kitchen. Now he could see the remains of a sliced loaf in its paper, a carton of eggs, a jar of coffee exactly like the one in which they kept their money.

There was no answer to his tap on the window, but if she were in the kitchen, she wouldn't hear. He played 'their tune' on the knocker, the tune which told whoever was in the house that this visitor was not the police or council, but one of their own.

He waited, then tried the knock again, then remembered where they had hidden a spare key after having once locked themselves out. He went to the back of the house, and found the key where they had hidden it in a flowerpot under some earth. She was not in the kitchen. Yet there would not be a light on if she had gone out.

Walter let himself in by the back door. In the kitchen greasy plates were soaking in the yellow plastic bowl they used for washing up. Two small pieces of bacon rind floated on top of the water. June always ate her bacon rind, even when it had 'Danish' written on it.

In the lighted living-room, he examined the remainder of the sliced loaf, which was fresh, and noticed that wood had recently been burned in the grate, but he could find no clothes or anything of June's.

There had been no light in Graham's room, and was not. He paused outside, lifted his fist to knock, then changed his mind, and walked about the hall. He tapped with his good foot against the skirting board, so as to be heard walking, and coughed three times. Then he shouted 'Hello' four times up the stairs, even though none of them ever went there, the stairs being unsafe.

Finally, he tapped on the door of Graham's room, and entered. There were blankets on the bed, and some text books on the floor. Had Graham left them behind?

Then he heard a key being turned in the front door.

'I went out for a drink. Couldn't stand this place any more.' Graham had drunk a great deal many more than one drink. 'Where did you get to, then?' Walter didn't answer. 'June and I thought you'd stay here.'

They were waiting for the kettle to boil. 'I'm sorry about what happened, but we really were in love.'

Walter looked at the kettle. What steam did was to escape from the kettle. Yet when it had escaped, it was no longer steam.

'She said she was sure you'd come back here, looking for her, and you have. She was very good about people, if not so very good to them.' Graham heaped two and a half teaspoons of Instant Coffee into each mug. He had never been able to remember that Walter could only drink coffee if it was very weak.

'No sugar for you, I'm afraid. Don't take it myself, as you'll remember, so didn't buy any. Not being as certain as she was that you'd come. Cheers!' Walter was handed a cup of strong sugarless coffee, and they moved into the lighted room, and sat on separate mattresses.

They sat in silence until Graham had drunk half his coffee. Finally he spoke. 'You'll be wondering.'

He waited for a reply, but got none.

'We went to another squat. Lots of people there. Much better than this place.' He thought. 'Must get out of here.' He thought again. 'Where was I? Oh, yes. Well, there was this girl I knew from college. Upset June. We had a row. Several, in fact. Then she did a bunk. June did. Never trusted anybody, did she, not even you?'

Walter realized that Graham was more than slightly drunk. When the light did not glitter on his spectacles, it could be seen that his eyes kept closing. Also his hands shook.

'I knew she had enough Valium for a couple of weeks, so I didn't run after her.' Silence. Graham's head was still. Was he staring into space, or had he closed his eyes again?

After a while, Graham's head dropped forward, and in an almost inaudible voice, he asked, 'What shall I do? Can you tell me?' Walter could not, and did not, but after a while, as the silence persisted, he realized that he was sitting close to the sliced bread. He had forgotten how hungry he was. But to get any bread, he would have to ask.

'I've got to work. Somehow. It's all there is really.'

'Can I have some bread, please?' He had spoken for the first time since Graham's arrival.

'Sorry?'

Walter indicated the sliced bread. 'Can I?'

'Yes, of course. There's butter and something ... something to put on it ...' But Walter already had four slices in his fist, rolled into one, and was eating. 'I remember there *was* something to ... Oh Christ!'

Walter stopped pushing bread into his mouth, and stood up. He supposed that he was standing because Graham was crying. He had stared wide-eyed at Walter eating, and then burst into tears, holding his spectacles between his thumb and index finger, biting at the back of his hand, and blubbering like a baby.

The crying became more extreme, more abandoned. Walter found that he was standing with Graham's arms around his neck, supporting most of Graham's weight.

Between the sobs, there were words. 'There's something ... you should see ... upstairs. Come upstairs.'

But no one ever went upstairs. The stairs were not safe.

Graham controlled himself, and found a torch. There were no lights upstairs. Going on all fours, and carefully avoiding the stairs without treads, they reached the landing of the first floor of the three-storey house.

Graham opened the door of one of the rooms. 'The floor's safe in here. It's been tested.' The beam of light from the torch swung round the empty room, and came to rest, illuminating a patch of wall close to the floor. Graham stood with his hand on the door-knob, while Walter clutched at his slices of bread, which had gained some dust during the climb.

'Go and look on the wall. Over there.'

Walter crossed the room cautiously, and bent down to look at the patch of wall in the circle of light. Someone had scratched writing on the wall with a nail.

'Can you read it?' Walter shook his head. Graham came over to him slowly, and stood behind him. Then he began to sob and whimper, making whining sounds like a dog, as he read aloud what was scratched on the wall.

'First day. I think. Can't move my legs or arms. Cried wolf but nobody came. Know you'll come back. Second day. Where are you, Pigeon? It's so cold. Third day. Please hurry.'

207

The beam of light moved from the wall, and zigzagged about the ceilings, floor and walls of the empty room, as Graham made his way back to the door. 'She came back here. It'd been very cold. She went all over the house, looking for things to burn – lino, wood, anything. She went right to the top of the house, striking matches to see her way.' He swung the beam of light so that it pointed to the ceiling, a large part of which had collapsed. 'She was lying where you are. Died in the ambulance. Internal bleeding.'

Walter placed the fingers of his right hand near his boots, and felt the floorboards.

'Better go down.'

They stood in the hall.

'I suppose she scratched that on the wall in case I didn't get here in time. I've used up all the Valium I brought for her. Got to get out of this place. Always felt there was something wrong with the house. Staying here won't bring her back. Really loved her, you know. Told me she had a baby up north. Wonder what'll happen to it.'

Time passed. They stood together in the dimly lighted hall. 'What will you do now?' Walter did not answer. 'I've got some money, if you want to go back up there, up to that hospital you came from.' No reply. 'She talked about you in the ambulance. She was very fond of you.' Graham waited for a response, and got none. 'I've got to work. Somehow.'

They were still standing in the hall. 'Funny name she called me – "Pigeon". Never called me that before. How will you manage?' No reply. Graham moved back into the lighted room. 'If there's anything else you need ... I mean, there's more to eat if you want it.'

Walter remained in the hall. He had left his bread on the floor upstairs.

4

Don't let me disturb you. Thought I'd give you something for a pillow.

The clouds were wispy and red, yet the ground was iron-hard beneath the snow, which had remained frozen into whatever shape had last been pressed into it. Many of the footprints had been there for weeks.

Walter lay on the snow in Gunnersbury Park, hardly denting it. Above him the red sky reminded him of Hell. The snow which pressed against the right side of his face, numbing it, was white and as cold as Heaven must therefore be.

Christmas had gone. He would be too late to wish Jesus a Happy Birthday. Walter himself had never had a birthday party. He wondered how many candles there would have been on Jesus's cake.

His body shivered, but the snow against his face had stopped the aching in his head, and would cool the hotness of his skin. He was sweating, but the sweat would freeze into a block of ice all round him, and he would be allowed to sleep for ever, since there would be no one left behind to wait for Jesus to decide. And Jesus would not turn him away. His mother had promised that he would go to Heaven if he were good, and he had not been bad. She had promised that they would meet together in Paradise, and there would be no reason for Jesus to feel embarrassed since Walter was not one of His Mistakes.

'What's it like, then?'

Walter blinked.

'Sleeping in the snow. What's it feel like?'

Grey dots floated down towards him.

There was a boy standing over him. A teenager.

More grey dots floated down like confetti, some landing on Walter's face. He brushed them aside.

'Must try it some time. Kipping in the snow.' The teenager was holding something in his left hand, and picking at it with the fingers of his right. The something was moving. Struggling. Walter saw that there poked out from between the fingers of the left hand the leg of a bird. 'Try anything once.'

The bird's leg withdrew quickly and reappeared as the teenager plucked. What was floating down on Walter were not grey dots, but the tiny grey breast-feathers of a bird, which was being plucked alive by the youth who stood over him.

'Always wanted to do this. See what it felt like.' A tail-feather floated down towards Walter.

Slowly Walter attempted to get to his feet, but the youth casually placed one of his own feet on top of one of Walter's hands. 'Don't let me disturb you. Thought I'd give you something for a pillow. Feathers.' There was no humour in his voice. He did not even look at Walter, but continued to pull out the feathers of the struggling bird as if he were unwrapping a parcel in the contents of which he was only minimally interested.

It seemed to give him no particular satisfaction to contemplate the raw purple skin of the bird, covering the network of veins and the projecting bones, or the bird's heart, beating faster, so large a pulse within so small a frame, getting faster and faster and faster, as each feather fluttered to the ground and panic grew with each successive pain.

'Don't even make a noise.' A beak appeared above the youth's thumb. It was opened in a silent scream. Walter knew that pigeons make no sound when they are in pain.

'Shit itself stupid when I picked it up.'

Now the bird was hanging from the youth's hand, and fluttering as he held it by one wing so as to make his choice of which flight-feather to pluck. Walter shouted, 'Don't!'

The youth looked first at Walter, and then upwards at the sky.

For a moment, Walter felt relief, believing that the youth was about to release the bird, and throw it back into the air.

The moment passed. The youth returned his gaze to Walter. A smile illuminated the youth's face. 'It's only a poxy pigeon. Too many of them. Spread disease.' And resumed plucking.

How could the bird understand that fingers of the same human kind from which in the past it had received bread and stale cake could now tear at its flesh? Using his free hand, Walter made a grab for the youth's ankle, and tugged as hard as he could.

The youth lost his balance, and toppled backwards. The pigeon fell chest first onto the snow, and was still. The youth swung back his right leg in preparation to kick the dying bird towards one of the sixty goal posts which stand in Gunnersbury Park. Walter made a dive for the pigeon, and clasped it, before the youth's shoe landed against the back of his hand. Then a second kick, intended for the groin, landed on Walter's right thigh. Walter was on his feet before the third, and the youth was retreating backwards like a boxer, jumping up and down, and laughing.

'It's bloody dead. Like you. Bloody deadbeat!'

At first Walter believed him. The bird was so still, the lower lids of its eyes almost closed. It seemed as if the layer of film which covers a bird's eyes in death was already present. Then by accident, his fingers touched the bird's raw breast, and its beak opened in another silent scream of pain.

It was still alive. Only he could save it. He could feel the bird's heart, beating against his fingers, thumping, thumping hard against them, as if trying to burst out.

Slowly Walter unbuttoned, and tucked the pigeon inside his shirt and up under his vest, until he could feel its heartbeat against the skin of his chest.

His own heartbeat would calm it, and their combined warmth would renew its wish to live.

Buttoning up his clothes against the bitter wind, he began to walk, and as he walked, he spoke gently to the pigeon which lay against his heart. 'I've no food for you. You should taste hemp seed. You'd like that. You should have tares and linseed, maple peas and maize.' His voice was like the sound of a fart in soapy water, but how should the bird know that?

Then he remembered the remainder of the sliced bread he had left on the floor of the room in which June had lain waiting for his return, and he changed direction.

'You'll be all right with me. We'll both be all right.'

He was walking again. He was talking again.

5

Finis

That is the end of the story of Walter, and as for June, she was never more than a part of it, and found at last by accident what she had so often tried to bring about deliberately.

He is still alive. He has returned – well, he has been returned to the Hospital; they have accepted him.

He watches television and the weekly film show. Sits. Speaks if someone speaks to him, but not much, and not always in a concentrated way. He never speaks of pigeons.

Only at night, in his dreams, the pigeons fly. Russian High-Fliers and Birmingham Rollers, Turbits, Long-Faced English Tumblers, White-Lace Fantails, Norman and Marlene, Marge and Lionel, Freda the favourite of all favourites, Clarice, Edna, William and Amy, they fly high in the air, swoop, glide, tumble and recover, flying forever in wide circles, clapping their wings as they wheel above the solitary figure looking up at them from below. All night they cut the clean air for their delight and his.

And when he awakes, his cheeks are wet with tears.